D0193836

modern french theatre

THE AVANT-GARDE, DADA, AND SURREALISM

MICHAEL BENEDIKT was educated at New York and Columbia Universities, and is at present Editorial Associate for *Art News* magazine and New York Correspondent for *Art International*. Mr. Benedikt is co-editor of *Post-War German Theatre* and editor of *Theatre Experiment*, two play anthologies that will be published in 1966. He has contributed translations from medieval French and German poetry to *Medieval Age*, and has also published many translations of contemporary French and German verse. His own poetry has most frequently appeared in *Poetry* (Chicago), and has also been published by *Art and Literature*, *The Lugano Review*, *Choice*, and *The Nation*, among other periodicals.

GEORGE E. WELLWARTH received his education at New York and Columbia Universities and took his doctorate at the University of Chicago. While at Chicago, Mr. Wellwarth began his professional acting career with the Chicago Court Theatre, and he has appeared in several off-Broadway productions. Since 1960 he has concentrated principally on translation and criticism. His translations of three plays by Jean Tardieu were produced at the VanDam Theatre in 1962. Mr. Wellwarth has published scholarly articles on such important theatrical figures as Beckett, Genet, Ionesco, Shaw, Duerenmatt, and Frisch. His book *The Theatre of Protest and Paradox* was recently published by the Gotham Library series of the New York University Press. At present Mr. Wellwarth is an Assistant Professor of English at The Pennsylvania State University.

MODERN FRENCH THEATRE was first published in 1964.

THE AVANT-GARDE,
DADA, AND SURREALISM

modern french theatre

AN ANTHOLOGY OF PLAYS

EDITED AND TRANSLATED BY

Michael Benedikt AND George E. Wellwarth

A Dutton
Paperback

E. P. DUTTON, NEW YORK

INDIVIDUAL COPYRIGHTS AND ACKNOWLEDGMENTS

ALFRED JARRY: *King Ubu.* English translation copyright © 1964 by Michael Benedikt and George E. Wellwarth. Originally published as *Ubu Roi* by Éditions Mercure de France, copyright 1896.

GUILLAUME APOLLINAIRE: *The Breasts of Tiresias.* English translation copyright © 1961 by Louis Simpson. Originally published as *Les Mamelles de Tirésias* by Éditions Sic copyright 1918. Reprinted by permission of Éditions Gallimard.

JEAN COCTEAU: *The Wedding on the Eiffel Tower.* English translation copyright © 1964 by Michael Benedikt. Originally published as *Les Mariés de la Tour Eiffel* by Éditions Gallimard, copyright 1923. Reprinted with the permission of Jean Cocteau and New Directions, who hold exclusive publications rights for this play in the United States. For amateur production rights please apply to New Directions, 333 Sixth Avenue, New York 14, New York.

RAYMOND RADIGUET: *The Pelicans.* English translation copyright © 1964 by Michael Benedikt. Originally published as *Les Pélican* in *Oeuvres Complètes* by Éditions Bernard Grasset, copyright 1952.

TRISTAN TZARA: *The Gas Heart.* English translation copyright © 1964 by Michael Benedikt. Originally published as *Le Coeur à Gaz* by Éditions G. L. M., copyright 1938.

ANDRÉ BRETON and PHILIPPE SOUPAULT: *If You Please.* English translation copyright © 1964 by George E. Wellwarth. Originally published as *S'Il Vous Plaît* in *Littérature*, No. 16, copyright 1920.

acknowledgments

THE EDITORS wish to express their sincere thanks to: Mr. Ralph J. Gladstone for his advice with respect to questions of translation from inception to completion of this anthology; Mr. Monroe Wheeler for his excellent suggestions regarding the rendering into English of Cocteau's *Les mariés de la Tour Eiffel*; Professor Hilde Jaeckel for her excellent suggestions regarding the rendering into English of *S'Il Vous Plaît* by Breton and Soupault; Marianne Sabados Benedikt for her inspiration seven years ago to translate one of the first of the plays eventually included in this anthology, Radiguet's *Les Pélican*; Mr. Anthony Linick for his always good advice; and Mr. Georges Borchardt for his monumental efforts in the pursuing and securing of the rights for the plays included here.

contents

* The dates in parentheses indicate the year in which the play was completed.

introduction

WHEN Alfred Jarry wrote *King Ubu* he effected what in literature amounts to a miraculous event. With no immediate literary antecedents, he created a genre of drama in which many of the most advanced poets and dramatists of his country—and many of the most talented—have worked; a genre which, indeed, has achieved a prominence today that Jarry himself could hardly have imagined. The *avant-garde* playwrights of the present have as their predecessors such important post-Jarry writers as Guillaume Apollinaire, Jean Cocteau, and Antonin Artaud, and have at their disposal a literary heritage which is traceable even in the works of more readily "acceptable" writers—such as Raymond Radiguet and Jean Anouilh—whose works are generally placed outside the stream of radical literary developments. It is all the more astonishing that this style of modern drama, which in the opinion of many critics is among the most important theatrical developments of the late nineteenth and twentieth centuries, should have come into being in its entirety through one public event: the first performance of Alfred Jarry's *King Ubu* at the Théâtre Nouveau in Paris, on December 11, 1896.

It is certainly not at all peculiar that the first performance of *King Ubu* should have been the cause of one of the most violent theatrical riots of all time. Alfred Jarry's approach to theatre must have appeared to many in the opening-night audience as virtually unprecedented in theatrical history; and it was, indeed, an approach without parallel in the theatre of the time.[1] When *Ubu*

[1] Not only were the aesthetics of *King Ubu* advanced theatrically, but the play precedes by over a decade the works in painting and music which are usually considered to have ushered in the modern era in their respective fields.

was written the dramatists who seemed most forward-looking were pursuing with determination the ideal of an increased physical or moral "realism." In *Ubu*, with an intransigence one would say is typical of the most inspired literary innovators—were there not so very few of them—Jarry embodied a theatrical aesthetics exactly the opposite of those preoccupying the most "progressive" dramatists of his day.

King Ubu draws its strength from Jarry's revolutionary rediscovery that theatre, in order to be viable, need not precisely reproduce the conditions of everyday life. If realism in the theatre may be characterized by its special concern with the reproduction of the details of everyday life, Jarry's theatre may be characterized by its strong feeling for the thorough exploitation of every available element of the theatrical machinery. It is, in fact, an exploration which the playwrights who followed Jarry have never ceased to continue, though in their own original and highly divergent ways.

In a letter to his producer, the already remarkably sympathetic Lugné-Poe, Jarry quite outspokenly recommends the simplifications and the symbolic suggestiveness which are perhaps the most outstanding charcateristics of all twentieth-century *avant-garde* drama—including that of today:

> It would be interesting, I think, to be able to stage the play . . . in the following manner.
> A mask for the chief character, Ubu . . .
> A cardboard horse's head, which he would hang around his neck, as in the old English theatre, for the only two equestrian scenes, both these suggestions being in the spirit of the play, since I intended to write a "guignol."
> The adoption of a single set, or better yet, of a single backdrop, eliminating the raising and lowering of the curtain within each individual act. A suitably costumed person would enter, as in puppet shows, to put up signs indicating the locations of the various scenes. (Note that I am convinced of the superiority from the point of view of "suggestiveness" of placards over sets. No set or contrivance could represent "the Polish army on the march in the Ukraine.")
> The elimination of crowds, which are a mistake on stage and hamper the mind. Thus, a single soldier in the review scene, a single soldier in the scuffle when Ubu says: "What a lot of people, what a retreat," etc.

Picasso's *Les Demoiselles d'Avignon* and Stravinsky's *Le Sacre du Printemps*, for example, date respectively from 1907 and 1913.

The adoption of an "accent," or better yet, a special "voice" for the chief character.

Costumes with as little specific local color reference or historical accuracy as possible (the better to suggest eternal things); modern, preferably, since the satire is modern; and sordid, since the drama will appear still more wretched and repugnant that way.[2]

Jarry's references to the popular form of French dramatic entertainment known as the "guignol" (or puppet show) and to the old English theatre are by no means gratuitous: it is to these forms of dramatic entertainment, rather than any "legitimate" nineteenth-century theatre, that *Ubu* may be related. In 1888, while a schoolboy in the *lycée* at Rennes, Jarry, with several of his classmates, collaborated in a rather informal variety of class play: a cycle of satires on one of their most despised instructors, a physics teacher named Hébert. The hapless Hébert's name was modified as it was bandied about to Hebe or sometimes to Heb'; and in one of these collaborative ventures, *Les Polonais*, performed as a puppet play by Jarry in a friend's attic, the rough draft of the play featuring Father Ubu, which overturned Paris eight years later, first saw the light. Since the text does not survive, probably having suffered dispersal shortly after performance, we cannot be sure which of the characteristics of Jarry's own Ubu cycle (which eventually included two other full-length Ubu plays, *Ubu Enchaîné* and *Ubu Cocu*), much less of Father Ubu himself, first appeared in what must have been the truly primordial dimness of that attic.

We can, however, be sure which characteristics of the guignol attracted Jarry to that popular variety of theatre. Even if Jarry had been so extraordinarily precocious in high school as to search for them elsewhere, the guignol contains elements which Jarry could not possibly have found in the "serious" theatre of his time.[3] In acting, highly mimetic; in setting, indicative of indifference to questions of realism; in structure, virtually as wayward as the "acts" in vaudeville or the circus—the guignol must have offered a unique

[2] "Lettre, 8 Janvier 1896," *Tout Ubu*, ed. Maurice Saillet (Paris: *Le Livre du Poche*, 1962).

[3] Although it seems highly unlikely that *Peer Gynt*, written a few decades before, could have been among Jarry's schoolbooks—any more than *King Ubu* is used as a text in English-speaking high schools today—Jarry had discovered Ibsen's "unrealistic" side by the time *Ubu*'s final version was completed. Jarry, in fact, in his role as assistant to the director Lugné-Poe, eventually assisted in the production of both *King Ubu* and *Peer Gynt*.

combination of attractive aspects to Jarry, not only while an unwilling student at the Rennes high school, but also later, as a fascinated student of the drama.

The old English theatre, which the young Jarry doubtless encountered in the classroom in the form of Shakespearean tragedies, suggests an approach to the stage which is curiously similar to that of guignol. The Elizabethan stage, with its violent shifts of mood and action, with its "dumb shows," and with its utter disinterest in the expression of reality by the exact imitation of its conditions, must have fascinated Jarry throughout his life. Indeed, there are many references to the outward aspects of Shakespeare's plays—particularly *Hamlet* and *King Lear*—throughout *King Ubu*. Jarry has even supplied *Ubu* with an epigraph hinting that the Englishman's tragedies were actually inspired by the exploits of Ubu. One might add that Jarry's non-theatrical works also place considerable stress on anti-realistic concepts.

In short, when the curtain was finally raised on *King Ubu*, most of the audience found itself confronted for the first time not only with a totally unrealistic stage, but with a stage that was militantly anti-realistic. Indeed, in both the plot and setting of *Ubu*, Jarry had represented a world which only a very few of even the most advanced poets of the era had ever dared envision, much less firmly embody. The plot of *Ubu* is a deliberately childish creation: a noble king murdered by a wicked usurper; the young and virtuous rightful heir to the throne as avenger; battles fought between armies resembling the little tin soldiers of a child's toy box; eerie (but not too eerie) "supernatural" events; a fight with a decidedly make-believe bear; and so on. Even to the most sophisticated literary people present, the experience of *Ubu* seems to have been overwhelming. The English *fin-de-siècle* poet and critic Arthur Symons has left us this impression of the première:

> The scenery was painted to represent, by a child's convention, indoors and out of doors, and even the torrid, temperate, and arctic zones at once. Opposite to you, at the back of the stage, you saw apple trees in bloom, under a blue sky, and against the sky a small closed window and a fireplace . . . through the very midst of which . . . trooped in and out these clamorous and sanguinary persons of the drama. On the left was painted a bed, and at the foot of the bed a bare tree, and snow falling. On the right were palm trees, about one of which coiled a boa constrictor; a

door opened against the sky, and beside the door a skeleton dangled from a gallows. Changes of scene were announced by the simple Elizabethan method of a placard. . . . A venerable gentleman in evening dress . . . trotted across the stage on the points of his toes between every scene and hung the new placard on its nail.[4]

W. B. Yeats, apparently equally stunned by Jarry's stage effects (he knew very little French, as he himself was the first to admit), later wrote:

> I go to the first performance of Alfred Jarry's *Ubu Roi.* . . . The audience shake their fists at one another, and [my friend] whispers to me, "There are often duels after these performances," and he explains to me what is happening on the stage. The players are supposed to be dolls, toys, marionettes, and now they are all hopping like wooden frogs, and I can see for myself that the chief personage, who is some kind of King, carries for Sceptre a brush of the kind that we use to clean a closet. Feeling bound to support the most spirited party, we have shouted for the play, but that night at the Hotel Corneille I am very sad, for comedy, objectivity, has displayed its growing power once more. I say, "After Stéphane Mallarmé, after Paul Verlaine, after Gustave Moreau, after Puvis de Chavannes, after our own verse, after all our subtle colour and nervous rhythm, after the faint mixed tints of Conder, what more is possible? After us the Savage God." [5]

Symons, in his somewhat puzzled identification of Jarry's over-all conception with "a child's convention," was, as we know now, making an accurate characterization indeed, while Yeats' prophecy of still harsher evocations of the primitive to come—after Jarry, if not as a direct result of him—was equally accurate.[6] The hero of

---

[4] *Studies in Seven Arts* (New York: Dutton, 1906), pp. 373–74.

[5] *The Autobiographies of W. B. Yeats* (Garden City, N.Y.: Doubleday, 1958), pp. 233–34.

[6] It is interesting that the leader of the then prevailing symbolist school of poetry, Stéphane Mallarmé—a literary idol of both Arthur Symons, who translated him, and W. B. Yeats—approved with fearless wholeheartedness of the boisterous *Ubu.* In a letter written to Jarry shortly after the opening night, Mallarmé identified Jarry's play in a way which first brought to it the perspective of tradition, as the work of "a sure, sober, dramatic sculptor"; Ubu himself Mallarmé identified as a new figure in "the repertory of the best taste." (Quoted in Roger Shattuck, *The Banquet Years: The Arts in France, 1885–1918* [New York: Harcourt, Brace, 1958], p. 177.) Mallarmé some years before had abandoned the writing of a virtually unplayable, anti-realistic monodrama, *Igitur.*

King Ubu is, in Jarry's own words, "un être ignoble," and in the untraditional indifference to nobility of this irrational king we see marked foreshadowings of the spectacular irrationality of approach which would be so important a part of the *avant-garde* theatre to come. With Ubu's rise to power, effected through the openhanded employment of a kind of childishly ingenuous deceit, a dreamlike atmosphere is evoked—not by any means the gloomy atmosphere of nightmares—full of the strange, the unlikely, and the scurrilously humorous. It is a half-comic, half-eerie atmosphere which the *avant-garde* theatre of the future would often re-create, particularly after the beginning of the Surrealist movement, which followed the first production of *King Ubu* by a matter of a little over two decades.

It will be seen that the ideals of Jarry and the implications of *Ubu* had little to do with the theatre as generally practiced in the 1890's; and, indeed, Jarry himself made little mark on the theatre of his time. Except in the memories of a few devoted friends, Jarry's remarkable literary personality remained unknown until World War I provided an unlikely impetus for his widespread revival.

Jarry's most important literary disciple, as well as one of the most important figures in the history of literature and painting in the early part of the twentieth century, was the poet and critic Guillaume Apollinaire. Apollinaire, who was literally one of the first critics to take serious account of Cubism—and who was thus one of the earliest proponents of twentieth-century non-objective painting—was a member of a group including painters such as Picasso and Braque and writers such as Max Jacob and André Salmon which regularly gathered around Jarry. Not the least of Apollinaire's critical accomplishments was the fact that he was one of the very few men of his day to understand the breadth of implication in Jarry's peculiar contribution to literature. After Jarry's death in 1907, Apollinaire wrote the following in an essay in devoted appraisal of his late friend:

> Someone once said within earshot of me that Jarry was our last author of burlesque. An error! . . . We don't even possess terms adequate to describe his peculiar kind of liveliness in which lyricism becomes satiric, or where satire in its operations upon reality surpasses its object so totally that it completely destroys it and

then climbs so high that Poetry itself can hardly keep up with it. . . . Jarry was the last of the sublime débauchés.[7]

The details of Jarry's personality seem to have been inherited by two men in particular. His most intimate lineaments, as Roger Shattuck notes in his superb study, *The Banquet Years*, were readily accepted by the young Picasso, who "adopted his eccentric, pistol-carrying habits and later acquired a valuable collection of Jarry's manuscripts."[8] His literary character was reflected with particular brilliance in the writing of Apollinaire, the extravagance of whose early work and the stage technique of whose first play, *The Breasts of Tiresias*, owe much to the immediate influence of Alfred Jarry.

The Breasts of Tiresias was begun in 1903, the year Apollinaire and Jarry first met, and completed in 1917, just one year before Apollinaire's death resulting from wounds sustained in the war. Here, Apollinaire concerns himself with Jarry's theatrical thinking more thoroughly than all but a few playwrights have since, and none ever did before. Judging from the evidence of the author's 1917 preface, Apollinaire at the outset approached the writing of his play with Jarryesque principles in mind:

> . . . it is legitimate, in my opinion, to bring to the theatre new and striking aesthetic principles which accentuate the roles of the actors and increase the effect of the production, yet without modifying the pathos or comedy of the situations, which must be self-sufficient. . . . May I say that, in abstracting from contemporary literary movements a certain tendency of my own, I am in no way undertaking to form a school, but above all to protest against that "realistic" theatre which is the predominating theatrical art today. This "realism" . . . is, I believe, as far removed as possible from the art of drama.

As if in deliberate opposition to these inclinations, Apollinaire chose as the theme of his drama a decidedly "realistic" problem:

[7] *Il y a*, pref. R. G. de la Serna (Paris: Messein, 1949), p. 176. Apollinaire's distinction between satire as means and as end is significant with respect both to Jarry's method and that of the theatre which followed him. While satirical elements are generally in evidence in much post-Jarry drama, as in *Ubu* itself, the importance of satire in this new French theatre has, in this writer's opinion, been much overemphasized. Apollinaire's recognition of the relationship of Jarry's theatre to Poetry in the broadest sense was insightful and right; Apollinaire's first play, *The Breasts of Tiresias*, itself proves that Jarry was anything but the last of the playwrights of his supra-satirical line.

[8] *The Banquet Years*, pp. 169–70.

female emancipation, and its relation (which seems to have wholly charmed Apollinaire) to population decline. The delightful verse in which this play is written (and into which it has been translated) thoroughly neutralizes the reality-bound implications of apparently so earnest a concern:

> Women at Zanzibar want political rights
> And suddenly renounce their reproductive rights
> No more children No more children you hear them shout
> To fill Zanzibar there are elephants about

Needless to say, *The Breasts of Tiresias* employs anti-realistic stagecraft throughout. We may isolate as a particularly daring example of the anti-realistic atmosphere evoked in this play Apollinaire's representation of the entire "people of Zanzibar" by a single character, doubtless a result of Jarry's recommendation that the Russian and Polish armies each be demobilized to a man. In the absence of King Ubu, this strange, brooding (yet democratic) background presence becomes himself the disconcerting central figure of Apollinaire's drama. As if to add to his mystery, he is not even allowed the few words Jarry permitted his genetic representatives: instead, "the people of Zanzibar" is supplied with a selection of noisemakers, which he employs during crowd scenes, and also uses as a kind of orchestral accompaniment to punctuate and underline the speeches of individuals.

For his total war on realistic theatre Apollinaire, as did Jarry, called for a new kind of delivery for his drama, requiring that many of the speeches be shouted through a megaphone. This newsboy-like diction, doubtless adopted as appropriate to the contemporaneous nature of the headline-making "themes" of the play (yet inexplicably applied to verse) is complemented by Apollinaire's use of a new kind of newspaper kiosk, with the proprietor represented by "a picture of the newspaper woman which is able to move its arm." Like a giant theatrical mask, Apollinaire's kiosk talks, sings, and even dances during the drama, as if determined to flaunt its ordinarily reality-bound function.

Structured along highly capricious lines, apt to resolve at any moment into apparently unrelated scenes, or into delightful nonsense songs—one of which is about Apollinaire's close friend, Pablo Picasso—the play is as completely removed from the con-

neologism, concatenation
nihilism, apostasy

ventions of ordinary "legitimate" stage reality as Jarry could have wished. Although wittily presented by its author as if it were another kind of drama entirely, a "problem play," with all the subservience to reality characteristic of that variety of theatre, *The Breasts of Tiresias* is most prophetically subtitled "Drame Surréaliste."

Although the strangely illogical ways of this play do evoke a new literary atmosphere, while harking back to Jarry, Apollinaire's explanation of what he meant by his newly coined term "Surréaliste" differs from that of the Surrealist poets and painters who began to form their movement a half decade after the first performance of this play. Although Apollinaire is often justifiably hailed as one of the most important French poets of the century, and one of the founders of Surrealism, his use of this term—to signify a possible reality beyond mere appearances—is intensely theatrical in both its recommendations and implications:

> To characterize my drama I have used a neologism. . . . I have invented the adjective *surrealist*. . . . The cheap idealism of the playwrights who followed Victor Hugo sought for verisimilitude in conventional local color, which as "photographic" naturalism produced comedies of manners, the originals of which may be found long before . . . in sentimental comedies. . . .
>
> And in order to attempt, if not a renovation of the theatre, at least an original effort, I thought it necessary to come back to nature itself, but without copying it photographically.
>
> When a man wanted to imitate walking he created the wheel, which does not resemble a leg. In the same way he has created surrealism. . . .[9]

Some years after the first performance of *The Breasts of Tiresias*, the young Jean Cocteau—who had been producing poems along the revolutionary lines of Apollinaire's, and critical articles further elaborating upon the new aesthetics—wrote his first play, *The Wedding on the Eiffel Tower*. Jarry's and Apollinaire's plays had

[9] The second early use of Apollinaire's neologism occurred in a similarly theatrical context, one month before the première of *The Breasts of Tiresias*. In a program note to the ballet *Parade* (music by Erik Satie, sets by Picasso, scenario by Jean Cocteau) Apollinaire wrote prophetically: "From this new alliance—for until now costume and scenery on one hand, choreography on the other, have been linked only artificially—there has resulted in *Parade* a kind of *sur-réalisme* which I see as the point of departure. . . ." (*Chroniques d'Art 1902–1918*, ed. L. C. Breunig [Paris: Gallimard, 1960], p. 426.)

not lacked for prefatory and/or other notes, and in his own combative preface Cocteau refers to the tradition of *King Ubu* and *The Breasts of Tiresias*. Here he identifies them as the first dramas to synthesize the "symbolic drama" and the "thesis drama," or problem play; yet, it must be remarked his own dependence on these two works indicates that he had as acute a perception of their original, anti-realistic aspects as he did of their synthetic characteristics.

The most remarkable aspect of *The Wedding on the Eiffel Tower* is the result of the realization of a concept latent in Apollinaire's representation of the people of Zanzibar by a single individual (to whom the role of one-man band is also assigned)—and perhaps even in Jarry's presentation of single individuals as entire armies. Both these plays suggest that precisely naturalistic numerical relationships between individuals who stand on the stage and characters in plays is not an absolute theatrical necessity, but rather an old theatrical habit. This realization resulted, in Cocteau's preface, in the brilliant, yet theatrical concept of the "universal athlete":

> A theatrical piece ought to be written, presented, costumed, furnished with musical accompaniment, played, and danced, by a single individual. This universal athlete does not exist. It is therefore important to replace the individual by what resembles an individual most: a friendly group.

Cocteau's theoretical tampering with the relationships among author, director, costume designer, composer, actor, and dancer is reflected in the play itself in a daring severing of the long unquestioned identity of speaker and actor. While the "actors" (actually, in the first, 1921 production, the Swedish Ballet) mime all the events of the drama, two narrators—identified by Cocteau with the master and mistress of ceremonies of the French vaudeville, or music hall—deliver dramatic recitations of what the characters might be speaking, or else furnish the audience with explanations of the actions on stage.[10] Rather in the manner of Apollinaire's

[10] Similar developments in the anti-realistic deployment of several theatrical elements at once occur consistently during this period in the works for the stage of Cocteau's close friend, Igor Stravinsky. The ballet-oratorio *Les Noces* (1914–21) describes a Russian wedding feast in a theatrically highly sophisticated way, placing the four formally garbed pianists of the orchestra on stage with dancers costumed in a primitive Russian style. For this work the writer

extraordinary realization of the theatrical mask (*Tiresias'* conversing kiosk), Cocteau's narrators are dressed as phonograph machines—bodies encased in boxes, with horns where their mouths should ordinarily be. As if in imitation of Apollinaire's anti-realistic newsboy delivery (itself a development of Jarry's plea for a "special" tone of voice), Cocteau's narrators speak "very loudly, very quickly." Aiding these extraordinary stage presences in the narration is an orchestra, supplied with instruments instead of noisemakers (with music written by men now at last generally considered to be among France's most distinguished twentieth-century composers); occasionally this raucous orchestra (reminiscent of that recommended by both Jarry and Apollinaire for their dramas) further punctures any realistic possibilities in the action with waltzes, polkas, funeral marches, fox trots, and other stylized—and stylizing—musical forms.

With *The Wedding on the Eiffel Tower* it would seem that Jarry's anti-realistic innovations, particularly in the department of stagecraft, could go no farther; and, indeed, while Cocteau was at work on his first play, he was also guiding his young friend, the extraordinarily gifted novelist and poet Raymond Radiguet, in the writing of a work which is relatively conventional from the point of view of staging, yet which is nevertheless well within the borders of Jarry's spiritual realm. *The Pelicans,* completed in 1921, is the story of an exceedingly kindly father with literary inclinations whose ungrateful offspring wish to become, respectively, a jockey and a photographer. Radiguet did effect a striking, if passing, relationship to modernity in his play by frequent references to several currently popular preoccupations. While Apollinaire related his play to his time by writing a prologue in which World War I was evoked, and Cocteau presented the Eiffel Tower, photography, bicycling, and a fashionable bathing beauty, Radiguet modernized what is essentially a delightful domestic comedy by devising a plot in which photography, swimming races, and an

C. F. Ramuz recalls that the composer had originally planned ". . . to place, in the wings, those giant music boxes which have been the style in the villages . . . wedding guests generally slip in two sous to start things going." (*Stravinsky in the Theatre*, ed. M. Lederman [special number of *Dance Index*, 1947], p. 245.) *L'Histoire du Soldat* (1917), with text by Ramuz, is a ballet "to be read, played, and danced," and utilizes the stage for simultaneous performances of narrator, actor-dancers, and orchestra.

attitude of utter flippancy toward familial matters play a large part. Perhaps more important is the fact that in the artlessness of the various dénouements, a characteristic which appears rarely in the few extant works of Radiguet (who died in 1923), there is a definite echo of an even more revolutionary literary current than that represented by his friend Cocteau—the Dada movement.

It remained for a group of refugees who fled from the battle-torn countries of World War I to neutral Switzerland to carry Jarry's immediate implications to a point of absolute no-return. The Dada movement was founded in a cabaret in Zürich in 1916 under the leadership of Tristan Tzara and a handful of friends. Thoroughly disgusted by what they considered to be the collapse of civilization, as evidenced by the war, the young Dada writers and painters felt that since the vaguely humanistic ethical values society claimed to hold were obviously proved false by its participation in world war, its literary values could no longer hold true. The Dadaists determined, in their poems, plays, collages, and frottages, as well as in their public performances at the Cabaret Voltaire, to meet the meaninglessness of contemporary civilization with a meaninglessness of their own: the movement's very name owes its existence to a reportedly random dip into a dictionary of French (the word itself stands for the childish nickname for "hobbyhorse" in that language). According to Tristan Tzara himself, writing in the 1918 edition of one of his many Dada manifestoes:

> Every product of disgust capable of becoming a negation of the family is Dada; a protest with the fists of its whole being engaged in destructive action: Dada; knowledge of all the means rejected up until now by the shamefaced sex of comfortable compromise and good manners: Dada; abolition of logic, which is the dance of those impotent to create: Dada; of every social hierarchy and equation set up for the sake of values by our valets: Dada; every object, all objects, sentiments, obscurities, apparitions and the precise clash of parallel lines are weapons for the fight: Dada; abolition of memory: Dada; abolition of archaeology: Dada; abolition of prophets: Dada; abolition of the future: Dada; absolute and unquestionable faith in every god that is the immediate product of spontaneity. . . .[11]

[11] *The Dada Painters and Poets*, ed. Robert Motherwell (New York: Wittenborn, 1951), p. 81.

The Dada attitude has been summarized more recently by Marcel Raymond:

> Dada thus appears as a desperate systematic skepticism leading directly to negation. Man is nothing. "Measured by the scale of eternity, any activity is futile," says Tzara. And André Breton: "It is inadmissible that man should leave a trace of his passage on earth." Everything is of equal insignificance. "What is beautiful? What is ugly? What is great, strong, weak? What is Carpentier, Renan, Foch? Don't know. What is myself? Don't know. . . ." These words by Georges Ribemont-Dessaignes are saluted by Breton as an act of great humility. To utter any judgement, to claim to distinguish the true from the false, is a mark of ridiculous presumption, for actually nothing can be contradicted. At about the same time Einstein's theory was encouraging people to believe that everything was relative to circumstance, to man, and that nothing in the world had any importance at all.[12]

It is obvious that this philosophy in its purest, most negative sense, as practiced in Zürich, and later in Paris, Berlin, and New York, might have little interest for us today had the destructive frolics of the Dadaists not taken on the form of something else: that of bona fide literary and artistic experiment. The best of the Dada writings (works of Tzara, Breton, and Aragon certainly among them), like the best of the Dada works of art (the collages of Ernst, Schwitters, the "readymades" of Duchamp, and the reliefs of Arp), make experiments with such "unartistic" devices as deliberate monotony and complete illogicality of structure in a way that is anything but permanently disorganizing to the imagination. Ubu himself had exclaimed at one point, "We won't have demolished anything at all if we don't demolish even the ruins!" In "demolishing even the ruins" the Dada writers, by their single-minded devotion to pointlessness, plunged their art into an atmosphere of experimentalism which, as many of them realized later as they continued to write, is not at all detrimental to the health of literature.

The postwar sequel to the activity at the Cabaret Voltaire was a series of "manifestations" and "Dada Festivals" staged by the Dadaist writers in various cabarets, halls, and theatres in Paris. At one of these "manifestations," which were frequently punctuated

---

[12] *From Baudelaire to Surrealism*, pref. Harold Rosenberg (New York: Wittenborn, 1950), p. 270.

by barrages of insults, and sometimes by rotten eggs, one of the most effective of Dada plays, Tristan Tzara's *The Gas Heart*, was first performed. *The Gas Heart* is, indeed, one of the few examples of Dada performances to survive today, since they were often staged merely to vary the program during evenings of reading of Dada poetry or to be played between demonstrations and riots, as it were.

Despite its author's modest introductory disclaimer, this play is a thoroughly innovative work and strikes us more with the force of pure visual and verbal spectacle than as what—even in the light of much later developments—can easily be considered theatre. *The Gas Heart* confronts us with a group of characters named after, of all things, parts of the head—a scheme which might have inspired a dramatist of more delicate fantasy to create conversations appropriate to nose, ear, mouth, neck, eye, and eyebrow. Instead, these characters speak without reference to their names, and generally at cross-purposes, repeating, as if obsessed, a simple verbal pattern or perhaps a proverb. While this ceremonial use of the banal is prophetic of the domestic verbal delirium employed by later writers especially for satirical purposes, the effect here is that of a concatenation of colliding chants, or of ritual.

Tzara's *The Gas Heart* received its first performance informally, with the leading Dadaists in the leading roles, in 1920. At its première with professional actors, in 1923, the poet Paul Eluard, representing Tzara's literary camp, came to blows on stage with André Breton, the leader of a new rival literary group which was soon to become, under his leadership, the Surrealist movement.

Ever since, critics have attempted to isolate the difference between Dada and Surrealism. It is now fairly clear that whereas Dada developed as an immediate result of the feelings of disappointment and disgust following World War I, the early years of Surrealism as a movement are related primarily to the literary preoccupations of André Breton; and that these preoccupations, unlike those of the Dada leaders, were anything but negative. Whereas many of the leading Dadaists were beginning to point out, around 1921, that a movement claiming to be devoted entirely to nihilistic gestures ought, as a final effort, to abolish even itself, Breton began in late 1921 to publicize his projected "Congress of the Modern Spirit," or "Congress of Paris," which he scheduled for 1922. It is no wonder that many Paris Dadaists, after five years of public negations, deserted to his literary camp when Breton announced his congressional plans. It is perhaps no wonder too that although this particular plan of Breton's miscarried shortly after it was conceived, Dada was already fatally disconcerted. Generally, those of its partisans who continued to write and paint continued their work independently, or else continued it as Surrealists.

Complicated as its history is, we can isolate as one of the most important elements in the early years of Surrealism, and of the *avant-garde* drama of the Twenties as well, Breton's intense interest in contemporary developments in psychiatry. Breton, a former student of medicine, returned to Paris after the war following a tour of duty as a psychiatric aide at a series of army neurological hospitals. He was a devoted disciple of Freud, with whom he actually secured an interview in 1921; and when, in 1924, as the unofficially accepted spokesman for the Surrealist movement, Breton issued the first of his *Manifestoes of Surrealism*, he outlined a Surrealist literary methodology which was far closer to psychiatry than even he could keep within his own work.

In the first of Breton's Surrealist manifestoes—which generally were to have the almost consistent effect of arousing various protests and apostasies within all factions of the Surrealist movement —he daringly outlined his curious theory of "Automatic Writing." Here, he couched his definition of Surrealism strictly in terms of psychiatric technique, drawing a literary parallel to the psychiatrist's encouragement of spontaneous speech in analysis. Surrealism was, Breton said, "A psychic automatism with the aid of which we propose to express the real functioning of thought, either orally, or in writing, or in any other way. A dictation of thought without any control of reason, outside all aesthetic or moral preoccupation." [13]

Breton's recommendation that literary primacy be given the subconscious is actually somewhat less revolutionary than it might appear to be. Jarry, whose hero crashes through all kingly conventions for the sake of the unashamed satisfaction of his whims, would have especially understood Breton's emphasis on the abolition of moral preoccupations in literature. Dada certainly might

---

[13] *Manifestes du Surréalisme* (Paris: Pauvert, 1962), p. 40.

have approved of the anti-artistic climate of Breton's manifesto, had it not resisted on principle the somewhat positivistic, pseudo-scientific aspect of the document. Nonetheless, few works were actually composed which strictly adhered to the automatic ideal. With few exceptions, the Surrealist eventually revealed himself as a determined artist, unwilling to abandon himself without considerable qualification to the winds of psychic chance. It is clear from the prose of Breton's manifesto itself—which is stylistically distinguished with respect to the very logical values Surrealism considered anathema—that Breton's own postwar surrender to the unconscious was anything but unconditional. Breton had discussed other aspects of Surrealism in his first manifesto (especially its relationship to the dream and trance, and what Breton called "the Marvelous"), and it is these aspects which captured the imaginations of most Surrealist writers, and eventually more fully occupied the imagination of Breton himself.

The text most often cited as the best example of pure automatic writing is *Les Champs Magnétiques*, written in late 1919 and early 1920 by Breton in collaboration with the poet Philippe Soupault. A second work composed by Breton and Soupault during this period is the play *If You Please*, which would appear to be one of the first Surrealist attempts to employ automatic writing in a modified form. Written before Surrealism as such officially existed, the play also exhibits many outward signs of the then contemporary movement, Dada, notably in the presentation of the following statement in place of act four: "The authors . . . do not want the fourth act printed." To add to the confusion, the literary style of the piece varies widely—perhaps less because of its collaborative origin than because of the desire of its authors to flaunt the usual literary goal of homogeneity of style. The play itself presents three separate sets of characters, in differing situations. An amusing picture of an office, with a busy executive administering a business which is at the same time a marriage agency, detective bureau, counseling service, and jewel thieves' clearinghouse creates, out of commercial nonsequiturs, a magically illogical reality in the second act. The first and third acts employ a highly irrational, freely associative speech to convey the thoughts of overwrought lovers. In employing the flamboyant linguistic flights of automatic writing to express the sentiments of individuals under intense emotional stress and strain, Breton evoked an important aesthetic value indeed: that of expressive appropriateness.[14]

The idea of using automatic writing in a suitably expressive way seems to have influenced Louis Aragon in the writing of his play *The Mirror-Wardrobe One Fine Evening*. This was written in 1923, when Aragon—who later attacked Breton, and of course abandoned anti-realistic techniques in his later, naturalistic novels—was a leading member of the Surrealist circle. The play's pretext, like that of the first and third acts of *If You Please*, is a dramatic situation so outworn, so common, as to suggest melodrama—if not bedroom farce. Here, a husband comes home to the suspicion that his wife's lover is hiding in the clothes closet. The tension between the daringly old-fashioned structure of the play proper and the irrationality of the actions of its characters (*this* husband delays opening the closet, as his wife constantly urges him to, by his brilliant speech-making) seems to bring fresh dimensions to both Surrealist theatre and domestic melodrama. It is perhaps further indicative of the increasing range of "irrational" theatre that the characters of the Prologue to the play (which relates only obliquely to the plot itself), among them a soldier, an unhappy mother, a general, and the President of the Republic, manage to reflect sharply the author's later aims as a political novelist.

One of the emerging characteristics of the new, post-Jarry theatre, of paramount importance in Aragon's play, is its increasing stress on purely verbal inventiveness. It would, of course, be possible to explain this tendency by directing our attention to the fact that the most adventurous of the playwrights who followed Jarry were in fact poets: with Apollinaire, Cocteau, Radiguet, Tzara, Aragon, Soupault, and Breton we have the list, excluding a

---

[14] In his *Second Manifesto of Surrealism* (1929) Breton assigned a relatively minor role to automatic writing. Gradually Breton and Soupault had both turned their interest from automatic writing to what might be termed "the automatic life." Breton's novel *Nadja* (1928) and Soupault's novel *Le Voyage d'Horace Pirouelle* (1925)—among their authors' best works—relate the "marvelous" adventures of their mysteriously motivated characters in prose of a strict, almost classical clarity. The techniques of psychic automatism may have been most fully embodied in the work of certain French Surrealist painters in the Thirties. Several of these came to the United States—as did Breton himself—during World War II; and partly through their influence automatism came to play a crucial role in the formation of the characteristic style of American Abstract-Expressionism, or "Action Painting."

very few, of the most distinguished French poets of the early part of the twentieth century. This verbally spectacular "poets' theatre" is probably equally explicable by the fact that Jarry himself, in emphasizing anti-realistic stagecraft, implied a challenge—unaccepted until the Twenties and the advent of Surrealism—to the concept of the play as an art form bound to theatrical actualization. It may well be that the use of a common plot in *The Mirror-Wardrobe One Fine Evening* represents an effort to keep the play in an actable form—to weight it, as it were, to the stage.

It is in several plays by authors whose work lies outside the official Surrealist movement—André Breton having in effect "excommunicated" them, or they themselves having from the first avoided the relationship—that we find an ultimate experimental exaggeration of the Dadaist and Surrealist tendency toward what is perhaps an ultimately untheatrical, purely verbal brilliance. Around 1922, while a young habitué of coffeehouse concerts, Armand Salacrou wrote, "as if to the music," several plays in the most advanced contemporary idiom of his time. One of two recently republished by its author, *A Circus Story*, is apparently from Salacrou's descriptions of its origins, as well as from evidence provided by the play itself, one of the earliest independent dramatic explorations of the automatic writing aesthetic. Completely extravagant in its plot, as well as in its suggestions of events to take place on stage (as would seem appropriate for the events in a circus tent), it has been termed by its author a "Pièce à Lire," a play for reading.

René Daumal and Roger Gilbert-Lecomte, who as young men were first to achieve notoriety as critics of orthodox Surrealism in their magazine, *Le Grand Jeu*, had earlier carried Surrealist methods to grotesque extremes in a series of playlets they wrote while schoolmates. Composed in 1924, when their authors were approximately the same age as Jarry when he first worked at *King Ubu*, Daumal's *En Gggarrrde!* and Gilbert-Lecomte's *The Odyssey of Ulysses the Palmiped* employ orthodox Surrealist techniques so lightheartedly they seem to satirize them. While the pretense of actability is maintained, and elaborate stage directions are conscientiously given, these short pieces are nevertheless unprecedently unproducible. Their emphasis on the ridiculous aspects of Surrealism perhaps places them closest in spirit to the nonsense writings now recognized as foreshadowing Surrealism, rather than to most other writings of that early Surrealist era.

With the unstageable "plays for reading" by Salacrou—as well as by Daumal and Gilbert-Lecomte—the Dadaist and Surrealist drama reached what might well be regarded as an aesthetic impasse. The newest branch of *avant-garde* theatre would almost certainly have atrophied fatally had not a theatrical theorist of genius appeared to provide the catalyst which not only continued it, but finally effected its rebirth as the *avant-garde* drama of today. When in 1938 Antonin Artaud published a selection of his essays on the theatre, *The Theatre and Its Double*, he crystalized into text theatrical implications which had arisen as early as the 1896 première of *King Ubu*. Indeed, the close relationship Artaud felt to Jarry is signified by the name he and Roger Vitrac gave to the experimental theatre they founded in Paris in 1927—the Théâtre Alfred Jarry.

Describing the program of the Théâtre Alfred Jarry at its inception, Artaud stated that it proposed ". . . to contribute by strictly theatrical means to the ruin of the theatre as it exists today in France."[15] He elaborated: "The Théâtre Alfred Jarry has been created . . . to return to the theatre that total liberty which exists in music, poetry, or painting, and of which it has been curiously bereft up to now."[16]

In *The Theatre and Its Double* Artaud placed the blame for the imaginative poverty of the conventional French theatre as squarely as possible on "culture." By culture, Artaud meant the patterns of artificiality which civilization—especially Western civilization—had imposed upon human nature; and, indeed, Artaud's concept of the theatre obviously stems from an intense desire to do justice to what he considered the essentials of the human personality, as much as from purely artistic considerations. Artaud's yearning for theatrical innocence, which hauntingly recalls Rousseau's belief that the human soul is crushed by the restraints imposed upon it by a corrupting civilization, had predictably revolutionary ramifications. To Artaud the hidden core of art was pure emotion: only the instinctive human desires (anger, hate, longing, and the most intense physical desires) are worthy of consideration by the artist.

[15] *Oeuvres Complètes*, Vol. II (Paris: Gallimard, 1962), p. 37.
[16] Ibid., p. 33.

The theatre must resist the artificial hierarchy of values imposed by "culture" by being consistently uninhibited; and it must demonstrate the true reality of the human soul, and the mercilessly savage conditions under which it operates, by what Artaud called a "Theatre of Cruelty."

Cruelty in the theatre does not mean, Artaud was careful to point out, the mere dramatization of the techniques of physical laceration. Artaud thought that, above all, theatrical expression had to be given to an impersonal, implacable cruelty, lying essentially outside of man: the cruelty of the universe itself, in all its natural, violent force. "Everything that acts is a cruelty," Artaud wrote. "It is upon this idea of extreme action, pushed to its limits, that the theatre must be built." [17]

Artaud realized that in order to express best his idea of primordial theatre, a stage would be necessary that would completely overwhelm its audience. He therefore recommended the abolition of all physical barriers between theatregoer and actor. "We abolish the stage and the auditorium and replace them by a single site," he wrote, "without partition or barrier of any kind . . . a direct communication will be re-established . . . the spectator, placed in the middle of the action, is engulfed and physically affected by it." [18] He also recommended the intensification of the theatrical means itself, and found an example of a stage utilizing the full resources of the theatre in ". . . the spectacle of the Balinese theatre, which draws upon dance, song, pantomime—and a little of the theatre as we understand it in the Occident. . . ." [19] The Balinese theatre, which was virtually wordless, or which used words in a ritualistic, incantatory sense, presented a perfect antidote to ". . . our purely verbal theatre, unaware of everything that makes theatre." [20] Emphasizing special vocal intonations, spectacle, ritual, actors' masks, as well as fresh concepts of lighting, scenery, and costuming—in short, as many techniques specifically at the disposal of the theatre as possible—Artaud outlined a system of almost totally anti-realistic drama. Even today, Artaud's dramatic prescriptions are among the most technically and philosophically

[17] *The Theatre and Its Double*, trans. Mary C. Richards (New York: Grove Press, 1958), p. 42.
[18] Ibid., p. 96.
[19] Ibid., p. 53.
[20] Ibid., p. 56.

revolutionary extant; and there are few *avant-garde* playwrights today to whom Artaud's comprehensive aesthetic crystallizations do not apply.

It is a curious, yet understandable, aspect of Artaud's view of the theatre that he did not emphasize the writing of fresh theatrical texts. Artaud himself wrote very few plays, preferring to devote himself to the form of pantomime, or to the textless restaging of older theatrical and even non-theatrical works. His short play, *Jet of Blood*, produced at the Théâtre Alfred Jarry in 1927, is one of the few original works we can turn to in order to see what Artaud may have ideally thought of as drama, in any conventional sense. Artaud, who did in fact work in the cinema, as actor, director, and adapter, seems to envision this play in terms of a vocabulary of pure theatrical impossibility. Here we have the disintegration of all values imposed by civilization spectacularly symbolized in the tumbling down of live pieces of human bodies, and whole temples; the revolt against all superimposed, man-made (and therefore unnatural) convention in the deliberately startling blasphemy of the whore biting God's wrist; and the "theatre of cruelty" in the frenziedly discontinuous activity which characterizes the entire play. Still, *Jet of Blood* escapes the classification "play for reading" by the narrowest of margins.

It remained for a play by Roger Vitrac, *The Mysteries of Love*, written about 1924, and directed by Antonin Artaud at the Théâtre Alfred Jarry in 1927, to represent both the culmination of the Surrealist drama and at the same time bring Artaud's own dramatic theories effectively to the stage. Subtitled "A Surrealist Drama," this play with its incessant lovers' quarrels has that much in common with Aragon's *The Mirror-Wardrobe One Fine Evening*, with which its composition is roughly contemporary (indeed, Aragon's play is dedicated to Vitrac). Described by Artaud himself as a "real dream," [21] Vitrac's first play uniquely employs the orthodox Surrealist elements it contains. Artaud himself had once written:

> It has always been far from our thoughts to consider Surrealism as a method capable of effectiveness solely through the means of automatic writing. Surrealism is perfectly consistent with a certain lucidity. In this lucidity a superior logic participates. . . . [22]

[21] *Oeuvres Complètes*, Vol. II, p. 38.
[22] Ibid., pp. 164–65.

The "superior logic" prevailing here is unquestionably that of Artaud's theatrical thinking. One of the most striking features of this amusing and also very violent drama is its highly innovative mingling of audience and performance. At the outset establishing the "direct communication" Artaud had called for, the play does not begin on the stage, but rather in a box overlooking the stage which simply comes to life at curtain time, almost as if the audience itself was being presented.[23] After the relocation of the action, which soon shifts to the stage, the audience is consistently invited in every way short of actual participation to enter into the play itself. Vitrac's methods of accomplishing this accelerated involvement range from the traditional theatrical device of the "aside," through the recurrent intervention of the "author" himself in his play (whom Vitrac ironically pictures as a rather conventional literary "type"), to the final violence of the denouement in which, in an unprecedentedly desperate effort to involve the audience in the action of a play, one member of the audience is shot (and killed) from the stage.

The relationship of the plays of Jean Anouilh to anti-realistic theatre has often and correctly been noted. In Anouilh's work, an ingenious and fanciful approach to the stage generally brings us to the borders, if not the interior, of the fantastic. The playwright's use of whimsical structural devices—disguises, mistaken identities, and denouements of sudden simplicity in which it is impossible to believe—reinforces the impression of this literary territory. Anouilh's presentation of harlequin-like sprites in his dramas and interpolated musical and balletic sequences (suggesting the *Commedia dell'Arte* and other time-honored genres of theatrical stylization) tend to place his virtuosic use of anti-realistic stagecraft conspicuously within the perspective of tradition.

In 1929, with the Surrealist movement still at its first full tide, Anouilh, in collaboration with the screen-writer Jean Aurenche, wrote one of his first plays, *Humulus the Mute*, in a way which appears to have been influenced directly by contemporary developments. Written when Anouilh was in his late teens, this play seems

---

[23] This device may reflect, together with the influence of Artaud, the ideas of Pirandello, whose *Six Characters in Search of an Author* was first presented in Paris in 1923.

to have been structured solely in order to vaporize at the play-wrights' pleasure with a bitterly silly, pointless joke, in the purest Dadaist tradition. The remarkably monstrous Duchess who mani-acally dominates the piece, the orchestra which comments rau-cously upon the action, the sudden descent of one character to the steps of the stage, and the bicycling scenes toward the close are among those features which most strikingly recall popular stage imagery of that time. Nor is this the only direct evidence we have of Anouilh's sympathy with radical theatrical developments of this period. In 1962, Roger Vitrac's second play, *Victor, ou Les Enfants au Pouvoir*, performed at the Théâtre Alfred Jarry in 1929, was revived in Paris under Anouilh's aegis.

Possibly the first masterpiece produced by Surrealism in the theatre is *La Place de l'Étoile* by Robert Desnos. Desnos, a brilliant poet whose skillful experiments in dream-dictated literature and in automatic (and semi-automatic) writing astonished even Breton himself, began this play in 1927; he completed it shortly before his arrest and deportation to the concentration camp where he was interned as a member of the French Resistance, and where he died. The world of dream is allusively and delicately evoked in this fantasy having in part to do with the proliferation of starfish in Paris. Despite the subtlety of its methods, the intention of *La Place de l'Étoile* is as ambitious as any drama in the post-Jarry theatre: the abolition on the stage of all boundaries usually ac-cepted for practical reasons—those lying between wakefulness and sleep, between the living and the dead, the possible and the im-possible, for example. Desnos more than vaguely accomplishes the evocation of the blatantly anti-realistic world of his beliefs in his play. It proceeds with a lyrical delicacy that is far more character-istic of the finest works of Surrealism than those who associate it invariably with the obvious heresies of a Dali might imagine it to be.

With the plays of Jean Tardieu, classified by their author under the headings "Chamber Theatre," or "Poems to be Played," we seem to enter one-room laboratories in which many of the most advanced experiments in the *avant-garde* theatre are taking place. With remarkable regularity, Tardieu's plays propose original the-atrical systems, briefly experiment with them, and then dismiss them—often never again to reappear in their author's work. *One Way for Another* is characteristic of this playwright's highly exacting technical method; yet at the same time the play is a delightful spoof of the arbitrary and perhaps ultimately meaningless conventions of social etiquette. Tardieu's picture of the upside-down world of the Nameless Archipelago, in which coughing is substituted for applause, insults take the place of compliments, and failure is the only form of success, is perfectly apt satire; yet even André Breton would have found it difficult to improve upon such solemn absurdities as Tardieu's representation of people greeting each other by shaking feet.

In Robert Pinget's *Architruc* we find ourselves again in the world of an irrational king. Like Ubu, Architruc inhabits a whimsically childish world; but instead of devoting himself to leading impossible troop movements or arranging assassinations of reigning sovereigns, Architruc spends his life on a nostalgic, other-worldly plane, in regretful rumination. He is returned to reality only by the refusals of his minister, Baga, to permit him sweets, liqueurs, overeating, or any other form of self-indulgence. In his meditative, conscience-stricken approach to all things, Architruc may be said to resemble Ubu turned, gently and sadly, inside out. Far from wishing to murder his predecessor, Architruc is above all concerned lest his own succession be ended, a situation that his touching relationship with his only real companion, his minister, emphasizes poignantly. The lonely life of this ruler, in which only memory has any potency, is plainly reminiscent of the spirit of certain works by Samuel Beckett; and Beckett, who translated Pinget's earlier play, *La Manivelle* (quite appropriately into Irish dialect, as *The Old Tune*), is a close friend of the author of *Architruc*.

It has often been pointed out that Samuel Beckett occupies a double position in literary history: one of the most powerful writers in the French theatre, he is also one of the most important figures in contemporary Irish—and perhaps English—literature, a worthy successor to James Joyce. Beckett excepted, the most familiar figure in the tradition of Jarryesque theatre in France today is, it seems safe to say, Eugène Ionesco. Although the entire *oeuvre* of this writer, his plays as well as his many remarkable essays on the theatre, exhibits qualities which would have delighted Jarry (no less than would Ionesco's possession of the rank of Transcendent Satrap in the Collège de 'Pataphysique [24]), perhaps in no play more than *The Painting* is Ionesco's concern with anti-naturalistic theatrical technique emphasized more unequivocally—both inside and outside the play proper.

In a brief introduction to *The Painting* (a work written in 1954, in the early years of its author's career), Ionesco states both the premises of his play and those of his work in general—and reasserts as well the premises of the whole theatrical movement of which he has become such an important part. In a manner somewhat atypical of recent Jarryesque writers (who, unlike Jarry and his immediate successors, Apollinaire, Cocteau, and Tzara, have not needed so greatly to preface their work with combative manifestoes) Ionesco remarks in his introduction about the first, evidently conventional performance of *The Painting*: "The interpreters had committed an important error: they had adopted for the first part of the play a realistic, even naturalistic manner. . . ."

In the particular anti-realistic style chosen for *The Painting* Ionesco seems to hark back specifically to the early days of the modern French *avant-garde* theatrical tradition. The play itself is subtitled "guignolade," and Ionesco here draws upon the same guignol, or puppet-play style Jarry adopted in *Ubu*, employing as a primary expressive means the knockabout, broadly humorous features of that variety of dramatic entertainment.

The Painting presents us with two self-styled devotees of what they consider to be art, in a situation which seems realistic enough. One individual is a wealthy patron of the arts, who believes that

---

[24] The Collège de 'Pataphysique might be described as an international society for artistic or other embodiment of 'pataphysical principles. It derives its name from the "science" of 'pataphysics, invented by Alfred Jarry (probably in ironic homage to Hébert, the physics teacher who served as model for the first Father Ubu) and described in Jarry's collection of meditations *Gestes and Opinions du Docteur Faustroll* (1898) as ". . . the science of the realm beyond metaphysics. . . . It will study the laws which govern exceptions and will explain the universe supplementary to this one; or, less ambitiously, it will describe a universe which one can see—must see perhaps—in place of the traditional one." Jarry defined 'pataphysics with witty gravity as ". . . the science of imaginary solutions, which symbolically attributes the properties of objects, described by their virtuality, to their lineaments" ([Paris: Fasquelle, 1955], p. 32). Among the officers of the Collège in France alone are the painters Joan Miro, Jean Dubuffet, and Marcel Duchamp, the poet Jacques Prévert, the poet and novelist Raymond Queneau, the cartoonist Siné, the filmmaker René Clair, and playwright Ionesco.

a painting should be an exact representation of reality; the other is the kind of "artist" who devotes himself to producing pleasant pictures of that reality, here in the form of a sentimentalized portrait of a pretty woman. Hovering over the painting, both men engage in a kind of linguistic and aesthetic slapstick, the senseless character of their dialogue (which Ionesco admittedly exaggerated by making even more senseless than it might have been) being paralleled outlandishly on the physical plane. It is clearly an important part of Ionesco's meaning that he urges, both in the introduction and within the play itself, that the most apt behavior for these individuals be exaggerated and preposterous in action and speech, in the manner of puppets or buffoons.

Although statements of aesthetics do appear in Ionesco's plays, and one entire play, *Improvisation, or the Shepherd's Chameleon*, is devoted to a discussion of theatrical theoretics, *The Painting* may be said to be increasingly atypical of Ionesco's dramatic preoccupations. In most of his later works, Ionesco has turned in more obviously outward directions—directions which might have seemed highly improbable both from the point of view of Ionesco's own earlier works as well as earlier post-Jarry theatre. In such plays as *Rhinoceros*, performed five years after the inappropriately naturalistic première of *The Painting*, we find Ionesco dealing unmistakably with social and political questions in a way which is as ingenious as it is dramatic, well within the context of techniques favored by the post-Jarry theatre.[25]

Indeed, the impression left by the foremost French playwrights today, as well as by their American and English cognates and derivatives, is far less that of rampant irrationality than of ultimately didactic intent. The most important practitioners of the post-Jarry theatre have, in one or another of their works, reclaimed for their own questions which might have seemed most appropriate within the naturalistic repertoire of "problems." To name some of the best known plays of the four most familiar playwrights of the current *avant-garde* French theatre: Ionesco's

[25] Ionesco's use of the technically virtuosic, highly sophisticated post-Jarry theatre to deal with events with a strong social and political flavor has interesting parallels in more or less recent developments in the other arts. Perhaps the most striking is Picasso's use of complex anti-realistic techniques refined from those of Cubism in his *Guernica* (1937). In a sense, *Rhinoceros*—if not the earlier *The Killer*—is Ionesco's *Guernica*.

Rhinoceros, among its other possible interpretations, may be read as an allegory having to do with the difficulty of remaining a balanced individual in a group gone mad; Beckett's *Waiting for Godot* appears to recommend increased humanity in a world deprived of a deity; Adamov's *Ping Pong* warns against allegedly soul-destroying systems operating in the world today; and Genêt's *The Blacks* seems to predict the doom of Western civilization unless "minorities" shortly receive their deserts.

It is perhaps this willingness to come to terms—no matter how complex the terms may be—with questions of wide public interest (although that very public, confused by the plays, may entirely miss the presence of those questions) that implies a fresh role for the post-Jarry theatre. The term *avant-garde* is a relative expression, defined by audience as well as by works of art, and despite the more than half-century-old traditions of the "new" French theatre, it is in the relative sense that we have used it here. The fact that Cubism or the classic works of the founders of twentieth-century music continue to outrage a surprising number of those who consider themselves sincere devotees of the arts, may indicate that this term, used in any contemporary context, has a long way to go before public approbation disqualifies it. However, judging from what appears to be a particularly great cultural lag in the theatre (for anti-realistic developments in such non-theatrical fields as painting, sculpture, the novel, poetry, and the film have for the most part been widely accepted, while precisely parallel phenomena in the theatre are just beginning to achieve general recognition) it would seem that this term is fated to an exceptionally long theatrical life.

The essential seriousness of much of the drama deriving from Jarryesque techniques is quite apparent. However, it is probable that the type of theatre implied by *Ubu* has not ended with the intensely didactic themes of its current practitioners. The remarkably generous legacy of Alfred Jarry's revolution in the theatre is sufficient to be an abundant source of theatrical originality for generations of playwrights to come.

MICHAEL BENEDIKT

POSTSCRIPT

No discussion of currents in the *avant-garde* French theatre would be complete without reference to the remarkable directors who have been responsible for its presentation. It was the role of such *metteurs en scène* as Jacques Copeau, Charles Dullin, Louis Jouvet, Gaston Baty, Georges Pitëoff, and today, Roger Blin and Jean-Louis Barrault, to achieve a luster in the area of anti-realistic production at least comparable to that of André Antoine and his celebrated naturalistic "Théâtre Libre" in Jarry's day. The elaborate production notes that Jarry issued to Lugné-Poë, the first director of *King Ubu*, and W. B. Yeats' contemporary account of the actual production suggest that *Ubu* was as much a reaction to the unimaginative styles of direction of that day as to the playwriting. Artaud's apparent casualness with regard to the creation of new texts of his own and the brief emphasis in the 1920's on the so-called *pièce à lire* point toward the fresh emphasis and new demands made on the director. Such recent phenomena as the now almost universally performed "Theatre Piece" (the theatrical performance based on literary material originally not meant for the stage) and the American-born "Happening" are doubtless related branches of this particular theatrical development.

M.B.

king ubu

by ALFRED JARRY

translated by Michael Benedikt and George E. Wellwarth

Then Father Ubu shakes
his peare, who was afterwards
yclept SHAKESPEARE by the
Englishe, and you have from
him in his own hand manie
lovely tragedies
under this name.

CHARACTERS AND COSTUMES

FATHER UBU: Casual gray suit, a cane always stuffed in his right-hand pocket, bowler hat. A crown over his hat at the beginning of Act II, Scene 2. Bareheaded at the beginning of Act II, Scene 6. Act III, Scene 22, crown and white hood, flaring to a royal cape. Act III, Scene 4, cloak, cap pulled down over his ears; same outfit, but with bare head in Scene 7. Scene 8, hood, helmet, a sword stuck in his belt, a hook, chisels, a knife, a cane still in his right-hand pocket. A bottle bounces at his side. Act IV, Scene 5, cloak and cap but without above weapons or stick. In the sailing scene a small suitcase is in Father Ubu's hand.

MOTHER UBU: Concierge's clothes or a toiletries saleswoman's ensemble. Pink bonnet or a hat with flowers and feathers and a veil. An apron in the feasting scene. Royal cloak at the opening of Act II, Scene 6.

CAPTAIN BORDURE: Hungarian musician's costume, very close-fitting, red. Big mantle, large sword, crenelated boots, feathery hat.

KING WENCESLAS: Royal mantle and the crown Ubu wears after murdering him.

QUEEN ROSEMONDE: The mantle and crown Mother Ubu later wears.

BOLESLAS, LADISLAS (sons of King Wenceslas and Queen Rosemonde): Gray Polish costumes, heavily frogged; short pants.

BOUGRELAS (the youngest son): Dressed as a child in a little skirt and bonnet.

GENERAL LASCY: Polish costume, with an admiral's hat with white plumes, and a sword.

STANISLAS LECZINSKY: Polish costume. White beard.

JOHN SOBIESKI, NICHOLAS RENSKY: Polish costume.

THE CZAR, EMPEROR ALEXIS: Black clothing, enormous yellow sword, dagger, numerous military decorations, big boots. Huge frill at the throat. Hat in the form of a black cone.

THE PALOTINS (GIRON, PILE, COTICE): Long beards, fur-trimmed greatcoats, shitr-colored; or red or green if necessary; tights beneath.

CROWD: Polish costume.

MICHAEL FEDEROVITCH: Same. Fur hat.

NOBLES: Polish costume, with cloaks edged with fur or embroidery.

ADVISERS, FINANCIERS: Swathed in black, with astrologers' hats, eyeglasses, pointed noses.

PHYNANCIAL FLUNKIES: The Palotins.

PEASANTS: Polish costume.

THE POLISH ARMY: In gray, with frogging and fur trimmings: three men with rifles.

THE RUSSIAN ARMY: Two horsemen: uniform like that of the Poles, but green, with fur headgear. They carry cardboard horses' heads.

A RUSSIAN FOOTSOLDIER: In green, with headgear.

MOTHER UBU'S GUARDS: Polish costume, with halberds.

A CAPTAIN: General Lascy.

THE BEAR: Bordure in bearskin.

THE PHYNANCIAL HORSE: Large wooden rocking horse on casters, or else cardboard horse's head, as required.

THE CREW: Two men in sailor suits, in blue, collars turned down, and so on.

THE CAPTAIN OF THE SHIP: In a French naval officer's uniform.

JAILER *

MESSENGER *

* Jarry did not include suggestions for the costuming of these two characters in these notes, which were published from manuscript by the Collège de 'Pataphysique in 1951.

COMPOSITION OF THE ORCHESTRA

Oboes
Pipes
Blutwurst
Large Bass
Flageolets   Transverse Flutes
Flute
Little Bassoon   Big Bassoon
Triple Bassoon   Little Black Cornets
Shrill White Cornets
Horns   Sackbuts   Trombones
Green Hunting Horns   Reeds
Bagpipes
Bombardons   Timbals
Drum   Bass Drum
Grand Organs

ACT I

SCENE 1

Father Ubu, Mother Ubu.

FATHER UBU: Shitr!

MOTHER UBU: Well, that's a fine way to talk, Father Ubu. What a pigheaded ass you are!

FATHER UBU: I don't know what keeps me from bouncing your head off the wall, Mother Ubu!

MOTHER UBU: It's not *my* head you ought to be cracking, Father Ubu.

FATHER UBU: By my green candle, I don't know what you're talking about.

MOTHER UBU: What's this, Father Ubu, you mean to tell me you're satisfied with the way things are?

FATHER UBU: By my green candle, shitr, madam, certainly I'm satisfied with the way things are. After all, aren't I Captain of the Dragoons, confidential adviser to King Wenceslas, decorated with the order of the Red Eagle of Poland, and ex-King of Aragon—what more do you want?

MOTHER UBU: What's this! After having been King of Aragon you're satisfied with leading fifty-odd flunkies armed with cabbage-cutters to parades? When you could just as well have the crown of Poland replace the crown of Aragon on your big fat nut?

FATHER UBU: Ah! Mother Ubu I don't know what you're talking about.

MOTHER UBU: You're so stupid!

FATHER UBU: By my green candle, King Wenceslas is still very much alive; and even if he does die he's still got hordes of children, hasn't he?

MOTHER UBU: What's stopping you from chopping up his whole family and putting yourself in their place?

Alfred Jarry

FATHER UBU: Ah! Mother Ubu, you're doing me an injustice, and I'll stick you in your stewpot in a minute.

MOTHER UBU: Ha! Poor wretch, if I were stuck in the pot who'd sew up the seat of your pants?

FATHER UBU: Oh, really! And what of it? Don't I have an ass like everyone else?

MOTHER UBU: If I were you, I'd want to install that ass on a throne. You could get any amount of money, eat sausages all the time, and roll around the streets in a carriage.

FATHER UBU: If I were king I'd have them build me a big helmet just like the one I had in Aragon which those Spanish swine had the nerve to steal from me.

MOTHER UBU: You could also get yourself an umbrella and a big cape which would reach to your heels.

FATHER UBU: Ah! that does it! I succumb to temptation. That crock of shitr, that shitr of crock, if I ever run into him in a dark alley, I'll give him a bad fifteen minutes.

MOTHER UBU: Ah! Fine, Father Ubu, at last you're acting like a real man.

FATHER UBU: Oh, no! Me, the Captain of the Dragoons slaughter the King of Poland! Better far to die!

MOTHER UBU (*aside*): Oh, shitr! (*Aloud.*) So, then, you want to stay as poor as a churchmouse, Father Ubu?

FATHER UBU: Zounds, by my green candle, I'd rather be as poor as a starving, good rat than as rich as a wicked, fat cat.

MOTHER UBU: And the helmet? And the umbrella? And the big cape?

FATHER UBU: And what about them, Mother Ubu?

He leaves, slamming the door.

MOTHER UBU (*alone*): Crap, shitr, it's hard to get him started, but, crap, shitr, I think I've stirred him up. With the help of God and of myself, perhaps in eight days I'll be Queen of Poland.

Scene 2

A room in Father Ubu's house, with a splendidly laid table.

Father Ubu, Mother Ubu.

MOTHER UBU: So! Our guests are very late.

FATHER UBU: Yes, by my green candle, I'm dying of hunger. Mother Ubu, you're really ugly today. Is it because company's coming?

MOTHER UBU (*shrugging her shoulders*): Shitr!

FATHER UBU (*grabbing a roast chicken*): Gad, I'm hungry; I'm going to have a piece of this bird. It's a chicken, I think. Not bad at all.

MOTHER UBU: What are you doing, you swine? What will be left for our guests?

FATHER UBU: There will be plenty left for them. I won't touch another thing. Mother Ubu, go to the window and see if our guests are coming.

MOTHER UBU (*going*): I don't see anything.

Meanwhile, Father Ubu takes a piece of veal.

Ah, here come Captain Bordure and his boys. What are you eating now, Father Ubu?

FATHER UBU: Nothing, a little veal.

MOTHER UBU: Oh! the veal! the veal! The ox! He's eaten the veal! Help, help!

FATHER UBU: By my green candle, I'll scratch your eyes out.

The door opens.

Scene 3

Father Ubu, Mother Ubu, Captain Bordure and his followers.

MOTHER UBU: Good day, gentlemen; we've been anxiously awaiting you. Sit down.

CAPTAIN BORDURE: Good day, madam. Where's Father Ubu?

FATHER UBU: Here I am, here I am! Good lord, by my green candle, I'm fat enough, aren't I?

CAPTAIN BORDURE: Good day, Father Ubu. Sit down, boys.

They all sit.

FATHER UBU: Oof, a little more, and I'd have bust my chair.

CAPTAIN BORDURE: Well, Mother Ubu! What have you got that's good today?

MOTHER UBU: Here's the menu.

FATHER UBU: Oh! That interests me.

MOTHER UBU: Polish soup, roast ram, veal, chicken, chopped dog's liver, turkey's ass, charlotte russe . . .

FATHER UBU: Hey, that's plenty, I should think. You mean there's more?

MOTHER UBU (*continuing*): Frozen pudding, salad, fruits, dessert, boiled beef, Jerusalem artichokes, cauliflower à la shitr.

FATHER UBU: Hey! Do you think I'm the Emperor of China, to give all that away?

MOTHER UBU: Don't listen to him, he's feeble-minded.

FATHER UBU: Ah! I'll sharpen my teeth on your shanks.

MOTHER UBU: Try this instead, Father Ubu. Here's the Polish soup.

FATHER UBU: Crap, is that lousy!

CAPTAIN BORDURE: Hmm—it isn't very good, at that.

MOTHER UBU: What do you want, you bunch of crooks!

FATHER UBU (*striking his forehead*): Wait, I've got an idea. I'll be right back.

He leaves.

MOTHER UBU: Let's try the veal now, gentlemen.

CAPTAIN BORDURE: It's very good—I'm through.

MOTHER UBU: To the turkey's ass, next.

CAPTAIN BORDURE: Delicious, delicious! Long live Mother Ubu!

ALL: Long live Mother Ubu!

FATHER UBU (*returning*): And you will soon be shouting long live Father Ubu. (*He has a toilet brush in his hand, and he throws it on the festive board.*)

MOTHER UBU: Miserable creature, what are you up to now?

FATHER UBU: Try a little.

Several try it, and fall, poisoned.

Mother Ubu, pass me the roast ram chops, so that I can serve them.

MOTHER UBU: Here they are.

FATHER UBU: Everyone out! Captain Bordure, I want to talk to you.

THE OTHERS: But we haven't eaten yet.

FATHER UBU: What's that, you haven't eaten yet? Out, out, everyone out! Stay here, Bordure.

Nobody moves.

You haven't gone yet? By my green candle, I'll give you your ram chops. (*He begins to throw them.*)

ALL: Oh! Ouch! Help! Woe! Help! Misery! I'm dead!

FATHER UBU: Shitr, shitr, shitr! Outside! I want my way!

ALL: Everyone for himself! Miserable Father Ubu! Traitor! Meanie!

FATHER UBU: Ah! They've gone. I can breathe again—but I've had a rotten dinner. Come on, Bordure.

They go out with Mother Ubu.

SCENE 4

Father Ubu, Mother Ubu, Captain Bordure.

FATHER UBU: Well, now, Captain, have you had a good dinner?

CAPTAIN BORDURE: Very good, sir, except for the shitr.

FATHER UBU: Oh, come now, the shitr wasn't bad at all.

MOTHER UBU: Chacun à son goût.

FATHER UBU: Captain Bordure, I've decided to make you Duke of Lithuania.

CAPTAIN BORDURE: Why, I thought you were miserably poor, Father Ubu.

FATHER UBU: If you choose, I'll be King of Poland in a few days.

CAPTAIN BORDURE: You're going to kill Wenceslas?

FATHER UBU: He's not so stupid, the idiot; he's guessed it.

CAPTAIN BORDURE: If it's a question of killing Wenceslas, I'm for it. I'm his mortal enemy, and I can answer for my men.

FATHER UBU (*throwing his arms around him*): Oh! Oh! How I love you, Bordure.

CAPTAIN BORDURE: Ugh, you stink, Father Ubu. Don't you ever wash?

FATHER UBU: Rarely.

MOTHER UBU: Never!

FATHER UBU: I'll stamp on your toes.

MOTHER UBU: Big shitr!

FATHER UBU: All right, Bordure, that's all for now; but, by my green candle, I swear on Mother Ubu to make you Duke of Lithuania.

MOTHER UBU: But . . .

FATHER UBU: Be quiet, my sweet child. . . .

They go out.

SCENE 5

Father Ubu, Mother Ubu, a messenger.

FATHER UBU: Sir, what do you want? Beat it, you're boring me.

THE MESSENGER: Sir, the king summons you.

He leaves.

FATHER UBU: Oh, shitr! Great Jumping Jupiter, by my green candle, I've been discovered; they'll cut my head off, alas! alas!

MOTHER UBU: What a spineless clod! And just when time's getting short.

FATHER UBU: Oh, I've got an idea: I'll say that it was Mother Ubu and Bordure.

MOTHER UBU: You fat Ubu, if you do that . . .

FATHER UBU: I'm off right now.

He leaves.

MOTHER UBU (*running after him*): Oh, Father Ubu, Father Ubu, I'll give you some sausage!

She leaves.

FATHER UBU (*from the wings*): Oh, shitr! You're a prize sausage yourself.

SCENE 6

The palace.

King Wenceslas, surrounded by his officers; Captain Bordure; the king's sons, Boleslas, Ladislas, and Bougrelas; and Father Ubu.

FATHER UBU (*entering*): Oh! You know, it wasn't me, it was Mother Ubu and Bordure.

KING WENCESLAS: What's the matter with you, Father Ubu?

CAPTAIN BORDURE: He's drunk.

KING WENCESLAS: So was I, this morning.

FATHER UBU: Yes, I'm potted, because I've drunk too much French wine.

KING WENCESLAS: Father Ubu, I desire to recompense your numerous services as Captain of the Dragoons, and I'm going to make you Count of Sandomir today.

FATHER UBU: Oh, Mr. Wenceslas, I don't know how to thank you.

KING WENCESLAS: Don't thank me, Father Ubu, and don't forget to appear tomorrow morning at the big parade.

FATHER UBU: I'll be there, but be good enough to accept this toy whistle. (*He presents the king with a toy whistle.*)

KING WENCESLAS: What can I do with a toy whistle at my age? I'll give it to Bougrelas.

BOUGRELAS: What an idiot Father Ubu is!

FATHER UBU: And now I'll scram. (*He falls as he turns around.*) Oh! Ouch! Help! By my green candle, I've split my gut and bruised my butt!

KING WENCESLAS (*helping him up*): Did you hurt yourself, Father Ubu?

FATHER UBU: Yes, I certainly did, and I'll probably die soon. What will become of Mother Ubu?

KING WENCESLAS: We shall provide for her upkeep.

FATHER UBU: Your kindness is unparalleled. (*He leaves.*) But you'll be slaughtered just the same, King Wenceslas.

SCENE 7

Father Ubu's house.

Giron, Pile, Cotice, Father Ubu, Mother Ubu, Conspirators and Soldiers, Captain Bordure.

FATHER UBU: Well, my good friends, it's about time we discussed the plan of the conspiracy. Let each one give his advice. First of all, I'll give mine, if you'll permit me.

CAPTAIN BORDURE: Speak, Father Ubu.

FATHER UBU: Very well, my friends, I'm in favor of simply poisoning the king by slipping a little arsenic in his lunch. At the first nibble he'll drop dead, and then I'll be king.

ALL: How base!

FATHER UBU: What's that? You don't like my suggestion? Let Bordure give his.

CAPTAIN BORDURE: I'm of the opinion that we should give him one good stroke of the sword and slice him in two, lengthwise.

ALL: Hooray! How noble and valiant.

FATHER UBU: And what if he kicks you? I remember now that he always puts on iron shoes, which hurt a great deal, for parades. If I had any sense I'd go off and denounce you for dragging me into this dirty mess, and I think he'd give me plenty of money.

MOTHER UBU: Oh! The traitor, the coward, the villain, and sneak.

ALL: Down with Father Ubu!

FATHER UBU: Gentlemen, keep calm, or I'll get mad. In any case, I agree to stick out my neck for you. Bordure, I put you in charge of slicing the king in half.

CAPTAIN BORDURE: Wouldn't it be better to throw ourselves on the king all together, screaming and yelling? That way we might win the troops to our side.

FATHER UBU: All right, then. I'll attempt to tread on his toes; he'll protest, and then I'll say, SHITR, and at this signal you'll all throw yourselves on him.

MOTHER UBU: Yes, and as soon as he's dead you'll take his scepter and crown.

CAPTAIN BORDURE: And I'll pursue the royal family with my men.

FATHER UBU: Yes, and be extra sure that you catch young Bougrelas.

They go out.

(*Running after them and bringing them back.*) Gentlemen, we have forgotten an indispensable ceremony: we must swear to fight bravely.

CAPTAIN BORDURE: How are we going to do that? We don't have a priest.

FATHER UBU: Mother Ubu will take his place.

ALL: Very well, so be it.

FATHER UBU: Then you really swear to kill the king?

ALL: Yes, we swear it. Long live Father Ubu!

ACT II

Scene 1

The palace.

King Wenceslas, Queen Rosemonde, Boleslas, Ladislas, and Bougrelas.

KING WENCESLAS: Mr. Bougrelas, you were very impertinent this morning with Mr. Ubu, knight of my orders and Count of Sandomir. That's why I'm forbidding you to appear at my parade.

QUEEN ROSEMONDE: But, Wenceslas, you need your whole family around you to protect you.

KING WENCESLAS: Madam, I never retract my commands. You weary me with your chatter.

BOUGRELAS: It shall be as you desire, my father.

QUEEN ROSEMONDE: Sire, have you definitely decided to attend this parade?

KING WENCESLAS: Why shouldn't I, madam?

QUEEN ROSEMONDE: For the last time, didn't I tell you that I dreamed that I saw you being knocked down by a mob of his men and thrown into the Vistula, and an eagle just like the one in the arms of Poland placing the crown on his head?

KING WENCESLAS: On whose?

QUEEN ROSEMONDE: On Father Ubu's.

KING WENCESLAS: What nonsense! Count de Ubu is a very fine gentleman who would let himself be torn apart by horses in my service.

QUEEN ROSEMONDE *and* BOUGRELAS: What a delusion!

KING WENCESLAS: Be quiet, you little ape. And as for you, madam, just to show you how little I fear Mr. Ubu, I'll go to the parade just as I am, without sword or armor.

QUEEN ROSEMONDE: Fatal imprudence! I shall never see you alive again.

KING WENCESLAS: Come along, Ladislas, come along, Boleslas.

They go out. Queen Rosemonde and Bougrelas go to the window.

QUEEN ROSEMONDE *and* BOUGRELAS: May God and holy Saint Nicholas protect you!

QUEEN ROSEMONDE: Bougrelas, come to the chapel with me to pray for your father and your brothers.

SCENE 2

The parade grounds.

The Polish Army, King Wenceslas, Boleslas, Ladislas, Father Ubu, Captain Bordure and his men, Giron, Pile, Cotice.

KING WENCESLAS: Noble Father Ubu, accompany me with your companions while I inspect the troops.

FATHER UBU (*to his men*): On your toes, boys. (*To the king.*) Coming, sir, coming.

Ubu's men surround the king.

KING WENCESLAS: Ah! Here is the Dantzick Horseguard Regiment. Aren't they magnificent!

FATHER UBU: You really think so? They look rotten to me. Look at this one. (*To the soldier.*) When did you last shave, varlet?

KING WENCESLAS: But this soldier is absolutely impeccable. What's the matter with you, Father Ubu?

FATHER UBU: Take that! (*He stamps on his foot.*)

KING WENCESLAS: Wretch!

FATHER UBU: Shitr! Come on, men!

CAPTAIN BORDURE: Hooray! Charge!

They all hit the king; a Palotin explodes.

KING WENCESLAS: Oh! Help! Holy Mother, I'm dead.

BOLESLAS (*to Ladislas*): What's going on? Let's draw.

FATHER UBU: Ah, I've got the crown! To the others, now.

CAPTAIN BORDURE: After the traitors!

The princes flee, pursued by all.

SCENE 3

Queen Rosemonde and Bougrelas.

QUEEN ROSEMONDE: At last I can begin to relax.

BOUGRELAS: You've no reason to be afraid.

A frightful din is heard from outside.

Oh! What's this I see? My two brothers pursued by Father Ubu and his men.

QUEEN ROSEMONDE: Oh, my God! Holy Mother, they're losing, they're losing ground!

BOUGRELAS: The whole army is following Father Ubu. I don't see the king. Horror! Help!

QUEEN ROSEMONDE: There's Boleslas, dead! He's been shot.

BOUGRELAS: Hey! Defend yourself! Hooray, Ladislas!

QUEEN ROSEMONDE: Oh! He's surrounded.

BOUGRELAS: He's finished. Bordure's just sliced him in half like a sausage.

QUEEN ROSEMONDE: Alas! Those madmen have broken into the palace; they're coming up the stairs.

The din grows louder.

QUEEN ROSEMONDE *and* BOUGRELAS (*on their knees*): Oh, God, defend us!

BOUGRELAS: Oh! That Father Ubu! The swine, the wretch, if I could get my hands on him . . .

SCENE 4

The same. The door is smashed down. Father Ubu and his rabble break through.

FATHER UBU: So, Bougrelas, what's that you want to do to me?

BOUGRELAS: Great God! I'll defend my mother to the death! The first man to make a move dies.

FATHER UBU: Oh! Bordure, I'm scared. Let me out of here.

A SOLDIER (*advancing*): Give yourself up, Bougrelas!

BOUGRELAS: Here, scum, take that! (*He splits his skull.*)

QUEEN ROSEMONDE: Hold your ground, Bougrelas; hold your ground!

SEVERAL (*advancing*): Bougrelas, we promise to let you go.

BOUGRELAS: Good-for-nothings, sots, turncoats! (*He swings his sword and kills them all.*)

FATHER UBU: I'll win out in the end!

BOUGRELAS: Mother, escape by the secret staircase.

QUEEN ROSEMONDE: And what about you, my son? What about you?

BOUGRELAS: I'll follow you.

FATHER UBU: Try to catch the queen. Oh, there she goes. As for you, you little . . . (*He approaches Bougrelas.*)

BOUGRELAS: Great God! Here is my vengeance! (*With a terrible blow of his sword he rips open Father Ubu's paunch-protector.*) Mother, I'm coming!

He disappears down the secret staircase.

Scene 5

A cave in the mountains.

Young Bougrelas enters, followed by Queen Rosemonde.

BOUGRELAS: We'll be safe here.

QUEEN ROSEMONDE: Yes, I think so. Bougrelas, help me! (*She falls to the snow.*)

BOUGRELAS: What's the matter, Mother?

QUEEN ROSEMONDE: Believe me, I'm very sick, Bougrelas. I don't have more than two hours to live.

BOUGRELAS: What do you mean? Has the cold got you?

QUEEN ROSEMONDE: How can I bear up against so many blows? The king massacred, our family destroyed, and you, the representative of the most noble race that has ever worn a sword, forced to flee into the mountains like a common brigand.

BOUGRELAS: And by whom, O Lord, by whom? A vulgar fellow like Father Ubu, an adventurer coming from no one knows where, a vile blaggard, a shameless vagabond! And when I think that my father decorated him and made him a count and that the next day this low-bred dog had the nerve to raise his hand against him.

QUEEN ROSEMONDE: Oh, Bougrelas! When I remember how happy we were before this Father Ubu came! But now, alas! All is changed!

BOUGRELAS: What can we do? Let us wait in hope and never renounce our rights.

QUEEN ROSEMONDE: May your wish be granted, my dear child, but as for me, I shall never see that happy day.

BOUGRELAS: What's the matter with you? Ah, she pales, she falls. Help me! But I'm in a desert! Oh, my God! Her heart is stilled forever. She is dead? Can it be? Another victim for Father Ubu! (*He hides his face in his hands, and weeps.*) Oh, my God! How sad it is to have such a terrible vengeance to fulfill!

And I'm only fourteen years old! (*He falls down in the throes of a most extravagant despair.*)

Meanwhile, the souls of Wenceslas, Boleslas, Ladislas, and of Queen Rosemonde enter the cave. Their ancestors, accompanying them, fill up the cave. The oldest goes to Bougrelas and gently awakes him.

Ah! What's this I see? My whole family, all my ancestors . . . how can this be?

THE SHADE: Know, Bougrelas, that during my life I was the Lord Mathias of Königsberg, the first king and founder of our house. I entrust our vengeance to your hands. (*He gives him a large sword.*) And may this sword which I have given you never rest until it has brought about the death of the usurper.

All vanish, and Bougrelas remains alone, in an attitude of ecstasy.

SCENE 6

The palace.

Father Ubu, Mother Ubu, Captain Bordure.

FATHER UBU: No! Never! I don't want to! Do you want me to ruin myself for these buffroons?

CAPTAIN BORDURE: But after all, Father Ubu, don't you see that the people are waiting for the gifts to celebrate your joyous coronation?

MOTHER UBU: If you don't give out meat and gold, you'll be overthrown in two hours.

FATHER UBU: Meat, yes! Gold, no! Slaughter the three oldest horses —that'll be good enough for those apes.

MOTHER UBU: Ape, yourself! How did I ever get stuck with an animal like you?

FATHER UBU: Once and for all, I'm trying to get rich; I'm not going to let go of a cent.

MOTHER UBU: But we've got the whole Polish treasury at our disposal.

CAPTAIN BORDURE: Yes, I happen to know that there's an enormous treasure in the royal chapel; we'll distribute it.

FATHER UBU: Just you dare, you wretch!

CAPTAIN BORDURE: But, Father Ubu, if you don't distribute money to the people, they'll refuse to pay the taxes.

FATHER UBU: Is that a fact?

MOTHER UBU: Yes, of course!

FATHER UBU: Oh, well, in that case I agree to everything. Withdraw three millions, roast a hundred and fifty cattle and sheep—especially since I'll have some myself!

They go out.

SCENE 7

The palace courtyard full of people.

Father Ubu crowned, Mother Ubu, Captain Bordure, flunkies carrying meat.

PEOPLE: There's the king! Long live the king! Hooray!

FATHER UBU (*throwing gold*): Here, that's for you. It doesn't make me very happy to give you any money; it's Mother Ubu who wanted me to. At least promise me you'll really pay the taxes.

ALL: Yes! Yes!

CAPTAIN BORDURE: Look how they're fighting over that gold, Mother Ubu. What a battle!

MOTHER UBU: It's really awful. Ugh! There's one just had his skull split open.

FATHER UBU: What a beautiful sight! Bring on more gold.

CAPTAIN BORDURE: How about making them race for it?

FATHER UBU: Good idea! (*To the people.*) My friends, take a look at this chest of gold. It contains three hundred thousand Polish coins, of the purest gold, guaranteed genuine. Let those who wish to compete for it assemble at the end of the court-yard. The race will begin when I wave my handkerchief, and the first one to get here wins the chest. As for those who don't win, they will share this other chest as a consolation prize.

ALL: Yes! Long live Father Ubu! What a king! We never had anything like this in the days of Wenceslas.

FATHER UBU (*to Mother Ubu, with joy*): Listen to them!

All the people line up at the end of the courtyard.

One, two, three! Ready?

ALL: Yes! Yes!

FATHER UBU: Set! Go!

They start, falling all over one another. Cries and tumult.

CAPTAIN BORDURE: They're coming! They're coming!

FATHER UBU: Look! The leader's losing ground.

MOTHER UBU: No, he's going ahead again.

CAPTAIN BORDURE: He's losing, he's losing! He's lost! The other one won.

ALL: Long live Michael Federovitch! Long live Michael Federovitch!

MICHAEL FEDEROVITCH: Sire, I don't know how to thank your Majesty. . . .

FATHER UBU: Think nothing of it, my dear friend. Take your money home with you, Michael; and you others, share the rest—each take a piece until they're all gone.

ALL: Long live Michael Federovitch! Long live Father Ubu!

FATHER UBU: And you, my friends, come and eat! I open the gates of the palace to you—may you do honor to my table!

PEOPLE: Let's go in, let's go in! Long live Father Ubu! He's the noblest monarch of them all!

They go into the palace. The noise of the orgy is audible throughout the night. The curtain falls.

ACT III

SCENE 1

The palace.

Father Ubu, Mother Ubu.

FATHER UBU: By my green candle here I am king of this country, I've already got a fine case of indigestion, and they're going to bring me my big helmet.

MOTHER UBU: What's it made out of, Father Ubu? Even if we are sitting on the throne, we have to watch the pennies.

FATHER UBU: Madam my wife, it's made out of sheepskin with a clasp and with laces made out of dogskin.

MOTHER UBU: That's very extraordinary, but it's even more extraordinary that we're here on the throne.

FATHER UBU: How right you are, Mother Ubu.

MOTHER UBU: We owe quite a debt to the Duke of Lithuania.

FATHER UBU: Who's that?

MOTHER UBU: Why, Captain Bordure.

FATHER UBU: If you please, Mother Ubu, don't speak to me about that buffroon. Now that I don't need him any more, he can go whistle for his dukedom.

MOTHER UBU: You're making a big mistake, Father Ubu; he's going to turn against you.

FATHER UBU: Well, now, the poor little fellow has my deepest sympathy, but I'm not going to worry about him any more than about Bougrelas.

MOTHER UBU: Ha! You think you've seen the last of Bougrelas, do you?

FATHER UBU: By my financial sword, of course I have! What do you think that fourteen-year-old midget is going to do to me?

MOTHER UBU: Father Ubu, pay attention to what I'm going to say to you. Believe me, you ought to be nice to Bougrelas to get him on your side.

FATHER UBU: Do you think I'm made of money? Well, I'm not! You've already made me waste twenty-two millions.

MOTHER UBU: Have it your own way, Father Ubu; he'll roast you alive.

FATHER UBU: Fine! You'll be in the pot with me.

MOTHER UBU: For the last time, listen to me: I'm sure that young Bougrelas will triumph, because he has right on his side.

FATHER UBU: Oh, crap! Doesn't the wrong always get you more than the right? Ah, you do me an injustice, Mother Ubu, I'll chop you into little pieces.

Mother Ubu runs away, pursued by Father Ubu.

SCENE 2

The Great Hall of the palace.

Father Ubu, Mother Ubu, Officers and Soldiers; Giron, Pile, Cotice, Nobles in chains, Financiers, Magistrates, Clerks.

FATHER UBU: Bring forward the Nobles' money box and the Nobles' hook and the Nobles' knife and the Nobles' book! And then bring forward the Nobles.

Nobles are brutally pushed forward.

MOTHER UBU: For goodness' sakes, control yourself, Father Ubu.

FATHER UBU: I have the honor to announce to you that in order to enrich the kingdom I shall annihilate all the Nobles and grab their property.

NOBLES: How awful! To the rescue, people and soldiers!

FATHER UBU: Bring forward the first Noble and hand me the Nobles' hook. Those who are condemned to death, I will drop down the trap door. They will fall into the Pig-Pinching Cellars and the Money Vault, where they will be disembrained. (*To the Noble.*) Who are you, buffroon?

THE NOBLE: Count of Vitebsk.

FATHER UBU: What's your income?

THE NOBLE: Three million rixthalers.

FATHER UBU: Condemned! (*He seizes him with the hook and drops him down the trap door.*)

MOTHER UBU: What vile savagery!

FATHER UBU: Second Noble, who are you?

The Noble doesn't reply.

Answer, buffroon!

THE NOBLE: Grand Duke of Posen.

FATHER UBU: Excellent! Excellent! I'll not trouble you any longer. Down the trap. Third Noble, who are you? You're an ugly one.

THE NOBLE: Duke of Courland, and of the cities of Riga, Reval, and the Mitau.

FATHER UBU: Very good! Very good! Anything else?

THE NOBLE: That's all.

FATHER UBU: Well, down the trap, then. Fourth Noble, who are you?

THE NOBLE: The Prince of Podolia.

FATHER UBU: What's your income?

THE NOBLE: I'm bankrupt.

FATHER UBU: For that nasty word, into the trap with you. Fifth Noble, who are you?

THE NOBLE: Margrave of Thorn, Palatin of Polack.

FATHER UBU: That doesn't sound like very much. Nothing else?

THE NOBLE: It was enough for me.

FATHER UBU: Half a loaf is better than no loaf at all. Down the trap. What's the matter with you, Mother Ubu?

MOTHER UBU: You're too ferocious, Father Ubu.

FATHER UBU: Please! I'm working! And now I'm going to have MY list of MY property read to me. Clerk, read MY list of MY property.

THE CLERK: County of Sandomir.

FATHER UBU: Start with the big ones.

THE CLERK: Princedom of Podolia, Grand Duchy of Posen, Duchy of Courland, County of Sandomir, County of Vitebsk, Palatinate of Polack, Margraviate of Thorn.

FATHER UBU: Well, go on.

THE CLERK: That's all.

FATHER UBU: What do you mean, that's all! Oh, very well, then, bring the Nobles forward. Since I'm not finished enriching myself yet, I'm going to execute all the Nobles and seize all their estates at once. Let's go; stick the Nobles in the trap.

The Nobles are pushed into the trap.

Hurry it up, let's go, I want to make some laws now.

SEVERAL: This ought to be a good one.

FATHER UBU: First I'm going to reform the laws, and then we'll proceed to matters of finance.

MAGISTRATES: We're opposed to any change.

FATHER UBU: Shitr! To begin with, Magistrates will not be paid any more.

MAGISTRATES: What are we supposed to live on? We're poor.

FATHER UBU: You shall have the fines which you will impose and the property of those you condemn to death.

A MAGISTRATE: Horrors!

A SECOND: Infamy!

A THIRD: Scandal!

A FOURTH: Indignity!

ALL: We refuse to act as judges under such conditions.

FATHER UBU: Down the trap with the Magistrates!

They struggle in vain.

MOTHER UBU: What are you doing, Father Ubu? Who will dispense justice now?

FATHER UBU: Why, me! You'll see how smoothly it'll go.

MOTHER UBU: I can just imagine.

FATHER UBU: That's enough out of you, buffrooness. And now, gentlemen, we will proceed to matters of finance.

FINANCIERS: No changes are needed.

FATHER UBU: I intend to change everything. First of all, I'll keep half the taxes for myself.

FINANCIERS: That's too much.

FATHER UBU: Gentlemen, we will establish a tax of 10 per cent on property, another on commerce and industry, a third on marriages and a fourth on deaths—fifteen francs each.

FIRST FINANCIER: But that's idiotic, Father Ubu.

SECOND FINANCIER: It's absurd.

THIRD FINANCIER: It's impossible.

FATHER UBU: You're trying to confuse me! Down the trap with the Financiers!

The Financiers are pushed in.

MOTHER UBU: But, Father Ubu, what kind of king are you? You're murdering everybody!

FATHER UBU: Oh, shitr!

MOTHER UBU: No more justice, no more finances!

FATHER UBU: Have no fear, my sweet child; I myself will go from village to village, collecting the taxes.

Scene 3

A peasant house in the outskirts of Warsaw. Several peasants are assembled.

A PEASANT (*entering*): Have you heard the news? The king and the dukes are all dead, and young Bougrelas has fled to the mountains with his mother. What's more, Father Ubu has seized the throne.

ANOTHER: That's nothing. I've just come from Cracow where I saw the bodies of more than three hundred nobles and five hundred magistrates, and I hear that the taxes are going to be doubled and that Father Ubu is coming to collect them himself.

ALL: Great heavens! What will become of us? Father Ubu is a horrible beast, and they say his family is abominable.

A PEASANT: Listen! Isn't somebody knocking at the door?

A VOICE (*outside*): Hornsbuggers! Open up, by my shitr, by Saint John, Saint Peter, and Saint Nicholas! Open up, by my financial sword, by my financial horns, I'm coming to collect the taxes!

The door is smashed in, and Father Ubu enters followed by hordes of tax collectors.

SCENE 4

FATHER UBU: Which one of you is the oldest?

A peasant steps forward.

What's your name?

THE PEASANT: Stanislas Leczinski.

FATHER UBU: Fine, hornsbuggers! Listen to me, since if you don't these gentlemen here will cut your ears off. Well, are you listening?

STANISLAS: But your Excellency hasn't said anything yet.

FATHER UBU: What do you mean? I've been speaking for an hour. Do you think I've come here to preach in the desert?

STANISLAS: Far be it from my thoughts.

FATHER UBU: I've come to tell you, to order you, and to intimate to you that you are to produce forthwith and exhibit promptly your finance, unless you wish to be slaughtered. Let's go, gentlemen, my financial swine, vehiculize hither the phynancial vehicle.

The vehicle is brought in.

STANISLAS: Sire, we are down on the register for a hundred and fifty-two rixthalers which we paid six weeks ago come Saint Matthew's Day.

FATHER UBU: That's very possible, but I've changed the government and run an advertisement in the paper that says you have to pay all present taxes twice and all those which I will levy later on three times. With this system, I'll make my fortune quickly; then I'll kill everyone and run away.

PEASANTS: Mr. Ubu, please have pity on us; we are poor, simple citizens.

FATHER UBU: Nuts! Pay up.

PEASANTS: We can't, we've already paid.

FATHER UBU: Pay up! Or I'll stick you in my pocket with torturing and beheading of the neck and head! Hornsbuggers, I'm the king, aren't I?

ALL: Ah! So that's the way it is! To arms! Long live Bougrelas, by the grace of God King of Poland and Lithuania!

FATHER UBU: Forward, gentlemen of Finance, do your duty.

A struggle ensues; the house is destroyed, and old Stanislas flees across the plain, alone. Father Ubu stays to collect the money.

SCENE 5

A dungeon in the Fortress of Thorn.

Captain Bordure in chains, Father Ubu.

FATHER UBU: So, Citizen, that's the way it is: you wanted me to pay you what I owed you; then you rebelled because I refused; you conspired and here you are retired. Horns of finance, I've done so well you must admire it yourself.

CAPTAIN BORDURE: Take care, Father Ubu. During the five days that you've been king, you've committed enough murders to damn all the saints in Paradise. The blood of the king and of the nobles cries for vengeance, and their cries will be heard.

FATHER UBU: Ah, my fine friend, that's quite a tongue you've got there. I have no doubt that if you escaped, it would cause all sorts of complications, but I don't think that the dungeons of Thorn have ever let even one of the honest fellows go who have been entrusted to them. Therefore I bid you a very good night and I invite you to sleep soundly, although I must say the rats dance a very pretty saraband down here.

He leaves. The jailers come and bolt all the doors.

SCENE 6

The Palace at Moscow.

The Emperor Alexis and his court, Captain Bordure.

ALEXIS: Infamous adventurer, aren't you the one who helped kill our cousin Wenceslas?

CAPTAIN BORDURE: Sire, forgive me, I was carried away despite myself by Father Ubu.

ALEXIS: Oh, what a big liar! Well, what can I do for you?

CAPTAIN BORDURE: Father Ubu imprisoned me on charges of conspiracy; I succeeded in escaping and I have ridden five days and five nights across the steppes to come and beg your gracious forgiveness.

ALEXIS: What have you got for me as proof of your loyalty?

CAPTAIN BORDURE: My honor as a knight, and a detailed map of the town of Thorn. (*Kneels and presents his sword to Alexis.*)

ALEXIS: I accept your sword, but by Saint George, burn the map. I don't want to owe my victory to an act of treachery.

CAPTAIN BORDURE: One of the sons of Wenceslas, young Bougrelas, is still alive. I would do anything to restore him.

ALEXIS: What was your rank in the Polish Army?

CAPTAIN BORDURE: I commanded the fifth regiment of the Dragoons of Vilna and a company of mercenaries in the service of Father Ubu.

ALEXIS: Fine, I appoint you second in command of the tenth regiment of Cossacks, and woe to you if you betray me. If you fight well, you'll be rewarded.

CAPTAIN BORDURE: I don't lack courage, Sire.

ALEXIS: Fine, remove yourself from my sight.

He leaves.

SCENE 7

Ubu's Council Chamber.

Father Ubu, Mother Ubu, Phynancial Advisers.

FATHER UBU: Gentlemen, the meeting has begun, and see that you keep your ears open and your mouths shut. First of all, we'll turn to the subject of finance; then we'll speak about a little scheme I've thought up to bring good weather and prevent rain.

AN ADVISER: Very good, Mr. Ubu.

MOTHER UBU: What a stupid fool!

FATHER UBU: Take care, madam of my shitr, I'm not going to stand for your idiocies much longer. I'd like you to know, gentlemen, that the finances are proceeding satisfactorily. The streets are mobbed every morning by a crowd of the local low-life, and my men do wonders with them. In every direction you can see only burning houses, and people bent under the weight of our finances.

THE ADVISER: And are the new taxes going well, Mr. Ubu?

MOTHER UBU: Not at all. The tax on marriages has brought in only eleven cents so far, although Father Ubu chases people everywhere to convince them to marry.

FATHER UBU: By my financial sword, hornsbuggers, Madam financieress, I've got ears to speak with and you've a mouth to listen to me with.

Shouts of laughter.

You're mixing me up and it's your fault that I'm making a fool of myself! But, horn of Ubu! . . .

A messenger enters.

Well, what do you have to say for yourself? Get out of here, you little monkey, before I pocket you with beheading and twisting of the legs.

MOTHER UBU: There he goes, but he's left a letter.

FATHER UBU: Read it. I don't feel like it, or come to think of it perhaps I can't read. Hurry up, buffrooness, it must be from Bordure.

MOTHER UBU: Right. He says that the Czar has received him very well, that he's going to invade your lands to restore Bougrelas, and that you're going to be killed.

FATHER UBU: Oh! Oh! I'm scared! I'm scared. I bet I'm going to die. Oh, poor little man that I am! What will become of me, great God? This wicked man is going to kill me. Saint Anthony and all the saints, protect me, and I'll give you some phynance and burn some candles for you. Lord, what will become of me? (*He cries and sobs.*)

MOTHER UBU: There's only one safe course to follow, Father Ubu.

FATHER UBU: What's that, my love?

MOTHER UBU: War!!!

ALL: Great heavens! What a noble idea!

FATHER UBU: Yes, and I'll be the one to get hurt, as usual.

FIRST ADVISER: Hurry, hurry, let's organize the army.

SECOND: And requisition the provisions.

THIRD: And set up the artillery and the fortresses.

FOURTH: And get up the money for the troops.

FATHER UBU: That's enough of that, now, you, or I'll kill you on the spot. I'm not going to spend any money. That's a good one, isn't it! I used to be paid to wage war, and now it's being waged at my expense. Wait—by my green candle, let's wage war, since you're so excited about it, but let's not spend a penny.

ALL: Hooray for war!

SCENE 8

The camp outside Warsaw.

SOLDIERS *and* PALOTINS: Long live Poland! Long live Father Ubu!

FATHER UBU: Ah, Mother Ubu, give me my breastplate and my little stick. I'll soon be so heavy that I won't be able to move even if I'm being chased.

MOTHER UBU: Pooh, what a coward!

FATHER UBU: Ah! Here's the sword of shitr running away first thing and there's the financial hook which won't stay put!!! (*Drops both.*) I'll never be ready, and the Russians are coming to kill me.

A SOLDIER: Lord Ubu, here's your ear-pick, which you've dropped.

FATHER UBU: I'll kill you with my shitr hook and my gizzard-saw.

MOTHER UBU: How handsome he is with his helmet and his breastplate! He looks just like an armed pumpkin.

FATHER UBU: Now I'll get my horse. Gentlemen, bring forth the phynancial horse.

MOTHER UBU: Father Ubu, your horse can't carry you—it's had nothing to eat for five days and it's about to die.

FATHER UBU: That's a good one! I have to pay twelve cents a day for this sway-backed nag and it can't even carry me. You're making fun of me, horn of Ubu, or else perhaps you're stealing from me?

Mother Ubu blushes and lowers her eyes.

Now bring me another beast, because I'm not going to go on foot, hornsbuggers!

An enormous horse is brought out.

I'm going to get on. Oops, better sit down before I fall off.

The horse starts to leave.

Stop this beast. Great God, I'm going to fall off and be killed!!!

MOTHER UBU: He's an absolute idiot. There he is up again; no, he's down again.

FATHER UBU: Horn of Physics, I'm half dead. But never mind, I'm going to the war and I'll kill everyone. Woe to him who doesn't keep up with me! I'll put him in my pocket with twisting of the nose and teeth and extraction of the tongue.

MOTHER UBU: Good luck, Mr. Ubu!

FATHER UBU: I forgot to tell you that I'm making you the regent. But I'm keeping the financial book, so you'd better not try and rob me. I'll leave you the Palotin Giron to help you. Farewell, Mother Ubu.

MOTHER UBU: Farewell, Father Ubu. Kill the Czar thoroughly.

FATHER UBU: Of course. Twisting of the nose and teeth, extraction of the tongue and insertion of the ear-pick.

The army marches away to the sound of fanfares.

MOTHER UBU (*alone*): Now that that big fat booby has gone, let's look to our own affairs, kill Bougrelas, and grab the treasure.

ACT IV

SCENE 1

The Royal Crypt in the Cathedral at Warsaw.

MOTHER UBU: Where on earth is that treasure? None of these slabs sounds hollow. I've counted thirteen slabs beyond the tomb of Ladislas the Great along the length of the wall, and I've found nothing. Someone seems to have deceived me. What's this? The stone sounds hollow here. To work, Mother Ubu.

Courage, we'll have it pried up in a minute. It's stuck fast. The end of this financial hook will do the trick. There! There's the gold in the middle of the royal bones. Into the sack with it. Oh! What's that noise? Can there still be someone alive in these ancient vaults? No, it's nothing; let's hurry up. Let's take everything. This money will look better in the light of day than in the middle of these graves. Back with the stone. What's that! There's that noise again! There's something not quite right about this place. I'll get the rest of this gold some other time—I'll come back tomorrow.

A VOICE (*coming from the tomb of John Sigismund*): Never, Mother Ubu!

Mother Ubu runs away terrified, through the secret door, carrying the stolen gold.

SCENE 2

The Main Square in Warsaw.

Bougrelas and his men, People and Soldiers.

BOUGRELAS: Forward, my friends! Long live Wenceslas and Poland! That old blaggard Father Ubu is gone; only that old witch Mother Ubu and her Palotin are left. I'm going to march at your head and restore my father's house to the throne.

ALL: Long live Bougrelas!

BOUGRELAS: And we'll abolish all taxes imposed by that horrible Father Ubu.

ALL: Hooray! Forward! To the palace, and death to the Ubus!

BOUGRELAS: Look! There's Mother Ubu coming out on the porch with her guards!

MOTHER UBU: What can I do for you, gentlemen? Ah! It's Bougrelas.

The crowd throws stones.

FIRST GUARD: They've broken all the windows.

SECOND GUARD: Saint George, I'm done for.

THIRD GUARD: Hornsass, I'm dying.

BOUGRELAS: Throw some more stones, my friends.

PALOTIN GIRON: Ho! So that's the way it is! (*He draws his sword and leaps into the crowd, performing horrible slaughter.*)

BOUGRELAS: Have at you! Defend yourself, you cowardly pisspot!

They fight.

GIRON: I die!

BOUGRELAS: Victory, my friends! Now for Mother Ubu!

Trumpets are heard.

Ah! The Nobles are arriving. Run and catch the old hag.

ALL: She'll do until we can strangle the old bandit himself! *Mother Ubu runs away pursued by all the Poles. Rifle shots and a hail of stones.*

SCENE 3

The Polish Army marching in the Ukraine.

FATHER UBU: Hornsass, godslegs, cowsheads! We're about to perish, because we're dying of thirst and we're tired. Sir Soldier, be so good as to carry our financial helmet, and you, Sir Lancer, take charge of the shitr-pick and the physic-stick to unencumber our person, because, let me repeat, we are tired.

The soldiers obey.

PILE: Ho, my Lord! It's surprising that there are no Russians to be seen.

FATHER UBU: It's regrettable that the state of our finances does not permit us to have a vehicle commensurate to our grandeur; for, for fear of demolishing our steed, we have gone all the way on foot, leading our horse by the bridle. When we get back to Poland, we shall devise, by means of our physical science and with the aid of the wisdom of our advisers, a way of transporting our entire army by wind.

COTICE: Here comes Nicholas Rensky, in a great hurry.

FATHER UBU: What's the matter with him?

RENSKY: All is lost. Sir, the Poles have revolted, Giron has been killed, and Mother Ubu has fled to the mountains.

FATHER UBU: Bird of night, beast of misery, owl's underwear! Where did you hear this nonsense? What won't you be saying next! Who's responsible for this? Bougrelas, I'll bet. Where'd you just come from?

RENSKY: From Warsaw, noble Lord.

FATHER UBU: Child of my shitr, if I believed you I would retreat with the whole army. But, Sir Child, you've got feathers in your head instead of brains and you've been dreaming nonsense. Run off to the outposts, my child; the Russians can't be far, and we'll soon be flourishing our arms, shitr, phynancial, and physical.

GENERAL LASCY: Father Ubu, can't you see the Russians down there on the plain?

FATHER UBU: It's true, the Russians! A fine mess this is. If only there were still a way to run out, but there isn't; we're up here on a hill and we'll be exposed to attack on all sides.

THE ARMY: The Russians! The enemy!

FATHER UBU: Let's go, gentlemen, into our battle positions. We will remain on top of the hill and under no circumstances commit the idiocy of descending. I'll keep myself in the middle like a living fortress, and all you others will gravitate around me. I advise you to load your guns with as many bullets as they will hold, because eight bullets can kill eight Russians and that will be eight Russians the less. We will station the infantry at the foot of the hill to receive the Russians and kill them a little, the cavalry in back of them so that they can throw themselves into the confusion, and the artillery around this windmill here so that they can fire into the whole mess. As for us, we will take up our position inside the windmill and fire through the window with the phynancial pistol, and bar the door with the physical stick, and if anyone still tries to get in let him beware of the shitr-hook!!!

OFFICERS: Your orders, Lord Ubu, shall be executed.

FATHER UBU: Fine, we'll win, then. What time is it?

GENERAL LASCY: It's eleven o'clock in the morning.

FATHER UBU: In that case, let's have lunch, because the Russians won't attack before midday. Tell the soldiers, my lord General, to take a crap and strike up the Financial Song.

Lascy withdraws.

SOLDIERS *and* PALOTINS: Long live Father Ubu, our great Financier! Ting, ting, ting; ting, ting, ting; ting, ting, ta-ting!

FATHER UBU: Oh, how noble, I adore gallantry!

A Russian cannon ball breaks one of the arms of the windmill.

Aaaaah! I'm frightened. Lord God, I'm dead! No, no, I'm not.

SCENE 4

The same, a Captain and the Russian Army.

A CAPTAIN (*entering*): Lord Ubu, the Russians are attacking.

FATHER UBU: All right, all right, what do you want me to do about it? I didn't tell them to attack. Nevertheless, gentlemen of Finance, let us prepare ourselves for battle.

GENERAL LASCY: Another cannon ball!

FATHER UBU: Ah! That's enough of that! It's raining lead and steel around here, and it might put a dent in our precious person. Down we go.

They all run away. The battle has just begun. They disappear in the clouds of smoke at the foot of the hill.

A RUSSIAN (*thrusting*): For God and the Czar!

RENSKY: Ah! I'm dead.

FATHER UBU: Forward! As for you, sir, I'll get you because you've hurt me, do you hear? You drunken sot, with your popless little popgun.

THE RUSSIAN: Ah! I'll show you! (*He fires.*)

FATHER UBU: Ah! Oh! I'm wounded, I'm shot full of holes, I'm perforated, I'm done for, I'm buried. And now I've got you! (*He tears him to pieces.*) Just try that again.

GENERAL LASCY: Forward, charge, across the trench! Victory is ours!

FATHER UBU: Do you really think so? So far my brow has felt more lumps than laurels.

RUSSIAN KNIGHTS: Hooray! Make way for the Czar!

Enter the Czar, accompanied by Captain Bordure, in disguise.

A POLE: Great God! Every man for himself, there's the Czar!

ANOTHER: Oh, my God, he's crossed the trench.

ANOTHER: Bing! Bang! Four more chopped up by that big ox of a lieutenant.

CAPTAIN BORDURE: So! The rest of you won't surrender, eh? All right, your time has come, John Sobiesky! (*He chops him up.*) Now for the others! (*He massacres Poles.*)

FATHER UBU: Forward, my friends! Capture that rat! Make mincemeat of the Muscovites! Victory is ours! Long live the Red Eagle!

ALL: Charge! Hooray! Godslegs! Capture the big ox.

CAPTAIN BORDURE: By Saint George, they've got me.

FATHER UBU: Ah! it's you, Bordure! How are you, my friend? I, and all the company, are very happy to welcome you again. I'm going to broil you over a slow fire. Gentlemen of the Finances, light the fire. Oh! Ah! Oh! I'm dead. I must have been hit with a cannon ball at least. Oh! My God, forgive my sins. Yes, it's definitely a cannon ball.

CAPTAIN BORDURE: It was a pistol with a blank cartridge.

FATHER UBU: Oh, you're making fun of me! All right, into the pocket you go! (*He flings himself upon him and tears him to pieces.*)

GENERAL LASCY: Father Ubu, we're advancing on all fronts.

FATHER UBU: I can see that. But I can't go on any more, because everyone's been stepping on my toes. I absolutely have to sit down. Oh, where's my bottle?

GENERAL LASCY: Go get the Czar's bottle, Father Ubu!

FATHER UBU: Ah! Just what I had in mind. Let's go. Sword of

Shitr, do your duty, and you, financial hook, don't lag behind! As for you, physical stick, see that you work just as hard and share with the little bit of wood the honor of massacring, scooping out, and imposing upon the Musovite Emperor. Forward, my Phynancial Horse! (*He throws himself on the Czar.*)

A RUSSIAN OFFICER: Look out, Your Majesty!

FATHER UBU: Take that! Oh! Ow! Ah! Goodness me. Ah! Oh, sir, excuse me, leave me alone. I didn't do it on purpose! (*He runs away, pursued by the Czar.*) Holy Mother, that madman is coming after me! Great God, what shall I do? Ah, I've got that trench ahead of me again. I've got him behind me and the trench in front of me! Courage! I'm going to close my eyes! (*He jumps the trench. The Czar falls in.*)

THE CZAR: God, I've fallen in!

THE POLES: Hooray! The Czar has fallen in!

FATHER UBU: I'm afraid to turn around. Ah! He fell in. That's fine; they've jumped on him. Let's go, you Poles; swing away; he's a tough one, that swine! As for me, I can't look. But our prediction has been completely fulfilled: the physical stick has performed wonders, and without doubt I would have been about to have killed him completely, had not an inexplicable fear come to combat and annul in us the fruits of our courage. But we suddenly had to turn tail, and we owe our salvation only to our skill in the saddle as well as to the sturdy hocks of our Phynancial Horse, whose rapidity is only equaled by its solidity and whose levitation makes its reputation, as well as the depth of the trench which located itself so appropriately under the enemy of us, the presently-before-you Master of Phynances. That was very nice, but nobody was listening. Oops, there they go again!

The Russian dragoons charge and rescue the Czar.

GENERAL LASCY: It looks like it's turning into a rout.

FATHER UBU: Now's the time to make tracks. Now then, gentlemen of Poland, forward! Or rather, backward!

POLES: Every man for himself!

FATHER UBU: Come on! Let's go! What a big crowd, what a stampede, what a mob! How am I ever going to get out of this mess? (*He is jostled.*) You there, watch your step, or you will sample the boiling rage of the Master of Phynances. Ha! There he goes. Now let's get out of here fast, while Lascy's looking the other way.

He runs off; the Czar and the Russian Army go by, chasing Poles.

SCENE 5

A cave in Lithuania. It is snowing.

Father Ubu, Pile, Cotice.

FATHER UBU: Oh, what a bitch of a day! It's cold enough to make the rocks crack open, and the person of the Master of Phynances finds itself severely damaged.

PILE: Ho! Mr. Ubu, have you recovered from your fright and from your flight?

FATHER UBU: Well, I'm not frightened any more, but, believe me, I'm still running.

COTICE (*aside*): What a turd!

FATHER UBU: Well, Sire Cotice, how's your ear feeling?

COTICE: As well as can be expected, sir, considering how bad it is. I can't get the bullet out, and consequently the lead is making me tilt.

FATHER UBU: Well, serves you right! You're always looking for a fight. As for me, I've always demonstrated the greatest valor, and without in any way exposing myself I massacred four enemies with my own hand, not counting, of course, those who were already dead and whom we dispatched.

COTICE: Do you know what happened to little Rensky, Pile?

PILE: A bullet in his head.

FATHER UBU: As the poppy and the dandelion are scythed in the flower of their age by the pitiless scythe of the pitiless scyther who scythes pitilessly their pitiful parts—just so little Rensky

has played the poppy's part: he fought well, but there were
just too many Russians around.

PILE *and* COTICE: Hey! Sir Ubu!

AN ECHO: Grrrrr!

PILE: What's that? On guard!

FATHER UBU: Oh, no! Not the Russians again! I've had enough of
them. And, anyway, it's very simple: if they catch me I'll
just put them all in my pocket.

SCENE 6

The same. Enter a bear.

COTICE: Ho! Master of Phynances!

FATHER UBU: Oh! What a sweet little doggie! Isn't he cute?

PILE: Watch out! What a huge bear! Hand me my gun!

FATHER UBU: A bear! What a horrible beast! Oh, poor me, I'm
going to be eaten alive. May God protect me! He's coming
this way. No, he's got Cotice. I can breathe again!

*The bear jumps on Cotice. Pile attacks him with his sword.
Ubu takes refuge on a high rock.*

COTICE: Save me, Pile! Save me! Help, Sir Ubu!

FATHER UBU: Fat chance! Get out of it yourself, my friend; right
now I'm going to recite my Pater Noster. Everyone will be
eaten in his turn.

PILE: I've got him, I'm holding him.

COTICE: Hold him tight, my friend, he's starting to let me go.

FATHER UBU: Sanctificetur nomen tuum.

COTICE: Cowardly lout!

PILE: Oh! It's biting me! O Lord, save us, I'm dead.

FATHER UBU: Fiat voluntas tua!

COTICE: I've wounded it!

PILE: Hooray! It's bleeding now.

While the Palotins shout, the bear bellows with pain and Ubu continues to mumble.

COTICE: Hang on, while I find my exploding brass knuckles.

FATHER UBU: Panem nostrum quotidianum da nobis hodie.

PILE: Haven't you got it yet? I can't hold on any longer.

FATHER UBU: Sicut et nos dimittimus debitoribus nostris.

COTICE: Ah! I've got it.

A resounding explosion; the bear falls dead.

PILE *and* COTICE: Victory!

FATHER UBU: Sed libera nos a malo. Amen. Is he really dead? Can I come down now?

PILE *(with disgust)*: Just as you like.

FATHER UBU *(coming down)*: You may be assured that if you are still alive and if you tread once more the Lithuanian snow, you owe it to the lofty virtue of the Master of Phynances, who has struggled, broken his back, and shouted himself hoarse reciting paternosters for your safety, and who has wielded the spiritual sword of prayer with just as much courage as you have wielded with dexterity the temporal one of the here-attendant Palotin Cotice's exploding brass knuckles. We have even pushed our devotion further, for we did not hesitate to climb to the top of a very high rock so that our prayers had less far to travel to reach heaven.

PILE: Disgusting pig!

FATHER UBU: Oh, you beast! Thanks to me, you've got something to eat. What a belly he has, gentlemen! The Greeks would have been more comfortable in there than in their wooden horse, and we very barely escaped, my dear friends, being able to satisfy ourselves of his interior capacity with our own eyes.

PILE: I'm dying of hunger. What can we eat?

COTICE: The bear!

FATHER UBU: My poor friends, are you going to eat it completely raw? We don't have anything to make a fire with.

PILE: What about our flintstones?

FATHER UBU: Ah, that's true. And it seems to me that not far from here there is a little wood where dry branches may be found. Sire Cotice, go and fetch some.

Cotice runs off across the snow.

PILE: And now, Sir Ubu, you can go and carve up the bear.

FATHER UBU: Oh, no. It may not be completely dead yet. Since it has already half-eaten you, and chewed upon all your members, you're obviously the man to take care of that. I'll go and light the fire while we're waiting for him to bring the wood.

Pile starts to carve up the bear.

Oh! Watch out! It just moved.

PILE: But Sir Ubu, it's stone cold already.

FATHER UBU: That's a pity. It would have been much better to have had him hot. We're running the risk of giving the Master of Phynances an attack of indigestion.

PILE (*aside*): Disgusting fellow! (*Aloud.*) Give me a hand, Mr. Ubu; I can't do everything myself.

FATHER UBU: No, I'm sorry I can't help you. I'm really excessively fatigued.

COTICE (*re-entering*): What a lot of snow, my friends; anyone would think this was Castile or the North Pole. Night is beginning to fall. In an hour it'll be dark. Let's make haste while we can still see.

FATHER UBU: Did you hear that, Pile? Get a move on. In fact, get a move on, both of you! Skewer the beast, cook the beast, I'm hungry!

PILE: Well, that does it! You'll work or you'll get nothing, do you hear me, you big hog?

FATHER UBU: Oh! It's all the same to me; I'd just as soon eat it raw; you're the ones whose stomachs it won't agree with. Anyway, I'm sleepy.

COTICE: What can we expect from him, Pile? Let's cook dinner ourselves. We just won't give him any, that's all. Or at most we'll throw him a few bones.

PILE: Good enough. Ah, the fire's catching.

FATHER UBU: Oh, that's very nice. It's getting warm now. But I see Russians everywhere. My God, what a retreat! Ah! (*He falls asleep.*)

COTICE: I wonder if Rensky was telling the truth about Mother Ubu being dethroned. It wouldn't surprise me at all.

PILE: Let's finish cooking supper.

COTICE: No, we've got more important problems. I think it would be a good idea to inquire into the truth of the news.

PILE: You're right. Should we desert Father Ubu or stay with him?

COTICE: Let's sleep on it; we'll decide tomorrow.

PILE: No—let's sneak off under cover of darkness.

COTICE: Let's go, then.

They go.

SCENE 7

FATHER UBU (*talking in his sleep*): Ah, Sir Russian Dragoon, watch out, don't shoot in this direction; there's someone here. Oh, there's Bordure; he looks mean, like a bear. And there's Bougrelas coming at me! The bear, the bear! He's right below me; he looks fierce. My God! No, I'm sorry I can't help you! Go away, Bougrelas! Don't you hear me, you clown? There's Rensky now, and the Czar. Oh, they're going to beat me up. And Mother Ubu. Where did you get all that gold? You've stolen my gold, you miserable witch; you've been ransacking my tomb in Warsaw Cathedral, under the moon. I've been dead a long time; Bougrelas has killed me and I've been buried in Warsaw next to Ladislas the Great, and also at Cracow next to John Sigismund, and also at Thorn in the dungeon with Bordure. There it is again. Get out of here, you nasty bear! You look like Bordure. Do you hear, you devilish beast? No, he can't hear me, the Salopins have cut his ears off. Disembrain them, devitalize them, cut off their ears, confiscate their money and drink yourself to death, that's the life of a Salopin, that's happiness for the Master of Phynances. (*He falls silent and sleeps.*)

ACT V

SCENE 1

It is night. Father Ubu is asleep. Enter Mother Ubu, without seeing him. The stage is in total darkness.

MOTHER UBU: Shelter at last. I'm alone here, which is fine, but what an awful journey: crossing all Poland in four days! And even before that, everything happened to me at once! As soon as that fat fool left, I went to the crypt to grab what I could. And right after that, I was almost stoned to death by that Bougrelas and his madmen. I lost the Palotin Giron, my knight, who was so stricken by my beauty that he swooned whenever he saw me, and even, I've been told, when he didn't see me, which is the height of passion. He would have let himself be cut in two for my sake, the poor boy. The proof is that he was cut in four, by Bougrelas. Snip, snap, snop! I thought I'd die. Right after that, I took to flight, pursued by the maddened mob. I flee the palace, reach the Vistula, and find all the bridges guarded. I swim across the river, hoping to escape my persecutors. Nobles come from every direction and chase me. I die a thousand deaths, surrounded by a ring of Poles, screaming for my blood. Finally I wriggle out of their clutches, and after four days of running across the snow of my former kingdom, I reach my refuge here. I haven't had a thing to eat or drink for four days. Bougrelas was right behind me. . . . And here I am, safe at last. Oh, I'm nearly dead of cold and exhaustion. But I'd really like to know what's become of my big buffroon—I mean my honored spouse. Have I fleeced him! Have I taken his rixthalers! Have I pulled the wool over his eyes! And his starving phynancial horse: he's not going to see any oats very soon, either, the poor devil. Oh, what a joke! But alas! My treasure is lost! It's in Warsaw, and let anybody who wants it, go and get it.

FATHER UBU (*starting to wake up*): Capture Mother Ubu! Cut off her ears!

MOTHER UBU: Oh, my God! Where am I? I'm losing my mind. Good Lord, no!

> God be praised
> I think I can see
> Mr. Ubu
> Sleeping near me.

Let's show a little sweetness. Well, my fat fellow, did you have a good sleep?

FATHER UBU: A very bad one! That was a tough bear! A fight of hunger against toughness, but hunger has completely eaten and devoured the toughness, as you will see when it gets light in here. Do you hear, my noble Palotins?

MOTHER UBU: What's he babbling about? He seems even stupider than when he left. What's the matter with him?

FATHER UBU: Cotice, Pile, answer me, by my bag of shitr! Where are you? Oh, I'm afraid. Somebody did speak. Who spoke? Not the bear, I suppose. Shitr! Where are my matches? Ah! I lost them in the battle.

MOTHER UBU (*aside*): Let's take advantage of the situation and the darkness and pretend to be a ghost. We'll make him promise to forgive us our little pilfering.

FATHER UBU: By Saint Anthony, somebody is speaking! Godslegs! I'll be damned!

MOTHER UBU (*deepening her voice*): Yes, Mr. Ubu, somebody is indeed speaking, and the trumpet of the archangel which will call the dead from dust and ashes on Judgment Day would not speak otherwise! Listen to my stern voice. It is that of Saint Gabriel who cannot help but give good advice.

FATHER UBU: To be sure!

MOTHER UBU: Don't interrupt me or I'll fall silent, and that will settle your hash!

FATHER UBU: Oh, buggers! I'll be quiet, I won't say another word. Please go on, Madam Apparition!

MOTHER UBU: We were saying, Mr. Ubu, that you are a big fat fellow.

FATHER UBU: Very fat, that's true.

MOTHER UBU: Shut up, Goddammit!

FATHER UBU: Oh my! Angels aren't supposed to curse!

MOTHER UBU (aside): Shitr! (Continuing.) You are married, Mr. Ubu?

FATHER UBU: Absolutely. To the Queen of Witches.

MOTHER UBU: What you mean to say is that she is a charming woman.

FATHER UBU: A perfect horror. She has claws all over her; you don't know where to grab her.

MOTHER UBU: You should grab her with sweetness, Sir Ubu, and if you grab her thus you will see that Venus herself couldn't be as nice.

FATHER UBU: Who did you say has lice?

MOTHER UBU: You're not listening, Mr. Ubu. Try and keep your ears open now. (Aside.) We'd better get a move on; it's getting light in here. Mr. Ubu, your wife is adorable and delicious; she doesn't have a single fault.

FATHER UBU: Ah, you're wrong there: there isn't a single fault that she doesn't have.

MOTHER UBU: That's enough now. Your wife is not unfaithful to you!

FATHER UBU: I'd like to see someone who could stand making her unfaithful. She's an absolute harpy!

MOTHER UBU: She doesn't drink!

FATHER UBU: Only since I've taken the key to the cellar away from her. Before that, she was drunk by seven in the morning and perfumed herself with brandy. Now that she perfumes herself with heliotrope, she doesn't smell so bad any more. Not that I care about that. But now I'm the only one that can get drunk!

MOTHER UBU: Stupid idiot! Your wife doesn't steal your gold.

FATHER UBU: No, that's peculiar.

MOTHER UBU: She doesn't pinch a cent!

FATHER UBU: As witness our noble and unfortunate Phynancial Horse, who, not having been fed for three months, has had to undergo the entire campaign being dragged by the bridle across the Ukraine. He died on the job, poor beast!

MOTHER UBU: That's all a bunch of lies—you've got a model wife, and you're a monster.

FATHER UBU: That's all a bunch of truth. My wife's a slut, and you're a sausage.

MOTHER UBU: Take care, Father Ubu!

FATHER UBU: Oh, that's right, I forgot whom I was talking to. I take it all back.

MOTHER UBU: You killed Wenceslas.

FATHER UBU: That wasn't my fault, actually. Mother Ubu wanted it.

MOTHER UBU: You had Boleslas and Ladislas killed.

FATHER UBU: Too bad for them. They wanted to do me in.

MOTHER UBU: You didn't keep your promise to Bordure, and moreover, you killed him.

FATHER UBU: I'd rather I ruled Lithuania than he. For the moment, neither of us is doing it. Certainly you can see that I'm not.

MOTHER UBU: There's only one way you can make up for all your sins.

FATHER UBU: What's that? I'm all ready to become a holy man; I'd like to be a bishop and have my name on the calendar.

MOTHER UBU: You must forgive Mother Ubu for having sidetracked some of the funds.

FATHER UBU: What do you think of this: I'll pardon her when she's given everything back, when she's been soundly thrashed, and when she's revived my phynancial horse.

MOTHER UBU: He's got that horse on the brain. Ah, I'm lost, day is breaking!

FATHER UBU: Well, I'm happy to know at last for sure that my dear wife steals from me. Now I have it on the highest authority. Omnis a Deo scientia, which is to say: omnis, all; a Deo, knowledge; scientia, comes from God. That explains this marvel. But Madam Apparition is so silent now! What can I offer her to revive her? What she said was very entertaining. But, look, it's daybreak! Ah! Good Lord, by my Phynancial Horse, it's Mother Ubu!

MOTHER UBU (brazenly): That's not true, and I'm going to excommunicate you.

FATHER UBU: Ah, you old slut!

MOTHER UBU: Such impiety!

FATHER UBU: That's too much! I can see very well that it's you, you half-witted hag! What the devil are you doing here?

MOTHER UBU: Giron is dead and the Poles chased me.

FATHER UBU: And the Russians chased me. So two great souls meet again.

MOTHER UBU: Say rather that a great soul has met an ass!

FATHER UBU: Fine, and now it's going to meet this little monster.

(He throws the bear at her.)

MOTHER UBU (falling down crushed beneath the weight of the bear): Oh, great God! How horrible! I'm dying! I'm suffocating! It's chewing on me! It's swallowing me! I'm being digested!

FATHER UBU: He's dead, you gargoyle! Oh, wait, perhaps he's not. Lord, he's not dead, save us. (Climbing back on his rock.) Pater noster qui es . . .

MOTHER UBU (disentangling herself): Where did he go?

FATHER UBU: Oh, Lord, there she is again. Stupid creature, there's no way of getting rid of her. Is that bear dead?

MOTHER UBU: Of course, you stupid ass, he's stone cold. How did he get here?

FATHER UBU (*bewildered*): I don't know. Oh, yes, I do know. He wanted to eat Pile and Cotice, and I killed him with one swipe of a Pater Noster.

MOTHER UBU: Pile, Cotice, Pater Noster? What's that all about? He's out of his mind, my finance!

FATHER UBU: It happened exactly the way I said. And you're an idiot, you stinkpot!

MOTHER UBU: Describe your campaign to me, Father Ubu.

FATHER UBU: Holy Mother, no! It would take too long. All I know is that despite my incontestable valor, everybody beat me up.

MOTHER UBU: What, even the Poles?

FATHER UBU: They were shouting: Long live Wenceslas and Bougrelas! I thought they were going to chop me up. Oh, those madmen! And then they killed Rensky!

MOTHER UBU: I don't care about that! Did you know that Bougrelas killed Palotin Giron?

FATHER UBU: I don't care about that! And then they killed poor Lascy!

MOTHER UBU: I don't care about that!

FATHER UBU: Oh, well, in that case, come over here, you old slut! Get down on your knees before your master. (*He grabs her and throws her on her knees.*) You're about to suffer the extreme penalty.

MOTHER UBU: Ho, ho, Mr. Ubu!

FATHER UBU: Oh! Oh! Oh! Are you all through now? I'm just about to begin: twisting of the nose, tearing out of the hair, penetration of the little bit of wood into the ears, extraction of the brain by the heels, laceration of the posterior, partial or perhaps even total suppression of the spinal marrow (assuming that would make her character less spiny), not forgetting the

punturing of the swimming bladder and finally the grand
re-enacted decollation of John the Baptist, the whole taken
from the very Holy Scriptures, from the Old as well as the
New Testament, as edited, corrected and perfected by the
here-attendant Master of Phynances! How does that suit you,
you sausage? (*He begins to tear her to pieces.*)

MOTHER UBU: Mercy, Mr. Ubu!

A loud noise at the entrance to the cave.

SCENE 2

*The same, and Bougrelas, who rushes into the cave with his
soldiers.*

BOUGRELAS: Forward, my friends. Long live Poland!

FATHER UBU: Oh! Oh! Wait a moment, Mr. Pole. Wait until I've
finished with madam my other half!

BOUGRELAS (*hitting him*): Take that, coward, tramp, braggart,
laggard, Mussulman!

FATHER UBU (*countering*): Take that! Polack, drunkard, bastard,
hussar, tartar, pisspot, inkblot, sneak, freak, anarchist!

MOTHER UBU (*hitting out also*): Take that, prig, pig, rake, fake,
snake, mistake, mercenary!

*The soldiers throw themselves on the Ubus, who defend them-
selves as best they can.*

FATHER UBU: Gods! What a battle!

MOTHER UBU: Watch out for our feet, Gentlemen of Poland.

FATHER UBU: By my green candle, when will this endlessness be
ended? Another one! Ah, if only I had my Phynancial Horse
here!

BOUGRELAS: Hit them, keep hitting them!

VOICES FROM WITHOUT: Long live Father Ubu, our Great Financier!

FATHER UBU: Ah! There they are. Hooray! There are the Father
Ubuists. Forward, come on, you're desperately needed, Gentlemen of Finance.

Enter the Palotins, who throw themselves into the fight.

COTICE: All out, you Poles!

PILE: Ho! We meet again, my Financial sir. Forward, push as hard as you can, get to the exit; once outside, we'll run away.

FATHER UBU: Oh! He's my best man. Look the way he hits them!

BOUGRELAS: Good God! I'm wounded!

STANISLAS LECZINSKI: It's nothing, Sire.

BOUGRELAS: No, I'm just a little stunned.

JOHN SOBIESKI: Fight, keep fighting, they're getting to the door, the knaves.

COTICE: We're getting there; follow me everybody. By conseyquence of the whiche, the sky becomes visible.

PILE: Courage, Sire Ubu!

FATHER UBU: Oh! I just crapped in my pants. Forward, horns-buggers! Killem, bleedem, skinnem, massacrem, by Ubu's horn! Ah! It's quieting down.

COTICE: There are only two of them guarding the exit!

FATHER UBU (*knocking them down with the bear*): And one, and two! Oof! Here I am outside! Let's run now! Follow, you others, and don't stop for anything!

SCENE 3

The scene represents the Province of Livonia covered with snow. The Ubus and their followers are in flight.

FATHER UBU: Ah! I think they've stopped trying to catch us.

MOTHER UBU: Yes, Bougrelas has gone to get himself crowned.

FATHER UBU: I don't envy him that crown, either.

MOTHER UBU: You're quite right, Father Ubu.

They disappear into the distance.

SCENE 4

The bridge of a close-hauled schooner on the Baltic. Father Ubu and his entire gang are on the bridge.

THE CAPTAIN: What a lovely breeze!

FATHER UBU: We are indeed sailing with a rapidity which borders on the miraculous. We must be making at least a million knots an hour, and these knots have been tied so well that once tied they cannot be untied. It's true that we have the wind behind us.

PILE: What a pathetic imbecile!

A squall arises, the ship rolls, the sea foams.

FATHER UBU: Oh! Ah! My God, we're going to be capsized. The ship is leaning over too far, it'll fall!

THE CAPTAIN: Everyone to leeward, furl the foresail!

FATHER UBU: Oh, no, don't put everybody on the same side! That's imprudent. What if the wind changed direction—everybody would sink to the bottom of the sea and the fishes would eat us.

THE CAPTAIN: Don't rush, line up and close ranks!

FATHER UBU: Yes, yes, rush! I'm in a hurry! Rush, do you hear! It's your fault that we aren't getting there, brute of a captain. We should have been there already. I'm going to take charge of this myself. Get ready to tack about. Drop anchor, tack with the wind, tack against the wind. Run up the sails, run down the sails, tiller up, tiller down, tiller to the side. You see, everything's going fine. Come broadside to the waves now and everything will be perfect.

All are convulsed with laughter; the wind rises.

THE CAPTAIN: Haul over the jibsail, reef over the topsail!

FATHER UBU: That's not bad, it's even good! Swab out the steward and jump in the crow's-nest.

Several choke with laughter. A wave is shipped.

Oh, what a deluge! All this is the result of the maneuvers which we just ordered.

MOTHER UBU *and* PILE: What a wonderful thing navigation is!

A second wave is shipped.

PILE (*drenched*): But watch out for Satan, his pomps and pumps.

FATHER UBU: Sir boy, get us something to drink.

They all sit down to drink.

MOTHER UBU: What a pleasure it will be to see our sweet France again, our old friends and our castle of Mondragon!

FATHER UBU: We'll be there soon. At the moment we've passed below the castle of Elsinore.

PILE: I feel cheerful at the thought of seeing my dear Spain again.

COTICE: Yes, and we'll amaze our countrymen with the stories of our wonderful adventures.

FATHER UBU: Oh, certainly! And I'm going to get myself appointed Minister of Finances in Paris.

MOTHER UBU: Oh, that's right! Oops, what a bump that was!

COTICE: That's nothing, we're just doubling the point of Elsinore.

PILE: And now our noble ship plows at full speed through the somber waves of the North Sea.

FATHER UBU: A fierce and inhospitable sea which bathes the shores of the land called Germany, so named because the inhabitants of this land are all cousins-german.

MOTHER UBU: That's what I call true learning. They say that this country is very beautiful.

FATHER UBU: Ah! Gentlemen! Beautiful as it may be, it cannot compare with Poland. For if there were no Poland, there would be no Poles!

CURTAIN

the breasts of tiresias

A SURREALIST DRAMA

by GUILLAUME APOLLINAIRE

translated by Louis Simpson

WITHOUT pleading for your indulgence, may I point out that this is a work of youth, for with the exception of the Prologue and the last scene of the second act, which were added in 1916, this work was written in 1903, that is to say, fourteen years before it was put on the stage.

I have called it a drama, meaning an action, to make clear what distinguishes it from those comedies of manners, dramatic comedies, light comedies, which for over half a century have provided the stage with works many of which are excellent but of the second rank and simply called plays.

To characterize my drama I have used a neologism which, as I rarely use them, I hope will be excused: I have invented the adjective *surrealist*, which does not at all mean *symbolic*, as Mr. Victor Basch has assumed in his article on the theatre, but defines fairly well a tendency in art which, if it is not the newest thing under the sun, at least has never been formulated as a credo, an artistic and literary faith.

The cheap idealism of the playwrights who followed Victor Hugo sought for verisimilitude in conventional local color, which as "photographic" naturalism produced comedies of manners the originals of which may be found long before Scribe, in the sentimental comedies of Nivelle de la Chaussée.

And in order to attempt, if not a renovation of the theatre, at least an original effort, I thought it necessary to come back to nature itself, but without copying it photographically.

When man wanted to imitate walking he created the wheel, which does not resemble a leg. In the same way he has created surrealism unconsciously.

However, I cannot possibly decide if this drama is serious or not. Its aim is to interest and entertain. That is the aim of every dramatic work. It also undertakes to emphasize a question of vital importance to those who understand the language in which it is written: the problem of repopulation.

I could have written on this subject, which has never before been treated, a play in the mock-melodramatic style which has been

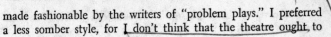

made fashionable by the writers of "problem plays." I preferred a less somber style, for I don't think that the theatre ought to make anyone feel desperate.

I might also have written a play of ideas and flattered the taste of the contemporary public, which likes to think that it thinks. I have preferred to give free rein to the fantasy which is my way of interpreting nature, a fancy which, like life from day to day, is sometimes more and sometimes less melancholy, satiric, and lyrical, but always, and as much as lies within my power, showing a common sense in which there is sometimes enough novelty to shock and anger, but which will be convincing to those who are sincere.

The subject is so moving in my opinion that it permits us to give the word *drama* its most tragic meaning; but it depends on the French whether, because they start making children again, in the future this work is to be called a farce. Nothing else could give me such great patriotic pleasure. I assure you, the reputation which would rightfully be enjoyed by the author of *The Farce of Master Pierre Pathelin*, if his name were known, keeps me awake at night.

It has been said that I have used some of the techniques of vaudeville: I don't really see where. Anyway there is nothing in that criticism that disturbs me, for popular art is an excellent basis and I would congratulate myself for having drawn on it if all my scenes followed the natural sequence of the fable I have imagined, of which the main idea, a man who makes children, is new to the theatre and to literature in general, but can be no more shocking than certain improbable inventions of novelists whose vogue depends on so-called science fiction.

Moreover, there is no symbolism in my play and it is transparent, but you are free to find in it all the symbols you want and to disentangle a thousand meanings, as with the oracles of the sibyl.

Mr. Victor Basch, who has not understood, or has not wanted to understand, that it was about repopulation, insists that my work is symbolic; he's free to think so! But he adds: "The first requirement for a symbolic drama is that the relationship between the symbol, which is always a sign, and the thing signified shall be immediately apparent."

Not always, however, and there are notable works in which the symbolism rightly has numerous interpretations which sometimes contradict one another.

I wrote my surrealist drama above all for the French as Aristophanes composed his comedies for the Athenians. I have warned them of the grave danger, recognized by everybody, that not making children holds for a nation that wishes to be prosperous and powerful, and to remedy the evil I have shown them what must be done.

Mr. Deffoux, a witty writer, but one who strikes me as being a belated Malthusian, finds a ridiculous connection between the rubber * of which are made the balloons and balls representing the breasts (perhaps this is where Mr. Basch sees a symbol) and certain articles recommended by neo-Malthusianism. To speak plainly, they have nothing to do with the matter, for there is no country where they are less used than in France, while in Berlin, for example, there isn't a day when they don't fall on your head as you walk in the street, so great a use do the Germans, a still prolific race, make of them.

The other causes to which, together with the prevention of pregnancy by hygienic methods, depopulation is attributed, alcoholism for example, exist everywhere else and in much larger proportions than in France.

In a recent book on alcohol, didn't Mr. Yves Guyot point out that if France took first place in the statistics of alcoholism, Italy, a notoriously sober country, came second? By this we can judge

* To clear myself of any reproach concerning the use of rubber breasts, here is an extract from the newspapers proving that these organs were absolutely legal:

"SALE OF NIPPLES OTHER THAN THOSE OF PURE RUBBER, VULCANIZED BY HEAT, PROHIBITED.—On the 28th of February last was issued in the *Official Journal* the law of February 26, 1917, modifying Article 1 of the law of April 6, 1910, which alluded only to the ban on feeding bottles with tubes.

"Revised Article 1 of this law is henceforth as follows: 'The sale, offering for sale, display and import of the following are forbidden:

" '1st. Feeding bottles with tubes;

" '2nd. Nipples and suckers made of materials other than pure rubber, vulcanized by any process other than vulcanization by heat, and not bearing, together with the brand of manufacturer or seller, the particular words: "pure rubber."

" 'Therefore only nipples and suckers made of pure rubber and vulcanized with heat are authorized.' "

how much trust may be placed in statistics; they are liars and you're a fool if you believe them. On the other hand, isn't it remarkable that the provinces of France where most children are made are precisely those which rank first in the statistics of alcoholism!

The fault is more serious, the vice has deeper roots, for this is the truth: we don't make children any more in France because we don't make love often enough. That's all there is to it.

But I won't enlarge any further on this subject. It would take a whole book and a social revolution. It is up to the authorities to act, to facilitate marriages, to encourage fruitful love above all else; the other important questions such as that of child labor will then be easily resolved for the good and honor of the country.

To get back to dramatic art, you will find in the prologue to this work the essential characteristics of the drama I propose.

Let me add that in my opinion this art will be modern, simple, swift-paced, with the short cuts or expansions that are needed to move the spectator. The subject will be general enough so that the dramatic work of which it is the basis may influence minds and manners in the direction of duty and honor.

Depending on circumstances, tragedy will prevail over comedy or vice versa. But I do not think that from now on you will be able to endure, without impatience, a theatre piece in which these elements are not balanced against each other, for there is such an energy in mankind today and in the writing of the younger generation that the greatest misfortune immediately seems understandable, as though it may be considered not only from the viewpoint of a kindly irony which permits laughter, but also from the perspective of a true optimism which at once consoles us and makes way for hope.

After all, the stage is no more the life it represents than the wheel is a leg. Consequently, it is legitimate, in my opinion, to bring to the theatre new and striking aesthetic principles which accentuate the roles of the actors and increase the effect of the production, yet without modifying the pathos or comedy of the situations, which must be self-sufficient.

Finally, may I say that, in abstracting from contemporary literary movements a certain tendency of my own, I am in no way undertaking to form a school, but above all to protest against that "realistic" theatre which is the predominating theatrical art today. This "realism," which is, no doubt, suited to the cinema, is, I believe, as far removed as possible from the art of drama.

I should like to add that, in my opinion, the only verse suitable for the theatre is a supple line, based on rhythm, subject matter, and breathing, and adaptable to all dramatic purposes. The dramatist will not scorn the music of rhyme, which in future must not be a constraint of which author and audience soon grow weary, but which may add beauty to the pathetic, the comic, in choruses, in certain cues, at the end of certain speeches, or to bring an act to a dignified conclusion.

Does not such a drama have infinite possibilities? It gives free play to the imagination of the dramatist who, while throwing off all the apparently necessary bonds or perhaps rediscovering a neglected tradition, does not think it useful to deny the greatest of his predecessors. Here he pays them the honor due to those who have raised humanity above the mere appearances of things, with which, left to itself, if it did not have geniuses who surpass it and point the way, it would have to be content. But these men reveal new worlds which, extending horizons, ceaselessly multiplying the vision of mankind, provide it with the joy and honor of advancing always toward the most astonishing discoveries.

To Louise-Marion

Louise-Marion you were wonderful
Inflating your many breasts with a new intelligence

Fecund reason squirted from my fable
No more sterile women and no more abortions
Your voice has changed the fate of the French nation
And bellies everywhere quiver with expectation

To Marcel Herrand

You were the husband sublime ingenious
Who making children raised up gods for us
Better armed united wiser more docile
Stronger and more adventurous than we
Victory watched their progress with a smile

And honoring in peace and prosperity
Your civic sense and your fertility
One day they all will be the pride of the City

To Yéta Daesslé

Did you like Zanzibar Mister Lacouf
Who died and died again without saying ouf

A traveling kiosk through which the news spread
You served as a head for every poor head

Among the spectators who weren't aware
They've got to have children or else cross the bar

Twice you served as the press that fecundates
Common sense in Europe as well as the States
Already they're all echoing your echoes

Thank you dear Daesslé
   The little Negroes
Who swarmed in the 2nd act of my play
Will be good little Frenchmen yours is the credit
As white and as pink as you are lady
   And there's our hit

To Juliette Norville

In this hour Madame we hear the men-at-arms
I'm one of them that's why sounding the alarms
I have spoken
   You on your fine horse astride
Were order in the valley and on the mountainside
Our efforts have revived in the French race
The taste for numbers in order to live at ease
As do the children of the husband of Thérèse

To Howard

You were the whole nation and maintained your silence
People of Zanzibar or rather of France
Sacrifice taste and keep your sanity
If you love your home you must make a journey
You must cherish courage and seek adventure
You must always think of France of the future

Don't hope for rest risk everything you own
Learn what is new for everything must be known
When a prophet speaks you must be looking on
And make children that's the point of my tale
The child is wealth and the only wealth that's real

CHARACTERS

With the cast of the first performance

DIRECTOR: Edmond Vallée
THÉRÈSE-TIRESIAS and THE FORTUNETELLER: Louise-Marion
HUSBAND: Marcel Herrand (Jean Thillois)
POLICEMAN: Juliette Norville
REPORTER FROM PARIS: Yéta Daesslé
SON: Yéta Daesslé
KIOSK: Yéta Daesslé
LACOUF: Yéta Daesslé
PRESTO: Edmond Vallée
PEOPLE OF ZANZIBAR: Howard
LADY: Georgette Dubuet
CHORUS: Niny Guyard, Maurice Lévy, Max Jacob, Paul Morisse, etc.

In present-day Zanzibar

*At the first performance the scenery and costumes were by Mr.
Serge Férat; Miss Niny Guyard was at the piano, the full score for
orchestra not having been executed because of the rarity of musicians during the war.*

PROLOGUE

*In front of the lowered curtain The Director, in evening dress and
carrying a swagger stick, emerges from the prompt box.*

DIRECTOR: So here I am once more among you
    I've found my ardent company again
    I have also found a stage
    But to my dismay found as before
    The theatre with no greatness and no virtue
    That killed the tedious nights before the war
    A slanderous and pernicious art
    That showed the sin but did not show the savior
    Then the hour struck the hour of men
    I have been at war like all other men

    In the days when I was in the artillery
    On the northern front commanding my battery
    One night when the gazing of the stars in heaven
    Pulsated like the eyes of the newborn
    A thousand rockets that rose from the opposite trench
    Suddenly woke the guns of the enemy

    I remember as though it were yesterday
    I heard the shells depart but no explosions
    Then from the observation post there came
    The trumpeter on horseback to announce
    That the sergeant there who calculated
    From the flashes of the enemy guns
    Their angle of fire had stated
    That the range of those guns was so great
    That the bursts no longer could be heard
    And all my gunners watching at their posts
    Announced the stars were darkening one by one
    Then loud shouts arose from the whole army
        THEY'RE PUTTING OUT THE STARS
        WITH SHELLFIRE

The stars were dying in that fine autumn sky
As memory fades in the brain
Of the poor old men who try to remember
We were dying there of the death of stars
And on the somber front with its livid lights
We could only say in despair
    THEY'VE EVEN MURDERED
    THE CONSTELLATIONS
But in a great voice out of a megaphone
The mouth of which emerged
From some sort of supreme headquarters
The voice of the unknown captain who always saves us cried
    THE TIME HAS COME TO LIGHT THE STARS AGAIN
And the whole French front shouted together
    FIRE AT WILL
The gunners hastened
The layers calculated
The marksmen fired
And the sublime stars lit up again one by one
Our shells rekindled their eternal ardor
The enemy guns were silent dazzled
By the scintillating of all the stars

There there is the history of all the stars

And since that night I too light one by one
All the stars within that were extinguished

So here I am once more among you
My troupe don't be impatient
Public wait without impatience

I bring you a play that aims to reform society
It deals with children in the family
The subject is domestic
And that is the reason it's handled in a familiar way

The actors will not adopt a sinister tone
They will simply appeal to your common sense
And above all will try to entertain you
So that you will be inclined to profit

From all the lessons that the play contains
And so that the earth will be starred with the glances of
    infants

Even more numerous than the twinkling stars
Hear O Frenchmen the lesson of war
And make children you that made few before

We're trying to bring a new spirit into the theatre
A joyfulness voluptuousness virtue
Instead of that pessimism more than a hundred years old
And that's pretty old for such a boring thing
The play was created for an antique stage
For they wouldn't have built us a new theatre
A circular theatre with two stages
One in the middle the other like a ring
Around the spectators permitting
The full unfolding of our modern art
Often connecting in unseen ways as in life
Sounds gestures colors cries tumults
Music dancing acrobatics poetry painting
Choruses actions and multiple sets

Here you will find actions
Which add to the central drama and augment it
Changes of tone from pathos to burlesque
And the reasonable use of the improbable
And actors who may be collective or not
Not necessarily taken from mankind
But from the universe

For the theatre must not be "realistic"

It is right for the dramatist to use
All the illusions he has at his disposal
As Morgana did on Mount Gibel
It is right for him to make crowds speak and inanimate things
If he wishes
And for him to pay no more heed to time
Than to space

His universe is his stage
Within it he is the creating god
Directing at his will
Sounds gestures movements masses colors
Not merely with the aim
Of photographing the so-called slice of life
But to bring forth life itself in all its truth

For the play must be an entire universe
With its creator
That is to say nature itself
And not only
Representation of a little part
Of what surrounds us or has already passed

Pardon me my friends my company

Pardon me ladies and gentlemen
For having spoken a little too long
It's been so long since I have been among you

But out there there's still a fire
Where they're putting out the smoking stars
And those who light them again demand that you
Lift yourselves to the height of those great flames
And also burn

O public
Be the unquenchable torch of the new fire

ACT I

The market place at Zanzibar, morning. The scene consists of houses, an area opening on the harbor and whatever else can evoke in Frenchmen the idea of the game of zanzibar.* A megaphone shaped like a dice box and decorated with dice is in the foreground. On the courtyard side, the entrance to a house; on the garden side, a newspaper kiosk with a large display and a picture of the newspaper woman which is able to move its arm; it is also decorated with a mirror on the side facing the stage. In the background, the collective speechless person who represents the people of Zanzibar is present from the rise of the curtain. He is sitting on a bench. A

---

* Zanzibar—commonly known as *zanzi*—a game of chance played with three dice and a dice box. Each player in turn throws the dice. An ace counts 100 points, a six 60, and the other numbers their face value. The player with the highest total wins. The game can be decided in one throw, in three throws, by leaving out one or two dice at each throw, or in several extra throws. In case of a tie, the players each throw once. There are many kinds of *zanzi*; the notorious *chemin de fer* is one of them—played with three throws of the dice; at each throw one of the dice is left out. [*Translator's note.*]

table is at his right, and he has ready to hand the instruments he will use to make the right noise at the right moment: revolver, musette, bass drum, accordion, snare drum, thunder, sleigh bells, castanets, toy trumpet, broken dishes. All the sounds marked to be produced by an instrument are made by the people of Zanzibar, and everything marked to be spoken through the megaphone is to be shouted at the audience.

Scene 1

The People of Zanzibar, Thérèse

THÉRÈSE (*blue face, long blue dress decorated with monkeys and painted fruit. She enters when the curtain has risen, but from the moment that the curtain begins to rise she attempts to dominate the sound of the orchestra*):
No Mister husband
You won't make me do what you want

(*In a hushing voice.*)
I am a feminist and I do not recognize the authority of men
(*In a hushing voice.*)

Besides I want to do as I please
Men have been doing what they like long enough
After all I too want to go and fight the enemy
I want to be a soldier hup two hup two
I want to make war (*Thunder*) and not make children
No Mister husband you won't give me orders
(*She bows three times, backside to the audience.*)

(*In the megaphone.*)
Because you made love to me in Connecticut
Doesn't mean I have to cook for you in Zanzibar

VOICE OF THE HUSBAND (*Belgian accent*):
Give me lard I tell you give me lard
Broken dishes.

THÉRÈSE: Listen to him he only thinks of love
(*She has a fit of hysterics.*)

But you don't understand you fool
(*Sneeze.*)

That after being a soldier I want to be an artist
(*Sneeze.*)

Exactly exactly
(*Sneeze.*)

I also want to be a deputy a lawyer a senator
(*Two sneezes.*)

Minister president of the state
(*Sneeze.*)

And I want to be a doctor or psychiatrist
Give Europe and America the trots
Making children cooking no it's too much
(*She cackles.*)

I want to be a mathematician philosopher chemist
A page in a restaurant a little telegraphist
And if it pleases me I want
To keep that old chorus girl with so much talent
(*Sneeze cackle, after which she imitates the sound of a train.*)

VOICE OF THE HUSBAND (*Belgian accent*):
Give me lard I tell you give me lard

THÉRÈSE: Listen to him he only thinks of love

Little tune on the musette.

Why don't you eat your old sausage feet

Bass drum.

But I think I'm growing a beard
My bosom is falling off
(*She utters a loud cry and opens her blouse from which her breasts emerge, one red, the other blue, and as she lets go of them they fly off, like toy balloons, but remain attached by strings.*)

Fly away birds of my frailty
    Et cetera
How pretty are feminine charms
They're awfully sweet
You could eat them
(*She pulls on the balloon strings and makes them dance.*)
But enough of this nonsense

Let's not go in for aeronautics
There is always some advantage in being virtuous
Vice is a dangerous business after all
That is why it is better to sacrifice beauty
That may be a cause of sin
Let us get rid of our breasts
(*She strikes a lighter and makes them explode; then she makes a face, thumbing her nose with both hands at the audience and throws them the balls she has in her bodice.*)
That is to say
It's not just my beard my mustache is growing too

She caresses her beard and strokes her mustache, which have suddenly sprouted.

What the devil
I look like a wheatfield that's waiting for the harvester

(*In the megaphone.*)
I feel as virile as the devil
I'm a stallion
From my head on down
I'm a bull

(*Without the megaphone.*)
I'll be a torero
But let's not reveal
My future to everyone hero
Conceal your arms
And you my husband less virile than I
You can sound the alarms
As much as you want
(*Cackling, she goes and admires herself in the mirror attached to the newspaper kiosk.*)

SCENE 2

The People of Zanzibar, Thérèse, The Husband

HUSBAND (*enters with a big bouquet of flowers, sees that she is not looking at him, and throws the flowers into the auditorium.*

From this point on, The Husband loses his Belgian accent):
I want lard I tell you

THÉRÈSE: Eat your old sausage feet

HUSBAND (*while he speaks Thérèse cackles louder and louder. He approaches as though to hit her, then laughing*):
Ah but it isn't my wife Thérèse
(*A pause then in a severe manner.*
In the megaphone.)
Who is this rascal who's wearing her clothes
(*He goes over to examine her and comes back.*
In the megaphone.)
No doubt he's a murderer and he has killed her

(*Without the megaphone.*)
Thérèse my little Thérèse where are you
(*He reflects with his head in his hands, then plants himself squarely, fists on hips.*)

But you, you base rascal who have disguised yourself like Thérèse
I will kill you

They fight, she overpowers him.

THÉRÈSE: You're right I'm no longer your wife

HUSBAND: Goodness

THÉRÈSE: And yet I am Thérèse

HUSBAND: Goodness

THÉRÈSE: But Thérèse who is no longer a woman

HUSBAND: This is too much

THÉRÈSE: And as I have become a fine fellow

HUSBAND: It must have escaped my attention

THÉRÈSE: From now on I'll have a man's name Tiresias

HUSBAND (*hands clasped*): Sweetiest

She goes off.

Scene 3

The People of Zanzibar, The Husband

VOICE OF TIRESIAS: I'm moving house

HUSBAND: Sweetiest

*She throws out of the window a chamberpot, a basin, and a
urinal. The Husband picks up the chamberpot.*

The piano
(*He picks up the urinal.*)

The violin
(*He picks up the basin.*)

The butter dish the situation is becoming grave

Scene 4

The Same, Tiresias, Lacouf, Presto

*Tiresias returns with clothes, a cord, various odd objects. She
throws down everything, hurls herself on The Husband. Upon the
last reply by The Husband, Presto and Lacouf, armed with cardboard revolvers, having emerged with a solemn bearing from below the stage, advance into the auditorium, while Tiresias over-
powering her husband, takes off his trousers, undresses herself,
hands him her skirt, ties him up, puts on the trousers, cuts her hair,
and puts on a top hat. This stage business goes on until the first
revolver shot.*

PRESTO: Old Lacouf I've lost at zanzi with you
    All that I hope to lose

LACOUF: Mister Presto I've won nothing
    And then what has Zanzibar got to do with it you are in Paris

PRESTO: In Zanzibar

LACOUF: In Paris

PRESTO: This is too much
  After ten years of friendship
  And all the bad things I've always said about you

LACOUF: Too bad did I ever ask you for a favor you are in Paris

PRESTO: In Zanzibar the proof is I've lost everything

LACOUF: Mister Presto we'll have to fight

PRESTO: We'll have to

  They go up solemnly on to the stage and take positions at the rear facing each other.

LACOUF: On equal terms

PRESTO: Fire at will
  All shots are natural

  They aim at each other. The People of Zanzibar fire two shots and they fall.

TIRESIAS (*who is ready, starts at the sound and exclaims*):
  Ah dear Freedom so you've been conquered at last
  But first let's buy a newspaper
  And see what has just happened

  She buys a newspaper and reads it; meanwhile the people of Zanzibar set up a placard on each side of the stage.

  PLACARD FOR PRESTO
  As he lost at Zanzibar
  Mister Presto has lost his pari
  Mutuel bet for we're in Paris

  PLACARD FOR LACOUF
  Mister Lacouf has won nothing
  Since the scene's at Zanzibar
  Just as the Seine's at Paris

  As soon as the People of Zanzibar return to their place, Presto and Lacouf get up, the People of Zanzibar fire a revolver shot, and the duelists fall down again. Tiresias throws down the newspaper in astonishment.

  (*In the megaphone.*)
  Now the universe is mine
  The women are mine mine is the government

I'm going to make myself town councilor
But I hear a noise
Maybe I'd better go away

*She goes off cackling while The Husband imitates the sound
of a locomotive.*

SCENE 5

The People of Zanzibar, The Husband, The Policeman

POLICEMAN (*while the People of Zanzibar play the accordion the
mounted policeman makes his horse caper, drags one dead
man into the wings so that his feet alone remain visible, makes
a circuit of the stage, does the same with the other body,
makes another circuit of the stage and, seeing The Husband
tied up in the foreground*):
I smell a crime here

HUSBAND: Ah! since at last there's an agent of the government
Of Zanzibar
I'm going to challenge him
Hey Mister if you've got any business with me
Be kind enough to take
My army papers out of my left pocket

POLICEMAN (*in the megaphone*): What a pretty girl
(*Without the megaphone.*)
Tell me pretty maiden
Who has been treating you so shamefully

HUSBAND (*aside*): He takes me for a young lady
(*To The Policeman.*)
If it's a marriage that you have in mind

The Policeman puts his hand on his heart.

Then begin by getting me out of this

*The Policeman unties him, tickling him; they laugh and The
Policeman continues to say* What a pretty girl.

SCENE 6

The Same, Presto, Lacouf

As soon as The Policeman begins to untie The Husband, Presto and Lacouf return to the spot where they fell.

PRESTO: I'm beginning to be tired of being dead
    Imagine there are people
    Who think it's more honorable to be dead than alive

LACOUF: Now you can see you were not in Zanzibar

PRESTO: Yet that's the place to live
    But it disgusts me to think that we fought a duel
    Certainly death is regarded
    Much too favorably

LACOUF: What do you expect people think too well
    Of mankind and its remains
    In the stool of jewelers
    Do you think there are pearls and diamonds

PRESTO: Greater marvels have been seen

LACOUF: So Mister Presto
    We don't have luck with pari-mutuels
    But now you can see that you were in Paris

PRESTO: In Zanzibar

LACOUF: Aim

PRESTO: Fire

The People of Zanzibar fire a revolver shot, and they fall. The Policeman has finished untying The Husband.

POLICEMAN: You're under arrest

Presto and Lacouf run off in the direction opposite where they entered. Accordion.

Scene 7

The People of Zanzibar, The Policeman, The Husband (*dressed as a woman*)

POLICEMAN: The local duelists
    Won't prevent me saying that I think it's
    Like a lovely ball of rubber when I touch you

HUSBAND: Kerchoo

Broken dishes.

POLICEMAN: A cold bewitching

HUSBAND: Kitchi

*Snare drum. The Husband removes the skirt, which is imped-
ing his movements.*

POLICEMAN: Loose woman
    (*He winks.*)

    So what if she's pretty

HUSBAND (*aside*): Really he's right
    Since my wife is a man
    It's right for me to be a woman
    (*To The Policeman bashfully.*)

I am a decent woman-mister
My wife is a man-lady
She's taken the piano the violin the butter dish
She's a soldier minister mover of shit

POLICEMAN: Mother of tits

HUSBAND: They've burst she's a lady psychiatrist

POLICEMAN: She's the mother of swans
    Ah, how they sing when they're dying
    Listen

Musette, a sad tune.

HUSBAND: After all it's a matter of curing people
    Music will do it
    As well as any other panacea

POLICEMAN: That's fine no resisting

HUSBAND: I refuse to continue this conversation
(*In the megaphone.*)

Where is my wife

VOICES OF WOMEN (*in the wings*): Long live Tiresias
No more childre no more children

Thunder and bass drum. The Husband makes a face at the audience and puts a hand to his ear like an ear trumpet, while The Policeman, taking a pipe out of his pocket, offers it to him. Bells.

POLICEMAN: Hey, Sweetheart, smoke a cigar
And I'll play my violin

HUSBAND: The baker of Zanzibar
Has a wife who changes her skin

POLICEMAN: She carries a joke too far

The People of Zanzibar hang up a placard with this ritornelle and it stays there:

Hey, Sweetheart, smoke a cigar
And I'll play my violin
The baker of Zanzibar
Has a wife who changes her skin
She carries a joke too far

POLICEMAN: Miss or Mrs. I'm crazy with love
For you
And I want to marry you I do

HUSBAND: Kerchoo
But don't you see that I am only a man

POLICEMAN: No matter what I could marry you
By proxy

HUSBAND: Nonsense
You'd do better making children

POLICEMAN: Hah! the idea

VOICES OF MEN (*in the wings*): Long live Tiresias
Long live General Tiresias

Long live Deputy Tiresias

The accordion plays a military march.

VOICES OF WOMEN (*in the wings*): No more children No more
children

SCENE 8

The Same, The Kiosk

The Kiosk with the moving arm of the newspaper woman pro-
ceeds slowly toward the other end of the stage.

HUSBAND: Famous representative of authority
        You hear I believe it's been said with clarity
        Women at Zanzibar want political rights
        And suddenly renounce their reproductive nights
        No more children No more children you hear them shout
        To fill Zanzibar there are elephants about
        Monkeys and serpents mosquitoes and ostriches
        And just as in beehives enough sterile bitches
        But bees at least make wax and bring in the honey
        Woman is only a neuter under the sky
        And you can take my word for it Mister gendarme
        (*In the megaphone.*)

        Zanzibar needs children
        (*Without the megaphone.*)

        go and sound the alarm
        Shout it at the crossroads and on the avenue
        In Zanzibar we'll have to make children anew
        Women won't make them Worse luck Let men populate
        But yes exactly I'm letting you have it straight
        And I'll make them myself

POLICEMAN *and* KIOSK: You

KIOSK (*in the megaphone which the husband holds out to her*):
        A story like this should go far
        It's much too good to restrict it to Zanzibar
        You that shed tears at the play
        Wish for children that conquer

Observe the measureless ardor
Born of the changing of sex

HUSBAND: Return this very night and see how nature can
Provide me with progeny without a woman

POLICEMAN: I shall return this night to see how nature can
Provide you with progeny without a woman
Don't keep me cooling my heels with no reward
I'm coming back tonight and take you at your word

KIOSK: What a jerk is the gendarme
Who's in charge of Zanzibar
The burlesque theatre and the bar
For this fellow hold more charm
Than repeopling Zanzibar

SCENE 9

The Same, Presto

PRESTO (tickling the husband): What do you think their name
should be
They are just the same as we
Yet they're not men as you can see

POLICEMAN: I shall return this night to see how nature can
Provide you with progeny without a woman

HUSBAND: Well then return this night and see how nature can
Provide me with progeny without a woman

ALL (in chorus. They dance, The Husband and Policeman to-
gether, Presto, and The Kiosk paired off and sometimes
changing partners. The People of Zanzibar dance alone play-
ing the accordion): Hey, Sweetheart, smoke a cigar
And I'll play my violin
The baker of Zanzibar
Has a wife who changes her skin
She carries a joke too far

CURTAIN

ACT II

SCENE 1

The same place, the same day, just as the sun goes down. The same scenery to which have been added several cradles containing the newborn. An empty cradle stands next to an enormous bottle of ink, a gigantic pot of glue, a huge fountain pen, and a tall pair of scissors.

HUSBAND (*he has a child on each arm. Continuous crying of children on the stage, in the wings and in the auditorium throughout the scene ad lib. The stage directions only indicate when and where the crying is redoubled*):
Ah! what a thrill being a father
40,049 children in one day alone
My happiness is complete
Quiet quiet

Crying of children in the background.

Domestic happiness
No woman on my hands
(*He lets the children fall.*)

Quiet

Crying of children from the left side of the auditorium.

Modern music is amazing
Nearly as amazing as the stage sets of the new painters
Who flourish far from the Barbarians
At Zanzibar
You don't have to go to the Ballet Russe or the Vieux-
        Colombier
Quiet quiet

Crying of children from the right side of the auditorium. Bells.

The time's come to swat 'em with belts on the bottom
But let's not rush matters I think that I'll go
And buy them bicycles and when they have got 'em

Then every virtuoso
May exercise
And vocalize
To the open skies

Gradually the children quiet down, he applauds.

Bravo bravo

A knock.

Come in

SCENE 2

The Same, The Reporter from Paris

REPORTER (*his face is blank; he has only a mouth. He enters danc-ing. Accordion*): Hands up
Hullo Mister Husband
I'm a Reporter from a Paris paper

HUSBAND: From Paris
Make yourself at home

REPORTER (*makes a circuit of the stage dancing*):
The papers of Paris
(*In the megaphone.*)
a town in America
(*Without the megaphone.*)

Hurrah

A revolver shot, The Reporter unfolds the American flag.

Have announced that you've discovered
The way for men
To make children

HUSBAND (*The Reporter folds the flag and wraps it around himself like a belt*): That's right

REPORTER: And how's it done

HUSBAND: <u>Willpower</u> sir that's the whole secret

REPORTER: Are they Negroes or like other people

HUSBAND: It all depends on how you look at it

Castanets.

REPORTER: You're wealthy I suppose
(*He does a dance step.*)

HUSBAND: Not at all

REPORTER: How will you bring them up?

HUSBAND: After they've been bottle fed
I hope that they'll feed me instead

REPORTER: In short you are something of a daughter-father
A maternalized paternal instinct I guess

HUSBAND: To the contrary Sir it's all pure selfishness
The child is the wealth of the family
It's worth more than cash and a legacy

The Reporter takes notes.

See that little fellow asleep in his cradle

The child cries. The Reporter tiptoes across to look at him.

His first name is Arthur and already he's made
A million for me in the curdled milk trade

Toy trumpet.

REPORTER: He's advanced for his age

HUSBAND: Joseph over there

The child cries.

he's a novelist

The Reporter goes over to look at Joseph.

His last novel sold 600,000 copies
Permit me to offer you one

A big book placard is lowered it has several pages on the first of which is printed:
                    What Luck!
                    A Novel.

Read it at your leisure

The Reporter lies down; The Husband turns the pages on which may be read one word to the page:
A lady whose name was Cambron.

REPORTER (*stands up and speaks into the megaphone*):
A lady whose name was Cambron
(*He laughs into the megaphone uttering the four vowels: a, e, i, o.*)

HUSBAND: Nevertheless it has a certain urbanity of expression

REPORTER (*without the megaphone*): Ah! ah! ah! ah!

HUSBAND: A certain precociousness

REPORTER: Eh! eh!

HUSBAND: That you don't find in the streets

REPORTER: Hands up

HUSBAND: Finally just as it stands
The novel has put in my hands
Almost two hundred thousand francs
Plus a literary prize
Consisting of twenty cases of dynamite
(*Backs away.*)

REPORTER: Good-bye

HUSBAND: Don't be afraid they're in my safety deposit vault

REPORTER: All right
Don't you have a daughter

HUSBAND: Sure I do this one divorced

She cries. The Reporter goes over to look at her.

From the potato king
Gets a hundred thousand dollars alimony
And this (*She cries.*) no one in Zanzibar is as artistic as she

The Reporter shadow boxes.

She recites lovely poems on gloomy evenings
Her fire and genius earn in a year
What a poet earns in fifty thousand years

REPORTER: Congratulations my dear
    But you've got some dust
    On your dust coat

The Husband smiles gratefully at The Reporter as he picks up the speck of dust.

Since you're so rich lend me a hundred sous

HUSBAND: Put the dust back

All the children cry. The Husband chases The Reporter kicking him. He goes off dancing.

SCENE 3

The People of Zanzibar, The Husband

HUSBAND: Ah yes it's as simple as a periscope
    The more children I have
    The richer I'll be and the better able to live
    It's said that the cod produces enough eggs in a day
    To supply the whole world for a whole year
    With cod paste and garlic
    Isn't it wonderful to have a numerous family
    Then who are those idiotic economists
    Who've made us believe that the child
    Means poverty
    Whereas it's just the opposite
    Did you ever hear of a cod that died in poverty
    So I'm going to keep on making children
    First we'll make a reporter
    So I'll know everything
    I'll predict the rest
    And invent the remainder
    (He starts tearing up newspapers with his teeth and hands; he tramples. His movements must be very quick.)

He must be adaptable to every job
And able to write for every party
(He puts the torn newspapers in the empty cradle.)

What a fine reporter he'll be
Reporting lead articles

Et cetera
He'll have to have blood from an ink bottle
(*He takes the bottle of ink and pours it into the cradle.*)

He'll need a backbone
(*He puts a huge fountain pen into the cradle.*)

A brain for not thinking with
(*He empties the glue pot into the cradle.*)

A tongue to drivel with
(*He puts the scissors into the cradle.*)

Also he'll have to be able to sing
Come on sing

Thunder.

SCENE 4

The Same, The Son

The Husband repeats: "One, two!" till the end of The Son's monologue. This scene goes very quickly.

SON: Dear daddy if you want a closer look
At the activities of every crook
You've got to let me have some pocket money
The tree of print is leafy every bough
Flaps like a banner the fruit hangs in bunches
Papers have grown you ought to pick them now
And make the little kiddies salad lunches
If you let me have five hundred francs
I won't tell what I know about you
If you don't I'll tell all for I'm frank
And I fix fathers brothers sisters too
When you marry I'll tell them that your bride's
Pregnant three times over
I'll compromise you and I'll write besides
That you've stolen killed given rung bored

HUSBAND: Bravo there's a vocalist

The Son gets out of the cradle.

SON: Dear parents in one man
  If you want to know what happened yesterday evening
  Here it is
  A great conflagration destroyed Niagara Falls

HUSBAND: So what

SON: Alcindor the engineer
  Put a gas mask on and played
  The horn till twelve o'clock or near
  For a murderous brigade
  Listen and you still may hear

HUSBAND: So long as he doesn't do it here

SON: The Princess of Bergame they say
  Is marrying a girl today
  Just a meeting on the subway

  Castanets.

HUSBAND: What's it to me do I know all those people
  I want reliable news about my friends

SON (*he rocks a cradle*): We hear from Montrouge
  That Mister Picasso's
  New picture can move
  As this cradle does

HUSBAND: Bravo bravo
  For the brush of Picasso
  O my son
  Some other time I know right now
  All that I need to know
  About yesterday

SON: I'm going away to make tomorrow's news

HUSBAND: Good luck

  Exit The Son.

SCENE 5

The People of Zanzibar, The Husband

HUSBAND: That one didn't work out
   I think I'll disinherit him

At this moment radio placards enter: Ottawa—fire j.c.b. industries STOP 20,000 prose poems destroyed STOP president expresses sympathy. Rome—h.nr.m.t.ss. director villa medicis finishes portrait SS. Avignon—great artist g..rg.s braque has just invented process intensive cultivation of paintbrushes. Vancouver delayed bulletin—Dogs mister Paul Léaut..d on strike.

Stop stop
That was a lousy idea trusting the Press
They'll drive me crazy
The whole damn day
It's got to stop
(*In the megaphone.*)

Hullo hullo Miss
I don't want your telephone service
I'm de-subscribing
(*Without the megaphone.*)

I'm changing my program no more useless mouths
Economize economize
First off all I'll make a little tailor
When I'm dressed up I can take a walk
And as I'm not so bad to look at
Attract a lot of pretty girls

SCENE 6

The Same, The Policeman

POLICEMAN: Fine things you've been up to
   You've kept your word
   40,050 children in a day
   You're rocking the boat

HUSBAND: I'm getting rich

POLICEMAN: But the population of Zanzibar
   Famished by this excess of mouths to feed
   Will soon be dying of hunger

HUSBAND: Give them cards that makes up for everything

POLICEMAN: Where do we get them?

HUSBAND: From The Fortuneteller

POLICEMAN: That's clear enough

HUSBAND: Of course for we're thinking of the future

SCENE 7

The Same, The Fortuneteller

FORTUNETELLER (*she enters at the rear of the auditorium. Her skull is lighted with electricity*):
Chaste citizens of Zanzibar here I am

HUSBAND: Still another
I just don't count

FORTUNETELLER: I thought that you wouldn't have any objections
To having your fortune told

POLICEMAN: You are well aware Madame
You're practicing an illegal occupation
It's amazing the things people do
To avoid working

HUSBAND (*to The Policeman*): No scandal in my house

FORTUNETELLER (*to a spectator*): You Sir will shortly
Give birth to triplets

HUSBAND: Competition already

A LADY (*in the audience*): Madame Fortuneteller
I think he's deceiving me

Broken dishes.

FORTUNETELLER: Keep him in the hay box

She climbs onto the stage; crying of children, accordion.

Look an incubator

HUSBAND: If you're the barber give me a haircut

FORTUNETELLER: The girls of New York
  Only pick mirabelles
  Only eat ham from York
  That's why they're such belles

HUSBAND: The ladies of Paris
  Beat all competitors
  Cats like little mice
  And ladies we like yours

FORTUNETELLER: That is your smiles

ALL (*in chorus*): And then sing night and day
  Scratch if you itch and choose
  The white or the black either way
  Luck is a game win or lose
  Just keep your eye on the play
  Just keep your eye on the play

FORTUNETELLER: Chaste citizens of Zanzibar
  Who have given up childbearing
  Listen to me wealth and honor
  Pineapple groves and herds of elephants
  By right will belong
  Before very long
  To those who will claim them with armies of infants

All the children start crying on the stage and in the auditorium. The Fortuneteller deals the cards and they come tumbling down from the ceiling. Then the children are quiet.

You who are so fertile

HUSBAND *and* POLICEMAN: Fertile fertile

FORTUNETELLER (*to The Husband*): You'll be a millionaire ten times over

The Husband falls down in a sitting position.

FORTUNETELLER (*to The Policeman*): You who don't make children
  You'll die in the most abject poverty

POLICEMAN: You've insulted me
  I arrest you in the name of Zanzibar

FORTUNETELLER: Laying hands on a woman shame on you
>   *She claws and strangles him. The Husband offers her a pipe.*

>   Hey, Sweetheart, smoke a cigar
>   And I'll play my violin
>   The baker of Zanzibar
>   Has a wife who changes her skin

FORTUNETELLER: She carries a joke too far

HUSBAND: I'm going to turn you in to the chief of police
>   Murderer

THÉRÈSE (*taking off her fortuneteller's costume*):
>   Dear husband don't you recognize me

HUSBAND: Thérèse or should I say Tiresias

>   *The Policeman revives.*

THÉRÈSE: Tiresias is officially
>   Head of the Army in Room A at City Hall
>   But don't worry
>   I'm bringing back in a moving van
>   The piano the violin the butter dish
>   And three influential ladies whose lover I have become

POLICEMAN: Thanks for thinking of me

HUSBAND: My general my deputy
>   Thérèse I meant to say
>   You're as flat-chested as a bedbug

THÉRÈSE: So what! Let's go where the berries
>   And banana blossoms are
>   Let's hunt elephants on safaris
>   As they do in Zanzibar
>   Come and rule the heart of Thérèse

HUSBAND: Thérèse

THÉRÈSE: Throne or tomb no matter what
>   But this I'm sure of that we've got
>   To love or I'll die on the spot

HUSBAND: Dear Thérèse you must no longer be
>   As flat-chested as a bedbug

(*He takes out of the house a bouquet of balloons and a basket of balls.*)

Here's a whole supply

THÉRÈSE: We've both of us done without them
Let's continue

HUSBAND: That's true let's not make matters complicated
Let's go and dunk our bread

THÉRÈSE (*she releases the toy balloons and throws the balls at the audience*): Fly away birds of my frailty
Go and feed all the children
Of the new population

ALL (*in chorus. The People of Zanzibar dance jingling bells*):
And then sing night and day
Scratch if you itch and choose
The white or the black either way
Luck is a game win or lose
Just keep your eye on the play

CURTAIN

the wedding on the eiffel tower

by JEAN COCTEAU

translated by Michael Benedikt

EVERY work of the poetic order contains what Gide, in his preface to *Paludes*, so aptly calls "God's part." This "part," which eludes the poet himself, holds surprises for him. A certain phrase, a certain gesture, which seemed to mean as little to him as the concept of the third dimension to a painter, has a hidden meaning which everyone will interpret for himself. The true symbol is never foreseen: it emerges by itself, as long as the bizarre, the unreal, do not enter into the reckoning.

In a fairy land, the fairies do not appear. They walk invisibly there. They can appear to mortals only in natural circumstances. The unsophisticated mind sees fairies more easily than others, for it will not oppose the marvelous with the resistance of hardheadedness. I may even say that the chief electrician, by means of his reflections, has often illuminated a piece for me.

I have been reading in Antoine's memoirs of the scandal provoked by the presence on the stage of real quarters of beef and a fountain of water. We are now in an era in which the public, convinced by Antoine, is displeased if real objects do *not* appear on stage, and if it is not subjected to a plot as complicated, and as tedious, as those from which the theatre should serve to distract us.

Les mariés de la Tour Eiffel, because of its candor, seemed more deceptive than a truly esoteric play. The mysterious inspires in the public a kind of fear. Here, I renounce the mysterious. I illuminate everything, I underline everything. Sunday vacuity, human beastliness, ready-made expressions, disassociation of ideas from flesh and bone, ferocity of childhood, the miraculous poetry of daily life: these are my play, so well understood by the young musicians who composed the score for it.

A remark of the photographer's might do well as my epigraph: "Since these mysteries are beyond me, let's pretend we're organizing them." That is our motto, par excellence. A prig always finds a last refuge in responsibility. Thus, for example, he will go on with a war after the phenomenon which caused it has ceased.

In *Les mariés*, God's part is considerable. The human phonographs at the left and right of the stage, like the classic chorus, like the *compère* and *commère* who act as masters of ceremonies on our music-hall stage, describe, without the least "literature," the absurd action which is unfolded, danced, and mimed between them. I say "absurd" because, instead of attempting to keep this side of the absurdity of life, to lessen it, to organize and arrange it as we organize and arrange the story of an incident in which we played an unfavorable part, I accentuate it, I emphasize it, I try to paint *more truly than the truth*.

The poet ought to bring objects and emotions out of their veiling mists, to display them suddenly, so naked and so quickly that they are hardly recognizable. It is then that they amaze us with their youthfulness, as if they had never become official dotards.

This is the case with commonplaces—old, powerful, and universally esteemed as masterpieces are, but whose beauty and originality no longer surprise us because of over-use.

In my play I rejuvenate the commonplace. My concern is to present it from angles which will recapture its teens.

A generation devoted to obscurity, to a faded reality, does not give way before a shrug of the shoulders. I know that my text may seem too simple, too *readably written*, like schoolroom alphabets. But, tell me, aren't we really in school? Aren't we still deciphering the elementary symbols?

The young music finds itself in an analogous position. It suggests a clarity, a simplicity, a good humor, which are all new. The ingenuous ear is deceived. It thinks it is listening to a café orchestra. The ear commits the error of an eye which can find no difference between a garish material and the same substance rendered by Ingres.

In *Les mariés*, we employ the same popular material which France seems to despise at home, but will approve when a foreign musician exploits it.

Do you think, for example, that a Russian can hear *Pétrouchka* the way we do? All considerations of the power of this musical masterpiece aside, he finds his childhood there, his Sundays in Petrograd, the songs his nurses sang.

Why should I deny myself this double pleasure? I assure you that the orchestra of *Les mariés de la Tour Eiffel* moves me more

than any number of Russian or Spanish dances. It is not a question
of awarding prizes here. I think I have sufficiently praised Russian,
German, and Spanish musicians (not to mention Negro orches-
tras) to permit myself this *cri de cœur*.

It is curious to see the French endlessly angrily rejecting whatever is truly French, and embracing unreservedly the local spirit
of foreign lands. It is curious too that, in the case of *Les mariés de
la Tour Eiffel*, an audience at a dress rehearsal should be scandal-
ized by a type of classic numbskull, placed in the wedding cortege
the way the commonplaces are used in the text.

Every living work of art has its own ballyhoo, outside the real
performance, and only this is seen by those who do not choose to
enter. In the case of a new work, this superficial impression will
often be too shocking, too irritating, too upsetting to bring the
spectator in. He is distracted from its essence by its appearance, by
the unfamiliar expressions which distract him as would a clown
grimacing at the door. It is this phenomenon which deceives even
those critics least enslaved by convention. They fail to realize that
they are witnessing a work demanding as much attention as they
would accord the latest popular drama. They think that they are
watching a street show, plain and simple. A conscientious critic
would not write, in description of one of these "legitimate"
dramas, "The Duchess kisses the butler," instead of "The butler
presents a letter to the Duchess"; yet he will not hesitate, in review-
ing *Les mariés*, to make the cyclist or the art collector come out of
the camera—which is just as absurd. And this absurdity has nothing to do with the organized absurdity, the willed, the good absurdity, but simply the absurd. He'll never recognize the difference.
Along among my critics, M. Bidou, more aware of contemporary
developments, explained to the readers of *Débats*, that my play
was rather a witty construction.[1]

The action of my play is pictorial, while the text itself is not. I
am attempting to substitute a "poetry of the theatre" for "poetry

[1] It was he, also, who later wrote that my *Orpheus* was a "meditation on
death."

in the theatre." Poetry in the theatre is a delicate lace, impossible
to see at any distance. Poetry of the theatre should be a coarse lace,
a lace of ropes, a ship at sea. *Les mariés* can have the frightening
appearance of a drop of poetry seen under a microscope. The
scenes are linked like the words of a poem.

The secret of theatrical success is this: set a decoy at the door
so that part of the audience can enjoy itself there while everybody
else is inside. Shakespeare, Molière, and the profound Chaplin
know this well.

After the hisses, the tumult, the ovations of opening night at
which the Swedish dancers performed, in the Théâtre des Champs-
Elysées, I would have put it all down as a failure if the "informed"
audience had not given way before the real public. This public always really listens to me.

After *Les mariés* was performed a lady complained to me that
the play did not, essentially, go beyond the footlights. Noticing
my astonishment (for masks and megaphones are better by far at
getting beyond the footlights than ordinary voices and faces), the
lady admitted that she so loved the ceiling of Maurice Denis, who
decorated the theatre, that she had taken the highest seats in the
house, which had prevented her from gathering much of what was
happening on stage.

I give this as an example of the response of that little headless
and heartless group whom the newspapers call "the élite."

Moreover, our senses are so unused to reacting together that the
critics—even my publishers—thought that this complicated machinery should have two or three pages of explanatory text. One
must also blame this lack of perspective on the absence of the development of "ideas," a development which the ear is accustomed
to hear, since the days of symbolic drama and the drama *à thèse*.
Jarry's *Ubu* and Apollinaire's *Les mamelles de Tirésias* are both
symbolic dramas and dramas *à thèse*.

The diction of my two phonographs, Pierre Bertin and Marcel
Herrand, has its share in the general misunderstanding: a diction
black as ink, large and clear as the lettering on a billboard. Here
—wonder of wonders—the actors attempt to satisfy the require-

ments of the text instead of satisfying themselves: still another
lyric novelty to which the audience is not accustomed.

Let us consider the accusation of buffoonery which has often
been hurled at me by this age, an age preoccupied with false sub-
limities, an age, after all, still in love with Wagner.

If cold signifies night, and hot signifies light, lukewarm signifies
dusk. Ghosts love the dusk. The public loves the lukewarm. Now,
aside from the fact that the spirit of buffoonery brings with it a
clarity ill-suited to ghosts (by ghosts I mean what the public calls
"the poetic"), aside from the fact that Molière proved himself
more of a poet in *Pourceaugnac* and *Le bourgeois gentilhomme*
than in his "poetic" verse dramas, the spirit of buffoonery is the
only attitude which permits certain extraordinary audacities.

People come to the theatre for diversion. It is easy to amuse
them, to show them dancing dolls, to please them with plays
reminiscent of the candies one uses to get medicine into stubborn
children. Once the medicine has been taken, we must go on to
other exercises.

With the advent of people like Serge de Diaghilev and Rolf
de Maré, we see developing in France, little by little, a theatrical
genre which is not properly speaking ballet, which has no place in
the Opéra, nor at the Opéra-Comique, nor in any of the fashionable theatres. It is there, in this margin, that the future is being
sketched. Our friend Lugné-Poë has pointed out, with some
apprehension, in one of his articles. This new genre, more con-
sonant with the modern spirit, remains unexplored land, rich with
possibility.

Revolution which flings doors wide open to explorers! The new
generation will continue its experiments in which the fantastic, the
dance, acrobatics, mime, drama, satire, music, and the spoken
word combine to produce a new form; they will present, with very
small means, plays which the official artists will take for studio
farces, and which nonetheless are the plastic expression and embodiment of poetry itself.

The mixture of good and bad humor in Paris produces an atmosphere which is the most vital in the world. Serge de Diaghilev

told me one day that he felt nothing like it in any other capital.

Hisses and cheers. Injurious press. Here and there an article of surprising approval. Three years later the scoffers are all applauding, without the least memory of having hissed. Such is the history of my *Parade*, and of all the other works which revised the rules of the game.

A theatrical piece ought to be written, presented, costumed, furnished with musical accompaniment, played, and danced, by a single individual. This universal athlete does not exist. It is therefore important to replace the individual by what resembles an individual most: a friendly group.

There are many cliques, but few of these groups. I had the good luck to form one with several young musicians, poets, and painters. *Les mariés de la Tour Eiffel*, as a whole, is the image of a kind of poetic spirit to which I am proud to have already contributed a good deal.[2]

Thanks to Jean Hugo, my characters, instead of being, as so often happens in the theatre, too tiny, too true to life to justify the extent of the lighting and décor, were constructed, corrected, built up, enlarged by every device of artifice to a resemblance of epic proportions. I rediscovered in Jean Hugo a certain atavism of monstrous reality. Thanks to Irene Lagut, our Eiffel Tower suggests forget-me-nots and flowery compliments.

George Auric's Overture, "The Fourteenth of July," marching bands whose music blares out at a street corner and moves on, also evokes the potent enchantments of the sidewalk, of popular fairs, of red-festooned grandstands like guillotines, around which drums and trumpets start stenographers dancing with sailors and clerks. And his *ritournelles* accompany the pantomime just as a circus band repeats a certain motif during an acrobatic act.

The same atmosphere pervades in Milhaud's "Wedding March," in Germaine Tailleferre's "Quadrille" and "Waltz of the Telegrams," in Poulenc's "The General's Speech" and "The Trouville Bathing Beauty." Arthur Honegger amused himself, in

---

[2] It is a matter of taking the silliness out of silliness, even that of the heart. The sublime will have its day. And then you will hear us, perhaps, rehabilitate Wagner.

Smugness

the "Funeral March," by making fun of what our musicologists gravely call Music. Needless to say that they all fell into our trap. Hardly had the first notes of the "March" sounded when all those long ears were lifted. No one noticed that this march was as beautiful as a sarcasm, written with great taste, with an extraordinary appositeness. Not one of the critics, all of whom praised this piece, recognized the waltz from *Faust* which served as its basis.[3]

How can I express my gratitude to MM. Rolf de Maré and Borlin? The former by his clairvoyance and generosity, the latter by his modesty, made it possible for me to crystallize a formula I had been experimenting with in *Parade* and *Le Bœuf sur le toit*.

[3] Astonishingly, all this music has disappeared. The scores are still undiscoverable.

makes judgments

SCENERY

First platform of the Eiffel Tower.

The backdrop represents a bird's-eye view of Paris.

To the right, upstage, a professional photographer's camera, the height of a man. The bellows of the camera forms a corridor joining the wings. At the front of the bellows the camera opens like a door, to let the characters enter and exit.

Downstage, right and left, half-hidden behind the proscenium arch, are stationed two actors dressed as phonographs, their bodies the cabinets, horns corresponding to their mouths. These phonographs narrate the play and recite the parts of the characters. They speak very loudly, very quickly, and pronounce each syllable very distinctly.

The action is simultaneous with the descriptions of the phonographs.

The curtain rises to a drumroll, on an empty stage.

FIRST PHONOGRAPH: You are on the first platform of the Eiffel Tower.

SECOND PHONOGRAPH: Look! An ostrich! It crosses the stage. It goes off. Here's The Hunter. He looks for the ostrich. He peers. He sees something. He aims. He fires.

FIRST PHONOGRAPH: Heavens! A telegram.

A large blue telegram falls from above.

SECOND PHONOGRAPH: The explosion wakes up The Manager of the Eiffel Tower. He appears.

FIRST PHONOGRAPH: So, Monsieur, you think you are out hunting?

SECOND PHONOGRAPH: I'm following an ostrich. I thought I saw it caught in the grillwork of the Eiffel Tower.

FIRST PHONOGRAPH: And so you killed a telegram on me.

SECOND PHONOGRAPH: I didn't do it on purpose.

FIRST PHONOGRAPH: End of conversation.

SECOND PHONOGRAPH: Here is The Official Eiffel Tower Photographer. He speaks. What does he say?

FIRST PHONOGRAPH: Didn't you just see an ostrich go by?

SECOND PHONOGRAPH: Yes! yes! I'm looking for it.

FIRST PHONOGRAPH: Well, believe it or not, my camera is out of order. Usually when I say, "Now, don't move, watch the birdie," a little bird is what they see. This morning, I say to a lady: "Watch the birdie," and an ostrich steps out. I'm trying to find the ostrich to get it to go back into the camera.

SECOND PHONOGRAPH: Ladies and gentlemen, now the plot thickens. The Manager of the Eiffel Tower suddenly notices that his address is on the telegram.

FIRST PHONOGRAPH: He opens it.

SECOND PHONOGRAPH: EIFFEL TOWER MANAGER STOP COMING FOR WEDDING BREAKFAST STOP KINDLY RESERVE TABLE

FIRST PHONOGRAPH: But this telegram is dead.

SECOND PHONOGRAPH: It's precisely because it is dead that everybody understands it.

FIRST PHONOGRAPH: Quick! quick! We've just time to set the table.
I cancel your fine. I appoint you official waiter of the Eiffel
Tower Restaurant. Photographer, to your post!

SECOND PHONOGRAPH: They spread the tablecloth.

FIRST PHONOGRAPH: Wedding March.

SECOND PHONOGRAPH: The procession.

*Wedding March. The phonographs announce the wedding
guests, who enter strutting like dogs in an animal act.*

FIRST PHONOGRAPH: The Bride, gentle as a lamb.

SECOND PHONOGRAPH: The Father-in-Law, rich as Croesus.

FIRST PHONOGRAPH: The Bridegroom, handsome as Apollo.

SECOND PHONOGRAPH: The Mother-in-Law, false as a bad penny.

FIRST PHONOGRAPH: The General, stupid as a goose.

SECOND PHONOGRAPH: Look at him! He thinks he's on his mare,
Mirabelle.

FIRST PHONOGRAPH: The Ushers, strong as Turks!

SECOND PHONOGRAPH: The Bridesmaids, fresh as roses!

FIRST PHONOGRAPH: The Manager of the Eiffel Tower extends his
hospitalities. He shows them a bird's-eye view of Paris.

SECOND PHONOGRAPH: I'm getting dizzy!

*The Hunter and The Manager carry in a table with plates
painted on it. The tablecloth sweeps the ground.*

FIRST PHONOGRAPH: The General shouts: To the table! to the
table! and the wedding party sits down around the table.

SECOND PHONOGRAPH: Only on one side of the table, so the audience
can see you.

FIRST PHONOGRAPH: The General rises.

SECOND PHONOGRAPH: The General's speech.

*The General's speech is performed by an orchestra in the pit,
which makes percussive noises. He gestures only.*

FIRST PHONOGRAPH: Everyone is deeply moved.

SECOND PHONOGRAPH: After his speech, The General recounts the mirage phenomenon from which he suffered in Africa.

FIRST PHONOGRAPH: I was eating a tart with the Duke of Aumâle. This tart was covered with wasps. In vain we tried to chase them away. Actually, they were tigers.

SECOND PHONOGRAPH: What?

FIRST PHONOGRAPH: Tigers. They were prowling around by the thousands. A mirage projected them in miniature above our tart, and we mistook them for wasps.

SECOND PHONOGRAPH: You would never think he was seventy-four years old!

FIRST PHONOGRAPH: But who is this charming Cyclist wearing culottes?

Enter a Cyclist. She jumps off her bicycle.

SECOND PHONOGRAPH (*voice of The Cyclist*): Pardon me, gentlemen.

FIRST PHONOGRAPH: Madame, may we be of any service?

SECOND PHONOGRAPH: Am I on the road to Chatou?

FIRST PHONOGRAPH: Yes, Madame. Simply follow the railway tracks.

SECOND PHONOGRAPH: It's The General who is answering The Cyclist. He takes her for a mirage.

The Cyclist climbs back on the seat and rides off.

FIRST PHONOGRAPH: Ladies and gentlemen, we have just witnessed a mirage. They are quite frequent on the Eiffel Tower. This Cyclist, in reality, is pedaling along the road to Chatou.

SECOND PHONOGRAPH: After this instructive interlude The Photographer steps forward. What does he say?

FIRST PHONOGRAPH: I am The Official Eiffel Tower Photographer and I'm going to take your picture.

FIRST *and* SECOND PHONOGRAPHS: Yes! yes! yes! yes!

FIRST PHONOGRAPH: Form a group.

The wedding party forms a group behind the table.

SECOND PHONOGRAPH: You are doubtless wondering where the ostrich Hunter and The Manager of the Eiffel Tower have gone.
The Hunter is running up and down the Eiffel Tower looking
for the ostrich. The Manager is looking for The Hunter and
is managing the Eiffel Tower. This is no mere sinecure. The
Eiffel Tower is a world in itself, like Notre-Dame. It's the
Notre-Dame of the Left Bank.

FIRST PHONOGRAPH: It's the Queen of Paris.

SECOND PHONOGRAPH: It was the Queen of Paris. Now it's the
handmaiden of the telegraph.

FIRST PHONOGRAPH: One must live.

SECOND PHONOGRAPH: Don't move. Smile. Look at the lens. Watch
the birdie.

*A Trouville Bathing Beauty appears. She wears a bikini, carries
a landing net, and has a picnic basket slung over her shoulder.
Colored lights flash on. The wedding party lifts its hands in
admiration.*

FIRST PHONOGRAPH: Oh! It's like a picture postcard.

The Bathing Beauty begins to dance.

The Photographer doesn't share in the delight of the wedding
party. It's the second time today that his camera has played
tricks on him. He tries to get The Trouville Bathing Beauty
to go back into the camera.

FIRST PHONOGRAPH: Finally, The Bathing Beauty returns to the
camera. The Photographer makes her think it's a cabaña.

*End of the dance. The Photographer throws a bathrobe over
the shoulders of The Bathing Beauty, who returns to the
camera hopping and throwing kisses.*

FIRST *and* SECOND PHONOGRAPHS: Bravo! bravo! Encore! encore!
encore!

FIRST PHONOGRAPH: If I only knew in advance what surprises my
broken camera had in store for me, I might put on a show.
As it is, I begin to shake every time I pronounce those terrible
words. Does one ever know what's coming next? Since these
mysteries are beyond me, let's pretend we're organizing them.

He bows.

FIRST *and* SECOND PHONOGRAPHS: Bravo! bravo! bravo!

SECOND PHONOGRAPH: Ladies and gentlemen, despite my earnest wish to satisfy your every desire, the lateness of the hour forbids my presentation a second time of that popular number: The Trouville Bathing Beauty.

FIRST *and* SECOND PHONOGRAPHS: Yes! yes! yes!

FIRST PHONOGRAPH: The Photographer lies in order to arrange everything and be a big success. He looks at his watch. Two o'clock already! and that ostrich still hasn't returned!

SECOND PHONOGRAPH: The wedding party forms another tableau. Madame, put your left foot on one of the spurs. Monsieur, hang that veil on your mustache. Perfect. Don't move. One. Two. Three. Look at the lens. Watch the birdie.

He presses the bulb. A fat little boy appears. He wears a green paper crown. Under his arms are coloring books and a basket.

FIRST PHONOGRAPH: Good morning Mama.

SECOND PHONOGRAPH: Good morning Papa.

FIRST PHONOGRAPH: Here is still another of the perils of photography.

SECOND PHONOGRAPH: This Child is the image of the wedding.

FIRST PHONOGRAPH: And just listen to this:

SECOND PHONOGRAPH: He's the image of his mother.

FIRST PHONOGRAPH: He's the image of his father.

SECOND PHONOGRAPH: He's the image of his grandmother.

FIRST PHONOGRAPH: He's the image of his grandfather.

SECOND PHONOGRAPH: He has our mouth.

FIRST PHONOGRAPH: He has our eyes.

SECOND PHONOGRAPH: My dear parents, on this auspicious occasion, accept all my vows of respect and love.

FIRST PHONOGRAPH: The same compliment, from another aspect.

SECOND PHONOGRAPH: Accept all my vows of love and respect.

FIRST PHONOGRAPH: He should have learned a more complicated compliment.

SECOND PHONOGRAPH: Accept all my vows of respect and love.

FIRST PHONOGRAPH: He'll be a captain.

SECOND PHONOGRAPH: Architect.

FIRST PHONOGRAPH: Boxer.

SECOND PHONOGRAPH: Poet.

FIRST PHONOGRAPH: President of the Republic.

SECOND PHONOGRAPH: A beautiful little victim for the next war.

FIRST PHONOGRAPH: What's he looking for in his basket?

SECOND PHONOGRAPH: Bullets.

FIRST PHONOGRAPH: What will he do with bullets? He seems to be very naughty!

SECOND PHONOGRAPH: He massacres the wedding party.

FIRST PHONOGRAPH: He massacres his own flesh and blood to get some macaroons.

The Child bombards the wedding party, which scatters with cries.

SECOND PHONOGRAPH: Lord!

FIRST PHONOGRAPH: When I think of the trouble we went through to bring him up.

SECOND PHONOGRAPH: Of all our sacrifices.

FIRST PHONOGRAPH: Wretch! I'm your father.

SECOND PHONOGRAPH: Stop! there's still time.

FIRST PHONOGRAPH: Haven't you any pity for your grandparents?

SECOND PHONOGRAPH: Haven't you any respect for rank?

FIRST PHONOGRAPH: Bang! Bang! Bang!

SECOND PHONOGRAPH: I forgive you.

FIRST PHONOGRAPH: Be damned.

SECOND PHONOGRAPH: There are no bullets left.

FIRST PHONOGRAPH: The wedding party is massacred.

SECOND PHONOGRAPH: The Photographer runs after The Child. He threatens him with a whip. He orders him to go back into the box.

FIRST PHONOGRAPH: The Child takes refuge. He shouts. He stamps. He wants to "live his own life."

SECOND PHONOGRAPH: I want to live my own life! I want to live my own life!

FIRST PHONOGRAPH: But what's this other disturbance?

SECOND PHONOGRAPH: The Manager of the Eiffel Tower. What does he have to say?

FIRST PHONOGRAPH: A little peace and quiet, please. Don't frighten the telegrams.

SECOND PHONOGRAPH: Papa! Papa! the telegrams.

FIRST PHONOGRAPH: There are some awfully big ones up there.

SECOND PHONOGRAPH: The wedding party reassembles.

FIRST PHONOGRAPH: One

SECOND PHONOGRAPH: Could hear

FIRST PHONOGRAPH: A

SECOND PHONOGRAPH: Pin

FIRST PHONOGRAPH: Drop.

SECOND PHONOGRAPH: Five telegrams flutter down to the stage. The entire wedding party runs after them and jumps on them.

FIRST PHONOGRAPH: There, I've got one of them. Me too. Help! Help me! She's got me! Hold on! Hold on!

SECOND PHONOGRAPH: The telegrams calm down. They form a line. The handsomest steps forward and makes a military salute.

FIRST PHONOGRAPH (*in the voice of a master of ceremonies*): And may I ask who you are?

SECOND PHONOGRAPH: I'm the wireless telegram and like my sister the stork I've come from New York.

FIRST PHONOGRAPH (*in the voice of a master of ceremonies*):
New York! City of lovers and dim lights.

SECOND PHONOGRAPH: Forward! Music!

Dance of the telegrams. Exit of the telegrams.

FIRST PHONOGRAPH: My son-in-law, you can thank me for all this. Whose idea was it to come to the Eiffel Tower? Whose idea was it to have the wedding on the Fourteenth of July?

SECOND PHONOGRAPH: The Child stamps his foot.

FIRST PHONOGRAPH: Papa! Papa!

SECOND PHONOGRAPH: What does he say?

FIRST PHONOGRAPH: I want to have my picture taken with The General.

SECOND PHONOGRAPH: General, surely you won't refuse our little Justin this pleasure?

FIRST PHONOGRAPH: Agreed.

SECOND PHONOGRAPH: Poor Photographer. With a heavy heart, he loads his camera.

FIRST PHONOGRAPH: The Child, astride his sword, pretends to be listening to The General, who pretends to read to him out of a book by Jules Verne.

SECOND PHONOGRAPH: Don't move. Perfect. Watch the birdie.

A lion appears.

FIRST PHONOGRAPH: Good Lord! a lion. The Photographer hides behind his camera. The wedding party climbs into the grill-work of the Eiffel Tower. The lion stares at The General, for The General, alone, does not move. He speaks. What does he say?

SECOND PHONOGRAPH: Don't be afraid. There can be no lion on the Eiffel Tower. Therefore, it is a mirage, a simple mirage. Mirages are, so to speak, the white lies of the desert. This lion is actually in Africa, just as the cyclist was on the road to Chatou. This lion sees me, I see him, and yet we each recognize that we are simply reflections.

FIRST PHONOGRAPH: To confound the incredulous, The General approaches the lion. The lion gives a great roar. The General runs off, pursued by the lion.

SECOND PHONOGRAPH: The General disappears under the table. The lion disappears behind him.

FIRST PHONOGRAPH: After a minute, which seems like a century, the lion comes out from beneath the tablecloth.

SECOND PHONOGRAPH: Horror! Horror! Ahhhhhh!

FIRST PHONOGRAPH: What's that in his mouth?

SECOND PHONOGRAPH: A boot, with a spur.

FIRST PHONOGRAPH: Having eaten The General, the lion goes back into the camera.

Dirge.

FIRST *and* SECOND PHONOGRAPHS: Ahhhh! Ahhhh . . .

FIRST PHONOGRAPH: Poor General.

SECOND PHONOGRAPH: He was so gay, so youthful in outlook. Nothing would have amused him more than this death. He would have been the first to chuckle at it.

FIRST PHONOGRAPH: Obsequies of The General.

Funeral March.

SECOND PHONOGRAPH: The Father-in-Law delivers the eulogy. What does he say?

FIRST PHONOGRAPH: Adieu, adieu, old friend.

From your first campaign, you gave proof of an intelligence beyond your rank. You never surrendered, even to evidence.

Your end is worthy of your career. We saw you, defying the beast, careless of danger, not even understanding it and not taking flight until the instant you understood it.

Once more, adieu, or rather au revoir, for your kind will perpetuate itself as long as there are men on this earth.

SECOND PHONOGRAPH: Three o'clock! and that ostrich hasn't come back yet.

FIRST PHONOGRAPH: She probably wanted to walk back.

SECOND PHONOGRAPH: That's stupid. Nothing is less fragile than the feathers of an ostrich.

FIRST PHONOGRAPH: Attention!

SECOND PHONOGRAPH: "Les mariés de la Tour Eiffel," quadrille, with music by the Garde Republicaine band.

FIRST *and* SECOND PHONOGRAPHS: Bravo! Bravo! Long live the Garde Republicaine! (*Quadrille.*)

SECOND PHONOGRAPH: Oof! What a dance.

FIRST PHONOGRAPH: Your arm.

SECOND PHONOGRAPH: Monsieur Photographer, surely you won't decline a glass of champagne?

FIRST PHONOGRAPH: You are too kind. I am overwhelmed.

SECOND PHONOGRAPH: Well, when in Rome, you know. But what does my grandson want?

FIRST PHONOGRAPH: I want someone to buy me some bread to feed the Eiffel Tower.

SECOND PHONOGRAPH: They sell it down below. I'm not going down.

FIRST PHONOGRAPH: I want to feed the Eiffel Tower.

SECOND PHONOGRAPH: It is only fed at certain hours. That's why it has grilles around it.

FIRST PHONOGRAPH: I want to feed the Eiffel Tower.

SECOND PHONOGRAPH: No and double no.

FIRST PHONOGRAPH: The wedding party cries out, for here is the ostrich. She was hiding in the elevator. She looks for another hiding-place. The Hunter approaches. The Photographer wishes it would hide in the camera.

SECOND PHONOGRAPH: He remembers that one has only to hide an ostrich's head to make it invisible.

FIRST PHONOGRAPH: He hides its head in his hat. In the nick of time.

The ostrich walks, invisible, a hat on its head. Enter The Hunter.

SECOND PHONOGRAPH: Have you seen the ostrich?

FIRST *and* SECOND PHONOGRAPHS: No. We haven't seen a thing.

SECOND PHONOGRAPH: That's strange. I was certain that she jumped onto this platform.

FIRST PHONOGRAPH: Perhaps it was a wave that you mistook for an ostrich.

SECOND PHONOGRAPH: No. The sea is calm. Anyway, I'm going to keep a lookout now from behind this phonograph.

FIRST PHONOGRAPH: No sooner said than done.

SECOND PHONOGRAPH: The Photographer approaches the ostrich on tiptoe. What does he say?

FIRST PHONOGRAPH: Madame, you haven't a moment to lose. He hasn't yet recognized you under your veil. Hurry, I have a carriage waiting.

SECOND PHONOGRAPH: He opens the cloth on the camera. The ostrich disappears.

FIRST PHONOGRAPH: Saved, my God!

SECOND PHONOGRAPH: You can imagine The Photographer's delight. He shouts with joy.

FIRST PHONOGRAPH: The wedding party questions him.

SECOND PHONOGRAPH: Gentlemen and ladies, at last I'm going to be able to photograph you in peace. My camera was broken; but now it works. Don't move!

FIRST PHONOGRAPH: But who are these two people coming over to distract The Photographer?

SECOND PHONOGRAPH: Look. The wedding party and The Photographer freeze. The entire wedding party is motionless. Don't you think they're a little . . .

FIRST PHONOGRAPH: A little wedding cake.

SECOND PHONOGRAPH: A little bouquet.

FIRST PHONOGRAPH: A little Mona Lisa.

SECOND PHONOGRAPH: A little masterpiece.

FIRST PHONOGRAPH: The Dealer in modern paintings and The Collector of modern paintings stop before the wedding party. What does The Dealer say?

SECOND PHONOGRAPH: I've brought you to the Eiffel Tower to show you, before anyone else, a truly unique piece: "The Wedding Party."

FIRST PHONOGRAPH: And The Collector answers:

SECOND PHONOGRAPH: I follow you blindly.

FIRST PHONOGRAPH: Well? Isn't it lovely? It's a kind of primitive.

SECOND PHONOGRAPH: Whose is it?

FIRST PHONOGRAPH: What's that? Whose is it? It is one of the latest works of God.

SECOND PHONOGRAPH: Is it signed?

FIRST PHONOGRAPH: God does not sign. But look at that paint! What texture! Look at that style, that nobility, that "joie de vivre!" It might almost be a funeral.

SECOND PHONOGRAPH: I see a wedding party.

FIRST PHONOGRAPH: Your vision is limited. It's more than a wedding. It's all weddings. More than all weddings: it's a cathedral.

SECOND PHONOGRAPH: What do you want for it?

FIRST PHONOGRAPH: It's not for sale, except to the Louvre, and to you. Take it, I'll let you have it at cost.

SECOND PHONOGRAPH: The Dealer has a big placard.

The placard bears the figure 1000000000000.

FIRST PHONOGRAPH: Will The Collector let himself be persuaded? What does he say?

The Dealer turns over the placard. One sees "SOLD," in large letters. He places it against the wedding party.

FIRST PHONOGRAPH: The Dealer addresses The Photographer.

SECOND PHONOGRAPH: Photograph this wedding party for me, with the placard. I'll get it into every magazine in America.

FIRST PHONOGRAPH: The Collector and The Dealer leave the Eiffel Tower.

SECOND PHONOGRAPH: The Photographer readies himself to take the picture, but—wonder of wonders!—his camera talks to him.

FIRST PHONOGRAPH: What does it say to him?

THE CAMERA (*in a remote voice*): I want . . . I want . . .

SECOND PHONOGRAPH: Speak, my lovely swan.

THE CAMERA: I want to give up The General.

SECOND PHONOGRAPH: He knows very well how to give up himself.

FIRST PHONOGRAPH: The General reappears. He is pale. He's missing a boot. In short, he arrives from far away. He recounts how he has returned from a mission about which he must maintain maximum security. The wedding party doesn't move. Head lowered, he crosses the platform and assumes a modest pose among the others.

SECOND PHONOGRAPH: Here is a fine surprise for The Collector of masterpieces. In a true masterpiece one never ceases to discover unexpected details.

FIRST PHONOGRAPH: The Photographer turns away. He finds the wedding party a bit too severe. If they can reproach The General for being alive, The General can certainly reproach them all for letting him be sold.

SECOND PHONOGRAPH: The Photographer is a man of feeling.

FIRST PHONOGRAPH: He speaks. What does he say?

SECOND PHONOGRAPH: All right, ladies and gentlemen, I'm going to count to five. Look at the lens. Watch the birdie.

FIRST PHONOGRAPH: A dove!

SECOND PHONOGRAPH: The camera is working.

FIRST PHONOGRAPH: Peace is achieved.

SECOND PHONOGRAPH: One.

The Bride and Groom detach themselves from the group, cross the stage, and disappear into the camera.

Two.

Same action for the Father-in-Law and the Mother-in-Law.

Three.

Same action for The Ushers.

Four.

Same action for The Bridesmaids.

Five.

Same action for The General, alone, head lowered, and The Child, who leads him by the hand.

FIRST PHONOGRAPH: Enter The Manager of the Eiffel Tower. He waves a megaphone.

SECOND PHONOGRAPH: Closing time! Closing time!

FIRST PHONOGRAPH: He goes out.

SECOND PHONOGRAPH: Enter The Hunter, hurrying. He starts to run past the camera. What does The Photographer say?

FIRST PHONOGRAPH: Where are you going?

SECOND PHONOGRAPH: I want to catch the last train.

FIRST PHONOGRAPH: It's too late. The gate is closed.

SECOND PHONOGRAPH: It's disgraceful. I'll complain to the manager of the railroad.

FIRST PHONOGRAPH: It's not my fault. There's your train, leaving right now.

The camera starts to move toward the left, followed by its bellows, like railroad coaches. Through various apertures one sees the wedding party waving handkerchiefs, and, beneath, feet walking.

CURTAIN

the pelicans

by RAYMOND RADIGUET

translated by Michael Benedikt

MONSIEUR PELICAN
MADAME PELICAN
ANSELME, son of Monsieur Pelican
HORTENSE, sister of Anselme
MADEMOISELLE CHARMANT, governess
MONSIEUR PASTEL, swimming instructor
MONSIEUR CHANTECLER, photography instructor
PARFAIT, valet

The play takes place in Paris after the turn of the century, in the apartment of Monsieur Pelican.

ACT I

A billiards room. In the center a billiards table. To the right, at the rear, a blackboard. A rope ladder dangles at the left.

Scene 1

Mademoiselle Charmant, Parfait

On the floor, stretched out, is Mademoiselle Charmant, who seems to have fainted. In her hand is a copy of La Vie Parisienne. *Next to her, a hammock. Parfait, feather duster in hand, leans forward and places his ear against Mademoiselle Charmant's chest.*

PARFAIT: I must have been out of my mind! Mistaking this hammock for a spider web! (*Pause.*) Is it my fault I'm near-sighted? And that my month's wages won't even pay for a pair of glasses? Besides, Madame *forbade* that miserable governess to use the hammock. Mademoiselle disobeyed. And why? To disappear and read the latest issue of *La Vie Parisienne* instead of instructing the little Pelicans. I would be wrong to blame myself. If Mademoiselle Charmant had listened to Madame and if I did not have to do the house-work, like the most miserable of servants, this little accident would never have happened.

A bell rings.

Madame rings!!!

Parfait lifts Mademoiselle Charmant, sits her upon a chair, climbs the rope ladder, and puts the hammock into perfect order. Mademoiselle Charmant now appears to be reading La Vie Parisienne. *Parfait leaves.*

Scene 2

Mademoiselle Charmant, Monsieur Pelican

MONSIEUR PELICAN (*a magazine in his hand*): Ah! Ah! Mademoiselle Charmant, you enjoy reading—so I have brought you another illustrated magazine. (*Pause.*) Are you angry,

119

dearest? (*Pause. To himself.*) Whatever could I have done to have displeased her so?

SCENE 3

Mademoiselle Charmant, Parfait

PARFAIT (*in street clothes, a suitcase in his hand. He glances about*): Nobody about. No one shall know my secret . . . unhappy secret, for I'm beginning to think she's dead. (*Pause.*) To give myself up, that would not help things any . . . on the contrary. (*He goes to the blackboard; he picks up a piece of chalk. He reads as he writes.*) Mademoiselle Charmant and I . . . we love each other madly. I have carried her off . . . in a week we shall be married.

Bell rings.

(*Parfait puts his signature at the bottom of the blackboard; after this he folds up the governess and puts her into his suitcase.*) In a few minutes Madame will be here for her swimming lesson. Best not to be surprised with Mademoiselle Charmant. I'm off to my native province!

He leaves whistling softly, suitcase in hand.

VOICE OFFSTAGE: Parfait . . . Parfait . . . I have been ringing for a quarter of an hour!

SCENE 4

MONSIEUR PELICAN (*alone*): So! My sulky beauty is no longer here. . . . (*He notices the blackboard, detaches it, and walks to the front of the stage to read.*) Ah! The little wretch! I understand now why she did not speak to me. (*He sits on a chair and buries his face in his hands. Then, resigned, lifting his head.*) It's my last love affair.

SCENE 5

Monsieur Pelican, Madame Pelican, Monsieur Pastel

Entrance of the swimming instructor, Monsieur Pastel, on all fours. On his back, Madame Pelican, in a bathing suit.

MADAME PELICAN: Heavens! My husband! (*She jumps down. Monsieur Pastel straightens up. Speaking to her husband, amiably yet aggressively.*) You finally decided to attend my lessons?

MONSIEUR PELICAN (*vigorously*): I bid you your good-bye, Monsieur Pastel.

MADAME PELICAN (*in a low voice to Monsieur Pastel*): I tremble, my dearest. He seems so unhappy; no doubt the poor man has found out that we love each other.

Monsieur Pastel leaves.

SCENE 6

Monsieur Pelican, Madame Pelican

Monsieur Pelican holds the blackboard before his wife. She reads it.

MADAME PELICAN: Didn't I tell you regularly that this girl was common? But you never listen to me.

MONSIEUR PELICAN: From now on, I will take charge of the education of our children.

MADAME PELICAN: Fine . . . but we cannot do without a valet. I'll put on a hat and run to the employment agency. (*She leaves.*)

SCENE 7

Monsieur Pelican, Hortense

Monsieur Pelican on a chair, his face in his hands. Hortense enters pulling a child's wagon loaded with hatboxes.

HORTENSE: So, Papa is asleep. I shall see if he is pretending. (*She puts a woman's hat on his head which will remain there until the end of the play. Monsieur Pelican doesn't stir. Hortense takes all the hats out of their boxes, tearing off the flowers and pinning them to the billiards table.*

SCENE 8

Monsieur Pelican, Hortense, Anselme

HORTENSE: Anselme, if you were nice, you would go and find Mama's green powder for me. I should so like to resemble a tree.

ANSELME: Autumn bleaches the hair of the trees. It is autumn and you are already blond.

Hortense begins to whistle.

MONSIEUR PELICAN (*getting up brusquely*): Hortense, your brother is right! A well-brought-up young lady should not whistle; you shall be deprived of dessert. (*Noticing the billiards table transformed into a garden.*) Yes . . . of dessert . . . until you are twenty-one . . . Your mother's new hats!

Hortense goes off into a corner, sniffling.

SCENE 9

Monsieur Pelican, Anselme, Hortense

Madame Pelican in a tailored suit.

MADAME PELICAN (*to Monsieur Pelican*): The idea! beating this child because she plays with my old hats.

MONSIEUR PELICAN (*shrugs his shoulders, then addresses his children*): We have discharged the governess and the valet; they were not well behaved. And I have decided to substitute at once for Mademoiselle Charmant.

Consternation of Hortense and Anselme.

But before beginning your lessons, tell me, my children, for what professions do you wish to prepare? Knowing this, ignoring no portion of your plans, I shall direct you all the better in the courses you have chosen. (*Moved by his own speech.*) Ah! if all fathers were like me.

ANSELME: I want to be a jockey.

HORTENSE: And I, a gardener.

MADAME PELICAN (*to Anselme*): Anselme, you're forgetting something. You're not even seventeen years old, and you weigh one hundred and sixty-five pounds. (*She leaves.*)

SCENE 10

The same, less Madame Pelican

MONSIEUR PELICAN: Anselme, you cannot be serious. If you knew how much pain you cause me! Two years ago you wanted to be a shepherd. For your birthday I gave you a shepherd's outfit and the *Eclogues* of Virgil. Was the lesson too subtle for you? Virgil should have proved to you that shepherds are poets.

ANSELME: That's why I no longer want to be a shepherd.

MONSIEUR PELICAN: And I, who would have so loved to have a poet son . . . (*Pause.*) My poor Anselme, I don't recognize you. Evil companions have changed you. But there is still time to stop you on the fatal decline. Choose: Poetry! or the reformatory.

ANSELME: With what pen name shall I sign my works?

MONSIEUR PELICAN: Ungrateful son! You know my feelings on this subject. My name—your name—must be famous. In school, on the first day of the term when the new students learned my name, they whispered those famous verses of Musset:

HORTENSE (*reciting*): When, tired after much traveling, the Pelican
In the mists of evening returns to the reeds
His little hungry ones run along the shore
Observing his distant descent to the waters.
Immediately imagining the sharing of their prey
They run to their father with cries of joy
Shaking beaks against hideous necks.
Stumbling to a heap of rocks
With drooping wing he shelters his brood.
Melancholy fisherman, he scans the skies.
Blood runs down his opened breast;
In vain he searched the ocean's depths;

The sea was empty, the beach like some desert:
The only nourishment here is his heart.
Grave and silent, stretched out on the stones
Dividing among his sons his fatherly substance
With divine love he soothes his grief;
Watching the flow of his bloody breast
He swoons at these feasts of death
Drunken with joy, fear, and tenderness.
But in the midst of the divine sacrifice sometimes
Exhausted by dying in so long a torment
He fears that his children will let him live;
Then he lifts himself, widens wings to the wind
And tears at his heart with a harsh cry
And flings into night so mournful a farewell
That sea birds desert the mainland
And the traveler, straying late on this strand
Commends himself, sensing death, to God.
Poet, this is the way of the greatest poets.
They let those be merry who live out their little hour only
But the human feasts they have at their celebrations
Closely resemble those of the Pelicans.

*Head bowed, Monsieur Pelican listens to the recitation.
Anselme shows obvious signs of impatience.*

MONSIEUR PELICAN: What a lesson for you, Anselme, (*Aside.*) and
for me. When I was only ten I swore that the name of Pelican,
in several centuries, would evoke no more laughter than that
of Racine or Corneille. Do you want to make your father a
liar? Of course you don't. Imagine the bursts of laughter of
children hearing the name of Racine or Corneille for the first
time—yes, I believe that in the seventeenth century children
were no better than children are today. A ridiculous name is
a blessing—it gives one the ambition that is necessary to become a great man. Hence I feel ambitious to make my son a
great poet. (*Pause.*) And you, Hortense, you are afraid to admit that you want to paint. Painting is an accomplishment
and therefore an honorable occupation. . . . But certain
colors are not without their dangers, and for a young lady
. . . (*He searches for an end to his sentence, does not find it,
and taps his foot.*) for a young lady, finally . . . yes . . . I
understand myself, that's the main thing. Hortense, become
a photographer. A poet, though his admirers be few, still must

plein d'emphase

distribute his photograph to them. What a saving for Anselme! Tomorrow I shall present your photography instructor to you.

Monsieur Pelican and Hortense go out.

SCENE 11

ANSELME (*alone*): I have few scruples—but I have never dared to dirty a clean sheet of paper. At school, this made my professors think me a dunce. But when one has a personality like mine (*He slaps his chest.*) to suffer in silence is best.

SCENE 12

Anselme, Monsieur Pelican

MONSIEUR PELICAN (*re-entering suddenly*): I listened behind the door; give me your hand; I understand: You are unaccustomed to writing and you are afraid of wasting all your paper in rough drafts. Your scruples are those of an honest boy. But do not go on tormenting yourself. At first you shall write your poems on this blackboard.

CURTAIN

ACT II

Two months later, Christmas Day. A girl's room, converted into a darkroom, dimly lit by a red lamp.

SCENE 1

Monsieur Chantecler, Hortense

HORTENSE: How I love you!

Someone knocks.

VOICE OF MONSIEUR PELICAN (*behind the door*): Well, my child, are the photographs successful?

HORTENSE (*alarmed, in a low voice to Monsieur Chantecler*): My God! My hair isn't even combed.

MONSIEUR CHANTECLER (*in a brisk voice, to Monsieur Pelican*): Don't come in, don't come in; the light will fog our negatives. Mademoiselle Hortense is making excellent progress.

Monsieur Pelican goes away. Hortense opens the shutters. It is daytime. Then she picks a daisy from a vase and begins to pluck off the petals.

HORTENSE: He loves me . . . he loves me not. . . . (*To Monsieur Chantecler.*) And now can you dare say that you love me?

MONSIEUR CHANTECLER: Certainly, little naïve one . . . I don't believe in the language of flowers.

He leaves curling the end of his mustache.

SCENE 2

HORTENSE (*alone*): I am unable to do anything now but kill myself. A firearm, the blade, some poison, yes . . . No, today is Christmas; the druggist's will be closed. My suicide could be risky; we have no antidotes at home. Wait! An idea! What if I threw myself in the river? We live only two steps from the Seine. Monsieur Chantecler doesn't love me? Well! I shall marry my rescuer! (*She throws kisses to the audience and curtsies gracefully.*)

SCENE 3

Monsieur Pelican, Madame Pelican, Anselme

Monsieur Pelican in coat with a big fur collar; Madame Pelican in a bathing suit; Anselme, very emaciated.

MONSIEUR PELICAN (*to Madame Pelican*): Shouldn't you be competing in the Christmas Day Race?

MADAME PELICAN: You're right! I let the starting time slip by accidentally. And besides, I was afraid the water might be a little cold.

MONSIEUR PELICAN: You will never get a reputation as a swimming champion by swimming on our billiards table. (*He goes out.*)

SCENE 4

The same, less Monsieur Pelican, but with Monsieur Pastel

ANSELME: Mama, if you are looking for Hortense, I met her in the hall. She told me she was going to drown herself, but I'm not worried. . . .

MADAME PELICAN: Is it possible that to tell me this, you've waited peacefully for your father to go—as if it were a matter of asking for pocket money? Ah! if this were not Christmas Day I would box your ears. (*Turning to Monsieur Pastel.*) You're a swimming instructor, go save her.

MONSIEUR PASTEL (*annoyed*): My dear friend, what do you take me for? I am not a master swimmer. I teach theory, but I don't know how to swim.

MADAME PELICAN: Let me see you no more, impostor. To seduce me, infamous person, you did not hesitate to convince me that you knew how to swim.

He leaves, hanging his head.

SCENE 5

Madame Pelican, Monsieur Chantecler, Anselme

MADAME PELICAN: Ah! Here is the photography instructor. Monsieur Chantecler, my daughter has thrown herself into the river. Go save her—there will be a nice reward.

MONSIEUR CHANTECLER (*annoyed*): Your daughter will soon be Madame Chantecler. A future mother-in-law should speak in quite another tone of voice. I shall go to save my Hortense, but promise first not to give me a reward.

MADAME PELICAN (*throwing herself on her knees*): Grief has made me forget the customs of society. Forgive me, my good Monsieur Chantecler.

Monsieur Chantecler throws his jacket, his vest, his tie and his false collar into the four corners of the room. He leaves, running.

SCENE 6

Madame Pelican, Monsieur Pelican, Anselme

MADAME PELICAN (*addressing the audience*): My husband has gone mad.

MONSIEUR PELICAN: And you, what little song do you sing over there? I have every right to display my joy.

MADAME PELICAN (*sobbing*): What . . . my God . . . Ah, Hortense . . . if you only knew.

MONSIEUR PELICAN: Yes, I know. . . . She has won the Christmas Day Race, and moreover, she saved the photographer instructor who tried to commit suicide. I hardly see any reason to weep.

MADAME PELICAN (*to Anselme, menacingly*): Then you've been lying to me. Ah! If it weren't Christmas. . . .

ANSELME (*to his mother*): A moment ago you interrupted me in the middle of a sentence. . . . If I didn't seem very anxious, it's because I knew that the Seine would be frozen over.

MADAME PELICAN: Miracle of miracles! My daughter wins the first prize in swimming on a day when the Seine is frozen.

MONSIEUR PELICAN: Hortense, who knows as little about swimming as you do, is an excellent skater. And when the Seine is frozen, it is the custom to change the swimming competition to a skating contest.

ANSELME: In any case, it's thanks to me that Hortense is a celebrity. I knew her passion for the photography instructor. Wondering how deeply Monsieur Chantecler loved her, she asked him for a bouquet of daisies as her Christmas gift. It was I, playing a trick on Hortense, who pulled a petal from every daisy.

MONSIEUR *and* MADAME PELICAN: What a poet!!!

ANSELME (*proudly*): And thanks to this diet, I have reached the weight appropriate for a jockey.

MONSIEUR PELICAN: I see it now perfectly. Seeing you mounted on your horse, I shall tell myself that you ride Pegasus. And I would have conducted myself like an old egotist! But why force you to become any kind of celebrity? Isn't our name already in the dictionary?

HORTENSE (*reciting*): When, tired after much traveling, the Pelican . . .

ANSELME (*vigorously*): Yes! Yes! We know it by heart. (*He leaves.*)

MONSIEUR PELICAN: Hortense, be a gardener, since that will amuse you.

HORTENSE: Ah! No, Papa! I would enjoy being a photographer much more.

MONSIEUR PELICAN: What are we to do with a photographer-daughter?

MADAME PELICAN: While you think, Hortense can photograph us. The family is all here.

HORTENSE: Yes, Mama . . . but I would very much like to appear in the group myself, with my fiancé.

MONSIEUR PELICAN: That can easily be arranged. Monsieur Pastel, over there, is not a member of the family.

CURTAIN

the gas heart

by TRISTAN TZARA

translated by Michael Benedikt

CHARACTERS

EYE
MOUTH
NOSE
EAR
NECK
EYEBROW

ACT I

Neck stands downstage, Nose opposite, confronting the audience. All the other characters enter and leave as they please. The gas heart walks slowly around, circulating widely; it is the only and greatest three-act hoax of the century; it will satisfy only industrialized imbeciles who believe in the existence of men of genius. Actors are requested to give this play the attention due a masterpiece such as Macbeth *or* Chantecler, *but to treat the author—who is not a genius—with no respect and to note the levity of the script which brings no technical innovation to the theatre.*

EYE: Statues jewels roasts
    statues jewels roasts
    statues jewels roasts
    statues jewels roasts
    statues jewels roasts
    and the wind open to mathematical allusions

    cigar pimple nose
    cigar pimple nose
    cigar pimple nose
    cigar pimple nose
    cigar pimple nose
    cigar pimple nose
    he was in love with a stenographer

    eyes replaced by motionless navels
    mister mygod is an excellent journalist
    inflexible yet acquatic a good-morning was drifting in the air
    what a sad season

MOUTH: The conversation is lagging isn't it?

EYE: Yes, isn't it.

MOUTH: Very lagging, isn't it?

EYE: Yes, isn't it?

MOUTH: Naturally, isn't it?

EYE: Obviously, isn't it?

MOUTH: Lagging, isn't it?

EYE: Yes, isn't it?

MOUTH: Obviously, isn't it?

EYE: Yes, isn't it?

MOUTH: Very lagging, isn't it?

EYE: Yes, isn't it?

MOUTH: Naturally, isn't it?

EYE: Obviously, isn't it?

MOUTH: Lagging, isn't it?

EYE: Yes, isn't it?

MOUTH: Obviously, isn't it?

EYE: Yes, isn't it?

NOSE: You over there, man with starred scars, where are you running?

EAR: I'm running toward happiness
I'm burning in the eyes of passing days
I swallow jewels
I sing in courtyards
love has not court nor hunting horn to fish up
hard-boiled-egg hearts with

Mouth exits.

NOSE: You over there, man with a scream like a fat pearl, what are you eating?

EAR: Over two years have passed, alas, since I set out on this hunt. But do you see how one can get used to fatigue and how death would be tempted to live, the magnificent emperor's death proves it, the importance of everything diminishes—every day—a little . . .

NOSE: You over there, man with wounds of chained wool molluscs, man with various pains and pockets full, pieman of all maps and places, where do you come from?

EYE: The bark of apotheosized trees shadows wormy verse but the rain makes organized poetry's clock tick. The banks filled with medicated cotton-wool. String man supported by blisters like

you and like all others. To the porcelain flower play us chastity
on your violin, O cherry tree, death is so quick and cooks
over the bituminous coal of the trombone capital.

NOSE: Hey you over there, sir . . .

EAR: Hey hey hey hey hey hey hey hey hey hey hey hey hey

NECK: Tangerine and white from Spain
I'm killing myself Madeleine Madeleine.

EAR: The eye tells the mouth: open your mouth for the candy of
the eye.

NECK: Tangerine and white from Spain
I'm killing myself Madeleine Madeleine.

EYE: Upon the ear the vaccine of serious pearl flattened to mimosa.

EAR: Don't you think it's getting rather warm?

MOUTH (*who has just come in again*): It gets warm in the summer.

EYE: The beauty of your face is a precision chronometer.

NECK: Tangerine and white from Spain
I'm killing myself Madeleine Madeleine.

EAR: The watch hand indicates the left ear the right eye the forehead the eyebrow the forehead the eyebrow the left eye the
left ear the lips the chin the neck.

EYE: Clytemnestra, the diplomat's wife, was looking out of the
window. The cellists go by in a carriage of Chinese tea, biting
the air and openhearted caresses. You are beautiful, Clytemnestra, the crystal of your skin awakens our sexual curiosity. You are as tender and as calm as two yards of white
silk. Clytemnestra, my teeth tremble. I'm cold, I'm afraid.
I'm green I'm flower I'm gasometer I'm afraid. You are married. My teeth tremble. When will you have the pleasure of
looking at the lower jaw of the revolver closing in my chalk
lung. Hopeless, and without any family.

NECK: Tangerine and white from Spain
I'm killing myself Madeleine Madeleine.

MOUTH: Too sensitive to approval by your good taste I have decided
to shut off the faucet. The hot and cold water of my charm

will no longer be able to divert the sweet results of your sweat, true love or new love. (*Exits.*)

EAR (*entering*): His neck is narrow but his foot is quite large. He can easily drum with his fingers or toes on his oval belly which has already served as a ball several times during rugby. He is not a being because he consists of pieces. Simple men manifest their existences by houses, important men by monuments.

NOSE: How true how true how true how true how true . . .

EYEBROW: "Where," "how much," "why," are monuments. As, for example, Justice. What beautifully regular functioning, practically a nervous tic or a religion.

NOSE (*decrescendo*): How true how true how true how true how true . . .

EYEBROW: In the lake dipped twice in the sky—the bearded sky— a pretty morning was found. The object fleeting between the nostrils. Acidulous taste of weak electric current, this taste which at the entrances to salt mines switches to zinc, to rubber, to cloth—weightless and grimy. One evening—while out walking in the evening—someone found, deep down, a tiny little evening. And its name was good evening.

NOSE: How true how true how true how true how true . . .

EYE: Look out! cried the hero, the two paths of smoke from those enemy houses were knotting a necktie—and it rose overhead to the navel of the light.

NOSE: How true how true how true how true how true . . .

EAR: Carelessly the robber changed himself into a valise, the physicist might therefore state that the valise stole the robber. The waltz went on continuously—it is continuously which was not going on—it was waltzing—and the lovers were tearing off pieces of it as it passed—on old walls posters are worthless.

NOSE: How true how true how true how true how true . . .

EYE: They kept catching colds with great regularity. For the regularity of his life a little death, too. Its name was continuity.

NOSE: How true how true how true how true how true . . .

EYE: Never had a fisherman made more assassinating shadows under the bridges of the city. But suddenly midnight sounded beneath the stamp of a blink and tears mingled in telegrams undecoded and obscure.

EYEBROW: He flattened out like a bit of tin foil and several drops several memories several leaves testified to the cruelty of an impassioned and actual fauna. Wind the curtain of nothingness shakes—his stomach is full of foreign money. Nothingness drinks nothingness: the air has arrived with its blue eyes, and that is why he goes on taking aspirin all the time. Once a day we give abortive birth to our obscurities.

EYE: We have the time, alas, time is lacking no longer. Time wears mustaches now like everyone, even women and shaven Americans. Time is compressed—the eye is weak—but it isn't yet in the miser's wrinkled purse.

MOUTH: Isn't it?

EYE: The conversation is lagging, isn't it?

MOUTH: Yes, isn't it?

EYE: Very lagging, isn't it?

MOUTH: Yes, isn't it?

EYE: Naturally, isn't it?

MOUTH: Obviously, isn't it?

EYE: Lagging, isn't it?

MOUTH: Yes, isn't it?

EYE: Very lagging, isn't it?

MOUTH: Yes, isn't it?

EYE: Naturally, isn't it?

MOUTH: Lagging, isn't it?

EYE: Obviously mygod.

CURTAIN

ACT II

EYEBROW: We're going to the races today.

MOUTH: Let's not forget the camera.

EYE: Well hello.

EAR: The mechanical battalion of the wrists of shriveled hand-shakes.

Mouth exits.

NOSE (*shouts*): Clytemnestra is winning!

EAR: What do you mean you didn't know that Clytemnestra was a race horse?

EYE: Amorous jostlings lead everywhere. But the season is propitious. Take care, dear friends, the season is satisfactory. It chews up words. It distends silences in accordions. Snakes line up everywhere in their polished eyeglasses. And what do you do with the bells of eyes, asked the entrepreneur.

EAR: "Seekers and curious people," answered Ear. She finishes the nerves of others in the white porcelain shell. She inflates.

NOSE: Fan having a seizure of wood,
light body with enormous laugh.

EYEBROW: The driving-belts of the mills of dreams brush against the woolen lower jaws of our carnivorous plants.

EAR: Yes, I know, the dreams with hair.

EYE: Dreams of angels.

EAR: Dreams of cloth, paper watches.

EYE: The enormous and solemn dreams of inaugurations.

EAR: Of angels in helicopters.

NOSE: Yes I know.

EYE: The angels of conversation.

NECK: Yes I know.

EAR: Angels in cushions.

NOSE: Yes I know.

EYE: Angels in ice.

NOSE: Yes I know.

EAR: Angels in local neighborhoods.

NOSE: Yes, I know.

EAR: The ice is broken, said our fathers to our mothers, in the first springtime of their life which was both honorable and gracious.

EYE: This is how the hour understands the hour, the admiral his fleet of words. Winter child the palm of my hand.

Mouth enters.

MOUTH: I've made a great deal of money.

NOSE: Thank you not bad.

MOUTH: I swim in the fountain I have necklaces of goldfish.

NECK: Thank you not bad.

MOUTH: I'm wearing the latest French coiffure.

NOSE: Thank you not bad.

EYE: I've already seen it in Paris.

NECK: Thank you not bad.

MOUTH: I don't understand anything about the rumblings of the next war.

NECK: Thank you not bad.

MOUTH: And I'm getting thinner every day.

NOSE: Thank you not bad.

MOUTH: A young man followed me in the street on his bicycle.

NECK: Thank you not bad.

MOUTH: I'll be on my ship next Monday.

NOSE: Thank you not bad.

EYE: Clytemnestra the wind is blowing. The wind is blowing. On the quays of decorated bells. Turn your back cut off the wind. Your eyes are stones because they only see the wind and rain. Clytemnestra. Have you felt the horrors of the war? Do you know how to slide on the sweetness of my speech? Don't you breathe the same air as I do? Don't you speak the same language? In what limitless metal are your fingers of misery inlaid? What music filtered by what mysterious curtain prevents my words from penetrating the wax of your brain? Certainly, stone grinds you and bones strike against your muscles, but language chopped into chance slices will never release in you the stream which employs white methods.

Mouth exits.

EAR: Doubtless you know the calendars of birds?

EYE: What?

EAR: Three hundred and sixty-five birds—every day a bird flies away—every hour a feather falls—every two hours somebody writes a poem—somebody cuts it apart with scissors.

NOSE: I've already seen it in Paris.

EYE: What a philosophy. What a poet. I don't like poetry.

EAR: Then you must love cold drinks? Or a countryside that rolls like a dancer's permanent waves? Or ancient cities? Or the black arts?

EYE: I know all about that.

NOSE: A little more life on the stage.

EYEBROW: Gray drum for the flower of your lung.

EAR: My lung is made out of lung and is not a mere cardboard front if you really want to know.

EYE: But, Miss.

EAR: Please, Sir.

EYE: Bony sacraments in military prisons painting doesn't much interest me. I like a quiet countryside with considerable galloping.

NOSE: Your piece is quite charming but you really don't come away enriched.

EYEBROW: There's nothing to be enriched by in it everything is easy to follow and even come away with. An outlet of thought from which a whip will emerge. The whip will be a forget-me-not. The forget-me-not a living inkwell. The inkwell will dress a doll.

EAR: Your daughter is quite charming.

EYE: You're very considerate.

EAR: Do you care for sports?

EYE: Yes, this method of communication is very practical.

EAR: You know of course that I own a garage.

EYE: Thank you very much.

EAR: It's spring it's spring . . .

NOSE: I tell you it's two yards.

NECK: I tell you it's three yards.

NOSE: I tell you it's four yards.

NECK: I tell you it's five yards.

NOSE: I tell you it's six yards.

NECK: I tell you it's seven yards.

NOSE: I tell you it's eight yards.

NECK: I tell you it's nine yards.

NOSE: I tell you it's ten yards.

NECK: I tell you it's eleven yards.

NOSE: I tell you it's twelve yards.

NECK: I tell you it's thirteen yards.

NOSE: I tell you it's fourteen yards.

NECK: I tell you it's fifteen yards.

NOSE: I tell you it's sixteen yards.

EAR: Thank you thank you very good.

EYE: Love—sport or indictment
summary of the directories of love—love
accumulated by centuries of weights and numbers
with its breasts of copper and crystal
god is a nervous tic of shifting sand dunes

nervous and agile leafs through countrysides and the pockets
of onlookers
the hair-do of death thrown on the flail
outwardly new
friendship with error delicately juxtaposed.

NOSE: I tell you love's seventeen yards.

NECK: I tell you it's eighteen yards.

NOSE: I tell you it's nineteen yards.

NECK: I tell you it's twenty yards.

NOSE: I tell you it's twenty-one yards.

NECK: I tell you it's twenty-two yards.

NOSE: I tell you it's twenty-three yards.

NECK: I tell you it's twenty-four yards.

NOSE: I tell you it's twenty-five yards.

NECK: I tell you it's twenty-six yards.

NOSE: I tell you it's twenty-seven yards.

NECK: I tell you it's twenty-eight yards.

NOSE: I tell you it's twenty-nine yards.

EAR: You have a very pretty head
you ought to have it sculpted
you ought to give the grandest of parties
to know nature better and to love nature
and sink forks into your sculpture
the grasses of the ventilators flatter the lovely days.

EYEBROW: Fire! Fire!
I think Clytemnestra's ablaze.

CURTAIN

ACT III

NECK: The sky is clouded
my finger is opened
sewing-machine these staring examinations

the river is opened
the brain clouded
sewing-machine these staring examinations.

MOUTH: We will make fine material for the crystal dress with it.

NOSE: You mean to say: "despair gives you its explanations regarding its rates of exchange."

MOUTH: I don't mean to say anything. A long time ago I put everything I had to say into a hatbox.

NECK: Everybody knows you, installation of conjugal bliss.

NOSE: Everybody knows you, tapestry of forgotten ideas, crystallization.

NECK: Everybody knows you, formula for a song, running board of algebra, insomnia number, triple-skinned machine.

MOUTH: Everybody does not know me. I am alone here in my wardrobe and the mirror is blank when I look at myself. Also I love the birds at the ends of lit cigarettes. Cats, all animals and all vegetables. I love cats, birds, animals and vegetables which are the projection of Clytemnestra in the courtyard, bedding, vases and meadows. I love hay. I love the young man who makes such tender declarations to me and whose spine is ripped asunder in the sun.

Dance of the gentleman fallen from a funnel in the ceiling onto the table.

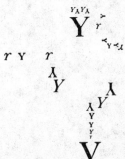

MOUTH: Dreams dampen the evening of stretched hide. (*Exits.*)

EYE: Imagine that my dear friend I no longer love him.

EAR: Which one do you mean?

EYE: I mean the one I've loved too long.

EAR: Me too I've lost an illusion. The prize horse in my stable has lost his energy.

EYE: Well then, my dear, his life must be renewed.

EAR: You're just bitter. (*Exits.*)

Enter Mouth.

EYE: Clytemnestra you are beautiful. I love you with the intensity of a diver . . . his seaweeds. My blood trembles. Your eyes are blue. Why can't you hear, Clytemnestra, the quiet laughter of my cells awaiting you, the violence of my breath and the sweet childish possibilities fate has in store for us? Are you perhaps awaiting further sensational revelations regarding my temperament?

Exit Mouth.

Eye falls to the stage.

NOSE: Huge.

NECK: Fixed.

NOSE: Cruel.

NECK: Broad.

NOSE: Small.

NECK: Short.

NOSE: Shrill.

NECK: Feeble.

NOSE: Magnificent.

NECK: Long.

NOSE: Narrow.

NECK: Strong.

NOSE: Sensitive.

NECK: Fat.

NOSE: High.

NECK: Slim.

NOSE: Trembling.

NECK: Fine.

NOSE: Clear.

NECK: Courageous.

NOSE: Thin.

NECK: Obscure.

NOSE: Timid.

NECK: Pretty.

NOSE: White.

NECK: Flexible.

NOSE: Deep.

NECK: Nasty.

NOSE: Ugly.

NECK: Heavy.

NOSE: Low.

NECK: Black.

NOSE: Superficial.

NECK: Scentless.

NOSE: Harmonious.

NECK: Smooth.

NOSE: Rigid.

NECK: Tangerine and white from Spain
I'm killing myself Madeleine Madeleine.

EAR: (*entering with Mouth, who crawls on all fours, and shouting*): Clytemnestra, race horse:
3,000 francs

Going once!
Going twice!!
Going thrice!!!
☞ Gone!

Eye goes up to Mouth, on all fours.

EAR: This will end with a lovely marriage.

EYE: This will end with a lovely marriage.

EYEBROW: This will end with a lovely marriage.

MOUTH: This will end with a lovely marriage.

NECK: This will end with a lovely marriage.

NOSE: This will end with a lovely marriage.

EAR: Go lie down.

EYE: Go lie down.

EYEBROW: Go lie down.

MOUTH: Go lie down.

NECK: Go lie down.

NOSE: Go lie down.

l' A mour

FINIS

if you please

by ANDRÉ BRETON *and*
PHILIPPE SOUPAULT

translated by George E. Wellwarth

ACT I

A drawing room. 5:00 P.M.

Door at the back. Windows at right and left.

Two armchairs. A cassock. A low table. A lamp. Mirrors.

> PAUL: Forty years old. Hairline mustache; stoops, has gray hair.
> VALENTINE: Twenty-five years old.
> FRANÇOIS: Twenty-seven years old, clean-shaven.

SCENE 1

PAUL: I love you. (*Long kiss.*)

VALENTINE: A cloud of milk in a cup of tea.

Pause.

PAUL: How hard do you think it is for me to choose between the passage of the Tropics and those more distant dawns that dazzle me as soon as you open your eyes? The white phosphorus of other women's lips had made love impossible for me up to now. Uncertain of finding you, I listened to the shower of tresses striking the windows of my idleness and only perceived the turbulence of manufactured breezes from afar. I must confess that for a long time I have given myself over to delusive arguments between that inseparable pair, the street-lamp and the gutter.

VALENTINE: Don't be afraid to speak. I know what you are going to say, but who cares! Our life rises so slowly with your eyes which look at me and forget me. You are still going to cradle me with "Remember!"—do you remember?

PAUL: You have to keep a certain distance from the wall to rouse an echo. With all those we love our hope is to be able to embrace the trunk of this supraterrestrial tree.

VALENTINE: The thousand and one nights sink into one of ours. I dreamed that we were drowning.

PAUL: It's a long time since the charming statue on top of the Tour Saint-Jacques let fall the crown of the immortals which

149

it held in its hand. . . . How do you like your new apartment?

VALENTINE: My husband's study has a view of the gardens of the Palais-Royal.

PAUL: Ah, yes! Staring at the bars again.

VALENTINE: Naughty. And those crumbs of bread for the birds: solitude? The regions of the imagination are so vast!

PAUL (*catching sight of one of his own grimaces in the mirror*): It's absolutely correct to compare certain looks to lightning: they flash against the same broken branches, they make the same blond young girls leaning against black furniture appear. . . . You are more beautiful than they.

VALENTINE: I know. You like the gleaming chestnuts buried in my hair.

Pause.

PAUL: Did you hear him come in?

VALENTINE: Current morality: it makes one think of a current of water.

PAUL: The charm lies in that lovely liquid song, the spelling out of the catechism by children. What do you talk about in a pinch?

VALENTINE: The patience of an angel. I have the patience of an angel. He rented a villa, a temporary one for the season. Lots of ivy. Like other men, he is the slave of his fatigue at one time and of his pleasure at another. (*Arranging a fold of her dress.*) Do you like my dress?

PAUL (*going to her*): A casket of arms lined with blue velvet.

VALENTINE: Love.

PAUL: Flesh or pearls. A diver in crystal waves. Everything hangs by a thread.

VALENTINE: It's the beginning of paradise, or so it seems. The gray, slaty day has blue automobile horns; at night one flies on a silvery frond.

PAUL: What are you doing tomorrow?

VALENTINE: The department stores will be open: the youth of so many women.

PAUL: You say to the elevator starter standing near the door: "Going up, sir, if you please?"

VALENTINE: The smiles of the salespeople. Yet another coquetry (*Pause.*) What are you thinking about?

PAUL: The sweetness of life. Everyone takes part in it. Gossamer at the height of a man's face, the song of capitals.

VALENTINE: You're like the workers who test the wheels with a hammer when the train stops.

PAUL (*distraught*): I've often asked myself what might be the speed, in a fast train or in love, of the flies which fly from the rear wall to the front wall of some sleeping compartment or other. (*Coming back brusquely to her.*) You're not cold?

VALENTINE: What time is it? (*Pause.*) Paul, my happiness is as sweet as starved birds. You can play at lowering your eyes or at clenching your fists. I agree to be in despair. I've thought of you so much since the other day!

PAUL: Speak.

VALENTINE: The brilliant words I would like to say stream in the sky like the stars which you were looking at. You don't want to laugh? When you are away from me it is your laugh I hear first of all.

SCENE 2

FRANÇOIS (*enters with hands extended*): My dear friends, I've come to say good-bye. (*To his wife.*) It's a pity that you're not tempted by a little promenade to Geneva. I can't resign myself to going alone.

VALENTINE: I'm so exhausted, my friend.

FRANÇOIS: Even more exhausted now?

VALENTINE: Yes. I feel dizzy. My head feels like a cash register. I feel lost around here. Before Paul came a ray of sun falling on a green plant kept me going like an exciting novel.

FRANÇOIS: You should take a cup of linden tea with a dash of brandy. Sometimes I feel the same way myself, and I always make myself a nice hot cup of linden tea and add several shots of brandy. It does wonders. Wouldn't you like to try it?

VALENTINE: No, thanks. I'll be all right. I feel better already. I wish you wouldn't bother about me—it makes me feel so silly.

PAUL: There's nothing silly about it. Would you like me to ring?

VALENTINE: Please don't bother.

PAUL: Really?

VALENTINE: Really.

FRANÇOIS: All the same, a little cup of linden tea with a little brandy wouldn't do you any harm.
    Pause.

VALENTINE: What time does your train leave?

FRANÇOIS: 7:33 P.M.

VALENTINE: Where will you be staying?

FRANÇOIS: Hotel Bristol, Geneva. I hope you won't be too bored. (*To Paul.*) See that you entertain her. (*Taking him by the arm.*) I rely on you, old chap.

VALENTINE: What are you going to do there?

FRANÇOIS: Do you remember John the Coalminer? I've owed him a visit for a long time. He used to be my best friend.

VALENTINE: You've often told me about him.

FRANÇOIS: You're the one who urged me to go, and now I almost regret it. It's so easy for me not to think of anything but us. If only you'd agree to leave Paris with me! Is it really so hard to give up these activities, these parties? I'd love to see the color come back to your face and not see these dark circles under your eyes.

VALENTINE: Listening to you one would think I was in critical condition.

PAUL: It will go away. It's nerves.
    Pause.

FRANÇOIS (*gets up, takes several steps, then stops in front of Valentine*): This time tomorrow I'll be far away from you. It will be a solitude both pleasant and warm. I will feel as if I had been away from you for weeks, months, years. People will speak and be excited. The caress of the water on the bank moves and excites me already! From the terrace of my hotel I see white sails pass by on the lake. That landscape intoxicates me at sunset. After having been the great, silent lake all day, at twilight it becomes an enchanted and supernatural country.

A knock on the door.

VALENTINE: Come in.

Enter a servant.

SERVANT: The carriage waits, sir.

François looks at his watch.

VALENTINE: You must not be late.

FRANÇOIS: Oh, I've got time.

The servant leaves.

FRANÇOIS (*changing his tone*): What if I telegraphed to John not to expect me? (*Pause. He appears to hesitate.*)

PAUL: Stay.

FRANÇOIS: One constantly retraces one's steps, which is understandable enough. I know that for me reality is here in your friendship, and uncertitude is out there among the chattering voices and the busy faces.

Valentine goes to the window and remains there until the beginning of the following scene, her forehead pressed against the glass.

The railroad stations are great temptations which one resists as much as possible. On what can you rest your eyes when they've ceased to exist? One doesn't carry away any remembrance, not even a scrap of wallpaper. Nothing but the dryness of the timetable and the ability to start a conversation with any stranger. (*Sighs.*) Ah! (*Calling out.*) Valentine!

VALENTINE: What?

FRANÇOIS (*arms extended*): I'm going.

VALENTINE: Till Thursday. (*She gives him her forehead to kiss.*)

FRANÇOIS (*to Paul*): So long, old chap. (*Shakes hands.*)

SCENE 3

Pause. Valentine is still at the window. The door closes.

PAUL: Valentine!

VALENTINE: What?

PAUL: A door closes and our life begins.

VALENTINE (*going to him*): I know that voice false as the clouds. *Noise of automobile going away.*

PAUL: Then you have not understood that all these gestures, all these words which come to you die, if you don't gather them.

VALENTINE: Look at me and I will believe in the sadnesses of each yes, in awakenings painful as sand.

PAUL: I have the right to lie to you.

VALENTINE: I have seen my image in each reflection and I am afraid not to believe you. You lie? And I want you to tell me no.

PAUL: What for? You know very well that you must suffer. One day, one hour, like a tree isolated in the country of your childhood, is worth all the distant months which are nothing but tomorrow. Doubt leans gently against you, and you will run away from it like an ingrate.

VALENTINE: I am going to find air and cold again, and I will finally know that you are no longer there.

PAUL: I am only sincere when I can lie to you. The words you love I know by heart.

VALENTINE: Speak, I beg you. Each moment of silence eats up my minutes. My heart beats as at the arrival of trains. I follow the roadbed of my dreams. The end is very near. We will not delay our partings, and sleep stretches around us.

PAUL: Listen. . . .

VALENTINE: You're smiling. . . .

PAUL: I cannot flee from my smile. It imposes itself on me like a dream.

VALENTINE: Do we know why I suffer? I don't even know why I tremble. I'm frightened. Do you hear?

PAUL (*dryly*): Yes, perfectly.

VALENTINE: I wanted to tell you . . .

PAUL (*same tone*): What?

VALENTINE: You know. Will you be able to come to see us often?

PAUL (*same tone*): I don't know. We'll see.

VALENTINE: I'd like to leave you right away and not hear your words, which fall heavily on my ears. The sound of your steps hurts me.

PAUL: You are so far away!

VALENTINE: I am as near to you as the ground.

PAUL: It's necessary to depart and not look back. It's a question of something else entirely. We are not concerned with tenderness: it's that vague fog which is not enough to hide the blood in our veins and the suffering of our hands.

VALENTINE: My head sinks; my eyes close. I'd like to be the horizon which you'll never reach. I would feel your painful desire and your looks.

PAUL: It's getting dark. You still seem to be speaking of the pretty moonbeams of our youth. The sky is beautiful, you say (*looking out of the side of the window*), but it's really just a sunset.

VALENTINE: At least right now tears can touch you.

PAUL: One glimpses adventure and destinies in the distance. And yet it's too near. The months, the color of eyes, and the reflections of rainy days beguile us. Sometimes, in the evening, I turn out my pockets.

VALENTINE: Do you really know how late it is?

PAUL: Since you only forget our silence and the moistness of our eyelids, night can come without my caring. Mystery leaves me as cold as the branches they'll throw on our graves the next day, and the vigil candle, the rain, and the bad weather. What does all that and everything else mean? These noises behind me—do you think I fear them? I prefer to read in your face the imaginary joys and sadnesses that I have known so well. My age doesn't interest me. (*He lights a cigarette.*)

VALENTINE: I still hear you. The skeleton that you are rattling and these words that make me clench my teeth—I love them like the final moments of the night. Even at the great distance between us your encircling arms suffocate me. Is the sequel worth living? The great fire which illuminates us and sings in our flesh leaves us a husk of helpless shadows. I'm not afraid of love. Perhaps only desire exists and I am the strongest in the final analysis. Look how I am protected! At this moment you can do nothing against any single one of my actions. (*She puts her hands behind her head and turns slightly to the right, her eyes closed. A mass of hair is seen falling on the right.*) What are you going to do with me?

Paul puts out his cigarette in an ash tray. Sound of an automobile stopping in front of the hotel. Paul slowly draws a revolver from his pocket, barely taking aim. Valentine falls without a sound. Several sharp rings are heard. Very calmly Paul puts the revolver away and relights his extinguished cigarette.

CURTAIN

ACT II

An office at four o'clock in the afternoon.

A huge map of France on the rear wall.

Window at rear. Doors at right and left.

Typewriter on table in front of window. A suitcase near the door.

Telephone and large notebook on the desk.

Armchairs, chairs.

LÉTOILE: Forty years old, clean-shaven, rosette of the Legion of Honor, horn-rimmed glasses.

A TYPIST: dark, pretty.

LEFEBVRE

A MAN

A LADY

TWO LADIES OF CHARITY

A YOUNG MAN

THREE MEN

TWO POLICEMEN

A POLICE INSPECTOR

AN OFFICE BOY

SCENE 1

LÉTOILE (*dictating*): I would be very much obliged if you would send me a favorable answer to this in the shortest possible time. Yours sincerely, etc.

The typist goes back to her desk and starts to type.

SCENE 2

LEFEBVRE (*having knocked several times without getting an answer, he opens the door and sticks his head in*): O.K. if I come in, Chief? (*He comes in.*) I haven't wasted my day, Chief. Got something here which I think'll interest you. This afternoon in the country I saw some people amusing themselves by starting up two sidetracked locomotives.

LÉTOILE: Very good.

LEFEBVRE: It wasn't as amusing a caper as those jokers had thought, since the locomotives overturned in a ditch. If they hadn't capsized they'd have run through two houses, which would have been the crowning joy for those jokers. (*Sanctimoniously.*) It is high time that people understood that all individual wealth and force contribute to the wealth and strength of everyone, and that people are simply depriving themselves when they drive locomotives into the streets or break the windows of the carriages when the train is late.

LÉTOILE: Idiot. Go and sit down in the waiting room next to the woman near the window. Get hold of her handbag and bring me the letters you'll find there. Thank you.

Lefebvre goes out.

Scene 3

LÉTOILE (*makes a telephone call*): Elysées 40–52. (*Pause.*) Hello! Is this the Bellègue Press? Létoile here. Take this down. I want the proofs delivered to me tomorrow at six. In the good old days, when an inhabitant of one of our little villages departed this life, the sacristan had the church bells rung. In order to let the other villagers know the age of the deceased, the number of times the death bell was tolled indicated the age of the departed, and people said, "How old he was!" Nowadays, if the sacristans of our big city parishes followed this old custom, we would hear all too often very short death tolls and we would frequently say, "Alas! How young he was!" Nowadays one dies young. The fault lies in the conditions of existence, which have changed. We overwork; we exhaust our strength by leading too busy a life. Let us therefore listen to the sound of other bells, joyous and comforting bells, those which we will call the happy carillon of idleness, that is to say, of the uselessness of effort. Send it to Létoile, 47 rue du Sentier. (*This whole speech must be delivered in a crisp tone of voice. Létoile hangs up. He puts an overcoat on, turns the collar up and puts his hat on the desk; then he rings.*)

A distinguished-looking man in his forties enters immediately.

Scene 4

LÉTOILE (*speaks heatedly; during the whole scene his eyes do not leave the other man*): Sir, I'm sorry to say I can't give you more than a few moments. I was about to go out when your card was sent in. Be so good as to take a seat. (*He remains standing.*)

THE MAN: Yesterday evening my wife and I came home after having been to the theatre. I should tell you that the dressing

room is quite some distance from our bedroom. Before un-
dressing, my wife put her necklace and rings on the mantelpiece. I remained in the study.

LÉTOILE: Excuse me, were you smoking?

THE MAN (*after taking time to reflect*): Yes. Several minutes
later . . .

LÉTOILE: Several minutes, you say.

THE MAN (*troubled*): Well, about ten minutes. The jewels had
disappeared.

Pause.

LÉTOILE: I would be interested in knowing to what I owe the honor
of this visit.

THE MAN (*worried*): You *are* Monsieur Létoile?

LÉTOILE: Absolutely.

THE MAN: I've come on the strength of your posters which paper
all the walls, whether broken-down or not. In time of need
these promises are sweeter than knowing how to swim. Everyone knows that Létoile is in possession of the same powers
as God: he sees all, hears all—and no one suspects it. For a
long time now I've considered you the hero of our modern
romance of knight errantry. You will pull me out of this mess
in the twinkling of an eye.

LÉTOILE: Matters such as this concern the police. At any other
time, my dear sir, it will be a pleasure to be of service to you.
(*He goes to open the door.*)

The man rises, bows, and leaves.

SCENE 5

Létoile takes off his overcoat.

*Lefebvre enters, gives him some letters, and goes out without a
word.*

Létoile puts the letters in a drawer.

Scene 6

A knock on the door. Enter the office boy.

THE OFFICE BOY: There's two ladies outside who want to speak to you about a charity.

LÉTOILE (*rubbing his hands*): Show them in at once.

The two ladies enter. They are old and shabby and carry little notebooks in their hands. Without a word Létoile shows them to a seat. He goes back to his armchair, lights a cigar, and waits. The first lady coughs.

(*In a cutting tone, blowing huge puffs of smoke.*) The smoke doesn't bother you?

The lady appears very bothered.

SECOND LADY: Have you sometimes, sir, when evening falls,
Observed the hungry creep along the walls?
Like a frightened ghost or spectre in the dark,
You see them pass and pass again outside the park.
Haggard, tattered, shielding with alarm
A little infant child to keep it from all harm:
A burden dear, with rags wrapped up in vain,
Which yet sleeps peacefully in snow and rain,
Finding, next to that breast so withered by her grief,
His only warmth, his one protective reef!
She holds her hand out to you. Suppliant and mute
Under the pale gas lamps which light her route,
She glides along with speed and in the shadowy halls
Of ruined houses, or along the walls
She flits, her face expressive of her grief . . .

LÉTOILE: How much do you want?

FIRST LADY: My God, your heart must dictate the amount, sir.

Létoile opens a drawer and offers them a banknote without saying a word. The two ladies thank him profusely, put away the money, and prepare to go.

LÉTOILE: One moment.

He rings. Enter the office boy.

Get two policemen instantly. (*To the ladies.*) You'll explain yourselves at the station house.

THE TWO LADIES (*nonplussed*): But sir, what do you take us for?

LÉTOILE: Yes or no, are you or are you not thieves?

FIRST LADY (*taking a card from her bag*): We are licensed by the Municipal Authorities.

LÉTOILE (*having carefully examined the card*): In that case, you'll give the 500 francs back.

The ladies tremblingly return the money. Létoile crumples it up while he keeps looking at them and then throws it into the fire. The ladies, discountenanced, sit down. A pause. Létoile opens a newspaper. The ladies leave, one behind the other. The first one drops her notebook and the second picks it up.

SCENE 7

Enter a lady wearing a small veil.

THE LADY: I would like to speak to you in confidence.

LÉTOILE: Very good, Madame. (*Turning to the typist.*) You will take down our conversation. (*Peremptorily.*) I am listening, Madame.

THE LADY (*holding a handkerchief*): I've been married scarcely a year and I now understand that my husband feels an honest and upright love for another woman. Doubtless he doesn't know it yet himself, but I can measure the depths of the enormous abyss that already lies between us better than anyone. There is nothing for me to do but to sacrifice myself. (*A pause; some tears.*) That's why, simply, I've come to see you. I must leave my husband. I will grant him his independence.

LÉTOILE: You are absolutely determined to get a divorce?

THE LADY: Absolutely.

LÉTOILE: Doubtless you believe that you will be making your husband happy. What a misapprehension! It is wrong to suppose that the more independent a man is, the happier he is. Happiness consists in balance; it involves habits, a routine—in brief, a curb on the need for pleasure. If a couple does not feel itself bound by an authority stronger than their own caprice, then the ease with which they can separate renders the least irritation intolerable to them. Liberty is beautiful as the sun, but it does not behoove you to draw your husband away from his habits. Everything in its place is a bond that is sweeter than woman's breath. Everything that exists today—the fold of a curtain, the light in its accustomed corner—is then once and for all dead to him. All that is left to him is a memory which pursues him like a ghostly bat. . . . You may count on me, Madame: in approximately two months the divorce will be decreed in your favor. I will call you in for the indispensable formalities.

THE LADY (*who has been giving signs of doubt*): Listen, I'm going to think it over again. I'll see.

LÉTOILE (*dryly*): I wouldn't advise it. Reflect—that's just always retracing your steps.

THE LADY: I don't know what to do anymore. (*Tears.*)

LÉTOILE (*energetically*): You have nothing to do. Just sign a few pieces of paper. (*He rises.*)

The lady rises in her turn, undecided. She leaves.

Scene 8

LÉTOILE: Take this down. (*He dictates.*) Publicity Office, 40 rue de Richard Lenoir. 100,000 francs REWARD. A mysterious theft has occurred during the last few days in the home of the Chardin-Lamothe family, 172 boulevard Péreire, Paris. A casket decorated with precious stones of an incalculable value disappeared under the most mysterious circumstances. Paragraph. Two young women going under the assumed names of Marcelle de Livry and Blanche Valfort, also known as Bigmouth, are suspected of having committed the crime. Paragraph. Since audacity is more than ever to be encouraged, one must predict a brilliant career for them. Anyone instrumental in uncovering their traces may put in his claim for the promised reward by communicating with Monsieur Létoile, 47 rue du Sentier. Period.

The bell rings.

Scene 9

The office boy enters and puts a vase of flowers on the desk. Létoile puts a flower in his buttonhole. Enter a smiling young man with a well-groomed blond mustache.

LÉTOILE (*after having shaken hands*): I think I may have what you are looking for. Delighted to be of service in any little thing. I find your company really agreeable.

THE YOUNG MAN: What color are her eyes?

He remains standing; Létoile leans easily against the desk.

LÉTOILE: Ah! People keep saying that society is going to the dogs, but it's organisms like yourself that reassure me of its health. In you, as in the woman I've destined for you, I distinguish the elements of a force which will find full scope for action in your marriage. Young man, you show signs of deep wisdom: life is a path full of twists and turns—the views are varied and the traveler loves to communicate his impressions. If the path is dull, it seems not so long when trodden with a companion. If several paths are seen, you consult together, and if some difficulty comes up you encourage each other and thus surmount the obstacle more easily. Singing together, the two companions climb up the first slope of the hill; when they reach old age, leaning on each other's arms, with halting steps they descend the opposite slope, chatting together of their memories of other times, their faces lighted up with an eternal smile.

THE YOUNG MAN: Is she musical?

LÉTOILE: In a very few days we will have the meeting in a public place—a teahouse, a park, a theatre. The presentation by Létoile. Smiles . . . compliments . . . what a happy coincidence! How often each one has heard the other spoken of! Charming!

THE YOUNG MAN (*moved*): How can I ever thank you, Monsieur Létoile?

LÉTOILE (*shaking his hand*): You owe me nothing, my friend; it's a pleasure for me.

SCENE 10

A knock on the door.

LÉTOILE: Come in.

Enter the office boy.

THE OFFICE BOY: The police are here, sir.

LÉTOILE: Good; have them come in. (*To the policemen.*) Arrest that man.

THE YOUNG MAN: What's going on? You're out of your mind.

LÉTOILE: Resistance is useless. (*To the policemen.*) I make a formal accusation against this man for murdering his mistress, Madame Valentine Saint-Cervan. My deposition will be brief. I will rejoin you at the station house in a moment. (*Calling them back.*) Take this suitcase with you. It contains the evidence for conviction.

SCENE 11

Létoile walks up and down for a moment and then stops in front of the map of France.

TYPIST: May I have the afternoon off tomorrow, sir?

LÉTOILE: I'll allow you to go to the Bois de Boulogne.

TYPIST: Thank you, sir.

LÉTOILE (*looking fixedly at her*): You are beautiful, my child.

She lowers her eyes.

Are you afraid of me?

She comes nearer.

Do you understand what goes on here? Fanaticism is a magic lantern in the light of which boredom takes on disquieting shapes like this map of France. You think of nothing but casual friends with whom one stretches out on the grass or makes jokes with. I see no other inconveniencing factor in that than the clouds of dust raised by the cars on the road.

TYPIST: We've had a wonderful time today.

LÉTOILE: It happens from time to time that I pace up and down in front of houses or among the trees on the square. The strollers smiled at my impatience, but I wasn't waiting for anyone.

TYPIST: I'll never forget you.

LÉTOILE: Like the wind, forgetfulness blows the leaves of bills over the doorsteps of credit, then chases them all away.

TYPIST: There are other whirlwinds—the intoxication of parties and the contradictory orders that you give. It's like when one is lying in the arms of pleasure close to midnight, when the concern of mother and brothers doesn't count any more; one loses all sense of wrongdoing and leans back with closed eyes against the comfort of a tree. The department stores could catch fire; all the prayers could be prayed: the earthly paradise is far. For the time being one returns to the brightly lit bars and in one's heart broods about the barbarous acts which are being committed all over the world.

LÉTOILE: Your way of unfolding the newspaper enchants me, but this young man whom I've had arrested hasn't done anything to you.

TYPIST: Chance dictates the colors that we like. It does not depend on us to stake our happiness on the green. (*She goes and cowers in a corner of the stage.*)

LÉTOILE: The appearance of danger is like your black hair and these little hands along the wall.

She extends her arms along the wall.

What's that supposed to mean: No Thoroughfare? Your adorable silences would tarnish your crown of martyrdom as easily as a little pocket mirror. But there is no exultation on my part. Action means as little to me as anything else, and if you will look carefully at my tie you will not believe that you see the pretty cashmere of lost illusions.

SCENE 12

LEFEBVRE (*enters without knocking*): Me and the boys would like to have a word with you, Chief.

Courtois, Hirsch, and Levy follow him in.

You've made us promise to follow your orders without arguing, but one can't always work without knowing what one's doing.

LÉTOILE: What do you want me to tell you?

HIRSCH: It's like in a prison around here. Moving a pile of rocks around by the sweat of your brow—if you're not condemned right away to do the opposite. As soon as you get on to one track, you're told to get off it.

LÉTOILE: What do you care? Aren't you getting paid?

COURTOIS: All the same, you don't feel right at having all that useless money pass through your hands, as if you were a bank teller. It's hard to give back the pocketbooks. When these acts of apparent honesty are carefully considered, who knows if they won't get the better of us?

Murmurs of approbation.

The other day you had us each disguise ourselves and follow each other around. (*Agitation.*)

LÉTOILE (*getting up and, with his hands in his pockets, looking out of the window*): I don't owe anyone an explanation. If you're not satisfied you can leave. (*He sits down again. A pause.*) Lefebvre, be at the Buttes-Chaumont at nightfall. See that you make yourself agreeable to the first person you see loitering on the bridge. Find means to bring him here. Understood?

LEFEBVRE (*questions his companions with his eyes*): Yes, Chief.

LÉTOILE (*to Levy*): A spherical drop of water takes two minutes to drop from the cloud where it is formed. Assuming that before falling this drop splits into ten separate drops of equal size, how long would it take this bunch of droplets to fall?

I need to know the answer to this problem before tonight. (*To the other two.*) Thank you very much.

They leave.

SCENE 13

The telephone rings.

LÉTOILE (*into the telephone*): Hello! Yes, it's me. . . . Not bad, thanks . . . Nothing . . . Later? Who knows . . . I've seen all the trees lose their leaves for a long time. . . . Over there that's all that one dreams, but over there doesn't exist. There will never be anything but here . . . I observe the drops of rain which are all the moments of my life run down the windowpanes. . . . The hours which will never return anymore seem like centuries. . . . So much the better! I no longer want the pleasures I've desired for such a long time because they are within my reach. I know tomorrow, the day after tomorrow, and all the other days. . . . The future is this same mirror that is always before one's eyes. . . . My ears buzz with the sound of the bells of pride. . . .

SCENE 14

LEFEBVRE (*rushing in*): The cops, Chief—you've just time to get out of here.

LÉTOILE (*in a faraway tone*): You're sure of what you're saying?

A knock at the door.

Who's there?

Silence.

Come in.

THE INSPECTOR: Monsieur Létoile?

LÉTOILE: That's me, in person.

THE INSPECTOR: I have a warrant for your arrest. You will please come with me.

LÉTOILE: Just the time to give one order and then I'm ready.

THE INSPECTOR: You are accused . . .

LÉTOILE: What does that matter to me?

CURTAIN

ACT III

A café at three o'clock in the afternoon.

Doors at rear and at left.

Clock at right. Two card players under the clock.

> MAXIME: thirty years old, blond, Vandyck beard.
> GILDA: A whore.
> AN ALGERIAN PEDDLER

When the curtain rises the card players are playing in silence. Gilda, who is sitting at another table, is drinking a red liqueur. It is raining.

SCENE 1

The waiter passes through and wipes one of the tables. He lifts the curtain and looks out.

FIRST PLAYER: Waiter, a beer.

> *The game starts again. The waiter brings the drink, sits down at the back, and opens a newspaper. Silence.*

SECOND PLAYER: If I'd known that, I wouldn't have trumped.

FIRST PLAYER: You made a mistake. (*He shuffles.*)

> *A newsboy is heard shouting, "La Patrie." Gilda takes a small mirror from her bag and puts on powder and lipstick.*

SCENE 2

Enter Maxime, an umbrella in his hand. He sits down in the back.

MAXIME: Let's see . . . give me a vermouth and something to write with. (*He seems to be groping for his words and keeps looking around. His observation of Gilda becomes more and more marked.*) It's too dark back there. (*He sits down nearer Gilda.*) What weather!

GILDA: It's raining.

A pause.

MAXIME: Aren't you bored?

GILDA: Why?

MAXIME: Are you waiting for someone?

GILDA: No. (*She smiles.*)

MAXIME (*sitting down opposite her*): With your permission.

A pause.

GILDA: I was dreaming that I was still in boarding school. I was wearing that lace collar one last time. They kept a sharp eye on my correspondence: an unknown man will climb over the garden wall this evening. He said to me: "You've been crying because of my mother-of-pearl cheeks." Night will fall. Soon there will be nothing but the windmills.

MAXIME: You can take it or leave it. Interior elegance and the maddest acts of despair. To leave the church throwing candy around.

GILDA: You're not like the others.

MAXIME: How can one not say to oneself several times every day: that won't come back again!

A pause.

GILDA: You haven't finished your letter.

MAXIME: What's the good of giving a sign of life for too long a time? It's 3:15 and I see you.

GILDA: The instinct to please is like a pit. Believe me, rings are nothing. In Paris, on the big boulevards, there is a slope so gentle that almost no one can stop himself from sliding down it.

MAXIME: The most touching maps of the world are the silver globes in which the waiter arranges a napkin from time to time. Caged birds love these little gleaming spheres. It comes to the same thing whether one sings with the street or the sewing machine.

GILDA: I recognize liberty by certain finer signs.

MAXIME: The kingdom of the skies is peopled with assassins. Higher up there's a swing which waits for you. Don't lift your head again.

GILDA: The photographer said: Let's not move.

MAXIME: I don't want to die.

GILDA: Someone has dared to sadden you?

MAXIME: I don't think so; I've only just come in.

GILDA: Are your eyes really that color?

MAXIME: Elbow on the table like naughty children. The fruit of a Christian primary education, if books don't lie, is everything that is golden.

GILDA: In the huts of fishermen one finds those artifical bouquets made up of periwinkles and even a bunch of grapes.

MAXIME: The globe must be lifted up if it is not transparent enough. The fountain of the Observatory at sunrise.

GILDA: The songs of the streets and of the woods are beautiful.

A *pause*.

MAXIME: I won't love you always.

GILDA: I don't ask for any other truth when I go out than the rainbow. Somebody once told me—it was such a long time ago—that I was beautiful; today I know that I am only pretty.

MAXIME: Observe the flight of birds or the wanings of the moon.

GILDA: The numbers that one throws into one's life, the dates of days of sadness are far from my lips.

MAXIME: Corridors and clouds are my whole life. I only know the glimmer of my lamp. You are near me.

GILDA: I am big tonight and only my head exists.

MAXIME: You are a child or the drowsiness of summer.

GILDA: When you say good-bye to me in a few minutes, I will follow you until death.

MAXIME: Past and future are only the present. The market pitchmen, thirst, and all these little quotidian insects. It is day and I am there.

GILDA: Words burn me like spotlights.

MAXIME: You're still thinking about dawns. You say: Over there. I am near you.

GILDA: I dream of forests.

MAXIME: The paths in the fields at dawn. Mad animals and blind beggars listening to us.

GILDA: Why do you laugh?

MAXIME: Midday: the hour of doves and, much later, the evening. Your look and your shoulders before me. The flowers which we both love. Heat dances at full speed. Again these same thoughts which fall and fly: the butterflies of suffering and a dream sweeter than agony.

A *pause.*

GILDA: Automobiles are silent. It will rain blood.

MAXIME: The rats chew up the vines without thinking of tomorrow. The peasant girls don't know fans. Give me your hand and I will love your life.

GILDA: Call me Gilda.

MAXIME: Listen, listen.

GILDA: I am there.

MAXIME: It's tomorrow.

GILDA: The distance, the network of cardinal points. Flags and immense expanses of bunting cover the earth. Fold your hands and breathe softly.

A pause. For some moments Maxime has been holding the stem of an empty glass between the index and middle fingers of his right hand and has been tracing eight diagonal lines on the marble with it. A peddler of carpets, shawls, belts, and so on, has entered. He has started to make his pitch to the card players.

SCENE 3

The Algerian goes to Maxime. He shows a tiger skin which he carries on his shoulders and under which he alternately stretches out and lets fall his arm. A pause.

ALGERIAN: Purse.

A pause. Maxime remains motionless.

Rug. (*A pause.*) Suspenders. (*He shows the suspenders.*)

A pause. The waiter enters and sees the Algerian.

WAITER: Let's go—get out of here.

The Algerian leaves slowly.

SCENE 4

MAXIME: Where do you live?

GILDA: No, no, don't.

MAXIME: What's the matter?

GILDA (*giving him her hand*): Let me leave alone.

MAXIME: Waiter.

WAITER: That'll be three francs, sir.

They get up.

GILDA: Don't insist, sweetheart. You'll regret it. I've got the syph.

MAXIME: Who cares?

They leave.

CURTAIN

A LONG INTERMISSION

ACT IV

NOTE: The authors of *If You Please* do not want the fourth act printed.

the mirror-wardrobe one fine evening

by LOUIS ARAGON

translated by Michael Benedikt

TO ROGER VITRAC

CHARACTERS

THE WOMAN
THE SOLDIER
THE PRESIDENT
THE GENERAL
THE TWO SISTERS
THE MAN
THEODORE FRAENKEL
JULES
LENORE
MADAME LEON

In front of the curtain, a French soldier, twenty years old, meets a nude woman wearing a large hat with flowers and carrying a baby carriage on her shoulders.

THE WOMAN: Soldier!

THE SOLDIER: At your service.

THE WOMAN: Have you seen a tree anywhere along this road? This bundle of mine is warm.

THE SOLDIER: You won't find any for at least a league, Madame or Mademoiselle?

THE WOMAN: Madame.

THE SOLDIER: But I could hold out my arms, and you could sit down in my shadow.

THE WOMAN: As if one God weren't enough. (*She sits down.*) It's a hard time, Soldier, we find ourselves living in. Life is no joke.

THE SOLDIER: Obedience is all I know.

THE WOMAN: And I, my baby carriage. Do you think we'll have another of those wars?

THE SOLDIER (*modestly*): I fire rifles magnificently, and some people even say nice things about me, but that's all foolishness.

THE WOMAN: I'm not very fond of people who fire rifles, because sooner or later it comes out in their behavior; you seem honest, though.

THE SOLDIER: Oh, I'm disciplined.

THE WOMAN: Happy?

THE SOLDIER: No I'm not happy. I'm disciplined.

THE WOMAN: So goes the whole world, it seems: you can't do two things at once. I don't feel much like doing anything.

THE SOLDIER: You mustn't let everything go to pieces, now.

THE WOMAN: It must be, it must not be: I think, sometimes, if I were in the Americas somewhere . . . But it would still be the same story.

177

THE SOLDIER: What's troubling you, little lady? You seem to be at loose ends.

THE WOMAN: It's the times we live in, I tell you: there is no place for us in this scheme of things. There's even too little elbow room in dreams.

THE SOLDIER: Sometimes I too feel that way. It is, however, not the fault of the government: some call them traitors, but their only concern is for the rest and happiness of the army. For instance, the other day in the town square, the President of the Republic . . .

THE WOMAN: Quiet, Soldier, here he is now with a Negro general.

The Woman and The Soldier stand off to one side. Enter The President, in evening clothes with the ribbon of the Legion of Honor, together with the Negro general. The latter wears white suede knee breeches, an ornamented jacket, an admiral's hat with red and green plumes, numerous medals, an unsheathed sword stuck in his belt, a pearl necklace around his throat, stars spangled on his sleeves; and in his left hand he holds an ocarina.

THE PRESIDENT: Yes, General, we are damned. Here I am the highest officer of the Republic; a fat lot of good it does me.

THE GENERAL: With that magnificent red scarf? In my country the same word signifies red and perfect contentment.

THE PRESIDENT: Have we ever been able to be happy? I know very little about it, but our era bears the brand of a red-hot iron.

THE GENERAL: Red and perfectly content, Paris is a lovely city.

THE PRESIDENT: In the depths of their hearts people grow poisonous plants. There is no longer peace for anyone: some vast change has come over the world today.

THE GENERAL: Red and perfectly content, your presidential Majesty, and all those pretty white Frenchwomen?

THE PRESIDENT: I've sampled every kind of debauch, General; I've even tried out virtue. Very soon, believe me, old humanity is going to become conscious of its cancer, and then we'll be the witnesses of its suicide.

THE GENERAL: Mr. President, I have never been sick a day in my life; I believe in duty, in hygiene, and in civilization (*He makes the motion of pressing a button.*): electric light. (*He laughs.*)

THE PRESIDENT: General, you are an idiot; I hereby promote you to field marshal.

The Siamese-twin sisters enter and curtsy before The President.

What can I do for you, ladies?

THE TWO SISTERS (*together*): I would like your autograph, Mr. President, for my album.

THE PRESIDENT (*signing the albums*): Anything else?

THE TWO SISTERS: Permission for us to get married separately.

THE PRESIDENT: Granted, granted. But please don't both speak at once.

The two Siamese sisters clap their hands and express their great joy in a dance.

Poor hideous pleasures of mankind! Here are two happy women. Saint Vitus' dance, would you say, General?

THE GENERAL: The rose O that rose, please excuse me Mr. President. (*He goes over to the sisters and begins to pay court to the one dressed in pink.*)

THE PRESIDENT: There goes my new field marshal off on a campaign. Let's not disturb him. (*He begins to go out but notices the soldier kissing the nude woman.*) So, those people too. A pitiful spectacle.

A man on a tricycle goes by: in sport clothes, with gray hair, fifty years old, in a cap, and with a nose so long that it touches his chest; he has to lift it to speak.

Well, sir, what do you think of these people?

THE MAN: I don't bother with people, and I didn't ask you any questions either. I have my own interests. There's an appropriate time for everything in this life of ours. (*He crosses the stage on his tricycle, and exits.*)

THE PRESIDENT: There are married people, and there are single people. There are also lovers.

The curtain opens to let Theodore Fraenkel come out, arm-in-arm with a woman dressed in the latest fashions, except for a medieval hennin she wears on her head; in her left hand she holds a metal banner which is painted red.

But who are these other people?

THEODORE FRAENKEL (*bowing*): Mr. President, it is I, Theodore Fraenkel; and naturally here with me is a fairy.

THE PRESIDENT: A fairy? There are still fairies in the twentieth century? It's certainly hard to keep up with all that goes on in just one epoch. But how can she be a fairy?

THEODORE FRAENKEL: She is a fairy because she is with me.

THE PRESIDENT: Tell me, is this lady mute?

THEODORE FRAENKEL: Naturally, since she is with me.

THE PRESIDENT: And what are you doing here in these barren climes?

THEODORE FRAENKEL: We have come to tell you that the play is about to begin and that you are boring everybody with your lamentations. Go, get out of here, shoo!

THE PRESIDENT: What's this? What's this? To the President of the Republic himself? (*To The General.*) Marshal, arrest this impudent fellow.

THE GENERAL (*without troubling himself to move, to The Soldier*): Soldier, hey! you there! You, trooper, take this couple into custody.

The Soldier, far too busy, does not move.

THE PRESIDENT: Well, will you look at this!

The stagehands bring out a big wardrobe with mirrors on the doors, running into and upsetting everybody.

THEODORE FRAENKEL: You see that you're hindering these maneuvers—disappear, you people of every description: the world must become the world again.

All exit, disturbed by the stagehands who carry the wardrobe onstage.

THE CURTAIN RISES

A vulgarly furnished room. To the right, a window facing the street, and a recessed door. To the left, upstage, a cupboard hidden by a flowery curtain. Downstage, a door, and, in a place cut out of the wall, a little dining alcove. Downstage a wardrobe with mirrored doors faces the audience. Some prints are on the walls, and a glossy cardboard calendar pictures "Springtime."

Lenore, leaning back spread-eagled against the wardrobe, eyes staring fixedly; Jules enters at the right.

JULES: Are the stars any less brilliant when he returns than when he leaves? Blue fly. (*He throws his hat on one of the chairs and pulls a hammer out of his pocket.*) I've bought a hammer.

LENORE: To kill with?

JULES: To drive in nails, for sure, and then to pull them out also.

LENORE (*cries out*): Claws!

JULES (*astonished*): You wept while I was gone?

LENORE: Nasty looks.

JULES: Afraid?

LENORE: Afraid, yes, that's the word for it. Of the wind and of space itself, of the birds between the sun and myself, my sun far off on the roads, buying hammers.

JULES: You little rat. But who's nailed you to the armoire? my little owlet, hoot, hoot. (*He takes a step toward her.*)

LENORE (*cries*): Don't come any closer.

JULES (*stops short*): It's the hammer (*He throws it on his hat.*): here are my two bare hands.

LENORE: Knock wood!

JULES: Oho, solitude depresses you, Madame; permit me lightly to touch the hem of your dress. (*He does, and Lenore pulls her hem away from him.*) Hey ho.

LENORE: Your breath.

JULES: The drama: but I'm going to clutch you in my arms as the young handsome Roman does the Sabine woman in the painting a copy of which is at the lady attorney's office. (*He takes a step forward.*)

LENORE (*cries*): Don't open the wardrobe, don't open the wardrobe!

JULES (*stops, as if suddenly struck with an idea*): Oh, well, that's different. (*He turns around, returns to stage right, takes off his jacket and hangs it up on one of the hooks; he unhooks his smoking-jacket; he puts it on, goes back to the table, takes some cigarettes out of the drawer, takes one out of the pack, taps it against the table and then suddenly stops, concentrating, places the cigarette on the table, and lets the contents of a box of matches which he had just opened fall to the floor.*) And why should I not open the wardrobe?

She stops crying.

My fingers are certainly supple enough to turn a key in a keyhole, my fingers of a strangler, you always say.

LENORE: If you open it, then the sun and the stars will go out, the rain will penetrate my bones and your black eyes; and nobody will come at night to install in these walls those venetian blinds that rattle, plock, plick, plick, in the wind.

JULES: So? So. Always to follow every whim of the little sage plant which grows in my house. Walk on your hands, sit down in the fireplace, you will not open the wardrobe—but come along now: you're only too happy, my friend, only too happy to be this dog lying beside Lenore of the Portals of Paradise. I will not open the wardrobe. (*He takes his cigarette from the table, looks at the floor, puts his cigarette back on the table, crouches, and begins to gather up the matches*)

Pause.

LENORE (*motionless still*): Blunderer, I have a lover; you can bet on it.

JULES (*throws the matches he's collected to the floor, kneels and begins to make two rows with them, one on the right, the other on the left*): One, two; one, two; one, two . . .

LENORE: The hammer, if I have a lover.

JULES: Not savage enough, one, two . . .

LENORE: You've loved me like the morning air.

JULES: One, two, the fragrance of strawberries, one, two . . .

LENORE: Fire, blood.

JULES: Blunderer: drama gone wrong, verbena from the crags. The carnivore has his confidence.

LENORE: A stupid confidence.

JULES (*lights his cigarette*): At the time of day for homecoming, the white walls are vast caresses for a man who's found only heaps of pebbles all day long, and ditches and signboards whose arrows say: Be on your way. It's sweet, too, that look flowing from your eyes, the honey which for ten years I've vainly pursued through the hives of villages and cities; and here is my honeybee now.

LENORE: Man? Man with the teeth of a wolf.

JULES: You speak, what would you speak?

LENORE: I do not want to lie.

JULES: With such lovely eyes?

LENORE: You see, you don't believe me. You see.

JULES: Oh, listen now, this hammer. (*He grasps it.*)

LENORE (*cries*): Don't hurt me.

JULES (*puts down the hammer*): So you think, then, that I'm running after some salamander, less lovely than you, always less lovely; go on now, I'm not so mad, even with all my folly.

LENORE: Ah, you Chinaman.

JULES: Today I saw the first chestnut seller. Since last year.

LENORE: One year.

JULES: But why do you stay crucified this way, Lenore? Don't you want to caress my face with your hands, so like daisies?

LENORE: Is there not one speck of dust in your eyes? Poor idiot that I am! There is only this hope: no matter what you say, you would like to open the wardrobe.

JULES: End this game, Lenore; I have nettles in my palms. Come here, and let's have no more talk about the wardrobe.

LENORE (*motionless, in a hollow voice*): To speak no more, to see no more, to think no more, is the promised land.

JULES (*in an outburst of anger*): Enough, enough, do you understand? The patience of an angel (*He stalks about.*): of an angel.

LENORE (*she bites her knuckles*): Oh, oh, here is his anger now. He'll begin to beat you, to crush you beneath his blows.

JULES (*in a fury*): You'd think that someone were listening to you in here.

LENORE (*glances furtively at the wardrobe*): Someone who listens to me in the depths of his own dark night.

JULES: The briefest jokes are the best.

LENORE: Don't pull my hair, don't clutch my neck, don't bruise my wrists.

JULES: Come on now, Leni, aren't you going to cook supper?

LENORE: Look at this fool thinking about eating now.

JULES: I'm telling you to stop playing this game.

LENORE: Sooner or later, let the wind howl or die down, he will want to open the wardrobe.

JULES: I'm in no mood to laugh or listen to you.

LENORE: You want to open it, I see the sun of wanting to open it rising in your eyes, black, red, and horrible. (*She screams.*)

JULES (*grasping his wife's right wrist*): Perhaps this will put an end to all this. Still, I've nothing to gain from it.

LENORE: All your life before this closed door without understanding why? There is always one moment when you'll want it opened.

JULES: Not one more word out of you. Do it yourself, then!

LENORE: No, I won't do that. The abyss, and this horror, myself, I can't. (*She hides her eyes beneath her left hand; Jules draws her over to him.*)

JULES: Come on now and cook supper: I can't stand these dramas we keep playing. They look too much like the face of life itself to me. A beautiful face, it's true. (*He kisses her forehead, and she recoils a little.*)

You little savage!

LENORE: You who know the hours of the conjunctions of planets, Jules. . . .

JULES: What?

LENORE: A woman married a man.

JULES: Obviously.

LENORE: No, no: suddenly nothing's able to hold her back, another man covers her with caresses and she's like a signal lost in the midst of the tracks. For a whole day forests could burn on the mountains, she no longer knows fire or water. Is it good, is it evil? A woman married to a man?

JULES: Good, evil what do they mean? But let them hide: and for sure the husband will kill them. Good, evil. (*Evasive gesture with his hand.*)

LENORE: For sure. At some moment misfortune comes in and it is like the nose in the middle of your face. She believes that she might know how to lie and suddenly she is thrown before the wardrobe.

JULES (*bursts into laughter*): I've guessed the meaning of this charade now. (*Deep voice.*) Madame, you're deceiving me. (*He moves toward the wardrobe; she stops him.*)

LENORE: One day in May with a light breeze blowing from the south the planter of Caïffa moved away down the road and we were alone beneath the willows and in the empty meadow.

JULES: What game are you stalking in my memory? Partridges in the woods.

LENORE (*wrings her hands*): To what end, here is the wardrobe where willows and partridges die.

JULES: Still at it? Your eyes are even red, calm yourself.

LENORE: Calm, calm as the willows. In the meadow, Lenore once, and a black man, strong as the willows over heads, Lenore once, and later they will say, Lenore again, poor Lenore. (*She sobs.*)

JULES (*takes her in his arms*): But you do weep now, Leni? It's my fault too; aren't I the one who gave you the taste for these endless fictions of yours. And that here you are caught in the net now, my swallow, in the net of my two arms. What has nested in your head while I traveled every road on my bicycle and acted the big businessman: and my oil tankers took on gasoline in the Gulf of Mexico; and then in all the stock exchanges of the world, what a great racket! The bankers paled before the little snakes of zeroes uncoiling upon their tables; and I, toward the house on the hill, when I returned, carried to my Leni a magnificent bronze allegorical group for a mantelpiece: Gasoline flowed from a well, in order to have a meeting with Happiness. Hammer in my pocket: when my hand met it, the gasoline all flew away. To chase away the monsters from your pretty head, we have only to open up their den. (*He reaches toward the wardrobe with one hand; his hand on the key, he pauses a long while; he looks at the motionless Lenore, eyes hidden behind her hand.*) You aren't going to stop me? Suddenly I don't even understand my own thoughts any more.

LENORE: Sometimes.

JULES: She outdoes me entirely (you can trumpet in pride). What's in the wardrobe, Lenore? When you look like that I could kill you. (*He jerks her by the wrist.*) I don't know what I'm doing any more. I'm a farmer, shaking you like a plum tree. And after all. (*Pause.*) Yes, but . . . Your words, I wasn't listening at first, the game, then everything comes back and takes shape: the wind, the stars, and the whole kit and caboodle. It's a stupid thing to say, Leni; it's stupid.

LENORE: Yes, don't make those spider eyes at me; open up instead.

JULES: You're the one who . . . But to be before it, myself, to have done with nights more than days, this milk where our arms form great infinity signs of clarity like this (*He draws in the air several 8's lying down.*), to have done with this skirt of the sky your dress, and the surprise while I sleep if I stretch a peach-like breast beneath my fingers which by degrees feel the hard pit through the fruit, to have done with our lies, this hide-and-seek, the hill and the roof over our heads, and with your hair my girl (*He roughly musses her hair; the hair falls down over Lenore's face; Jules's hand stays as if caught there; he lifts it again with the veil of hair tangled in it, then.*), oh, no, my little one, I'm not the person you took me for.

LENORE: Don't break my heart.

JULES (*abjectly*): Tell me what's in the wardrobe, then.

LENORE: You know very well what I always say about your fingers. The key.

JULES: The key to the mystery, yes; Leni, keep me from opening that door, or I'll become mad as the mad can ever be.

LENORE: Like madmen with red eyes? The hammer. Open.

JULES: What if I killed you before I opened it?

LENORE (*cowers and hides her face in her hair*): That is the final horror.

JULES (*picks up the hammer*): All this staggers the imagination. I was coming home with my riches, I, the builder of villages far off in the west. Customs officers chalked signs on my tank cars. Here was I, the upset mind of this now unkempt cat (*He makes the motions of washing his hands.*) was there, on the floor, and in the wardrobe there is something most distasteful, if we are to believe Lenore, a highly sensible person. Open it? No.

LENORE: Are you joking?

JULES: Joking? Speak for yourself. Since you're so eager to.

LENORE: Open it.

JULES: There's food for thought. All this haste! I obey. (*He reaches out, then changes his mind.*) You didn't flinch one bit. *His* suffering, therefore, is more odious to you than death. . . . He's smothering, isn't he? Yes, that's it. Who is he?

LENORE: Why are you asking me? Open it.

JULES: Who is he?

LENORE: Open it now, you won't believe me.

JULES: For example, who? For example, a hunchback, with you swooning as you know to do so well, your eyes, and your hand furtively upon his hump—to bring you luck.

LENORE: Open it.

JULES: The expression on his face now must be quite something, there in that box of his. (*He brandishes his hammer in the air.*) Do you hear me, you ox? I called him an ox. His name?

LENORE: The red front.

JULES: I've sought in vain . . . some peasant, the carcass.

LENORE: Jules.

JULES: Madame will excuse me. Yesterday I had the milky way in my eyes. His name, and I open it. Wall. Is he very handsome, at least? he who is about to die. You're afraid for him, eh? Let's guess what he looks like. Fair or dark? Thin lips? Well, then, a redhead. Well built, I'll bet. And with fine teeth—on this point you're quite demanding. Does he kiss to the death? Has he my arms, my hands which carry you God knows where? Like a sunflower you were, and you would blush. You won't say anything?

LENORE: Speak to the fire.

JULES: Filthy wretch.

A woman's head appears at the window: he changes his tone of voice.

Oh, look, it's Madame Leon, how is Madame Leon today?

MADAME LEON (*through the window*): Well, now, I'm tired; can I come in?

JULES: By all means.

Madame Leon disappears; Jules pushes Lenore into the alcove.

Your hair is a mess.

Lenore goes out; Jules opens the door.

MADAME LEON: You're alone?

JULES: Lenore.

MADAME LEON: Have you seen Leon lately? I've been after him since early this morning.

JULES: Sit down, Madame Leon, I haven't seen anybody.

MADAME LEON: Don't mind if I do. (*She sits down.*) He didn't come home for lunch, and I've been alone all day and here it is the evening.

JULES: I was in town: buying this hammer here.

MADAME LEON: A fine-looking hammer.

JULES: Isn't it? and so well made. No, nobody. But who knows, Lenore. (*Shouting.*) Lenore, Madame Leon! Even she's been afraid lately.

MADAME LEON: Afraid?

JULES: Oh, you know how it is, a creaking door, a lonely house.

MADAME LEON: I know how that feels—in broad daylight, too.

JULES: In broad daylight, obviously in broad daylight. A regular child, and when the night comes . . .

MADAME LEON: At night you're home.

JULES: Yes, alone with a man in a lonely place, at night.

MADAME LEON: Right, her husband. Ah, me.

JULES: You can picture that easily I can see, Madame Leon. (*He laughs loudly.*) With Leon.

Lenore appears, hair pulled back tightly, a handkerchief clasped in her left hand.

MADAME LEON: Good afternoon, neighbor.

LENORE: Good afternoon, Madame.

All three sit down, Jules in the middle.

MADAME LEON: Well, I see something's happened to your hair-do.

JULES (*noticing it suddenly*): Why, look! She's like the old saying come to life: not one hair out of place.

MADAME LEON: Such a pity, your hair was so pretty.

LENORE (*absent-mindedly runs her hand through her hair, and smiles*): It's of so little importance, so little.

MADAME LEON: Right, Madame Jules, but how does your husband feel?

JULES: It's not his hair.

Madame Leon laughs.

Have you seen Leon today?

LENORE: Me?—I haven't seen anybody.

JULES: No fibs now, my love, Leon I mean.

LENORE: Leon? Never Leon, certainly.

MADAME LEON: That means I've run over here again for nothing —and that's quite a climb, that hill of yours. I'm done in.

LENORE: You're looking for your husband?

MADAME LEON: Ever since this morning when he left me saying: in just two little minutes. Probably he's wandering around, drunk, getting ready to come back to me in a great state, or worse—and babbling to anybody who'll listen, and who'll have to revive him for me.

LENORE: Really, Madame Leon, aren't you ashamed, in front of us, who'll probably laugh the moment you're out the door? You know yourself there's no finer thing, even if he's un- faithful or untruthful, than your better half, whether he re- turns early or late.

MADAME LEON: Neighbor, you're always defending him, and he's always reminding me you are, in a way that could make a saint jealous.

JULES: The old fox!

LENORE: Do you think you're going to find this lost Leon under my skirts perhaps? You could sleep as soundly as you please; and he could go on staring as much as he wants.

MADAME LEON: It's been known to happen. . . .

LENORE: Look under the furniture, open all the closets.

MADAME LEON: Without even dreaming of quarreling, neighbor, I was going by, and, since I was going by, stopped for a bit of a rest and a bit of a visit. Two birds with one stone. But I'm leaving you right now, and you can stop laughing at me right now, you who are always together on earth. Good-bye, neighbor. Monsieur Jules.

After shaking hands, Jules accompanies her to the door, while Lenore slowly wanders across the stage.

JULES: There's no finer thing, even if he's unfaithful or untruthful, mumble and bumble and huff and puff, is that the way you put it? And under the furniture and in ALL the closets. Quite a speech.

LENORE: Her husband isn't the only man in the world.

JULES: You mean there's some other man besides me?

LENORE: Hundreds and hundreds, sweet as berries, muscular as subways, tender as needlework.

JULES: Very provocative. But, if you please, what about our little indoor Vesuvius?

LENORE: Go and open it.

JULES: Right now, caterpillar. You're yawning? You're obviously pretending.

LENORE: Pretending?

JULES: The ingenue part. Then fix your hair like a nun's. Undo it, and rid me of that, go on, go on.

She eludes his grasp.

LENORE: As ugly as can be, as ugly as can be, is that to be it? For my friend the hunchback, position's the only problem (*She stands on a chair and bursts into laughter.*): he's like a husband.

JULES: A husband, it's a question of me, then. Descend, O arc of the sky, so I may unroll you with only one foot. (*He trips her up, she falls to her knees; a long pause; he musses her hair again.*) Sorceress, with your hair your single defect. Your beautiful hair.

LENORE: The jasmine.

He turns her over, face to the floor.

JULES: It's the perfume he breathed in all day while somebody else was looking for him where still other intoxicants are sold, your handsome Leon, snow of chimneys, and here he dragged that great body of his; and placed his lips. A fine specimen.

LENORE: Leon?

JULES: Not him? Whomever you want. What's his name to me? I can see him gnawing your shoulder from here. (*He gnaws at her shoulder.*) His name, in God's name.

LENORE: Peasant, peasant, I'm bleeding. (*She rubs her shoulder and examines her fingers.*) Open it and let's have some peace.

JULES: You never deviate one moment! Listen, this creaks too. (*He grinds his teeth near Lenore's ear; she bounds up and runs toward the wardrobe.*)

LENORE: Idiot, look.

He stops her by brandishing his hammer.

JULES: One more step and you'll get this hammer.

LENORE: You're just trying to scare me.

He walks slowly toward her; she watches him approaching, hammer raised, in the mirror; she tries to cry out, and cannot; he indicates the mirror with his hammer.

JULES: This vertical lake separates you, my little lambs. She looks deep within the mirror for the look she is still quite drunken from, but sees only her own shell, emptied by terror—and it's all to make me feel pity.

LENORE: Believing unbeliever, believing, believing.

JULES: Do you think he can hear you? In spite of it all—how it lasts—an insane hope—but suppose he should have to sneeze?

Lenore laughs.

You're laughing; stand back, he might signal to you. How? I know about all those tricks. Once, before I became your harness, I had my period of stepping through windows, slipping into closets—and those passionate gleams in women's eyes. Seven hours once—seven deadly winter hours—I stayed in a darkened room, prevented from leaving or even breathing. Somewhere in the mountains, where people are hard and quick to use firearms. And so I reach into a dim past, and cannot be told: you were there or there on such and such a day; no, not by anyone. I myself have forgotten—pffft! And tomorrow, speaking of Leon, or of anybody else, and you, I'll be able to say: you are precisely there, and the hole longer than it is wide, and the soil carefully heaped up, and the four elements over your accursed heads. His name, quickly, for the sake of good manners. (*He steps back and sees himself in the mirror.*) Look at you, Jules, a man who wants to rule. (*He steps away.*) You feel it in your back, a sweating body that has been rolling about with your wife. Smash him between yourself and the wall. (*He hurls himself upon his image, arms outspread.*) Jules the husband. (*He obscures the reflection of his face with his breath on the mirror, raises the hammer, strikes; the glass shatters; Lenore cries out.*) That could penetrate your heart, slivers of glass. But only a star, a large star, bars my way. Or a spider, evening spider. Who of us three can now still nourish the least flea of hope in his heart—(*Turning toward Lenore.*) can you?

LENORE: The glass is broken; whose the glove? Seven years. What a face the hammer has. Jules, Jules. You know at night when birds' wings tap against the roof tiles and I press against your body and you murmur in my hair sleepy words like revolving beacons . . . my little breasts and how nervously I laugh when you stroke my back right where the shoulders die away. Jules, when I take off my dress, and you sit down, looking at me, swinging your hand, Jules, when your face starts to dance . . . I'm too afraid. (*She dashes toward the door; Jules throws the hammer across the stage; it falls at Lenore's feet; she stops and looks at it.*)

JULES: It's a remarkable sight; it's quite out of the ordinary. The hammer on the floor, overhead the roof, and over the roof the sky, all the summer evening sky, all the last sky of your life, vast, vast with its small bullfinch singers of regret after regret, a thousand joyous thoughts, bravo the single cloud of gold, and the sun which will never again set or rise, but will run henceforth like a madman along the roads and into the beds of shameless women, laughing, endlessly laughing. His arms are ready to defend you, his fine strong arms of some other day, prisoners it's sad to say, behind a broken glass. There are my hands—and my rage—one summer's night. You know them, these thick hands, opium and machinery, coming to meet you, these hands which used to make you feel like some warm breeze in the suburbs.

He chases her while speaking to her, as far as the alcove. They pause; then go out. A long pause. While night falls, the calendar on the wall becomes luminous, bats enter through the window and land in the curtains. Jules comes in again, his hair in disorder, tie unknotted. He wipes his mouth. He looks at his hands, the alcove, then at the wardrobe. He goes very calmly toward the wardrobe, then changes his mind and returns, whistling quietly, and searches for the hammer in front of the door. Once again before the mirror, he notices his tie undone, places the hammer on the floor, painstakingly reties his knot, smoothes down his hair, picks up the hammer and, holding it high in his left hand, quickly opens the right hand door of the wardrobe. It is nearly night. Visible coming out of the wardrobe are all the characters of the prologue holding one another by the hand; they walk forward while darkness slowly falls on the stage and while the curtain falls. They join arm in arm then and dance a jig, then all sit down on the ground. Theodore Fraenkel rises.

THEODORE FRAENKEL: It's a perfect moment to talk politics.

He leads The President to the prompter's box, then sits down again—music.

THE PRESIDENT (*sings*): The tree in love with a housemaid
To the passer-by sang this refrain
Ivies reduce the fear
Of the woman we have here

My arms of bark my arms of birds
Clasp the air I breathe,
Her two legs are a scissors
On which the wind is cut

Into the kitchen a ship
Comes each evening
And it is the sun which goes overturning
Upon its skin.

The red hands the bloody hands
Whose hands

Sun's hands. Unoccupied hands
Will fly away

A force leans toward the water
The trees
She has picked the sweet clover
As far as my shadow.

The room and the stage are in total darkness. When the lights go on again, the stage is empty and the orchestra begins to play regimental band music.

a circus story

A PLAY FOR READING

by ARMAND SALACROU

translated by Michael Benedikt

CHARACTERS

THE ACROBAT
THE EQUESTRIAN
THE RINGMASTER
THE MAGICIAN
THE YOUNG MAN
MR. LOYAL
FIRST CLOWN
SECOND CLOWN
THIRD CLOWN
AUDIENCE
A JUGGLER, nonspeaking part
A GIRL
EIGHT MEN IN EVENING DRESS, nonspeaking parts
THE HEARSE DRIVER, one of the Eight Men in Evening Dress

In the tent of a traveling circus.

From stage right an Acrobat in red tights runs on; an Equestrian in white tights runs on from stage left.

Bows. The Audience applauds. The music begins a new rhythm. The Acrobat and The Equestrian, face to face, bow to each other elaborately—then each seizes his flying trapeze. The two trapezes swing closer and closer together; The Acrobat and The Equestrian exchange trapezes in mid-air.

Much applause.

The Equestrian wipes her hands on the handkerchief left by The Acrobat on his trapeze; The Acrobat picks up the handkerchief left by the rider on hers. Another silent exchange of trapezes.

THE ACROBAT (*shouting to The Equestrian over the music as he passes high about her*): Love of my life!

> *The Equestrian hears and, smiling now, catches her trapeze once again; she wipes her hands on the handkerchief. Below, on the circus platform, two clowns hug themselves, as if thrilled by such a show of dexterity. The Acrobat looks down at them.*

An embrace and death!

> *The music grows agitated, the trapezes fly; The Equestrian risks disaster now. The Audience stares open-mouthed; and The Acrobat nearly faints at every simulated fall.*

> *At last, within the arcs of the aerial circles, they are both ready. A bow. A second bow. The exchange of trapezes is nearly complete . . . No. The Acrobat has flipped like a pancake: he throws himself bodily at The Equestrian between the two trapezes, and the couple fall, perpendicularly.*

Admirable geometrical figure.

> *The Acrobat has landed on his back. The Equestrian untangles herself from the body, and, foot on the stomach of her friend, arms folded across her chest, she shouts to The Audience.*

THE EQUESTRIAN: And there you are!

> *The Audience, reassured, applauds. The two clowns carry off their poor dead friend.*

THE RINGMASTER: She's really done that once too often.

Final bow.

The rider returns to throw a kiss.

Alas! The young man has seen The Equestrian's eyes.

Different music. Tables covered with a wide variety of disconcertingly unrelated objects are carried on—and a Man in Evening Dress steps forward.

MAN IN EVENING DRESS: I am the Magician. (*At once he picks up a saxophone and begins to blow smoke out of it, puffing like a Turk; then he takes out his watch, and throws it in the air. The two golden covers on both sides open up and begin to beat like wings: it has become a cuckoo which flies around for a few moments before finding its niche below a dial; every quarter-hour it appears for a breath of air.*)

Finally The Magician taps the table with his magic wand.

THE MAGICIAN: Ladies and gentlemen, I can, if you will, make things materialize anywhere you wish.

Wriggling over the hats of protesting ladies, walking on the eyes of children, and steadying himself by holding onto the breasts of young women, a tall figure climbs down from the heights of the circus tent: a Young Man who finally sprawls before The Magician's table.

What a lot of fuss!

THE YOUNG MAN: Nevertheless, sir, I'll do what I can—only, unfortunately I can't do very much. I was well brought up but now I've lost my good manners. (*He notices The Equestrian; he wants to throw her a kiss, and gestures elaborately. But, with the motion of his kiss, his dirty gauntlet is thrown in the air; it flies up and then falls back again, like a muddy leaf.*) I was well brought up—but now I've lost. . . .

THE MAGICIAN (*whispering*): Are you the new ringmaster?

THE YOUNG MAN: I am in love.

THE MAGICIAN (*somewhat disturbed*): What do you want here? Do you want a rabbit to come out of your hat?

The Young Man removes his hat; but no rabbit is there.

. . . Or your fingers to turn into cigarettes?

But The Young Man has never chewed his fingernails.

. . . Or coins to appear in your handkerchief?

THE YOUNG MAN: Oh! The handkerchief, yes, the handkerchief . . .

THE MAGICIAN (*becoming more and more disturbed*): Ladies and gentlemen, we will now see, out of a simple, ordinary pocket handkerchief . . .

THE YOUNG MAN: No, I want her handkerchief. (*He points to The Equestrian's handkerchief.*)

THE MAGICIAN (*whispering*): Are you trying to make a fool of me?

THE YOUNG MAN (*very loudly*): Yes or no, are you able to make things materialize anywhere you want?

THE MAGICIAN (*in a small voice*): Yes . . .

THE YOUNG MAN: Then send my love to The Equestrian's breast, and into her heart . . . her heart.

THE MAGICIAN (*reassured, but still whispering*): You'll pay for that, you pig.
Ladies and gentlemen, all this is mere child's play. We'll speed up now to get to the really hard part. I have barely, up to now, given you a glimpse of my power. . . .

THE AUDIENCE: No, no, do what the lover wants!

THE MAGICIAN (*picking up a rifle and a bullet*): Note well that if this is an ordinary rifle I have here, the kind you might even kill yourself with, this is not an ordinary bullet. Compounded with utmost care for your amazement, I put it in the barrel of this rifle. . . . (*The Magician puts the rifle to his shoulder, and fires. Out of the barrel emerges, first of all, a long coil of black material, which, at the sound of the explosion, expands: it becomes an umbrella which The Magician holds out to the spectators.*) Is this not truly unprecedented?

THE AUDIENCE: The lover! The lover! The lover!

THE MAGICIAN (*whispering*): Ah! You pig! Get out of here. Now then, ladies and gentlemen, and you too, my dear young ladies, I shall begin. First of all I need a soap bubble, a pure bubble, imprisoning a sigh of love. (*The Magician begins to blow into a white pipe, in the direction of The Equestrian. From the froth concealed in the pipe a large bubble forms, gleaming. With great dexterity The Magician substitutes a large silver ball for it.*) Here it is, but it looks to me as if somebody's already been tampering with it. (*He taps the ball with his magic wand; it breaks open.*)

(*Inside is another ball, green, and a little smaller than the first. Another tap, another ball, yellow in color. Another tap, another ball, this one pink. Rather like a rose shedding its petals. Finally there remains only a tiny purple ball.*) And there you are. Now, Young Man, swallow it.

THE YOUNG MAN (*putting the ball in his mouth and making strenuous efforts*): I don't know how to swallow.

THE MAGICIAN (*whispering*): Oh, you swine, you swine!

The Young Man, frightened, crunches down on the ball, rips his gums, bleeds, and spits out blood.

(*To save the situation.*) He's bleeding? Isn't that already the beginning of love? Madame's heart is inside his breast.

The Young Man nearly faints.

And now the second, and most difficult, section of the operation . . . (*The Magician picks up a plate upon which he balances a bowl. A deft spin. He puts this assemblage on top of another spinning plate. The entire assemblage rotates faster and faster, until it looks like a white flower.*)

The Magician, to applause from The Audience, places it in the trembling hands of The Young Man and says to him:

Offer it to Madame, on your knees, and your prayers will be answered.

The Young Man brings the flower to The Equestrian, who laughingly accepts it and pins it to her white costume. There it disappears. White on white, as all the painters will tell you . . .

Do you feel your love for this Young Man now, Madame?

THE EQUESTRIAN: A deep, unforeseen, unalterable love . . .

The Young Man nearly faints again.

THE YOUNG MAN: My beloved!

Laughter and applause.

THE EQUESTRIAN: The Young Man will now try, for the love of me, and for the first time, the flying trapeze. . . . Up you go—I wish it.

THE MAGICIAN: Well done, my little pig.

The Young Man catches one of the trapezes. He is very clumsy. The Audience is convulsed.

THE EQUESTRIAN: Change trapezes!

The Young Man tries to leap into space. He even catches the other trapeze, but his feet stay caught to the one he would leave behind. There he remains, stretched over emptiness, fixed by his hands and feet to two motionless trapezes.

The Magician swiftly unhooks the tension wire. The trapeze retaining the feet of The Young Man falls. The Young Man tries to get a better grip on the other, but slips off it. Fall. Laughter of The Audience. He is on his knees before The Equestrian. The Audience applauds.

THE YOUNG MAN (*to The Equestrian*): I did the best I could.

The Audience cheers.

THE EQUESTRIAN: And now your number's over.

THE YOUNG MAN: What, you're not going to love me for the rest of our lives?

The Young Man turns sadly to The Magician, who, sleeves rolled up, hands held out in the spotlight, is wiggling his fingers: out fall cigars, oranges, coins, eggs. Suddenly fingers begin to fall from his fingers, then hands from his hands. Every time he opens his hand a new hand appears inside. . . . Now he presents two staffs of interwoven hands rising erect as hyacinths, colored like flesh.

He plants the two newest hands in the ground, raises his legs in the air; his feet touch the ceiling of the tent and attach themselves there.

Then, from hand to hand, his utensils are passed upward.

The platform is empty. A clash of a cymbal.

Darkness.

A note on the saxophone, very prolonged.

Light.

The platform is covered with old pairs of gloves, with thousands of old gloves.

MR. LOYAL: Here come the clowns!

A big fat Clown walks with great difficulty across the hills of gloves.

His performance begins as he takes off his huge overcoat and takes out of his trouser pockets two little Clowns, holding them by their arms.

The three Clowns gather up the gloves. As if they do not know where to put them, they begin putting them on, one after and over another. Their hands become gigantic. Beneath the last of the gloves they find The Young Man stretched out. The Clowns stare at The Young Man; then begin a discussion.

FIRST CLOWN: Kill him?

SECOND CLOWN: Hang him?

THIRD CLOWN: From the rafters?

FIRST CLOWN: By the neck?

SECOND CLOWN: From a nail?

THIRD CLOWN: Got any string?

FIRST CLOWN: No.

SECOND CLOWN: No.

The Third Clown sits down on The Young Man, and cries.

THE YOUNG MAN: Alas!

FIRST CLOWN: Did he say something?

SECOND CLOWN: He's not dead?

At these words The Third Clown immediately rises.

THIRD CLOWN: Then we don't have to kill him.

Seeing The Young Man begin to cry, the three Clowns start crying also.

FIRST CLOWN (*tearfully*): We must make him laugh.

The three Clowns form a circle, sobbing.

Barriers are brought out for the horses.

The first little Clown reaches back and grasps his heels, belly sticking out. The second little Clown does the same: two fine wheels for which The Young Man acts as the axle, arms out.

The big Clown picks up The Young Man's feet and pushes his wheelbarrow toward the exit.

Clash of cymbals.

The wheelbarrow falls apart.

The three Clowns, each standing on one foot, throw kisses to the audience, and then return, bowing, for a brief reprise.

The Young Man remains stretched out at the exit.

The Clowns return to him. He looks at his reflection in the sun on the costume of the big Clown, patting down his hair, adjusting his tie.

THE TWO OTHER CLOWNS (*offering their costume suns to The Young Man*): Would you like a triple mirror?

THE YOUNG MAN: No, it's The Equestrian I'd like to see.

THE BIG CLOWN: At your service.

The three Clowns disappear. The Equestrian, mounted on a superb white horse, leaps over The Young Man.

THE YOUNG MAN: Cruel!

The Young Man holds out his arms to The Equestrian, in her white tights glittering with spangles. Galloping past him, she lashes him with her whip.

Yes—I want to be your horse!

The horse, however, doesn't seem very happy.

The music continues, very rhythmically.

The dance of the horse continues also.

The Young Man leans against one of the barriers. The approaching horse jumps badly—The Equestrian tumbles in the air, and would have fallen on bare ground, had not The Young Man caught her in his arms.

At last! My love!

The Audience applauds the happy result of this trick, which it thinks has been planned.

THE EQUESTRIAN: You again?

THE YOUNG MAN: And if I hadn't been there?

THE EQUESTRIAN: So you think you're an indispensable part of my life? First of all, where do you come from?

THE YOUNG MAN: I come from . . . can I say? I feel that I am immortal and that I've just come from being born.

THE EQUESTRIAN: And what can you do?

THE YOUNG MAN: I can act on your every whim.

THE EQUESTRIAN: That doesn't interest me—unless you plan to act on all of them—all at once.

A Juggler comes out, with colored clubs; he begins to perform silently.

THE YOUNG MAN: Is he a mute?

THE EQUESTRIAN: What would he want to say?

THE YOUNG MAN: Do you want to see me charm the violins?

The Young Man takes the place of the Juggler, picks up his clubs, chases him out, and shouts:

Mr. Loyal, bring me some violins!

MR. LOYAL: Did you say violins?

THE YOUNG MAN: Ten violins. Ten. Yes. And don't get upset: I'll have no need for bows. (*He announces to The Audience.*) And now a serenade in honor of my lovely one, played as if I were under her very balcony.

Ten violins are brought out.

The Young Man juggles with them. Soon all ten are in the air. They reach as far as the loge opposite the orchestra.

Then, throwing them into the air again, The Young Man gives a lightly different twist to each. The air caresses the chords in different ways so that they reverberate strangely.

All the violins dance to this slow song.

(*Sings.*) Quant'é belle giovanezza
Che si fugzé tutta via
Chi vuol esser'lieto, sia
Di doman, non c'é certazza.*

Then he lets the violins fall with a clatter—and shatter; the orchestra accompanies this with the traditional drum roll.

One violin has not fallen, caught by its tuning keys in a rope ladder, at a great height.

A bow! I'll play that one yet.

THE EQUESTRIAN (*conquered at last*): A bow! Quick, go get a bow, Mr. Loyal. But how will he get to the violin? A bow. Hurry up!

A bow is brought out.

Here, my dearest, here!

THE YOUNG MAN: Oh, no! How do you expect me to play with this useless thing? A bow, I said. A longbow, with arrows, naturally.

Mr. Loyal, stupefied, brings out a longbow and arrows. The Young Man shoots at the violin. One after another the arrows graze the strings. A melody.

THE EQUESTRIAN (*baring her breast*): Shoot at my heart now!

But The Young Man does not hear. He is listening to his music. He pays no attention whatsoever to The Equestrian, but when he has shot his last arrow he stares at a girl leaning over the edge of the loge opposite the orchestra.

The Girl smiles.

Then The Young Man climbs into his longbow and shoots himself into the loge. And in the shadows of the loge The Girl welcomes him.

THE YOUNG MAN: How I've lacked dignity! Under your eyes, a veritable clown, alas! . . .

* How beautiful is youth, yet so fleeting; let he who wishes be happy, of tomorrow there is no certainty.

THE GIRL: You're much less handsome out of the spotlight, so near like this.

The Young Man cries out; at the rear of the loge he sees Eight Men in Evening Dress, with sinister expressions.

THE YOUNG MAN: Who are all those?

THE GIRL: My court.

Disgusted, The Young Man turns away and sees, in the spotlight, The Equestrian balancing upon a wire stretched above the platform. Feet together, he leaps onto the wire.

The wire slips out from under the feet of The Equestrian; she clings to her parasol and begins, almost as if weightless, to descend slowly. The Young Man has meanwhile bounced from the wire to the ground; immediately he falls to his knees before The Equestrian.

THE YOUNG MAN: Forgive me, forgive me. Oh, how miserable are the lives serious and respectable childhoods foretell! Why haven't I always lived in baggy pants, surrounded by the tears of these Clowns!

THE EQUESTRIAN: Have you quite finished playing the violin to that pretty young lady?

THE YOUNG MAN: I love only you; and I've come back to you.

THE EQUESTRIAN: Yes, but at this very moment it's she you're looking at and thinking about.

THE YOUNG MAN: Alas! Life is slipping through my hands. . . .

THE EQUESTRIAN: Enough. You're just a fly-by-night.

MR. LOYAL (*running out*): Ladies and gentlemen! Unfortunate events never seem to end: the Acrobat who died at the beginning of tonight's performance has left a will. The Director had the regrettable idea of looking into it at once, to spite the old superstition, and now, consequently, he cannot bring himself to ignore the stated wishes of the deceased. Now, this rather peculiar Acrobat demanded that his body, in its hearse, be pulled about by circus horses one last time around the circus ring before being thrown into a common grave.

Let things be done, therefore, according to the will of a man who desired so little during his lifetime.

The hearse moves forward, a first-class hearse covered with flowers. The Audience runs to the exits, in total disorder. The Young Man bows to the dead, and the black plumes at the corners of the hearse seem to bend in response.

THE YOUNG MAN: Let the dead move on!

But the well-trained horses are following the orchestra, and the music being played is Chopin's "Funeral March."

If they keep going that way the flowers will be withered before they reach the cemetery.

A cloud of butterflies rises from the wreaths. Revealed, the wreaths are only skeletons of wire.

The butterflies seem to dance, thrown into the air by invisible hands of jugglers.

Then their patterns grow more complicated; the hearse moves into the coalescing cloud and soon The Young Man distinguishes letters of the alphabet, and then a name: his own.

THE HEARSE DRIVER: What presumption! There is more than just one bear in this circus called Martin.

THE YOUNG MAN: First of all my name isn't Martin.

The Young Man falls silent; he has recognized in the person of The Hearse Driver one of the Eight Men in Evening Dress in the loge where The Girl was.

He looks up; the loge is empty. The hearse goes out. Behind it are the seven other Men in Evening Dress. They assume hieratic postures, arms raised to heaven. The Young Man looks for The Equestrian. He sees nothing but the ripples of the canvas circus tent swaying in the wind.

He is surrounded by snow and seven black trees, coated with snow, rising toward a low sky of writhing arms. Music is heard in the distance. The snow falls in squalling gusts.

Trees stripped bare, like my heart—but why, O sky, are your tears so brilliant and gaudy? My two friends, I have not known how to stay with you, nor how to choose otherwise.

He kneels down. The snow seems attracted by his despair and quickly covers his figure. A gang of children run in. They begin to throw snowballs at the snowman. . . . The Young Man tries not to move, and then falls asleep, numbed.

THE CURTAIN *falls slowly to the joyous cries of the children.*

en gggarrrde!

by RENÉ DAUMAL

translated by Michael Benedikt

A SMALL DRAMA
BY A GOOD LITTLE (NO LESS)
BOY:
AND FOR HIS REWARD
HE WILL HAVE A BRAND-NEW
CHOO-CHOO TRAIN
MADE OF SUGAR

CHARACTERS

MYGRAINE, a woman in a hennin
NAPOLEON, Napoleon
A TOOTHBRUSH
BUBU, a little angel
URSULE, a depraved young thing
SOME SNAILS
A CIGAR, pure Havana ("Romeo and Juliet")
A LEECH
A SOCIOLOGIST
A PERNOD WITH SUGAR
CLEOPATRA, a person not to fool around with
THE AUTHOR: Me!

The set represents the field between the poles of an electromagnet. From a nearby garden, the wailing of a newborn child is heard.

THE AUTHOR (*arrives on all fours, on the run—his clothing consists of an enormous eggshell and a mushroom growing in his hair —he slobbers piteously and says in a quavering voice*): I'm going to horsewhip you all! all! all!!!

CURTAIN

SCENE 1

The inside of a snail's shell.

Napoleon, Bubu, The Sociologist, The Leech, The Pernod with Sugar, and The Toothbrush are in discussion—all are wearing roller skates.

THE SOCIOLOGIST: My dear friends, I'm getting married next week.

ALL (*in disgust*): Eugghhaugghh!

A tense silence—The Sociologist falls asleep.

NAPOLEON (*to Bubu*): Don't put your tongue in the eyes of my girl friend The Toothbrush or I'll make you eat by my old nanny!

BUBU: I won't, so there! (*He climbs onto The Leech, and cries.*) Gentlemen, you are the object of an abominable machination! There are strawberries in the world, don't forget! . . . Well, then, your duty is clear!

ALL (*except The Sociologist, who is still asleep at the rear of the stage, floating several yards above the ground*): Let's go and sprinkle sugar on our strawberries, right now!

They go out in a conga line, to the sound of "The Marseillaise."

SCENE 2

The raft from the Medusa *or something along those lines.*

The same characters are stretched out dead drunk. Only The Pernod with Sugar runs over their bodies and sucks greedily at their feet.

THE PUBLIC (*horrified*): Encore!

> *A ship arrives, with the rest of the cast of characters; it stops near the raft.*

MYGRAINE (*climbs onto the raft, coughs and cries out*): On the very paws of my black dog, a mushroom is growing!

> *The individuals on the raft stand on their heads—The Pernod with Sugar, discreetly, disappears inside a sea gull, whistling an obscene tune.*

CLEOPATRA (*wandering among the masting, to Ursule who is doing a belly dance in front of The Leech*): The face of the moon does not have prettier legs, O Ursule, daughter of the local police force!

URSULE (*who's making fun of him, to The Leech*): Ah! Ah! Ah! Hi! Hi! Hi! Who's the little girl to do all these things?

THE LEECH (*filled with love*): Ursule!

THE TOOTHBRUSH (*parading her dignity*): Vive la France! (*She sinks.*)

THE CIGAR (*frisking about*): She certainly deserved it.

BUBU: The promise having been given us for this mutiny, in my opinion something's now going to happen.

> *Something happens.*

> *The curtain falls—one still hears sobs, rumbling noises, splashing, whistling, sudden collisions, bellowings, and so on.*

SCENE 3

The fly clique.

NAPOLEON (*alone, in an armchair*): To die for one's country is not so good, after all is said and done, as a good pipe.

URSULE (*falling on her knees*): Ah! Ah!

THE PUBLIC (*worn out*): Enough!

Ursule is reviled.

CLEOPATRA (*becoming visible to Napoleon*): My poor friend, you're getting lousier.

A SNAIL (*slobbering*): Stop, you're going to create diplomatic complications. As for me, I much prefer false rumors.

Rows of snails appear everywhere and make a big circle around the stage.

THE SOCIOLOGIST (*coming down head first*): Ah! We're going to enjoy ourselves, all right! Just like little rabbits.

Behind him descend, in a group, The Cigar, The Toothbrush, The Pernod with Sugar, and Mygraine.

MYGRAINE: To fill up the little spaces
Between my green toes
I've inserted wedge-shaped ices.
Moreover, I want to be the play's most sympathetic character!

THE CIGAR (*to The Toothbrush*): Let's blow our noses!

They blow their noses.

Mutually!

They blow their noses mutually.

THE PERNOD WITH SUGAR (*moved, tears in his eyes*): Oh! I've suffered so much!

NAPOLEON (*smiling idiotically, holding his hands over his ears*): I have three ants in my garden

The first is long, long . . .
The second is pink, pink . . .
The third is in its childhood, and it's that one that I prefer!
that I prefer! I prefer! prefer! refer! fer! er! r r r . . .

THE SNAILS (*have formed a circle around everybody. Ferociously*):
Ahhhah! Kiki's going to laugh now?

ALL (*with an unexpected simultaneity*): Who cares? I'm cir-
cumcised!

BUBU (*who, the nasty little thing, stood herself with the snails*):
M'sieur author! A neat denouement!

THE AUTHOR (*falls from Limbo, leaping—in a voice laden with
emotion*): Agag . . . gag . . . Agai . . . ga . . . Achoo!

*Fireworks, overturned paintpots, the sound of trombones in
the wings.*

FINAL CURTAIN

A GENTLEMAN IN THE AUDIENCE (*to his son [eight years old]*): Let
that teach you, Arthur, to always follow the right road!

THE END

the odyssey of ulysses the palmiped

by ROGER GILBERT-LECOMTE

translated by Michael Benedikt

SCENE 1

ULYSSES (*in his aquarium* [*or* "tub" *in lunar dialect*])

MONOLOGUE OF THE PALMIPED IN QUESTION:

(*He sticks his index finger in his nose, then with a sudden thrust inserts his arms to the shoulder in his appendix while shouting*): It is I the Stupefied Mystic! (*Then he augments his sibylline bellow with this phrase befitting the Kingly vocabulary of a process server's assistant.*) I'll accord no credence to the authenticity of CAUSAL LINKS until I CAN HANG MYSELF BY MEANS OF THE AFORESAID.

A VOICE (*coming like an old camembert out of his right sock*): Nitchevo! Nitchevo!!!

SCENE 2

The inside of a delicatessen meat store.

Two cross-legged tailors are completing a pair of oxford trousers of a bizarre material smelling of old coldcuts for Ulysses.

A TAILOR (*with a horrified gesture* [*eyes and toes shaking in a synchronous tremble*] *explains to the other how Ulysses obtained the material*):
In fact! Now then in fact!
Here is, here is the story
From the bag of purulent pus known as the Pearpear
Ulysses cut out
A big pair of drawers from some leather-like skin from
Auvergne. Ah!

The other tailor stands up to have the pleasure of falling in a dead faint.

SCENE 3

The Gibbet

An Auvergnian jury has condemned Ulysses to death.

Instead of a rope: the causal link, at the end of which Ulysses hangs, without pants.

A SARDINE *(forgotten in an old can beneath the gibbet)*: De profundis!

SCENE 4

The scene takes place in the Mystics' Paradise.

In the distance is heard the jazz combo of the spheres. In the foreground a vegetable garden: the disincarnated Ulysses slobbers with tenderness before a cabbage leaf on which three pale-blue snails play delightedly at "fly away birdie" by means of their flexible horns —for all eternity. Ulysses, ecstatic, would like to speak to describe the perfection of his heavenly bliss.

But he cannot.

Then

CURTAIN

jet of blood

by ANTONIN ARTAUD

translated by George E. Wellwarth

CHARACTERS

THE YOUNG MAN
THE YOUNG GIRL
THE KNIGHT
THE NURSE
THE PRIEST
THE SHOEMAKER
THE SEXTON
THE WHORE
THE JUDGE
THE STREET PEDDLER
A THUNDEROUS VOICE

THE YOUNG MAN: I love you, and everything is beautiful.

THE YOUNG GIRL (*with a strong tremolo in her voice*): You love me, and everything is beautiful.

THE YOUNG MAN (*in a very deep voice*): I love you, and everything is beautiful.

THE YOUNG GIRL (*in an even deeper voice than his*): You love me, and everything is beautiful.

THE YOUNG MAN (*leaving her abruptly*): I love you. (*Pause.*) Turn around and face me.

THE YOUNG GIRL (*she turns to face him*): There!

THE YOUNG MAN (*in a shrill and exalted voice*): I love you, I am big, I am shining, I am full, I am solid.

THE YOUNG GIRL (*in the same shrill tone*): We love each other.

THE YOUNG MAN: We are intense. Ah, how well ordered this world is!

A pause. Something that sounds like an immense wheel turning and blowing out air is heard. A hurricane separates the two. At this moment two stars crash into each other, and we see a number of live pieces of human bodies falling down: hands, feet, scalps, masks, colonnades, porches, temples, and alembics, which, however, fall more and more slowly, as if they were falling in a vacuum. Three scorpions fall down, one after the other, and finally a frog and a beetle, which sets itself down with a maddening, vomit-inducing slowness.

(*Shouting as loud as he can.*) The sky has gone mad! (*He looks at the sky.*) Let's get out of here. (*He pushes The Young Girl out before him.*)

Enter a knight of the Middle Ages in an enormous suit of armor, followed by a nurse holding her breasts in both hands and puffing and wheezing because they are both very swollen.

THE KNIGHT: Leave your breasts alone. Give me my papers.

THE NURSE (*crying shrilly*): Ah! Ah! Ah!

THE KNIGHT: Shit, what's the matter with you?

THE NURSE: Look! Our daughter—there—with him!

THE KNIGHT: Bah! There's no girl there!

THE NURSE: I tell you, they're screwing each other.

THE KNIGHT: What the hell do I care if they're screwing each other?

THE NURSE: Incest.

THE KNIGHT: Old woman.

THE NURSE (*plunges her hands into her pockets, which are as large as her breasts*): Pimp! (*She throws the papers at him.*)

THE KNIGHT: Bitch! Let me eat.

The Nurse runs off. The Knight gets up again and pulls an enormous slice of Gruyère cheese out of each paper. Suddenly he coughs and chokes.

(*His mouth full.*) Ehp! Ehp! Show me your breasts. Show me your breasts. Where did she go to?

He runs off.

THE YOUNG MAN (*re-enters*): I have seen, I have learned, I have understood. Here are the public square, the priest, the cobbler, the street peddlers, the threshold of the church, the red light of the whorehouse, the scales of justice. I can't any more!

A Priest, a Shoemaker, a Sexton, a Whore, a Judge, and a Street Peddler enter like shadows.

I have lost her. . . . Give her back to me.

ALL (*in various tones*): Who, who, who, who?

THE YOUNG MAN: My wife.

THE SEXTON (*very sexton-like*): Your wife . . . Phooey! Clown!

THE YOUNG MAN: Clown! You're talking about *your* wife, maybe!

THE SEXTON (*tapping his forehead*): That may be true.

He runs off. The Priest leaves the group and puts his arm round The Young Man's neck.

THE PRIEST (*in a confessional tone*): To what part of your body would you say you refer most often?

THE YOUNG MAN: To God.

The Priest, put out of countenance by this answer, imme-diately starts talking with a Swiss accent.

THE PRIEST (*with a Swiss accent*): But that doesn't go any more. We don't listen to that sort of thing any more. It's necessary to ask such things of volcanoes and earthquakes. We others feed ourselves on the dirty little stories we hear in the confessional. And that's all there is—that's life!

THE YOUNG MAN (*very impressed*): Ah, yes, there we are, that's life! Oh, well, it all goes down the drain sooner or later.

THE PRIEST (*still with his Swiss accent*): But of course.

Night suddenly falls. Earthquake. Thunder shakes the air, and lightning zigzags in all directions. In the intermittent flashes of lightning one sees people running around in panic, em-bracing each other, falling down, getting up again, and run-ning around like madmen.

At a given moment an enormous hand seizes The Whore's hair, which bursts into ever-widening flames.

A THUNDEROUS VOICE: Bitch, look at your body!

The Whore's body appears completely nude and hideous un-der her dress, which suddenly becomes transparent.

THE WHORE: Leave me, God.

She bites God's wrist. An immense jet of blood shoots across the stage, and we can see The Priest making the sign of the cross during a flash of lightning that lasts longer than the others.

When the lights come up again, all the characters are dead and their bodies lie scattered over the ground. Only The Young Man and The Whore are left. They are eating each other's eyes.

The Whore falls into The Young Man's arms.

THE WHORE (*with a sigh as if she were at the point of orgasm*): Tell me how this happened to you.

The Young Man hides his face in his hands.

The Nurse comes back carrying The Young Girl in her arms like a parcel. The Young Girl is dead. The Nurse lets her fall to the ground, where she is crushed flat as a pancake.

The Nurse no longer has any breasts. Her front is completely flat. At this moment The Knight comes out and throws himself on The Nurse, shaking her violently.

THE KNIGHT (*in a threatening voice*): Where have you put it? Give me my Gruyère!

THE NURSE (*cheerfully*): Here you are. (*She lifts her dress. The Young Man tries to flee but freezes at the sight like a petrified marionette.*)

THE YOUNG MAN (*as if suspended in mid-air and with the voice of a ventriloquist's dummy*): Don't hurt Mummy.

THE KNIGHT: Accursed woman! (*He covers his face in horror.*)

An army of scorpions comes out from under The Nurse's dress and swarms over his sex, which swells up and bursts, becoming glassy and shining like the sun. The Young Man and The Whore flee.

THE YOUNG GIRL (*reviving as if dazzled*): The virgin! Ah, that's what he was looking for.

CURTAIN

the mysteries of love

A SURREALIST DRAMA

by ROGER VITRAC

translated by Ralph J. Gladstone

TO SUZANNE

—*The women who love us
renew the true Sabbath.*

—ALFRED JARRY
(*L'Amour absolu*)

CHARACTERS

PATRICK, twenty-three years of age
LEAH, twenty-one years of age
MRS. MORIN, Leah's mother
FIRST FRIEND OF PATRICK
SECOND FRIEND OF PATRICK
THIRD FRIEND OF PATRICK
DOVIC (diminutive of Ludovic), thirty years old
THE NEIGHBORS
THE VIRGIN (not a speaking part)
THE YOUNG MAN, an actor
THE OLD MAN, an actor
THE THEATRE MANAGER
THÉOPHILE MOUCHET, author of the drama
THE LIEUTENANT OF DRAGOONS (role taken by Patrick)
LLOYD GEORGE (role taken by Dovic)
THE CHILD OF RED AND YELLOW CLOTH (not a speaking part)
THE CHILD SAWED OFF AT THE SHOULDERS (not a speaking part)
THE WOMAN IN BLACK (role taken by Mrs. Morin)
THE MAN WITH A MILITARY HAIRCUT AND CHECKERED TROUSERS:
  Mr. Morin
THE BUTCHER
THE AUTHOR
GUILLOTIN, son of Patrick and Leah (not a speaking part)
A WHITE FOX TERRIER
A GRAY BULLDOG
MUSSOLINI (role taken by Patrick)
THE CONDUCTOR
THE CHAMBERMAID
TWO COOKS (not speaking parts)
A MAN IN EVENING DRESS
THE WOMAN WHO SELLS YARD-GOODS
SEVERAL GHOSTS (not speaking parts)
HOTEL LODGERS
TWO POLICEMEN
THE HOTEL MANAGER
THREE CHILDREN
A SPECTATOR (not a speaking part)

PROLOGUE

The stage represents a public square. The weather is cloudy. It has been raining. On the wall of a house is painted the portrait below. The mouth is black. The cheeks are red like lips. The eyes are pale.

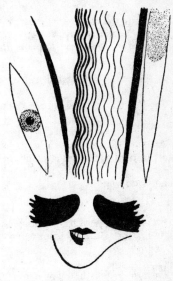

As the curtain rises, Patrick, crouching, is tracing sinuous lines in the mud with a stick. A Policeman enters.

THE POLICEMAN: You there! What are you doing?

PATRICK: As you see, sir, I am just finishing off her hair.

He leaves, tracing a sinuous line.
The curtain slowly falls.

END OF THE PROLOGUE

ACT I

First Tableau

A box overhanging the stage. The proscenium lights are out. The house lights, a chandelier above the audience, are lighted. To the right and left: black draperies. Framing the box: white lace, in festoons.

As the curtain rises, Leah is seated. Patrick is at her knees.

PATRICK: For heaven's sake! Confess, Leah.

LEAH: You're right.

PATRICK: Aren't I, Leah? Now at last you're being reasonable. Confess it, then. Believe me, sooner or later, you would have to. Don't be obstinate like a child. You don't want to make me angry, do you?

LEAH: Patrick! What are you doing?

PATRICK (*still kneeling*): Why, nothing, Leah, nothing. You can see: I'm out for a walk. Ah! But will you confess now?

LEAH: No.

PATRICK: Then do accept these few flowers. (*He slaps her.*)

LEAH (*laughing*): Mama, Mama, Mama!

PATRICK (*cupping his hands as a megaphone*): Mrs. Morin! Mrs. Morin!

Enter Mrs. Morin.

MRS. MORIN: Excuse me, madam, sir, if I am disturbing you.

LEAH: Oh, Mother!

PATRICK: I'm in the way, aren't I?

MRS. MORIN: What! You young snake! Tell me right off to go away. (*To Leah.*) He's as cool as a coconut.

PATRICK (*holding out a chair to her*): As for me, I'm going to take a stroll down by the waterside. (*He sits down and looks at the audience.*)

LEAH (*softly*): Mother! If you only knew how Patrick loves me.

PATRICK (*shouting*): Look out! You're going to fall.

MRS. MORIN: Why, that's fine, my dear.

PATRICK (*still shouting*): Is it you, the ox?

MRS. MORIN: And you, do you love him?

LEAH: Why, naturally.

PATRICK (*still shouting*): Go blow that lobster your father's nose, Girlie!

MRS. MORIN: Perhaps he will grow up, dear. But as for me, I have too much to do with my dogs. Six little dogs, Leah!

LEAH: Now you're getting on my nerves. Is it my fault if Old Man Morin wouldn't let me take my first communion? How spiteful!

MRS. MORIN: You will nevertheless have to decide.

LEAH: I don't dare.

PATRICK: Aha! Now it's the goat!

MRS. MORIN: Do you want me to speak for you?

LEAH: Pretty smart; you'll take him from me.

MRS. MORIN: Take that.

She slaps her, then goes off.

LEAH (*crying*): Patrick! Patrick! Patrick!

PATRICK: Devil take animals and the dining room.

LEAH: You are alone in the world, Patrick.

PATRICK: Oh, you! Have respect for those who are close to me!

LEAH: Ah! I hear you quite well now. Therefore I'll tell you everything.

PATRICK: Well, well, well . . .

LEAH: It's up to you to question me.

PATRICK: That doesn't matter; Mrs. Morin, you certainly do have a thick navel.

LEAH: Is that all? You're cruel!

PATRICK: I like that! That's a good one. What do you mean, Leah?

LEAH: I confess.

PATRICK: Ah! A thousand thanks, Leah. Thank you, thank you a thousand times.

Enter Patrick's three friends.

FIRST FRIEND: I'm happy, you know. (*They shake hands.*)

PATRICK: Thanks a lot.

SECOND FRIEND: Pity. She was made for me. Must be made of wood, Patrick.

PATRICK: Thanks a lot. (*They shake hands.*)

THIRD FRIEND: Ah! The children's children. Save one for me.

PATRICK: Thanks, and you?

The three friends go off.

I'll have the necktie. The circular saw-toothed necktie. And I'll make a bridge out of my blood, Leah.

LEAH: You are good.

PATRICK: Do you see, for a moment I took the lamb's part. It was bleating. Baa . . . Baa . . . Baa . . . The grass was getting off the train. It was putting on airs. The lamb pissed all over it. That's what it's like to be young. (*Pause.*) Oh, but pardon me! You confessed. Didn't you confess?

LEAH: Yes. But to what?

PATRICK: That's true, to what?

LEAH: Will you wait for me a moment? (*She goes off and returns immediately with a basket filled with small dogs.*) My mother is dogging you this basket for the way.

PATRICK: Thanks. (*He throws both dogs and basket into the audience.*) Because I, you know, and religion . . . (*A pause.*

Gesticulating.) What beautiful sunshine! What beautiful sunlight! (*Pause.*) Really, Leah? May I die of it on the spot! Oh! My friends.

Enter the three friends.

(*Still gesticulating.*) Will you leave, all you others?

The three friends leave.

Do you see, Leah, I'm happy. I don't need anything else. I'm stifling. It's the oysters. Do you hear? (*Shouting.*) It's the oysters. But what is the lemon doing? Ah, Leah, will you hide that leg, that knee! Will you hide that thigh! (*Screaming.*) Oh! Oh! Oh! Oh! I will shout it out. I will shout it out from the rooftops, from the stars, from above the stars! (*Taking the audience into his confidence.*) Leah loves me, Leah loves me, Leah loves me. She confessed it. She loves me. (*To Leah.*) It's your turn now. Shout it out, Leah. Go on my little Leah, my Lele, my Leah-Leah. Shout it out, now, shout it, my Leahleahleah.

LEAH (*to the audience*): I love Patrick. Oh! I love his guts. Oh! I love the clown. I love the clown. From every viewpoint, from every seam, from every form. Look at them, Patrick. Listen to them. Oh! Oh! Oh! . . . (*She bursts into laughter.*)

A VOICE (*in the audience*): But why? Merciful heavens! Why? Are you both ill?

LEAH: Madly.

THE VOICE: Are you both mad?

PATRICK: Madly.

A VOICE (*in the audience*): Do you hear them, Martine?

A shot.

ANOTHER VOICE: Do you hear them, Marie?

A shot.

ANOTHER VOICE: Do you hear them, Julie?

A shot.

ANOTHER VOICE: Do you hear them, Theresa?

A shot.

ANOTHER VOICE: Do you hear them, Michelle?

A shot.

ANOTHER VOICE: Do you hear them, Esther?

A shot.

SEVERAL VOICES: Kill me! Kill him! Kill her! Mercy! Pardon! The Child!

Tumult, cries, shots. Suddenly the house lights go off. Instant silence. The box alone is half-lighted.

PATRICK: Listen. A stroll in the mountains. The spruce trees are frozen. Ah, youth! Chandeliers under ice. And then the swamps! The swamps? So many beds with childless women. And suddenly there's the sparrowhawk. It's he. He is dead, I tell you. He falls like a flashing of lightning. There are no wings on either side of his naked body on the ground. There are two eyes. Isn't it so, Leah?

LEAH: It isn't Leah.

PATRICK: And yet it is she. The rest of the body, you'll say? Oh! See! She flies an ensign of blood. Do as she does, ladies. Hold onto your skin while removing your black mourning furs. Let it remain attached. You, Leah, above all, don't do it. Don't do it here. Your muscles would get cold and your nerves would become consumed. Oh, it's just that I don't allow myself to be surprised, that's all. Not me. Don't worry, my bed will smell neither of fulminate nor of powder, the way it does here.

LEAH: What! It already smells like brains.

PATRICK: Some good advice. Throw some sound and sweep under the armchairs. This mud is an infection.

LEAH: Stop it, Patrick.

PATRICK: Order, damn it all! Tidy things up a bit. The women, please, lay them out on the right. The men standing on the left. And the children in the middle, in the sauce.

LEAH: My big hero is right.

PATRICK: Shut up. And now, Commissioner, please chain all these fine people up for me.

A VOICE (*in the audience*): Mr. Patrick, you are a criminal.

PATRICK: I, sir? No, sir. Are you deaf? I love Leah. You should have shouted out that you love Julie, Marie, Theresa, Michelle, or Esther, and Leah would naturally have been among them. And I would experience a voluptuous pleasure in my wrists.

LEAH: And I wouldn't have to sleep with phosphorus tonight.

PATRICK: You little bird-brain.

LEAH: Stop, Patrick.

PATRICK (*very casually*): My dear, there will be a lot of people here tonight.

LEAH: So much the better, so much the better.

PATRICK: They're all signaling to us.

Leah and Patrick make friendly gestures to the audience. The house lights come on.

LEAH: And the face?

PATRICK: Come, now! You remind me of a slashing knife. A wound.

LEAH: Ah! That animal that pissed, how dear it is to your heart.

PATRICK: No, Leah. I swear it. It was right in the forehead. Besides, it's of no importance.

LEAH: The face, Patrick?

PATRICK: Oh! Sirens! You all have it, you're all fishheaded.

LEAH: Be a little discreet. If you force me to it, I'll be stark naked.

PATRICK: How useless it all is. Only clothing interests me. An empty dress or suit or shirt walking about. All these constructions of chalk, wax, wood, bone and flesh should be incinerated. A hat gliding along six feet above the sidewalk, have you ever seen that?

LEAH: What shitabed notions! And help!

PATRICK: Leah! Leah!

LEAH: What's the matter?

PATRICK: Nothing to worry about. My plaster hurts.

LEAH: Your plaster?

PATRICK: My hollow space.

LEAH: So?

PATRICK: Oh! So you can take your place at the pump.

LEAH: Why, Patrick?

PATRICK: Why, to pump up the red, my dear child.

LEAH: Bladders and lanterns, my love?

PATRICK: Isn't that always the way with bearded women! The intelligence of the extremities.

Pause.

Enter Dovic. Patrick looks at Leah dully. He is entirely indifferent to the scene that is to follow.

DOVIC (*to Leah*): Absolutely, positively, no.

LEAH: What's all this fuss?

DOVIC: You jealous liar, that's it.

LEAH: And all a-tremble, and all a-sweat, and all in tears.

DOVIC: Now, which one did you want, the animal, machinery or the child?

LEAH: But he was opening up my belly, that one.

DOVIC: You mean your noodle.

LEAH: With his beard.

DOVIC: Oh, no! No scandal here, right? I protest, Leah. (*Slapping her.*) I've always loved you. (*Pinching her.*) I still love you. (*Biting her.*) Give me credit for that? (*Pulling her ears.*) Did I have cold sweats? (*Spitting in her face.*) I caressed your breasts and your cheeks. (*Kicking her.*) Everything I had was yours. (*Making as though to strangle her.*) You left me. (*Shaking her violently.*) Did I hold it against you? (*Striking her with his fist.*) I am good-natured. (*Throwing her on the ground.*) I have already forgiven you. (*He drags her around the box by the hair.*)

Patrick rises.

LEAH (*presenting Dovic to him*): You know, Patrick, Dovic is a real gentleman.

PATRICK: Who is this Dovic?

DOVIC: That's me, sir.

LEAH (*whispering to Patrick*): He has ants on the back of his head.

PATRICK: Very good. And what interests you in life, Mr. Dovic?

DOVIC: Love. Love really.

PATRICK: Funny idea, coming to call. For without doubt you are dining with us?

LEAH: Did I invite him?

DOVIC: I'm used to the stairs, and the key is always in the door.

PATRICK: Perfect. (*To Leah.*) Close the windows and set the table. (*To Dovic.*) And love in what aspect?

DOVIC (*pointing to Leah*): See for yourself.

Without another word, Patrick and Dovic come to blows. They roll on the ground and strike each other violently.

LEAH (*following the combat*): Look out for the statue. Lean over to the right or you'll knock the armchair over. Now to the left. You're rolling into the fireplace. Look out for the plants, Patrick! Dovic, your nose is bleeding, you're getting spots on the tablecloth. The dishes are in pieces. Oh, my God! Bravo, both of you.

A doorbell rings.

Patrick, Dovic, stop it right now. Someone's ringing. Get up, Patrick! Get up, Dovic!

Enter a few neighbors. Patrick and Dovic get up. Dovic is bloody.

PATRICK (*to Dovic*): Go away. (*To the neighbors.*) And you too.

DOVIC (*showing a place in the box*): That palm is mine.

Exit Dovic and the neighbors shrugging their shoulders.

LEAH: I've got a migraine.

PATRICK: Never mind. Look, what sunshine!

LEAH: Tell me: You won't ask me anything about my past life, Patrick?

PATRICK: No.

Pause.

Enter a woman dressed in a long nightgown. Her face, hands and feet are blue.

PATRICK: Good day, Madame.

LEAH: In our room? What are you doing there, Patrick?

PATRICK: Why not?

LEAH: Who's this tart?

PATRICK: She's the virgin, Leah; she's the virgin. Are you happy?

Exit the woman in the nightgown.

The three knocks, traditional to French stagecraft, are heard. The house lights go off. The proscenium lights go on. The box is plunged into darkness. For a few seconds the curtain is strangely shaken. With each shake, the most diverse cries are uttered in the audience. Finally the curtain rises slowly. The stage is white. On the backdrop appears this inscription:

> IT'S ALWAYS POSSIBLE
> TO DIE
> TWO HOURS AT A TIME
> CIGARETTES: SILK

From the left, enter a Young Man in evening dress. From the right, an Old Man with his beard trailing on the ground. The Young Man divests himself of his cane, his hat and his gloves, which he places on the floor of the stage. The Old Man raises his arms heavenward, and smiles.

THE YOUNG MAN (*pulling a bird out of his pocket*): Dad, you have before you one who is about to die.

THE OLD MAN: Then you will spread out my beard on the sheet. It needs to dry out.

THE YOUNG MAN: Don't you ever wash it? Look how dirty it is!

THE OLD MAN: Ah! When I was a child, Justin, it was as white as milk.

The Young Man opens his hand. The bird flies off. Both go off stage to the left, weeping.

The curtain falls abruptly. A shot is heard. A few protests arise in the audience. The Theatre Manager appears immediately.

THE THEATRE MANAGER: Ladies and gentlemen, the play is over. The drama which it has been our privilege to present to you is by Mr. Théophile Mouchet. Mr. Théophile Mouchet has just killed himself.

The Manager disappears. Stupor, then sudden and increasing laughter.

A VOICE: Author! Author!

ALL THE AUDIENCE (*in chorus*): Author! Author! Author!

The curtain rises again. The Author appears. He is in his shirt-sleeves. His face and clothing are covered with blood. He laughs. He laughs heartily. He laughs with all his might, holding his sides. Both curtains suddenly fall.

Second Tableau

The stage represents, on the left, the Quai des Grands-Augustins in Paris. To the right, a bedroom. In the center stands a small cabin with a porthole overlooking the Seine. In the background, in the space which should be occupied by the Palais de Justice, stands an advertising sign bearing this inscription in large blue letters: Le Petit Parisien. On the parapet, booksellers' stalls affecting the shape of coffins. Above, red tugboat stacks. The bedroom has closed windows, formed like narrow arches, the tops of which are lost in obscurity; they are adorned with very white muslin curtains. In front of the fireplace and a couple of yards from the entrance to the room stands a stove of the "salamander" variety. But it is from the fireplace that, from time to time, blue flames emerge. The bed is entirely covered by the sheets. A table. Chairs. A pedestal lamp with a green shade on the table. A glass-fronted sideboard is filled with dishes. In a corner, some old newspapers. A package of medicated cotton wool stands in front of the stove.

I

QUAI DES GRANDS-AUGUSTINS

*Enter The Lieutenant of Dragoons and Leah, carrying in her arms
a cloth doll, half red, half yellow.*

PATRICK (*as The Lieutenant of Dragoons*): I don't like people's
children.

LEAH: Look at her, Patrick. She has my eyes, my nose, my mouth.
They've cut her hair like this. It's sad. Is she a little Chinese
girl? I happen to be a blonde. But you know that she's really
yours.

*She blows into a child's toy trumpet. The doll weeps. Enter
Lloyd George. He looks like the former English prime
minister.*

LLOYD GEORGE: Psstt . . . Pstt . . . Pstt . . . Pstt . . .

PATRICK: Ah! What a terribly tragic conclusion.

*He seizes the doll, deposits it in the river, and disappears.
Lloyd George goes into his room. Leah follows him.*

II

LLOYD GEORGE'S ROOM

LEAH: I'm frightened, Dovic.

*Lloyd George crosses the room, raises the bedsheets, and re-
veals to a horrified Leah a little girl's head resting on the
pillow.*

LEAH: Mr. Lloyd George—I recognize her!

*With a sudden gesture, Lloyd George completely removes the
sheets and uncovers the child. Naturally, it is only a bust of
flesh which has been sawed off at the shoulders; the rest of the
body has disappeared. Enter Patrick as The Lieutenant of
Dragoons. His cheeks are hollow and his eyes deeply sunken.
Leah rushes into the small cabin and begins to utter piercing
shrieks, for the space of a few seconds. Lloyd George and
Patrick remain facing each other, petrified. Leah rejoins them.*

(To Patrick.) Go on, go on, I can see you're not a party to these goings-on.

Patrick slips into the bed beside the girl's bust.

LLOYD GEORGE *(to Leah)*: Ah! Now let's see a sample of my savoir-faire.

He goes off stage to the right and returns immediately carrying a young man under his arm. He deposits him on the table, and saws off his head. During this operation, terrifying crashing sounds, and the sound of bells, are heard.

(Carrying off the pieces.) There's a tidy bit of work, if I do say so myself.

Leah shrugs her shoulders. She bends over the bed and removes the little girl's eyes. They are as big as ostrich eggs.

LEAH: My eyes, Patrick! My eyes!

PATRICK *(turning toward the wall)*: I don't want to see it. I don't want to see it.

Enter Lloyd George. He is carrying a black suitcase, which he holds out to Leah.

LLOYD GEORGE: Here, Madame, are the miraculous remains of the well-beloved.

Leah crosses the Quai des Grands-Augustins. She weeps and disappears.

Enter Mrs. Morin, in mourning; and the late Mr. Morin. He has a military haircut and wears checkered trousers. The lamp lights of itself. All sit at the table. Patrick alone remains lying in the bed. Lloyd George sets four places. He brings numerous dishes: lobsters, chickens, dressed roasts, sherbets, pyramids of fruit. From time to time, he releases some birds. Leah returns. She takes her place. All eat and gesticulate in silence. Mr. Morin has removed his coat and is in his shirtsleeves. Mrs. Morin, her lips outrageously made up, a crepe hat on her head, remains motionless.

LLOYD GEORGE *(to Leah)*: Go over and arrange The Young Officer of Dragoons' knees below the little girl's shoulders. No one must notice that the child has been sawed off at the shoulders. The sheets, fallen in where the thighs and legs ought to produce natural protuberances, might give away the crime.

LEAH: That's true. (*She rises and arranges the knees of The Young Officer of Dragoons as Lloyd George has directed her. Then she returns to the table. Mr. Morin and Mrs. Morin have been pretending not to see anything.*)

LLOYD GEORGE (*to Leah*): Madame, kindly look at the sideboard.

Leah raises her eyes and sees Patrick's head looking at her from on top of the sideboard.

(*Lloyd George rises, takes Leah by the arm, pulls her to the front of the stage, and says to her*): How hard it's raining! I won't repeat it again. You are my unwilling accomplice, and if you talk, you will be handed over to the police. Besides, we must put an end to this. I propose the river.

LEAH: Decidedly, this is becoming a mania with you. What I would prefer are those booksellers' chests along the Seine that close with a padlock and are covered over with a sheet of zinc.

LLOYD GEORGE: My, my, can you see that?

LEAH: Too late!

Patrick as The Officer of Dragoons comes down from his observation point and goes over to the fire. The package of medicated cotton wool catches ablaze. Mrs. Morin utters a loud cry. Patrick calmly returns to his place on top of the sideboard.

LLOYD GEORGE (*laughing*): Ha ha ha ha ha ha ha ha! The assassination victims themselves fail in their attempt.

All resume eating. Lloyd George rises only to fetch new dishes.

MR. MORIN: However, that evening the sea was rough. Sardines were being taken by the netful. But the night, the thunder, the lightning, and especially the Negroes in the boiler room, not to mention the leopard . . . Eh, my wife? Surely you won't deny, Mrs. Morin, my wife, that one's ever eaten so well.

LLOYD GEORGE: I know quite well, sir, how to handle all this. But tell me—which way is the harbor?

Leah suddenly rises and, with the gestures of a sleepwalker, without being noticed, draws her chair near the dresser and covers Patrick's head over with a newspaper. She returns to the table and continues eating with the others.

MR. MORIN: Still, you must take some interest in my stories. However, that evening, the sea was rough. Sardines were being taken by the netful. But the leopard and the captain's knife and all the glasses were shattered . . .

At that moment the wind carries off the newspaper covering Patrick's head. Leah utters a loud cry. Mr. Morin rises and, taking Lloyd George by the arm, pulls him off toward the Quai des Grands-Augustins.

She's mad, sir. What, ho! See the crazy woman! See the crazy woman!

LLOYD GEORGE: Oh, my! The crazy woman! Oh! The crazy woman!

They go offstage.

MRS. MORIN: I've seen everything. Leah, come on over here.

They go toward the bed where two arms are being raised which resemble two dead branches, but whereon are flowering two enormous, very white hands.

Ah! My daughter! Don't come any closer. She has leprosy.

Leah kneels.

LEAH: She has my slanted eyes. My blond hair. My gleaming mouth. You must agree that you don't die of love.

END OF THE SECOND TABLEAU AND OF THE FIRST ACT.

ACT II

THIRD TABLEAU

The stage represents a hotel room. A bed. A table. Chairs. A wardrobe, and so on. Leah is stretched out on the bed. Patrick is at her bedside.

PATRICK: It's turning. It's turning.

LEAH: What's turning?

PATRICK: Not the table, obviously.

LEAH: The earth is turning.

PATRICK: Be quiet. The daylight is in my left eye.

LEAH: Oh!—he's starting that again!

PATRICK: I said, the daylight is in my left eye.

LEAH: Did I say it wasn't? (*A pause.*) And in your right eye, Patrick?

PATRICK: There is a mountain.

LEAH: Can I see?

PATRICK: If you want.

Leah bends over Patrick's eye, and looks.

LEAH: What is it?

PATRICK: It's a wheel.

LEAH: And behind it?

PATRICK: Behind it, there's a white quarry.

LEAH: Yes, the workers are taking it easy.

PATRICK: Aren't they, though!

LEAH: What's that shining among the stones?

PATRICK: Their tools. They're pretty, aren't they? They're made of nickel. The smallest one looks like a pink fingernail, and the biggest one like an ax. One of the men is holding the ax. Do you see him, Leah?

LEAH: Very well. He seems tired.

PATRICK: Still, he's got food and drink there.

LEAH: He's taking a bath. That's curious.

PATRICK: What's so curious about that?

LEAH: He's melting. He's white. Now the animals are eating him.

PATRICK: Poor creatures.

LEAH: Poor creatures? Those vipers? Those flaming, scaly things?

PATRICK: They haven't done anything to you.

LEAH: In that case, kiss my hands.

Patrick kisses her hands but suddenly leaps back.

PATRICK: Ouch!

LEAH: What have I done?

PATRICK: You've burned me.

Smoke is rising from Leah's hands. Leah goes toward the washstand and plunges them into the water.

LEAH: And you—you frightened me!

PATRICK: So in the future take care of your eyes, and leave mine alone.

Leah weeps.

That's no reason to cry.

LEAH: The world bores me.

PATRICK: Where is this world?

LEAH: Here I am, Patrick; here I am.

PATRICK: Pardon, Leah. The world, if you please.

Leah stretches out on the bed.

LEAH: Come, Patrick.

PATRICK: Oh! How long it is. (*Pointing to an electric lamp.*) The equator on a grid. And what lands have you protected, Madame? Tahiti, Tahiti, where change-purses drop like ripe bananas? Where lace is a valued auxiliary on the ambassadors' legs, Tahiti the shoe of spring?

LEAH: Tahiti? My hips. You boor!

PATRICK: Pull yourself together a bit, Leah. It's turning.

LEAH: Not the table, obviously, you idiot.

PATRICK: The earth is turning. The daylight is in my left eye.

LEAH: Why don't you get a grip on yourself and listen to me?

PATRICK: And yet it does turn.

LEAH: You're imagining things.

PATRICK: I'm not doing anything any more. I am the machine that is to turn in a vacuum. That's the brain, you say? It's poisoned by work. It's at the stage of tetanus. A nice animal, that one. Only yesterday I could still eat. Today, Leah, it's all over. The brain is in the belly. We let that outcast do anything. The heart? You can look for it in the bed. The stomach? It licks my feet beneath the table. The liver makes faces in the mirrors. The spleen is in the drawer next to the corkscrew, and my lungs are having fun making holes in your canaries. My poor brain, that divine dough, bends under any yoke. It's not Leah who's complaining, is it?

LEAH: Well! There's one who turns quickly, yet not at all awkwardly. Nevertheless, I didn't want this warfare.

The doorbell rings.

PATRICK: Come in.

Enter The Butcher.

THE BUTCHER: Is there anything for me, little lady?

LEAH: Yes, Casper. You will find everything wrapped up on the kitchen table.

THE BUTCHER: Very good, Miss Leah.

Exit The Butcher.

PATRICK: Who is that fellow?

LEAH: He's a man of sorrows.

PATRICK: And what does he do?

LEAH: He slaughters cattle.

PATRICK: Poor creatures!

LEAH: No calling is to be despised.

Re-enter The Butcher.

THE BUTCHER: Well now, Miss Leah, I'll not be coming to your place any more. Not worth the bother. Just some bones where even a whore wouldn't find a pittance! You can keep your garbage for the soldiers. You could give me the skin with the hair and nails on it now, and I still wouldn't give you another penny. You robber!

Exit The Butcher.

PATRICK: What does that man come to do here?

LEAH: Nothing, dear. He's very talented, Casper is. He reupholsters the chairs and replaces the windowpanes.

PATRICK: It seems to me I've seen his face before.

LEAH: Come now, Patrick, don't say that. You always insist that I have to turn out the light before you go to bed.

PATRICK: Who, me?

LEAH: Yes, you. And that brain that you're so proud of. There's certainly a good-time Charlie: before a meal, all he dreams about is knife wounds, animals dying in the forest—and such language! And after that there's the prairie, the country with its delicate herbs where Mr. Patrick lies down like the cloud called cirrus which in shape looks like a pike and in color like fire.

PATRICK: Go on! Next time our drainpipes won't dry up quite so quickly.

LEAH: So it would seem.

PATRICK: Only last night, someone was shouting: "Are you through cutting each other's throats up there?" I get up in my nightshirt and I answer, "This is August, dear sir, the month of the shower of stars." And do you know what our neighbor answers?

LEAH: What did our neighbor answer?

PATRICK: "When you have enough blood to go into business you should become a painter, not go around scandalizing people!"

LEAH: You see.

PATRICK: You, naturally, are going to suppose that he's being reasonable.

LEAH: What are you talking about?

PATRICK: The reasons of lodgers.

LEAH: Pardon me, I misunderstood.

PATRICK: Would you dare suppose that I don't have my reason?

LEAH: Far from it. Reason is balance, isn't it? You climb ladders well enough.

PATRICK: Oh! That hair, what battles!

LEAH: But how cosmetic!

PATRICK: You said it. You could have seen through every pore in the skin. A diamond millstone, that chest. And it's fortunate. Women today select pink underthings! You, it's the mouth that lights your way. It's like a quarry of blood.

LEAH: What nonsense! What about poetry?

PATRICK (*slaps her*): Take that!

LEAH: I'm not happy with you.

PATRICK (*slaps her again*): And now?

LEAH: I'm unhappy.

PATRICK (*dragging her around by the hair*): I'd be interested to know if I'll be a clock all my life. Or rather a clock's pendulum, or even pendent from a clock.

LEAH: Have mercy, Patrick; have mercy! I won't start up again. I'll always be happy.

PATRICK: Look at me, Leah. I'm not bad looking—maybe I have something missing?

LEAH: What would that be?

PATRICK: Fortune. Fortune for every care and garments for the skin. Fortune? Did I say fortune, Leah? Yes, I said fortune. What's most important of all is underwear. I go into a café. Faces are hidden behind pulled-up skirts. They are on the ceiling like pears. And suddenly everyone's kissing. They stick pins into the fleshy parts of their legs, and I hear on all sides: "How good-looking he is!" Chance, that pearl—I find it on the staircase. No, Leah, it's the fragrance that guides me. That house, I gild it every morning, for the evening before it is a ship in which we have both gone down. Open the door, for God's sake! And let the gesture accompany it. I said fortune. Fortune for every care and garments for the skin.

LEAH: The skin!

PATRICK: Ah! Don't touch on that one. My skin! My parchment? And also, skin yourself.

LEAH: You're hard, Patrick. You're heartless.

PATRICK: Well, I get along as I can—that's no one's lookout but my own. My behavior is my own. What was it someone once said? Love: the need to come out of oneself, someone once said. And that is why I ask you this: Are you through looking for what has been left me? Are you through looking at my skeleton? You're certainly quite an X-ray.

LEAH: What I have to listen to!

PATRICK: Ah, bah! What are you listening to? Are you really listening to this walking scaffold? A spinning top! Oh! The Skeleton and the Spinning Top (a fable):

A skeleton six feet tall
Happened to run out of plaster
The worms no longer cared for it it had become so brittle
and lovely
And the rest what did you do with it
When sitting down at the table
We made animals out of it
And the reason is this speed supplied
By the momentum of my darling's heart
That top
(The heart or the darling?
—Both.)

LEAH: Think of the future, rather.

PATRICK: The child you bear in your bosom, Leah, infinitely disturbs me. You may remove it.

LEAH: Rest assured, it's only temporary.

Exit Leah.

PATRICK (*alone*): What a business! But what sunlight!

Enter Mrs. Morin.

MRS. MORIN: Good day, Mr. Patrick.

PATRICK: Mrs. Morin! I'm happy to see you.

MRS. MORIN: You may believe that your pleasure is shared, my dear son-in-law.

PATRICK: Son-in-law, do you say? Please be seated, and remain calm. You're no doubt bent on death.

MRS. MORIN: On life, do you mean?

PATRICK: On life, on death, I know that tune. Your daughter, Mrs. Morin, is an eel on that theme.

MRS. MORIN: She has someone to take after.

PATRICK: I have hinted at it, Madame: she takes after death.

MRS. MORIN: But what sort of man *are* you, Mr. Patrick?

PATRICK: Ah there we are!

Enter Dovic.

MRS. MORIN: There's Dovic. (*To Dovic.*) Good day, son-in-law.

DOVIC: Leave me alone, you. (*To Patrick.*) Patrick, I'm quite fond of you.

PATRICK: Just one question, Mr. Dovic. You doubtless know the author of this play?

DOVIC: He's my father.

PATRICK: No.

DOVIC: At any rate, he's my best friend.

PATRICK: Well, then, please have him step over here a moment.

DOVIC: Hey, there! Author! Author!

ALL (*singing in chorus*): Why, there's the author, how are you, old lady?
Why, there's the author, how are you, my love?

Enter The Author.

THE AUTHOR: Good day, Mrs. Morin. Good day, Dovic; and good day to you, Patrick.

PATRICK: You've come just at the right time: how do you want all this to end?

THE AUTHOR: Well now, my lad, you seem quite involved in this.

PATRICK: Don't I, though? One word more.

THE AUTHOR: Go ahead.

PATRICK: You betray yourself, sir. Am I to conclude that we are to go ahead?

THE AUTHOR: Resolutely.

PATRICK: Then it's useless to talk. No one here may have the floor.

THE AUTHOR: Listen, my boy, your case doesn't interest me very much. It doesn't interest the public very much, either.

PATRICK: You don't think so?

THE AUTHOR: I understand myself as well as you understand me, and as well as you understand it.

DOVIC: I beg your pardon?

PATRICK: You leave us alone. Tend to the women. I am speaking with the gentleman. (*To The Author.*) Just one little word of advice, if you please?

THE AUTHOR: My friend, do you really want me to tell you something? Well, I am about to reveal my greatest weakness: in this particular case, I would behave as you do. But, in this particular case, permit me to withdraw.

Exit.

PATRICK: By Hercules! Let's go ahead.

He seizes a chair and breaks up everything. He knocks down Dovic and Mrs. Morin. The stage is spattered with blood. The light goes out. He continues to flail about furiously in the dark.

LEAH (*offstage*): Ah! Ah! Mo—Mo—Mother, Mother, Mother, Mother, Mother, aaaaah . . .

The light goes on again. Patrick is in tatters. Dovic and Mrs. Morin are stretched out on the floor. Enter Leah, a child in her arms.

LEAH (*joyfully*): It's a boy. (*Taken aback with shock.*) Oh, our apartment! And while I was giving birth to your son!

PATRICK: Yes, now you see. You leave me alone and you see what happens. Let's see the child.

LEAH: It didn't take me too long?

PATRICK: He seems well enough put together. Don't you think he'll be too cold on the marble mantelpiece?

LEAH: I'll clean the mirror and I'll make a fire every morning. But he'd be better off in the bed, between us.

PATRICK: It's warm enough right there! You can sweep away the broken statues. (*Taking his son and raising him up above him.*) Guillotin, you will be called Guillotin, and all your life you will occupy the place of a masterpiece, there, between our two rooms, on the pedestal of the Venus de Milo.

LEAH: What do you mean to do with your son? With your little sonny-boy, your Gui-gui, your Guiguillollo, your Guillo?

PATRICK: Well, that's a nice role you've got ready for me. (*Placing the child on the mantelpiece.*) Hold steady. And now, Guillotin, come into my arms.

The child risks a movement, loses its balance, falls and is killed.

LEAH: Ah! Ah! Ah! . . . Murder! Murder! That one, my lover, my daddy, my daddy, my Patrick, who's gone and murdered my Guigui, my Guigui, my Guillotin. (*Her tone changes.*) By the way, you could have given him some other name. You infanticide!

PATRICK: Enough, Leah. You will light the torches and prepare my traveling gear. I have things to do in the neighborhood.

LEAH: Good night, Patrick.

Exit Patrick.

A POLICEMAN (*entering*): Are you the one that's making all the noise? What's the matter with you, Madame? You're crying? Has someone beaten you?

LEAH: Oh, it's nothing, Officer; it's the little one who fell and caught the scarlet fever.

The curtain falls abruptly.

END OF THE THIRD TABLEAU

FOURTH TABLEAU

The stage simultaneously represents a railway station, a dining car, the seashore, a hotel lobby, a yard-goods shop, the main square of a provincial town. To be suitably arranged are signal discs, telegraph wires, several laid tables, large pieces of cotton wool to simulate the foaming waves, ships' masts, green plants, garden chairs, a sign bearing the inscription "Yard-Goods" and an explorer's statue. A projector will light up each part of the stage according to the location of the action.

As the curtain rises, Leah is alone in the center of the stage. Enter Mrs. Morin in full mourning. She is holding a child in her arms. By her side, both tied to the same leash, trot two dogs: a white fox terrier and a gray bulldog.

MRS. MORIN: Pardon me, Madame, would you hold my child a moment?

LEAH: I should hardly think so, Madame; my train leaves in five minutes.

MRS. MORIN: Have no fear! I'll be back soon. Just long enough to pick up tickets for my dogs, and then I'll be back. Besides, what are you afraid of? My husband is in this coach.

Darkness, then light. Mussolini is seated at a table. Enter Leah, the child in her arms and the dogs following her. Several passengers are eating. Leah sits, and the two dogs stretch out at her feet. A Conductor passes.

LEAH: Is it luncheon time already?

THE CONDUCTOR: It's five after twelve.

LEAH: At what time will we arrive?

THE CONDUCTOR: At three.

Whistles. Steam noises. The train starts.

LEAH (*at the door*): Stop! Stop! Stop! I've been given a child. . . .
Yes, the child isn't mine . . . the woman . . . there!

THE CONDUCTOR (*laughing*): Come now, Madame, that one's been
tried on us before. You keep the child; you'd come to regret it
later on.

Leah sits down again.

LEAH: What have they done? Me, a child-stealer? I should say not!
But now how to get rid of it? A cherub is such a nuisance!

MUSSOLINI (*from his place*): The sea air will do the child good.

LEAH: That's true.

MUSSOLINI: You understand, you can't . . .

LEAH (*interrupting him*): Excuse me, sir, but you are mistaken.
Your wife, I suppose it was, entrusted me with this child and
these animals. Only you will readily understand that I cannot be burdened with a child, with dogs, and with a man,
at my age.

MUSSOLINI: Well! You *could* say a man, a child, and dogs.

Darkness, then light.

MUSSOLINI (*alone*): The sea! What foam! Not a drop of water.
Just foam. Foam up to the roofs of the houses. It rises at
regular intervals. I've never seen anything so impressive! And
this town, built on a bridge! The sea, where is the sea? It's two
feet below, the sea. I'm frightened.

*Darkness, then light. Enter Leah from the left with the child
and the dogs. An old Chambermaid enters from the right.*

LEAH: Funny country.

THE CHAMBERMAID (*sitting on one of the steps to the stage*): You're
not obliged to stay here.

LEAH: Could I have a few bones for my dogs?

*A Cook enters from the left. He is peeling some vegetables.
A second Cook follows him; he too is peeling vegetables.
Finally, the last to enter is a Man in Evening Dress, with
white gloves, also peeling vegetables.*

THE MAN IN EVENING DRESS (*to The Chambermaid*): Answer the lady! Yes, Madame, you'll be given some bones.

Leah manifests great joy. She places the child and the dogs underneath her dress (without being afraid to show her legs) and shakes them in all directions.

LEAH: The bulldog is unhappy. Why, I hadn't noticed his paws. He has paws like a tiger's.

Enter Musssolini; the Cooks and the Man in Evening Dress who seemed interested in Leah's actions are seized with panic, and flee. Leah places the dogs on the floor. She keeps the child in her lap. Mussolini kicks the fox terrier and sends it rolling into the wings.

You brute! You've bashed his snout in, and his ear!

MUSSOLINI: Doctors aren't for dogs: better have him taken care of.

Leah places the child on the floor.

LEAH: Oh, how horrible are these black shoes, these laced shoes, and these black stockings! I'm going to buy him some others.

MUSSOLINI: No, it's useless.

LEAH: You're right: I'd better go.

Darkness followed by light. The yard-goods shop.

LEAH: I'd like some white leather booties for the child.

THE SHOPKEEPER: Sky-blue would be prettier.

LEAH: No, white! I want white booties!

THE SHOPKEEPER: What taste!

LEAH: Everyone to his taste. (*She examines the booties.*) Why! The soles are made of cork. They can't be very practical. They'd soak up the water.

THE SHOPKEEPER: And what about wine-bottle corks when you push them under water?

LEAH: All right, I'll take the sky-blue ones.

Darkness followed by light.

LEAH (*seated*): I'm going to Saint Affrica, in Africa. I can't take you.

MUSSOLINI: Complain! I advise you to complain. A husband without looking for one, a child you haven't borne, and dogs
you haven't bought.

LEAH: He has curls. He's blond. He has large black eyes. He looks
like the one I have at home, like my Patrick. I'm keeping the
child. He's too pretty.

Darkness, then light.

LEAH (*holding the child by the hand*): The light is opaque; the
atmosphere is heavy. It is the city of wills-o'-the-wisp. And
those people, those black phantoms. It is all very disturbing.
(*She runs.*) There! I've got one! It's Mussolini.

MUSSOLINI: Well! It's obvious you've never had a child before.
You're running like a madwoman, running as though you were
alone, and you're dragging the brat on the floor.

LEAH: Yes, you're right. I'd forgotten him. I was holding him by
the hand. But, first, please call me "Madame." I can't stand
disrespect.

MUSSOLINI: There she goes again!

Mussolini, the child, and the dogs begin to weep.

LEAH: What's wrong with you? Why are you crying?

MUSSOLINI: Ah, I don't hold it against you. (*Taking the child's
black shoes from his pocket.*) Here, put his old shoes, his
black shoes, back on him. Some day he may be able to race
along with you. But just now he needed them.

LEAH: Oh, my God! If I could only change my heart! (*She throws
away the blue shoes and places the black ones on the child's
feet.*) And the hair falling straight down over his forehead—
where are his lovely blond curls?

MUSSOLINI: Yes, he had on a wig.

*Leah begins to walk rapidly around the stage holding the
child by the hand and saying:*

LEAH: Oh—it's true! Now he runs as fast as I, he runs as fast as I,
he runs as fast as I. (*She stops and takes the child into her
arms.*) My little one, my little one, now we will never part
again. You will have no more wigs. And so that you may pass
unrecognized I will dye your hair black.

Exit Leah followed by the dogs. Mussolini sits down and holds his head in his hands. The curtain slowly falls.

END OF THE FOURTH TABLEAU AND OF THE SECOND ACT

ACT III

FIFTH TABLEAU

The stage represents a hotel lobby at midnight. As the curtain rises, a clock is heard to strike, bells ring, there are footsteps and shouts on the stairs. The elevator filled with lodgers goes up and down at full speed. People in evening gowns, evening dress, shirt-sleeves, and so on.

SEVERAL VOICES: —It's number 53. —It's on the fourth. —On the fourth. —53? —A woman. —Do they know who she is? — She's living alone. —She's an actress. —An American. —A housewife. —A prostitute. —The poor woman; what's wrong with her? —She's gone mad. —There's nothing wrong with her. —She's hysterical. —She's wrecking everything. —She's wrecking the furniture. —She's breaking the windows. —She's about to set fire to the whole building.

ONE LOUDER VOICE (*from above*): We can't get it open. Will you open up? (*A pause.*) No? (*A pause.*) Break down the door.

A loud cry, followed by absolute silence. The elevator comes down. Leah, her hands dripping blood, her white dress in tatters, is in it between Two Policemen. Jostling on the stairs as the lodgers rush down to watch.

FIRST POLICEMAN (*to The Manager*): What's her name?

THE MANAGER: We don't know. Here we call her Madame Leah.

SECOND POLICEMAN: Hasn't she filled in a police form?

THE MANAGER: Police matters are your concern.

FIRST POLICEMAN: That's right. In that case, Madame Leah—since Madame Leah it is—kindly follow us.

LEAH (*exaltedly*): I will follow you to the ends of the earth, to the ends of the earth. (*Bursts of laughter.*)

SECOND POLICEMAN: Either she's crazy or she's drunk. Do you know if she has any vices, sir?

THE MANAGER: I've been trying to tell you that I don't know her at all.

FIRST POLICEMAN: That's no answer. Couldn't she be injecting herself or inhaling drugs?

THE MANAGER (*to Leah*): Do you inject yourself? Do you inhale drugs?

LEAH: I neither inject myself nor do I inhale drugs.

FIRST POLICEMAN (*to the lodgers*): Does anyone here know Madame Leah? Is there someone here who can tell us anything about her?

ALL: Madame Leah? Madame Leah? Madame Leah? . . .

FIRST POLICEMAN: Now, then, what has she done, this Madame Leah?

THE MANAGER: She smashed the wardrobe. She made a shambles of the bathroom. She strangled the goldfish in their tank. She set fire to the curtains in her room. That's what she's done, this Madame Leah. She'll have to pay for it too, this Madame Leah.

FIRST POLICEMAN: Did you hear what he said, Madame? You will admit these facts, I assume?

LEAH (*to The Manager*): I did not come here, sir, to occupy a number, not even Number 53. You say I smashed the wardrobe: Patrick had promised to take me to the pole. Did he do it? You say I made a shambles of the bathroom? Patrick had promised me some stars which he had made himself. You press on a coiled spring: you're supposed to see the sea, the trees, and the clouds. What did I see? You say I strangled the goldfish in their tank? I sold all I could of Saint Patrick's body. The rest had gone on a trip. Has the rest come back? If it has, why hasn't someone told me? I will build you artificial grottoes at my own expense and I will buy you clocks made of silk and human flesh. And I will stock your holy-water pond in which carp and Holy Sacraments will swim. As for your curtains, sir, I set them ablaze to please you. Marlborough, Marlborough died in the wars. It's only right that you should resurrect his mouth on the balcony of your hotel. I did what I could to open his eyes. But your walls are of iron, sir, your walls have nickel pupils. They have stripped off the flesh from my insect hands, my little Frenchwoman's frogs.

SEVERAL VOICES: Charming! Mad? Charming! Mad, but charming.

The lodgers slowly withdraw.

THE MANAGER: Ladies and gentlemen, kindly, I beseech you, return to your apartments. May I ask that you be a little discreet? I myself am mortified by this scandal. Happily, it's all over. All's well that ends well, isn't that right, gentlemen? Good night, ladies. (*To The Policemen.*) See what you can do with her. No more scenes, right? I don't want to make an issue of this. I just want to be left in peace. Good night.

FIRST POLICEMAN: Madame Leah, please come with us.

SECOND POLICEMAN: Come with us.

LEAH: Officers! (*Pointing to the door.*) Look at that door.

FIRST POLICEMAN: So what?

SECOND POLICEMAN: I see it.

LEAH: It's about to open. It must open.

FIRST POLICEMAN: That's right, it must open. I'm going to open it myself right away.

LEAH (*sadly*): Don't trouble yourself, Officer. It will open by itself.

The door opens by itself.

Just look at the power of words.

POLICEMEN (*together*): What about the power of words?

LEAH: You'll see. Say the word "light."

POLICEMEN (*together*): Light.

LEAH (*disconcerted*): Now you have followed the light. Not a thing changed. The light keeps shining. It keeps shining all by itself.

The Policemen shrug their shoulders.

And now, say: "the night."

POLICEMEN (*together*): Let's humor her. "The night."

LEAH: It's waiting for you, just as your shadows wait for you to
follow you. The night gets along without us. It passes all by
itself. But I, I say, I am going to say, that I carry him . . .
and he passes . . . as though molded by my throat and sprung
from my mouth: "Patrick."

Enter Patrick. The Policemen flee in terror.

Ah! Patrick, what joy!

They kiss.

PATRICK: Weren't you still waiting for me? Were you still waiting
for me?

LEAH: I was hardly waiting for you at all. Still, yesterday while I
was eating strawberries I said to myself: "Will I ever see the
cream on the table again? Patrick in his place?" And I took
some sugar.

PATRICK: And you took some sugar?

LEAH: I took some. Ah! All that sugar I wasted!

PATRICK: And the house?

LEAH: Now it's in the hands of the electricians.

Clap of thunder.

PATRICK: What is that sound?

LEAH: It's thunder.

PATRICK: But the sky is like lead.

LEAH: Today is Corpus Christi day.

PATRICK: Today is Corpus Christi day.

Enter some Children.

FIRST CHILD: Mr. Patrick, what did you bring in your shoes?

PATRICK: Elephants beneath the palms.

SECOND CHILD: And that lion looking at us?

PATRICK: That, my boy, is liberty.

THIRD CHILD: And the automobile, is it for us?

PATRICK: It's unbreakable and deep.

FIRST CHILD: Are you giving us any new scents?

PATRICK: Take these birds.

SECOND CHILD: Give us something more.

PATRICK: Leah, don't you have anything for these children?

LEAH: Children, leave your father alone.

THE CHILDREN: But Patrick isn't our father!

PATRICK: Who is your father, then, children?

FIRST CHILD: Mine is the bakery's horse.

SECOND CHILD: Mine is my mother's sewing machine.

PATRICK (to the Third Child): And who is yours?

THIRD CHILD: My father, Mr. Patrick? Rather say my son who is
off fighting the Arabs. He has a large face like an apple tart
and giant's ears. My son's beard grows in his wallet and he has
eyes in all his pockets. They say he's quite a character. But,
then, what don't they say? Isn't that right, Mr. Patrick? They
also say you buy Negresses to make grape preserves and that
you sell the leavings to the goldsmiths. Such a disgusting trade
fairly makes me retch. My son will never get over it when he
finds out. He's a good friend of Leah's, isn't he, my girl? This
is what he said to me before he went away: "Be happy, little
father! Leah is the finest of the finest, and it won't be long
before Patrick smashes the terrace of the house against her
face." I didn't say anything to such nonsense. Leah forbids
me to talk about it, but she thinks a lot of characters like me.
Isn't that right, children?

THE CHILDREN (together): Yes, sir. Long live the colonel's father!

PATRICK: Ah! sir! Your son is a colonel?

THIRD CHILD: We've been knocking ourselves out repeating it.
My son is a colonel of Zouaves.

PATRICK: Go on, dear child, assemble your troops and leave me in
peace.

THIRD CHILD: By my command! Fall in!

The Children line up side by side. The colonel's father pulls a revolver from his pocket and kills them point-blank.

Write that down in your hunting record, Mr. Patrick!

PATRICK: Oh, my son, my son! Think of the future of our line! Come here and let me decorate and embrace you properly.

THIRD CHILD: What do you want, Papa? I was the father of a colonel of Zouaves by accident, but I'll always be a child of love.

Clap of thunder.

PATRICK: Begin reading the proclamation.

LEAH: My God, you've given me the breasts of a cow—give me today the crested helmet of rebellion, for Patrick and my child have forsaken me.

Clap of thunder.

THIRD CHILD: Rise, Madame. Your Patrick has lost nothing in his travels. The Nile flows through many lands, and I was my family's joy before the age of reason. Give thanks to your son while you accept mine. If Patrick had met the colonel of Zouaves, he would have lacked for nothing. He would have been restored to you a eunuch, Leah. And my father would today have that bayonet-like voice which is the sign of imminent genius.

LEAH: Thank you, little one. You speak like a book.

THIRD CHILD: Mother, books don't speak.

PATRICK: What do they do, my son?

THIRD CHILD: They read.

Clap of thunder.

PATRICK: Go away, you swarm of flies. Miniature graybeards. Go blow your noses. They get on my nerves, these children. They exasperate me.

LEAH: Yes, they're killing each other. I'm fed up with it too.

PATRICK: A fine bonnet, that crown of newborn babes, one of whom already has a son who is a colonel of Zouaves. But how do I fit into the story? And the final outcome?

LEAH: You've put on weight, Patrick.

PATRICK: The outcome?

LEAH: Ah! I've waited so long already!

PATRICK: The outcome?

LEAH: How impatiently!

PATRICK: Yes, that's right. But to conclude . . .

LEAH: To conclude what?

PATRICK: To love each other.

LEAH: I'm hungry.

PATRICK: Oh, my dear, what big teeth you have!

LEAH: The better to rock you with, my child.

PATRICK: Well, then let's go to sleep.

LEAH: No, I want you to tell me a story.

PATRICK: Well, then, I'll tell you one. It will be the last. The factory chimneys are harvested at the end of November. First they are polished by being rolled in sand. They come out smooth and bright after that operation. Some are set aside for reproduction, on the right; the others are placed on the left. The latter are divided into two parts. One part is for armaments. Cannons are made from them. The rest are sold at auction. These are therefore scattered. But as they change hands they wear out and soon nothing is left of these former factory chimneys. All that remains are the factories and the cannons. Then the cannons are aimed at the factories. A cannon is given away to every lady who asks for one, so that finally not a single cannon remains.

LEAH: And, dear Patrick, what do the ladies do with all those cannons?

PATRICK: My dear, you don't have to believe me—but they eat them.

LEAH: It's not true.

Enter The Author.

THE AUTHOR: Hey there! Patrick!

LEAH: Who are you?

PATRICK: He's The Author.

THE AUTHOR: Do you need me?

PATRICK: No, thank you.

THE AUTHOR (*handing him a revolver*): Here, take this; you'll need it.

PATRICK: You're right. (*He fires at The Author.*)

THE AUTHOR: It's no use, my dear Patrick! Those bullets can't penetrate me. And it's a shame!

PATRICK: Well, then, keep the thing. I have no use for it.

THE AUTHOR: Please. If you won't do it for me, then do it for the sake of the drama you are enacting. I assure you that a shot at the end of the play is absolutely necessary for the development of the plot.

PATRICK: Do you think so?

THE AUTHOR: I'm sure of it.

PATRICK: Then I will obey you. Good-bye, sir.

THE AUTHOR: Farewell, Patrick.

LEAH (*to The Author*): Tell me something.

THE AUTHOR: Madame?

LEAH: Aren't you going to give me anything?

THE AUTHOR: That's a reasonable question. Take this. (*He hands her another revolver.*)

LEAH: Is it loaded, at least? (*To Patrick.*) I'm sure you haven't examined your weapon.

THE AUTHOR: Have no fear; they are both suitably provided.

LEAH (*to Patrick*): Don't you think the gentleman takes after Dovic a little?

PATRICK: The gentleman has all his parts properly in place. That's enough, Leah.

THE AUTHOR: You should make allowances, Patrick. Leah is a woman.

PATRICK: What did you say?

THE AUTHOR: I said: Leah is a woman.

PATRICK: I'm a woman too, then. What would you say to that?

THE AUTHOR: What I say is this: I know more about it than you do, but I must say I didn't think you'd turn out so well.

PATRICK: See how white my skin is.

THE AUTHOR: That wouldn't prove very much.

PATRICK: It wouldn't prove anything, actually, if it were not for the perpetual snows. The perpetual snows, sir, if you care to know, have taught me to see clearly into this. The mountains, it is true, did somewhat disturb me. But do you know what I did with the mountains?

THE AUTHOR: What did you do with the mountains?

PATRICK: I turned them into men.

THE AUTHOR: Your words make everything impossible, my friend.

PATRICK: Well, then, write plays without words.

THE AUTHOR: Did I ever intend to do otherwise?

PATRICK: Yes, you put words of love into my mouth.

THE AUTHOR: You should have spat them out.

PATRICK: I tried to, but they turned into gunshots or dizzy spells.

THE AUTHOR: That's hardly my fault. Life is like that.

PATRICK: Leave life alone, then, and increase the size of your brain.

THE AUTHOR: Without fail.

PATRICK: When it gives birth, save a little brain for me.

THE AUTHOR: You can count on me.

PATRICK: I can really do without it, but it will amuse Leah's child.

THE AUTHOR: Don't you have anything else to ask me?

PATRICK: No.

LEAH: May I ask you for something too?

THE AUTHOR: If you don't ask for too much.

LEAH: Then give us two little brains. One for the child and the other for me.

THE AUTHOR: For you?

LEAH: Yes, that will give me three.

THE AUTHOR: How is that?

LEAH: Mine, Patrick's, and yours.

THE AUTHOR (*hastily*): Count on me, count on me. (*To Patrick, in low tones.*) One bit of good advice, my friend; use that thing you're holding. Your future depends on it. (*He runs away.*)

PATRICK: Where are you running off to? Where are you running off to?

THE AUTHOR: I'm going to give birth. Good night.

A long pause. Patrick and Leah look at each other.

PATRICK: Ah, Leah, there's still love!

LEAH: Love worn down to the bare rope, and the rope to hang yourself. Love: the secret work of wear. There's just you, Patrick.

PATRICK: Me, let's talk about it! Me, a little cork of marrow bobbing on a string. There's you, Leah.

LEAH: Ah, Patrick: the beautiful architecture of wrath! I would be quite willing to live on roses: they have a flowery odor. I need coal and bedsheets. There is pain, Patrick.

PATRICK: Pain? A burning drop of oil engendering a body. The curving of the earth is the pain of the world, as the tongue is the pain of thought, as the isthmus of the neck is the pain of the body and, when it is sliced through, the most painful criminals are severed from life. Pain? The great genesis. But there is kindness, Leah.

LEAH: Kindness? No, Patrick. Kindness, a gift at the end of a rubber band, the flabby malady of death. Fat cheeks and overburdened knees. Don't try to touch me with that. The trained-dog factory. But there is forgiveness, Patrick.

PATRICK: Forgiveness, like the sun. Forgiveness, like returning. Forgiveness, like a boomerang. Forgiveness, like births. Forgiveness, like the seasons. Forgiveness, without any ill-feelings.

LEAH: There is death.

PATRICK: Yes, death. But death like forgiveness. Like snow on the mountain. Forgiveness, like fire you slice with a knife. Forgiveness, like the water houses are made of. Forgiveness, like the murderer other crimes are made of. Forgiveness, like the living other dead are made of. Forgiveness, like the secret the storms are made of. Forgiveness, like the horse fortunes are made of. Forgiveness, like the old man the clouds are made of. Forgiveness, like me, whom I am making a criminal of. Forgiveness, like you whom I am making a deadly acid of. The heart is red already. Flow. Leah. Hands on the copper of shadows. The heart is red already as far as the end of the theatre where someone is about to die.

LEAH: Enough, Patrick! (*She fires a shot.*)

PATRICK: What have you done, Leah? What have you done? You've just killed a spectator.

END OF THE FIFTH TABLEAU AND THE THIRD ACT

humulus the mute

by JEAN ANOUILH *and* JEAN AURENCHE

translated by Michael Benedikt

Characters

THE DUCHESS
HECTOR DE BRIGNOC
HUMULUS, as a child, then as an adolescent
THE TUTOR
THE MAIDS, at least three
HÉLÈNE

Scenery

The Duchess's salon
The central fixture of which is the Duchess's armchair
Then a road bordered by plane trees
Then a public garden
But none of these settings is indispensable.

The Duchess, an extraordinary individual who sits in an enormous wing chair with emblazoned wings. Beside her, Uncle Hector, a tall, thin, gamy country-squire type, who puts his monocle alternately to his right and left eye, with little apparent effect either way. An orchestra is heard.

THE DUCHESS: Hector, I enjoy this little party of ours more every year.

HECTOR: The orchestra is charming.

THE DUCHESS: Yes, the musicians are horribly expensive. I had to haggle with them like a shopkeeper.

Enter the maids, single file, carrying bouquets.

My friends. I am touched by your presence here and by your good intentions. But there are traditions which a Brignoc does not flaunt. I ought to receive the compliments of my children before those of my people. Show a little patience; my grandson, Mr. Humulus, should be here before long. Hector, do you remember my little Humulus?

HECTOR: Very vaguely. He was, I believe, eighteen days old when I left for the Indies.

THE DUCHESS: You will find him quite changed. He's a good little boy, a bit timid. If it weren't for his infirmity, he would make a delightful duke.

HECTOR: Do I seem to recall that the poor little fellow is mute?

THE DUCHESS: Was, Hector, was! It's obvious that you've returned only yesterday. God has wrought a miracle during your stay in the Indies.

HECTOR: God has always protected the Brignocs.

THE DUCHESS: An English physician, after much effort, has enabled him to pronounce one word each day.

HECTOR: Only one word?

THE DUCHESS: Yes, but then he's still so very little. As he grows, we hope he'll be able to say still more. Note too, Hector, that if

271

my little Humulus abstains one day from speaking his word, he can speak two the next day.

HECTOR: Would it be possible, then, do you think to teach him one of those little fables that children of his age ordinarily know by heart?

THE DUCHESS: I have often dreamed of just that. But it would take too long. To say "honor above all," the Brignoc motto, my dear Hector, he must remain silent three days. . . . I make this little sacrifice every year during our regional festival, but I just don't know how I can go on much longer without hearing him say his word. For I have absolutely insisted that Humulus come and say his word to me every morning. Yesterday, Friday, for example, he came up to me and said "codfish."

Enter Tutor.

Well now, Tutor, is my grandson ready?

THE TUTOR: Madame, here he is. We'd been looking for quite a while for just the right thing for Mr. Humulus to say, this year, on New Year's Day. There are of course no lack of recitations suitable for young people, but they were all quite obviously too long. That is why I thought that the most appropriate, expressive, and I dare say, the most concise word, Madame, might be "happiness."

THE DUCHESS: A perfect choice, Tutor.

The Tutor goes out and returns pushing Humulus, a gawky boy still wearing short pants, who is virtually concealed by the enormous bouquet he carries. A buzz from the maids lined up and leaning forward to look at him.

(*Stopping him with a gesture at the head of the row of maids.*)

My grandson, even before you offer your grandmother your good wishes, your grandmother would convey to you her tenderness, at the threshold of this new year. Since your poor mother is dead, Humulus, I am the one who is left to love you. You have a grandmother, and you must take advantage of her advice. Be good and be valiant, like a true Brignoc. Cherish me always, and don't be upset if I see you only on state occasions, and festivals. All my time is taken up by my poor people. And

now, kiss me and speak your word to me. Tutor, have the
music stopped so that my grandson may speak his word to me.

*The Tutor goes out. The music stops. He returns to his place
again, and discreetly claps his hands. Then Humulus, blush-
ing, eyebrows knitted, slowly begins to walk toward the Duchess. Everyone smiles with compassion. Before the last maid,
at the very end of the line, he drops his bouquet. The maid
picks it up and hands it back to him. Then, in the silence,
after having struggled for a moment, crimson, between several
equally well-impressed lessons.*

HUMULUS: Thanks!

*A dreadful uproar from the orchestra. All assembled hide
their faces in their hands with consternation.*

THE TUTOR: Hapless child! You've spoken your word. Now how are
you going to say "happiness" to the Duchess?

THE DUCHESS: Mr. Humulus, you are a bungler.

*She exits, followed by Uncle Hector and all the maids. Humu-
lus remains alone, in the middle of the stage, with his bouquet.
The Tutor sits disconsolately on the steps to the stage.*

SCENE 2

*Same scenery. The characters stand as they were at the opening
curtain. But they are considerably aged. A little groom has been
added at the end of the row of maids. Music.*

THE DUCHESS: My friends, I am touched by your presence here and
by your good intentions. But there are family traditions which
a Brignoc does not flaunt. I ought to receive the compliments
of my children before those of my people. Show a little
patience; my grandson, Mr. Humulus, should be here before
long. In your opinion, Hector, what can he possibly be doing?

HECTOR: Perhaps he's practicing his word before a mirror?

Enter Tutor.

THE DUCHESS: Well, Tutor?

THE TUTOR (*who appears nervous*): Madame, Mr. Humulus requests the honor of presenting his good wishes to you. Mr. Humulus will pronounce the word "prosperity."

The Duchess smiles indulgently. The orchestra falls silent. Humulus, who is now a young man, is ushered in. The Tutor coughs. Humulus says nothing.

THE DUCHESS: Speak your word, my dear child.

Silence. All look at one another.

Don't upset yourself, dear Humulus. A grandmother is always indulgent. (*Pause.*) What does this mean, Tutor?

THE TUTOR (*stammering*): I am extremely surprised, Madame.

THE DUCHESS: Humulus, have you already spoken your word? The word, which at the threshold of the new year, you should have reserved for your grandmother?

HECTOR: The little rogue probably swore while trying to knot his tie.

THE TUTOR: You can't know my pupil very well, Baron. Mr. Humulus does not swear.

THE DUCHESS: Tutor, a word just doesn't get lost by itself like that. Have you watched over my grandson closely this morning?

THE TUTOR: I did not leave Mr. Humulus this morning, Madame, except for a moment in the clothes closet, and I can certify . . .

Humulus jabs him with his elbow.

THE DUCHESS: It seems to me that the two of you are in connivance. You're hiding something from me, Tutor.

THE TUTOR: Here's the whole truth, Madame. May heaven be my witness that I thought I was doing no harm when I consented to what Mr. Humulus proposed.

THE DUCHESS: What he proposed? Explain yourself, Tutor. What did he propose?

THE TUTOR: His proposals were actually commands, Madame.

THE DUCHESS: What commands? Hector, can you make anything of what the Tutor is talking about?

HECTOR: I hesitate among several equally painful hypotheses.

THE DUCHESS: Tutor, I call upon you to explain yourself clearly.

THE TUTOR: I shall, Madame, as much to unburden my conscience as to give some expression to the wishes of Mr. Humulus. Mr. Humulus has asked me to read you this note, Madame. (*He reads.*) "Madame, my grandmother, I am passionately in love with a woman named Hélène . . ."

The Duchess, with a terrible cry, faints. Uproar from the orchestra. Tumult, disorder, people running in all directions.

THE DUCHESS (*straightening up*): Hector, have my people leave me.

Hector pushes everybody out.

Tutor, your insolence has made me faint before my staff; I will never forget the humiliation you've caused. Continue.

THE TUTOR: With all due respect, if I may be allowed, Madame . . .

THE DUCHESS: You may be allowed nothing; continue.

THE TUTOR (*beginning to read*): "I am passionately in love with . . ."

THE DUCHESS: Take care to leave out the unseemly passages. . . .

THE TUTOR: ". . . with a woman named Hélène. I intend to declare my love to her as soon as possible. Since my sad infirmity allows me to say only one word a day, I have decided, beginning today, to abstain from pronouncing my daily word for a period of one month. My tutor and I thought . . ." That isn't quite correct, Madame.

With a wave of her fan, she signals him to continue.

"that thirty words would suffice to make this declaration. . . . Therefore I must excuse myself, Madame, my grandmother, for not being able, this New Year's Day, to come and speak to you the word 'prosperity.'"

THE DUCHESS: Tutor, you may stop. Such ingratitude disgusts me. I refuse to hear any more, and I shall not appear at the party tonight. Mr. Humulus, you are a scamp. What have you to say to that?

THE TUTOR: You know very well that he can't say anything, Madame . . .

THE DUCHESS: Tutor, you are an idiot. (*She goes out.*)

HECTOR: Bravo, you sly little dog. You're a true Brignoc. At your age, I myself had a mistress who played in the musical comedy.

THE TUTOR: You force me to play such painful roles, my dear pupil. Your fantasies will be the death of me. (*He goes out.*)

SCENE 3

The curtain rises on a road bordered by plane trees; Hélène appears, on a bicycyle. She carries a little black box on her handlebars. Behind her, Humulus, also on a bicycle. It is obvious that he is following her. They circle around a bit, then she dismounts. Humulus dismounts too.

HÉLÈNE: Excuse me, sir, can you tell me how many miles it is from here to the beach?

Humulus bows silently, hand on his heart.

Thank you very much, sir, that's not very far at all. I'll be able to get there before lunchtime.

She gets on her bicycle again and departs, smiling at him. He gets on his bicycle again and follows her. Their bells jingle away into the distance.

SCENE 4

A public garden. The Tutor enters, a piece of paper in his hand, and goes over to Humulus.

THE TUTOR: Mr. Humulus, I've worked very hard, believe me; I didn't sleep a wink last night, putting the finishing touches on this document. To frame a declaration of love in thirty words is no easy job. My dear pupil, please don't reproach me for not putting enough passionate phrases into the text. There are indeed prepositions here, and articles and conjunctions, which are admittedly neutral words, but only those absolutely necessary for the comprehensibility of the text. Here it is (*He reads.*): "Miss. Overwhelming love seized my entrails the other day. May my tears and sighs move your cruel beauty to pity! A single word from you would heal all my wounds." That makes thirty. I certainly shouldn't lend myself to this folly—but I too have loved, and this adventure calls sweet memories to mind. (*He takes out his watch.*) The young lady can't be long now. . . . Would you like me to stay here to prompt you, should it prove necessary, or shall I withdraw a stone's throw?

Humulus makes a motion; The Tutor withdraws. Standing there, alone, Humulus rereads his message, making passionate gestures. Hélène enters on her bicycle and for a moment circles around him, without his responding. Finally, Hélène's presence brings him out of his dreams; he pales, walks toward her, rereading his message one last time. Hélène has dismounted and watches him approaching, smiling.

HUMULUS (*in a rather unexpected, orator's voice*): Miss, I was the one behind you the other day on the bicycle. You asked the way. It was ten miles to the sea. (*He stops, turned white; then, dismayed, as if in spite of himself*): By the shortcut . . . (*His voice is choked off, and he begins feverishly to count on his fingers.*)

Hélène continues to watch him, smiling.

HUMULUS (*who has only three words left to say*): I love you.

HÉLÈNE (*smiling still*): Please excuse me, sir, but I'm a little hard of hearing, and I didn't hear a thing. (*She takes a large ear trumpet out of the little black box on the handlebars, and puts it to her ear; then, politely*): Would you mind repeating what you said, please?

Humulus stares at her, and an uproar from the orchestra hides his despair as the curtain falls.

la place de l'étoile

AN ANTIPOEM

by ROBERT DESNOS

translated by Michael Benedikt

—*Look, my son; if the remainder of my body were concealed, I could pass for one of the cherubim gliding through the skies.*
—JAMES BERESFORD

Characters

THE BARKEEPER
FIRST DRINKER
SECOND DRINKER
THIRD DRINKER
THE DOORMAN
MAXIME
THE CUSTOMER
THE POLICEMAN
THE WAITER
FABRICE
ARTHUR
FIRST MAN
SECOND MAN
THIRD MAN
ATHENAIS
A VOICE IN THE STREET
FIRST FIREMAN
SECOND FIREMAN
GÉRARD
FIRST RAGPICKER
SECOND RAGPICKER
LAMPLIGHTER
CONCIERGE
TWELVE WAITERS, nonspeaking
THREE MEN, nonspeaking

ACT I

A bar.

THE BARKEEPER: The twelfth of January, an anniversary for me.

A DRINKER: An anniversary?

THE BARKEEPER: Anniversary.

A DRINKER: Anniversary of what?

THE BARKEEPER: An anniversary . . . that's all.

ANOTHER DRINKER: A woman?

THE BARKEEPER: Oh, you're all so terribly concerned with women. An anniversary? Of what? A woman, a woman naturally . . . Misery!

ANOTHER DRINKER: Then, this anniversary of yours—what's it an anniversary of?

THE BARKEEPER: An anniversary for me.

FIRST DRINKER: Very mysterious, all right.

THIRD DRINKER: Well, he can keep his secrets.

THE BARKEEPER: Oh! Secrets! You know . . .

SECOND DRINKER: Right, right. Doorman! The phonograph.

THE BARKEEPER: You really enjoy that contraption, don't you?

FIRST DRINKER: It passes the time.

THE BARKEEPER: To pass the time . . . Misery!

THE PHONOGRAPH: "The pleasure of love lasts but a moment."

THE DOORMAN: Bad needle there.

SECOND DRINKER: Funny little song.

THE BARKEEPER: A woman . . .

FIRST DRINKER: That's no song to play in a bar.

THIRD DRINKER: And that machinery, always machinery . . . "The pleasure of lo-o-ve lasts but a mo-ment." Just to pass the time.

281

THE DOORMAN: And so?

FIRST DRINKER: Forget about it, forget about it.

Enter Maxime. He walks through the barroom, passes before a seated customer, retraces his steps and stops in front of him.

MAXIME: You, I want to see you about something.

THE CUSTOMER: I don't know why, Maxime. We've always gotten along without it in the past.

MAXIME: I want to see you to tell you that you're a rotter and a swine.

THE CUSTOMER (*getting up*): You fathead! Rotter!

MAXIME (*slapping him*): Lout! Filth!

Battle, overturned table. From behind it one hears the thudding of fists and Maxime's voice repeating: Filth! Filth! Filth! The Drinkers at the bar have turned around; The Barkeeper and the waiters separate the battlers. The Doorman returns with a Policeman.

THE BARKEEPER (*to The Policeman*): The idea, fighting like that!

MAXIME: How do you like my fist in your face, you skunk!

THE CUSTOMER: Just try it. And first of all, how'd you like to be arrested? Thief! Crook! (*Seeing The Policeman.*) Officer, arrest this man at once.

THE POLICEMAN: First of all, who do you think's giving the orders around here? Your papers, please.

THE CUSTOMER (*smiling wryly*): Here they are, but aren't you going to ask for his?

MAXIME: Informer, fumbler.

THE POLICEMAN (*to The Customer*): You're not the one who's giving the orders around here, you know. Causing a scandal like this! First of all, what did he steal from you?

MAXIME: I didn't steal anything from him.

THE POLICEMAN (*still to The Customer*): What did he steal from you?

THE CUSTOMER: He didn't steal anything from me. But this character . . .

THE POLICEMAN: Why are you calling him a thief, then? He might lodge a complaint against you, if he felt like it.

THE CUSTOMER: You're absolutely right; I said it in the heat of my anger.

THE POLICEMAN: Oh, don't try to make it up to me now. Angry or not, there are penalties for causing scandals. Get out of here. (*To Maxime.*) Do you want to lodge a complaint?

MAXIME: Me? Certainly not.

THE CUSTOMER: Well! That's a good one.

THE POLICEMAN: What do you mean, "that's a good one"? Come on, get out of here.

THE WAITER: Wait, he hasn't paid me yet.

THE POLICEMAN: He'll pay outside.

He thrusts The Customer out into the street; The Waiter follows them. Maxime shrugs his shoulders and goes toward a table to sit down; he sees Fabrice who had stood up during the incident and who approaches him.

FIRST DRINKER: Was that policeman stupid!

THE BARKEEPER: Quite, quite hilarious.

THIRD DRINKER: It serves that rat right. No man should turn another over to the police.

MAXIME: Fabrice!

FABRICE: Good evening . . . as usual.

MAXIME: It does me good, you know.

FABRICE: What had that fellow done to you?

MAXIME: Oh, it's quite complicated and very dull.

FIRST DRINKER (*to The Barkeeper*): That little fellow certainly gave it to the big one!

THIRD DRINKER: You know him?

THE BARKEEPER: I've seen him around, from time to time.

SECOND DRINKER: Do you know why they were fighting?

THE BARKEEPER: No.

THIRD DRINKER: A woman . . .

THE BARKEEPER: A woman . . . Misery!

FABRICE: Can you stay a moment?

MAXIME: As long as you like. How've you been? Happy? Satisfied?

FABRICE: Who, me? You know . . .

MAXIME: Always the same.

> *A long pause. The noises of the traffic outside are heard and, sporadically, the conversations of The Drinkers*

FIRST DRINKER: Do you know Lily?

SECOND DRINKER: Who? Little Lily?

THE BARKEEPER: Misery . . .

FIRST DRINKER: Yes, sometimes I wonder what became of her.

THIRD DRINKER: Rich?

SECOND DRINKER: Poor?

THE BARKEEPER: Lily? Rich . . . Poor . . . Misery . . .

FABRICE: And you, Maxime? As usual? As . . .

MAXIME: Please don't laugh, Fabrice. It's obvious enough that to you, I'm only . . . Nothing, skip it.

FABRICE: You're only? . . .

MAXIME: Nothing, nothing, nothing. And still you'll go on liking me.

FABRICE: As usual!

MAXIME: As usual!

FABRICE: Impossible!

FIRST DRINKER: That little Lily, all the same.

SECOND DRINKER: All the same, what?

FIRST DRINKER: I don't know.

THIRD DRINKER: You make me laugh with your crazy conversations.

THE BARKEEPER: Oh, it's just a manner of speaking. You have to kill the time somehow.

FABRICE: Maxime, I'm waiting . . . I'm waiting for someone.

MAXIME: I'm sorry I disturbed you. Besides, I have an urgent appointment that I forgot. Thanks for reminding me of it. So long, Fabrice.

THIRD DRINKER: Look, that young man just went out.

THE BARKEEPER: Misery!

ACT II

Maxime's room. Bed, table, several wardrobes, armchairs, chairs, a window and a door. The room is empty. Maxime enters, takes off his overcoat and hat. He seems to be looking for something. Finally he sits down in the armchair. Arthur comes in noiselessly and stands motionless behind him.

MAXIME: Arthur!

ARTHUR: Sir?

MAXIME: My starfish.

ARTHUR: You wish your starfish? It was on the mantelpiece. Look, it's gone now.

MAXIME: Where is it, then?

ARTHUR: No idea.

MAXIME: Ah! Ah! no idea, no idea. Why are inert objects always contradicting the desires of men? We've got to find that starfish!

Arthur and Maxime look for the starfish. They turn back the bedclothes, the carpet, upsetting the wardrobes, from which they withdraw an assortment of odd items: papers, books, clothing, tin things, birdcages, fans, ostrich plumes, and so on . . . which occasionally spill out on their heads.

That star, I must have it. I want it tonight. I won't stop until I've found it.

ARTHUR: Very good, sir.

MAXIME: Where is it! I'll wreck the whole house. . . .

They go on looking.

ARTHUR (*picking up the starfish from the mantelpiece*): Sir, here it is.

MAXIME: Where was it?

ARTHUR: On the mantelpiece.

MAXIME: You just looked there, though.

ARTHUR: I did, sir.

MAXIME: And?

ARTHUR: Sir?

MAXIME: And? And why didn't you see it there before?

ARTHUR: Because it wasn't there before.

MAXIME: You mean to tell me it walked there all by itself?

ARTHUR: No idea.

MAXIME: No idea! No idea! Get out of my sight!

ARTHUR: Very good, sir.

He goes out.

MAXIME (*seated before the mantelpiece, the starfish in his hand*): Five points! Five fingers on one hand, five senses, here they all are. That's not saying very much, I must say—but it's not entirely stupid! (*A pause.*) Fabrice. There we are. Oh, hell, no; it's not entirely stupid.

The door opens; enter The First Drinker.

FIRST DRINKER: Good day.

MAXIME: You just came in the door?

FIRST DRINKER: How are you supposed to come in?

MAXIME: By the door.

FIRST DRINKER: Well, then?

MAXIME: Well, then? Well, then, nothing. (*Pause.*) Is there something you'd like?

FIRST DRINKER: Give me your starfish.

MAXIME: You're obviously joking.

FIRST DRINKER: Please, give it to me.

MAXIME: It's a real comedy.

FIRST DRINKER: Give me your starfish.

MAXIME: No, absolutely not! Do you hear me? No!

FIRST DRINKER (*falling to his knees*): Maxime, in the name of life and death, give me your starfish.

MAXIME: No!

FIRST DRINKER (*getting up*): Too bad!

MAXIME: No, no, I tell you, no no no.

The door opens; enter a Policeman.

THE POLICEMAN: Sir!

MAXIME: What now?

THE POLICEMAN: Would you kindly give me your starfish?

MAXIME: What's this masquerade all about? You're not getting my starfish and you'll never get it, period.

THE POLICEMAN (*on his knees*): In the name of my dead wife and of my little one lying in her cradle, give me your starfish!

During this speech Arthur enters.

ARTHUR: You rang, sir?

MAXIME: For God's sake! I don't want anything! Leave me alone.

Arthur goes out.

THE POLICEMAN (*still on his knees*): Give me your starfish!

Enter The Second and Third Drinkers.

SECOND and THIRD DRINKERS (*together*): Don't give it to him.

MAXIME: Have no fear.

SECOND *and* THIRD DRINKERS (*together*): Give it to me!

SECOND DRINKER: To me, not to him!

THIRD DRINKER: No, to me!

MAXIME: What can this possibly mean?

THE POLICEMAN: That you have to give it to me.

MAXIME: No.

SECOND DRINKER: You see, argument is useless.

THIRD DRINKER: Just wait until he gives it to me.

MAXIME: To nobody.

THE POLICEMAN (*rising and addressing the two drinkers*): It's your fault. You're under arrest. (*He takes them by the arms.*) You're going to have to pay for this.

Enter The Barkeeper.

THE BARKEEPER: All this just over a little starfish.

The Policeman and The Two Drinkers exit, just as The Door-man enters.

(*To The Doorman.*) What are you doing here?

THE DOORMAN: Shhh . . . speak very quietly. I'm looking for a starfish, a beautiful starfish with five points. A magnificent starfish, still salty, fat, fresh from the sea. Virtually alive. I've come . . .

THE BARKEEPER: Are you feeling all right?

THE DOORMAN: Quiet! Not so loud! I've come to steal it while no one is looking.

THE BARKEEPER: I'm going to pull your ears for you. (*Shouting.*) You little punk!

They shove each other out the door.

(*Closing the door behind him.*) Misery! All that over a piece of flotsam . . .

A pause.

MAXIME (*alone*): Five fingers, five senses, five points. Fabrice!

FABRICE (*entering*): Maxime?

MAXIME (*standing up*): Just as it should be. Give me your hand, your hands. . . . (*He kisses her hands.*) . . . Two stars.

FABRICE: As usual!

MAXIME: Usual . . . Fabrice, I'm giving to you the thing I hold most dear in all this world. A starfish. Five points, five fingers, five senses . . . (*He gives her the starfish.*)

FABRICE: How pretty it is! So delicate, so plump. It smells of salt. It's like a cat. It smells of the depths of the sea. How pretty it is . . .

MAXIME: I give it to you.

FABRICE: Yes, Maxime, and I thank you for it. But what do you want me to do with it? I'd risk injuring it dancing, breaking its tips. No, keep it. It's better off with you. Don't be angry. I'd like it better knowing it's here. I'll come to see it. Don't be angry. Be as you are, as usual. I'll come back to see it. I swear to you I will.

MAXIME: It will always be here. (*He opens the window. Sound of an automobile in the street.*) It will always be here. (*He picks up the starfish and throws it out the window.*)

FABRICE: As usual.

MAXIME: Always. Good-bye, my poor dear.

Fabrice goes out.

(*Alone.*) All the same it's not completely stupid.

Enter The Policeman.

THE POLICEMAN: Sir, I've just found, down there, on the sidewalk, under your window, while passing, your starfish. And I'm returning it.

MAXIME: Just as it should be. Thank you!

The Policeman goes out. Enter The Three Drinkers.

TOGETHER: Sir!

MAXIME: You again! I thought you were all arrested.

TOGETHER: No. We've found . . .

MAXIME: What now?

TOGETHER: The starfish. (*Each gives him a starfish.*)

MAXIME: Just as it should be, thank you!

They go out, leaving Maxime alone. Enter The Doorman.

THE DOORMAN: Sir, sir, sir, I bring you your star . . . your star-fish.

Enter Twelve Waiters from the café carrying trays loaded with starfish. There are hundreds of them, and they scatter them everywhere: over the furniture, on the mantelpiece, and so on.

There we are.

MAXIME: Thank you!

THE BARKEEPER (*entering*): Misery of miseries! What a night! What a night! Ah! They're all there. Let them stay out there. It's impossible to walk in those starfish-infested streets. Now, let's go.

The Barkeeper, The Doorman, and The Twelve Waiters exit.

MAXIME (*alone*): Just as it should be.

ARTHUR (*entering*): What a job it will be cleaning up now!

MAXIME: Arthur!

ARTHUR: Sir?

MAXIME: You may go now.

ACT III

In a bar.

FIRST DRINKER: By the way, whatever became of him?

THIRD DRINKER: He's dead.

FIRST DRINKER: Of what?

SECOND DRINKER: Him, dead? When did it happen?

THIRD DRINKER: He died four or five months ago, but I don't know what the trouble was.

FIRST DRINKER: Are you sure?

SECOND DRINKER: Don't believe it. I saw him, flesh and blood, last week.

THIRD DRINKER: That's impossible. I attended his burial.

SECOND DRINKER: I tell you I ran into him last week. I even spoke to him. No question of it. I'm not crazy, am I? He had on that same peculiarly shaped hat of his, and the same baggy suit. No two men wear their clothes the same way. We perpetuate the characteristics of our body in the clothing we wear.

FABRICE: In Spain . . . I love the bullfights. And then there was that special feeling to everything, all so astonishing . . . the women . . .

THIRD DRINKER: I'm not crazy either. I went to his funeral. I saw his body; I even saw him die.

FIRST MAN: You're right, Fabrice . . . the sun, the withering heat, what could be more beautiful?

FABRICE: You're making a mistake. I never said that.

SECOND DRINKER: I saw him. He had a violin case under his arm.

SECOND MAN: Yes, Fabrice, I understand you. The Spanish people would be so beautiful if they were moved to Norway!

FABRICE: You're a good fellow. . .

FIRST DRINKER: He knew how to play the violin?

FABRICE: . . . which is to say, an imbecile. (*She turns her back to him.*)

THIRD DRINKER: I don't know, but I don't believe it.

SECOND DRINKER: I didn't say there was a violin in the violin case. You could use it for other things . . . for foodstuffs.

THE BARKEEPER: I had a customer, as a matter of fact, who used to go shopping with a violin case.

FABRICE (*to The Third Man*): You've nothing to say, now? No Norway? No Spain?

THIRD MAN: Oh, me, well, I'm not really much of a traveler.

FIRST DRINKER: Really, now, is he alive or is he dead?

FABRICE: That's no reason not to talk about Norway.

THIRD MAN: I don't understand.

FABRICE: It's quite simple.

THIRD DRINKER: After all, one thing is certain: ghosts don't exist.

THE BARKEEPER: Ghosts don't exist? I had a customer once . . .

Fabrice's voice rises over the end of the sentence.

FABRICE: You don't see how very simple it is?

SECOND DRINKER: It's all just a bunch of stories! Ghosts don't exist: therefore he is alive.

THIRD DRINKER: Therefore he's dead.

FIRST DRINKER: Ghosts don't exist? Absolutely? Not in the least . . .

THE BARKEEPER: Misery! Ghosts don't exist any more, today!

THIRD MAN: No, I don't understand, but I know that you're wearing a pretty dress and that you are beautiful and that you have the most extraordinary eyes.

FABRICE: Do run on, good fellow.

THIRD MAN: Why don't you believe me, dear Fabrice? You are beautiful and your relationships are as delicate as your sense of humor.

FABRICE: How simple it is, isn't it?

THIRD MAN: Don't you think I'm sincere?

FABRICE: Oh! Certainly.

THIRD MAN: Then?

FABRICE: Then, you're the one who's taking me for an idiot.

THIRD MAN: Oh, Fabrice . . .

FABRICE: So long. (*She walks toward the bar.*)

THE BARKEEPER (*to The Drinkers*): Perhaps you're not talking about the same person.

SECOND DRINKER: Yes, we are.

Fabrice sits down at the bar.

MAXIME (*approaching her*): Hello, Fabrice.

FABRICE: Hello. What's new?

MAXIME: Nothing, of course . . . I'm bored.

FABRICE: Ah! Boredom! . . .

FIRST DRINKER: Ghosts, ghosts . . .

Pause.

FABRICE: And your love life?

MAXIME: As usual.

FABRICE: That's not reasonable.

MAXIME: It's too reasonable.

Meanwhile Athenais has approached Maxime from behind and suddenly put her hands over his eyes.

ATHENAIS: Guess who.

MAXIME: Athenais, of course.

ATHENAIS: You win again!

MAXIME: My dear Fabrice, this is Athenais. And now I'll leave you two together. (*He walks away.*)

FABRICE: Why did he leave so quickly?

THIRD DRINKER: Athenais? A real ghost's name.

ATHENAIS: I'm very happy to know you. Maxime's friends have often mentioned you. I'm a bit jealous.

FABRICE: Has Maxime ever spoken to you of me?

ATHENAIS: Never. Have you known Maxime long? Funny fellow, isn't he? Sometimes he spends hours looking at his starfish and his hands, saying nothing. He's nice, isn't he? Have you known him long? I've always thought that he had a lovable sort of face. . . . I've seen you before. Wait a minute, don't you have a dark red dress, with some braid on it? And then I have a friend, I don't quite know which one, who met you once, I don't quite remember where. And have you known Maxime long? I was a bit jealous. Oh, I'm not really too bad. I'd like to be a good friend to you.

FABRICE: And I'd like to be a good friend to you, too. You were a bit jealous, you say, but you aren't any more?

ATHENAIS: Absolutely not. You know why? You're the kind of woman you can respect. Always surrounded by admirers. Who were you with just now? They seem fine fellows, these three chaps. Would you be good enough to introduce me to them?

FABRICE: Nothing could be simpler. So Maxime never spoke to you about me.

ATHENAIS: Absolutely not. You know him, with his starfish and his bottles. Always looking at his hands. A funny kind of life. Oh, not wicked, or anything, of course. Tell me, why is he always fighting with people? I live friends with everybody. Let everybody live as he likes, don't you think? But I like him well enough. After all, I may have a few queer notions myself—I think I like him out of curiosity.

FABRICE: But why were you jealous?

ATHENAIS: I don't know.

Meanwhile The Three Men have approached.

FIRST MAN: Well, Fabrice, still angry with me?

FABRICE: No, of course not, no.

SECOND MAN: And me either?

THIRD MAN: And me?

FABRICE: No, of course not. How odd you all are!

SECOND MAN: So, let's end the evening together.

ATHENAIS: Maxime! Maxime!

MAXIME: What is it?

ATHENAIS: Fabrice is leaving.

FABRICE: Good-bye, Maxime, see you soon.

MAXIME: See you soon.

ATHENAIS: Good-bye, see you soon. I want very much to be a good friend of yours.

FABRICE: Same here—good night.

ATHENAIS: Maxime.

MAXIME: What is it?

ATHENAIS: Why didn't you ever speak to me about Fabrice? I was a bit jealous, you know.

MAXIME: Jealous, jealous . . . you're all the same.

ATHENAIS: Are we going now?

FIRST DRINKER: Come on, tell me now what he wanted with that violin case.

THE BARKEEPER: Oh! You know those stories about gangsters . . .

THIRD DRINKER: Ghosts don't exist.

ACT IV

Maxime's room.

MAXIME (*alone*): To sleep alone. What a delight!
    Enter Athenais in a dress of era 1860.

ATHENAIS: Am I pretty, Maxime?

MAXIME: Like a ray of moonlight.

ATHENAIS: Why don't you ever speak to me about Fabrice?

MAXIME: You're a bit jealous, aren't you?

ATHENAIS: No, I'm afraid. Always looking at those starfish, and then your hands. There are too many starfish, too many things from the sea in here. My coral jewelry, and that mirror, and this whole room . . .

MAXIME: Look at the bed. This foaming sheet crashing on the pillow, that we drown in. It's a beautiful voyage, you know, with a wreck eventually certain.

ATHENAIS: Maxime, Maxime, don't talk like that; I'm afraid of the sea; I'm afraid of the night. Will I ever again dare to go to bed?

In the street a far-off hunting horn is heard.

MAXIME: There aren't any forests around here.

The clock strikes.

ATHENAIS: This hunting horn, those starfish . . . it all brings bad luck.

MAXIME: But whatever are you wearing? What's the meaning of that costume, Athenais?

A clamor in the street. Shouts: "Fire, fire!" Footsteps, broken windows.

ARTHUR (*entering*): Sir! sir! The staircase is cut off.

MAXIME: The staircase is cut off?

ARTHUR: Yes, sir—there's a fire, there's a fire!

MAXIME: A fire?

ARTHUR: The house is on fire; the stairs are cut off by the flames; we're lost!

ATHENAIS: God! . . . Oh! Burned alive! (*She starts to cry.*)

Maxime opens the door. The crashing of broken glass is heard. He opens the window.

MAXIME (*shouts*): Get out, get out! Fire, fire!

Distant sound of a fire-engine siren.

We've got to jump out the window. (*Shouting.*) Bring a mattress over here!

ARTHUR: Sir, sir! I could never jump down there.

MAXIME: I didn't ask for your opinion. (*He grabs him and literally throws him out the window.*) Athenais, you're next.

ATHENAIS: Never! Never! I'd rather die.

MAXIME: Oh, how you people trouble me! (*He takes Athenais in his arms and carries her to the window.*)

A VOICE IN THE STREET: Let's go, don't be afraid.

Maxime throws Athenais out and climbs onto the railing.

Let's go now!

Maxime jumps down. Meanwhile the sound of fire sirens has increased. Their noises fill the street, and the stage. A red ladder is raised in front of the window. A Fireman goes past on it without stopping. The clock strikes twice. A Fireman comes in the door, an ax in his hand, followed by another dragging a fire hose.

FIRST FIREMAN: Nothing here.

SECOND FIREMAN: That's funny, it's burning upstairs and downstairs, but not in here.

FIRST FIREMAN: And the fire seemed to stop suddenly when that character jumped out.

Pause.

SECOND FIREMAN: Look at this: what a starfish collection!

FIRST FIREMAN: He's probably a fisherman.

SECOND FIREMAN: I'm thirsty!

FIRST FIREMAN: What a job. Putting out fires. Now I ask you! Really—what's the use of all this!

SECOND FIREMAN (*turning to him slowly*): You're an utter maniac.

Pause. Enter Maxime.

MAXIME: Good evening. I hope I'm not disturbing you.

FIRST FIREMAN: No, no. You're in luck. Nothing caught fire here.

SECOND FIREMAN: I'd almost say that you put the fire out when you jumped out the window.

MAXIME: Oh, well, fire and I are very good friends.

FIRST FIREMAN: We'll be bidding you a very good evening, now.

SECOND FIREMAN: Pardon, sir, but are you a fisherman?

MAXIME: Why?

SECOND FIREMAN: All these starfish . . .

MAXIME: You're quite right, I am a fisherman, in fact.

FIRST FIREMAN: You were lucky you didn't kill yourself jumping out the window like that. It would have been particularly pointless since the fire never came in here.

MAXIME: Yes, you're right.

THE FIREMEN: Good evening, sir . . .

They go out. Enter Arthur and Athenais.

ARTHUR: I'd like to thank you, sir, for saving my life.

MAXIME: You mean I came within a hairsbreadth of killing you.

ARTHUR: Oh, no! I know that if we'd stayed here, we would have been roasted; that's the fact of the matter.

MAXIME: Not really!

ARTHUR: And also we see now how courageous you are, sir. A decision had to be made quickly, and I'd like to thank you, sir, despite that extraordinary punch you gave me.

MAXIME: You may go now.

ARTHUR: I do so, but thanking you, and thanking you again, sir.

ATHENAIS: My dearest, my dearest, how devoted to life you are . . . You must love me terribly to throw me out like that! Oh! I'll always see you above me and I in your arms and the street down there and the fire engines and bang . . . into the mattress. You must really love me, don't you? And when you climbed out the window . . . Oh! I closed my eyes, really, and when I opened them, you were there, hands in your pockets, a cigarette in your mouth.

MAXIME (*casually*): What did you feel like doing?

ATHENAIS: Do you want to come to the bar? I'd like to tell my friends about this.

MAXIME: Better go yourself. I'm tired.

ATHENAIS: Really, you don't want to come? Yes, go and rest. I'll be back in an hour.

MAXIME: Fine.

Athenais leaves.

MAXIME: Ah! Can it be that I'm dreaming?

ARTHUR: I can confirm, sir, that you're not dreaming.

ACT V

In the bar.

THE BARKEEPER: So, then, you still don't agree?

FIRST DRINKER: No!

SECOND DRINKER: No!

THIRD DRINKER: What we do all agree, is that ghosts don't exist.

SECOND DRINKER: Therefore, he isn't dead.

THIRD DRINKER: Therefore, he is dead.

THE BARKEEPER: Ah! You're still at it!

FIRST DRINKER: What a miserable life! Not even knowing if one of our close friends is dead or alive . . .

SECOND DRINKER: To feel one's foot slipping along a toad's back, the toad taken for a stone at twilight.

THIRD DRINKER: To put one's foot in a little rut by accident and spatter the woman you love . . .

FIRST DRINKER: At the theatre, to be seated behind a giant, huge as a big chest of drawers and high as a great closet . . .

SECOND DRINKER: At the moment the train is pulling out, to realize you forgot to pack the cigarettes . . .

THIRD DRINKER: To approach a woman who, seen from the back, seems to be charming, and to discover, facing her, the pock-marked face of some old whore . . .

FIRST DRINKER: To climb a staircase with slippers so large that they slip off at every step, from the lobby to the seventh floor . . .

SECOND DRINKER: To eat a tiny egg out of a drinking mug as if it were an egg cup . . .

THIRD DRINKER: To find oneself at a café seated beside a ruffian who simultaneously balances himself on his tilted-back chair, taps his foot like a knifegrinder, beats time on the table with his finger and whistles some military march . . .

FIRST DRINKER: To try, in the dead of winter, to spread cold butter on soft bread . . .

SECOND DRINKER: To have garters that constantly slip . . .

THIRD DRINKER: To be seated in an armchair missing one leg, the tilted seat of which sends you closer and closer toward the floor . . .

FIRST DRINKER: To wear a trouser-leg too tight . . .

SECOND DRINKER: To have the shaving soap keep slipping out of your hand: and finally to fish it out from under some piece of furniture, covered with dust, hair, and feathers . . .

THIRD DRINKER: Miserable life!

THE BARKEEPER: To have customers like you. Ah—you're not in the least amusing.

SECOND DRINKER: No, we're not amusing.

Pause.

FIRST DRINKER: No.

THE BARKEEPER: Wait a minute! A musician . . .

Enter a character dressed in a baggy suit and carrying a violin case under his arm.

SECOND DRINKER (*after turning around for a moment—addressing The Third Drinker*): A thousand francs that he's not dead.

THIRD DRINKER: It's a bet.

SECOND DRINKER: Turn around, he's behind you now.

THIRD DRINKER: Not really!

FIRST DRINKER: I'm not at all sure that that's him.

SECOND DRINKER: Gérard?

GÉRARD: Sir?

SECOND DRINKER: Why do you call me 'sir'?

GÉRARD: Because I don't know you.

THIRD DRINKER: Ha! I've won.

SECOND DRINKER: Excuse me, but you must be Gérard. Don't you recognize me? Your friend Gustave?

GÉRARD: No.

SECOND DRINKER: Don't you recognize Gabriel and Casper?

GÉRARD: No, but I think I've seen you before once some place.

FIRST DRINKER: That's funny, I'm not at all sure that I know you. I must say, if you're not Gérard, you certainly look like him.

GÉRARD: My name does happen to be Gérard.

FIRST DRINKER: It's incredible.

GÉRARD: It seems to me I may know you, but I don't quite remember where and when we met.

THIRD DRINKER: Now I've won my bet.

SECOND DRINKER: Not at all, he's Gérard all right.

THE BARKEEPER: As a matter of fact, it seems to me, he certainly is the person you're looking for—it's just that he doesn't remember you! In my opinion, it's no bet.

THIRD DRINKER: Not at all, you owe me a thousand francs.

SECOND DRINKER: Not at all, you owe it to me.

FIRST DRINKER (*to Gérard*): And you're a musician?

GÉRARD: No.

FIRST DRINKER: But this violin case . . .

GÉRARD: I'm bringing my spare linen to the laundry in it, and carrying a few old books.

THE BARKEEPER: That's not in the least surprising to me; many people do as you're doing. (*Pause. He looks up.*) Ah, there they are, coming back again. They certainly haven't been gone long. It must have been only a small fire.

FIRST DRINKER: Doesn't matter at all, it's really quite amusing. (*To Gérard.*) Will you have a drink with me?

THE BARKEEPER: In my time, they had magnificent fires. When the Charity Bazaar burned down, I happened to be in the neighborhood. I was strolling along the riverbanks. Suddenly I heard cries, a great deal of noise, and smoke and firemen appeared everywhere. That was a great fire, all right. There was the coachman of this marquise who saved his mistress' life by pulling her skirts up over her head and bringing her out on his shoulders.

GÉRARD: You saw that with your own eyes?

THE BARKEEPER: Yes, and after that the fire at the Opera House, and the two great department-store fires; and during the war the one at Saint Paul's. I saw the Opera House fire one evening while returning from work. I was on the upper deck of an omnibus, and for at least ten minutes the sky was a deep red, deep red. And all over the city you could hear the sound of fire engines in the distance. During those days the fire engines were horse-drawn. Beautiful creatures. How they galloped!

FIRST DRINKER: Doesn't matter at all, it's really quite amusing.

Enter Athenais.

What a beautiful dress, Athenais!

ATHENAIS: What do you mean? It's the one I wear every day.

FIRST DRINKER: The one you wear every day?

ATHENAIS: Of course.

GÉRARD: Everything is surprising when one sees without looking or rather when one looks without seeing unless it's the other way around.

FIRST DRINKER: It's curious, I feel too that I've met you before . . . but ask me where?—and I don't know where! and I know your name! Your name is Gérard and you look like my friend Gérard, and this one says that you're dead . . . excuse me . . . that he is dead . . . and that one says that he's met him, several days ago, that he had a violin case under his arm, that he spoke and here you are. Your name is Gérard, we know you and you don't know us. And, moreover, you're really he.

THE BARKEEPER: It's fortunate that ghosts don't exist.

ATHENAIS: I've just narrowly escaped a fire.

GÉRARD: Where?

ATHENAIS: At the burning building. The staircase was cut off. Jump . . . I'm afraid . . . You too . . . I'd rather die . . . Jump . . . and then a big deep hole. Crowds and lights. Maxime on the ground beside a smashed mattress . . . He was smoking his cigarette as if it was all nothing at all. That's a man for you!

FIRST DRINKER: It's very strange. Where the devil have we met before?

THE BARKEEPER: Really? There's been a fire? You didn't have to jump out the window, did you?

ATHENAIS: Yes, and so did Maxime. Always looking at his starfish, and then his hands . . . one, two, three, four, five, and then . . .

GÉRARD (to himself): These people must be drunk, thinking that they know me! They may know my name, but I'm not going to go on much longer letting the imaginations of three absurd alcoholics run on this way about me. As for this young lady, with her dress like something out of her grandmother's trunk, her agitation doesn't speak well for her. I like sensible, peaceful people. I don't in the least care for these eccentric women who frequent dens of iniquity and who affect misplaced fellowship with men.

FIRST DRINKER (slapping Gérard on the back): You're absolutely magnificent!

GÉRARD: Excuse me, I have to go now. Good-bye gentlemen, have a very pleasant evening. . . . Good-bye, Miss, enjoy yourself.

THIRD DRINKER: Fortunately, ghosts don't exist.

FIRST DRINKER: Perhaps they do.

SECOND DRINKER: Have you gone mad! Ghosts exist, indeed!

ATHENAIS: You mean you took that fellow who just went out with
his violin case for a ghost? Really, a ghost's not like that in
the least. A ghost is a skeleton with a greenish glow around
his head and wrapped in a big shroud.

FIRST DRINKER: It wouldn't surprise me if he turned out to be a
ghost. He looked exactly like I always thought a ghost would.

ATHENAIS: Don't talk about it any more, don't talk about it any
more; I'm getting frightened.

THIRD DRINKER: Don't pay any attention to him. He's either crazy
or crocked.

FIRST DRINKER: Have it your own way.

SECOND DRINKER: You'd have to be a complete moron to even suppose that ghosts could exist. It's absolutely absurd.

THE BARKEEPER: But, after all, was he your friend or wasn't he?

SECOND DRINKER: It was he, all right. He was trying to play a joke
on us. You owe me a thousand francs.

THIRD DRINKER: It wasn't he. That was some kind of double with
the same name, and that's all there is to it, and you're the
one who owes me the thousand francs.

THE BARKEEPER: To put you both at peace again, let us cut the child
in two. You owe one another 500 francs.

THIRD DRINKER: Fine!

SECOND DRINKER: Then we're quits?

THIRD DRINKER: We're quits.

ATHENAIS: It isn't true, is it? There really aren't any ghosts?

FIRST DRINKER: I'm not exactly sure, not sure at all.

ACT VI

*A street, at dawn. A sidewalk, a gas lamp. The Policeman walks
up and down, stamping his feet, blowing on his fingers. Finally he
dozes off, leaning against a streetlight pole. Then, in Indian file,
The Twelve Waiters from the café pass, each carrying, with one*

*hand held overhead, an empty tray. They go by without speaking;
then Athenais walks by. She stops a moment; The Three Drinkers
pass.*

FIRST DRINKER: Good evening, Athenais.

SECOND DRINKER: Good evening, my lovely one.

THIRD DRINKER: Good evening, my lovely one, don't dream of fires
now.

SECOND DRINKER: Nor of ghosts.

ATHENAIS: Good evening, good evening. I don't feel like sleeping.

THIRD DRINKER: Take care at night, my very lovely one.

They pass by.

ATHENIAS (*going out, in the opposite direction*): Don't feel like
sleeping, don't feel like sleeping.

The Two Firemen arrive.

FIRST FIREMAN: Wine, my friend? A glass of wine?

SECOND FIREMAN: All the cafés are closed now.

FIRST FIREMAN: I'm thirsty.

SECOND FIREMAN: Let's go to sleep, sleep, the only thing we can
do, while the fires are smoldering in readiness. The night is
too calm not to end in flames.

FIRST FIREMAN: Is it night? Is it day? I don't know any more, I
don't know any more.

They pass by.

*Three Men in top hats and capes pass by next, silently and
without stopping. From one direction Maxime appears, from
another, Fabrice.*

MAXIME: Alone?

FABRICE: Everyone has his own mystery.

MAXIME: Later? Always tomorrow, the next high tide, the next full
moon.

FABRICE: Everybody's asleep.

MAXIME: Not everybody, the city would be beautiful then. Solitude makes one wish for still more solitude.

FABRICE: Solitude?

MAXIME: The lover and his mistress could say that when they are together they are alone.

FABRICE: Are they?

MAXIME: But we don't love one another.

FABRICE: Ah, don't insist on it! Be quiet!

MAXIME: Good-bye, my dear Fabrice.

FABRICE: Hush, silence. This night is too calm to end without some nightmare.

MAXIME: No nightmares, even . . . They're for other dreams than ours.

    They go off. . . . The Barkeeper and The Doorman arrive. Their dress is half professional, half everyday.

THE BARKEEPER: A good day's work, my little fellow?

THE DOORMAN: I'm sleepy and bored.

THE BARKEEPER: Misery . . . That's life.

THE DOORMAN: Some day we may revolt.

THE BARKEEPER: Some day, perhaps . . .
    Enter Arthur.

ARTHUR: A game of cards, my friends?

THE BARKEEPER: Who's that?

THE DOORMAN: That face . . . I recognize it. . . .

ARTHUR: A game of cards?

THE BARKEEPER: Go your way as we go ours.
    The Doorman and The Barkeeper go out.

ARTHUR (*alone*): Not so friendly, those friends! . . . (*He calls out.*) Friends! Friends! Hey! Friends! (*He leaves the stage, running. In the distance.*) Friends! Friends!

    Enter Gérard.

GÉRARD: This night is too noisy, too noisy. These shouts: Friends! Friends! . . . I really don't know what I've become.

THE POLICEMAN (*waking up*): What are you doing there?

GÉRARD: Mine is a peaceful disposition.

THE POLICEMAN: Who are you?

GÉRARD: Mine is a peaceful disposition, very peaceful.

THE POLICEMAN: Your papers, please.

GÉRARD: Mine is a peaceful disposition, very peaceful, and I'm going . . .

THE POLICEMAN: No explanations. What's in that violin case?

GÉRARD: Mine is a peaceful disposition, very peaceful, and I'm going out under the stars.

THE POLICEMAN: Are you making fun of me? Watch out!

GÉRARD: Mine is a peaceful disposition, very peaceful, and I'm going out under the stars and into the depths of the night.

THE POLICEMAN: So, you're not going to answer me? Come on now, let's go . . .

GÉRARD: Mine is a peaceful disposition, and I'm not to be arrested like that.

THE POLICEMAN: What?

GÉRARD: You stay there now; be good, do you hear me? Be good and don't move.

THE POLICEMAN: That I'd like to see!

GÉRARD: Good evening.

He goes away . . . while The Policeman remains motionless, as if frozen stiff.

A long pause.

THE POLICEMAN (*coming to suddenly*): What! What! What's happened to me? Come on now, Hector, you're not crazy, are you? Oh, I'd better take better care of myself; I need some rest.

Re-enter Gérard. He crosses the stage, walks before The Policeman without looking at him. The Policeman stares at him, bewildered.

GÉRARD: Mine is a peaceful disposition, very peaceful, and I'm going out under the stars and into the depths of the night.

He goes off.

ACT VII

The stage is hung with black velvet. On a console table, an antique bust—of anyone at all—a bust with staring eyes, the sort you see in lawyers' offices; a divan, a large stuffed bird (a stork, or a pink flamingo, and so on), and a very large, old-fashioned map of the world.

FABRICE: Happy are those who sleep.

FIRST MAN: Are you happy?

FABRICE: It's not me. It's another Fabrice who lives in dreams, another . . . a life so marvelous. With nothing in common with life, life, do you hear me, with its limited connotations that you give to it. And I would sleep and dream forever.

FIRST MAN: But, Fabrice, you're happy, even in your own life, beautiful . . . beloved . . .

FABRICE: Beloved! Beloved! You dare tell me that I'm beloved? I will be some day, perhaps, but my love and . . . his is a love which is a kind of catastrophe. Everything could be so simple.

FIRST MAN: But I love you, Fabrice, and my two friends love you too. It's only up to you to be happy.

FABRICE: Happy? Do you think I can be happy? When your peace, your pleasure, your innermost satisfaction is my anguish, my terror?

SECOND MAN: What are you afraid of? Everyone loves you, everyone.

FABRICE: You dare to tell me everyone loves me! To love me as you do . . . is to love flimsily, to love at reduced rates! What am I afraid of? Not of life, certainly, not even of its pitfalls, but of a certain cloudy sky where birds of ill-omen fly; afraid of the inclinations of my heart and my soul . . . If eternal salvation really existed, a damnation and a last judgment, my anguish would rise above even that. Something else entirely troubles me—for there is no paradise and no such thing as sin.

FIRST MAN: Happy Fabrice! And no hell, naturally.

FABRICE: How exasperating you are! No hell, of course! No hell. And perhaps my anguish lies right there.

FIRST MAN: Such thoughts never trouble me in the least. Eternal salvation, paradise! Why, that's a smile from you.

THIRD MAN: Fabrice, you're afraid of mere fantasies . . . of ghosts.

Enter Gérard.

GÉRARD: Hello, Fabrice; hello, gentlemen. (*He leans his violin case against the console table with the bust.*)

FABRICE: Hello . . . No, I'm not afraid of ghosts. Simply cage all the birds in the world, and then I'll be satisfied.

THIRD MAN: You, satisfied? You're never satisfied with anything or with anybody . . . not even yourself.

SECOND MAN (*to Gérard*): Sir, please help us. . . . Fabrice is bored, Fabrice is sad and, for this reason, we're bored and sad too; she must be comforted. She says things that are silly and dangerous. Paradise, the last judgment and eternal salvation . . . What more need I say?

FABRICE: You—keep quiet, you never understand anything.

GERARD: And me too now, Fabrice; I never understand anything any more.

FABRICE: And you're more intelligent than all the others, as a result.

GÉRARD: Everybody knows me. There are even men whom I don't recognize, whom I've never even seen and who nevertheless are my intimate friends, who can prove it to me, and to whom not a single detail of my life—not even the most intimate—is unknown.

FABRICE: If it were only a question of that! As for me, I'm more unknown by those who surround me than if I were lost on a desert island. Unknown to all, except for one, and this knowledge is exactly what will always separate us.

GÉRARD: Nobody ever knows anybody.

FABRICE: True love is nevertheless this very knowledge, and I tell you that he knows me.

FIRST MAN: Who, him?

GÉRARD: Love? It's the illusion of knowledge.

FABRICE: That's right. And when we think we are mistaken, and I abandon you, and you abandon me . . . it's from another that we separate.

GÉRARD: It's an illusion.

FABRICE: I think you know better than that. Illusion? In love? But, then, what is there that's really true?

GÉRARD: I'm too peaceful a personality to be known well, and my own words sound strange to me as I speak them. They must have done a bad job of winding up the mechanism this morning.

SECOND MAN: What mechanism?

GÉRARD: I'm a peaceful personality, and you mustn't attach too precise a sense to my words.

He leaves in haste.

THIRD MAN: He forgot his violin case.

FIRST MAN: Who, he? Who knows you?

FABRICE: I certainly don't mean you.

FIRST MAN: Fabrice!

FABRICE: Enough of all these miserable secrets. You have been and you are my lover.

FIRST MAN: Fabrice!

FABRICE: Fine, then! It's over. You're obviously far too troublesome a creature. Oh, virtually nothing at all—a stone in the road. Over, over, do you hear me? Over forever!

FIRST MAN: Fabrice!

FABRICE: Farewell!

FIRST MAN: Fabrice!

FABRICE: Farewell, I tell you.

The First Man walks slowly away.

SECOND MAN: My dear Fabrice, you've been very hard on him, but I don't blame you. He wasn't worthy of you.

FABRICE: Don't talk about it any more. At least I never loved him. No regrets. Not even a trace.

SECOND MAN: You understand that? Know you? Why, I know you. And so well, so tenderly. Fabrice, will you permit me to be your devoted servant?

FABRICE: You! Farewell, and be quick about it.

Exit The Second Man.

And you, the last one! Will you accept a tragic love? If I told you: I love you—would you abandon everything?

THIRD MAN: Fabrice, why do you dramatize what's so simple? I too love you.

FABRICE: You must love me without reservation.

THIRD MAN: That is the way I love you.

FABRICE: Leave everything behind. Not only accustomed ways . . .

THIRD MAN: Why dramatize it? One can love so easily, without tragedy.

FABRICE: Because one can love me in no other way.

THIRD MAN: You're happy this way—let's love this way! Why do you want to complicate everything?

FABRICE: I beg of you! I love you! You see, I'm telling you that. You will abandon your accustomed ways.

THIRD MAN: All right, Fabrice; I will abandon them.

FABRICE: Your fortune, your name, your family, your friends, your most familiar thoughts. I beg you, let's depart, depart, not only to change the scenery, but to throw our whole beings to the winds. Another man, another woman and, in ten or twenty years, if we want to, we'll return to see what became of our corpses.

THIRD MAN: Fabrice, we're agreed, but I need just a little delay, to put a few things in order.

FABRICE: Does death wait? It's sudden, immediate!

THIRD MAN: Fine then! Yes—I'll obey you. I love you too much. You love me! You love me! I'm a different man.

FABRICE: Idiot! Idiot! Idiot! What do you take me for—a school-teacher? A fine fellow this is—you have to persuade him to love. Love isn't like that! And I've taken you in! I, Fabrice, begging you! Giving you reasons! Having patience! Oh, go away and never cross my path again, do you hear, never!

THIRD MAN: If only I understood what you meant by this scene! . . .

FABRICE: Idiot! Idiot! (*Pause. To herself.*) There go three monstrosities who'll bother me no longer. (*Pause.*) Drink! (*She takes a bottle and glass from behind the bust. She drinks several glasses, one after another.*) And now Fabrice is as drunk as the commonest whore. If any of those idiots were here, they'd say that I do it to forget my troubles. . . . To what end . . . fair Fabrice . . . no more cares . . . no more troubles . . . And here's love, ladies . . . I must certainly buy some flowers.

Some flowers . . . some flowers . . . no, that's stupid. . . . Flowers, and then an engine and a somersault . . . to buy a somersault.

The fair Fabrice is as potted as a Polack. . . . There we are. . . . Good morning, how are you? . . . As usual? . . . No, something has changed today. And you, as usual? Yes . . . Then . . . Then, you love me . . . I love you. . . . (*Pause.*) No! it's too funny! He loves Fabrice, the adorable Fabrice. . . . No, but do you believe that it's true?

It's too silly. . . . I will buy a somersault and some flowers . . . some flowers. . . . No, plants can be idiots. . . . (*She stretches out on the couch.*) And I will say: give me flowers and not toadstools, because toadstools aren't flowers. . . .

(*Pause. Fabrice seems asleep. She sits up suddenly.*) Mush-rooms are somersaults and not flowers . . . Oh! a drinking fountain! (*She lies down again, and closes her eyes.*)

ACT VIII

A square shaded by trees, in a quiet neighborhood. Some Rag-pickers are going through an ash can. Dawn is near. Gérard and Athenais arrive together.

FIRST RAGPICKER: Arthur, when you finish tying up your papers this morning, come and help me load the tin.

SECOND RAGPICKER: Do you have hammers?

ATHENAIS: It's almost day.

GÉRARD: It's the ragpickers.

ATHENAIS: I'm in a rush to get home. (*She rings at the door.*) Do you still love me a little?

GÉRARD: Is that a question?

ATHENAIS: And do I love you? (*The door opens. She steps in.*)

GÉRARD: Athenais.

ATHENAIS: Good night. Go straight home now. (*The door closes.*)

FIRST RAGPICKER: Don't bother about the straw. The yard is full of it.

SECOND RAGPICKER: All the same . . .

GÉRARD: Pardon me, what time is it?

SECOND RAGPICKER: About to strike five.

LAMPLIGHTER: Good evening, friends. Not too early this morning.

FIRST RAGPICKER: Don't worry about the drinks. We're closing up shop on time.

LAMPLIGHTER: Drinks? Or something else?

SECOND RAGPICKER: Of course. Are you through?

LAMPLIGHTER: Just that one over there to put out.

GÉRARD: Is there a bar open now?

FIRST RAGPICKER: Yes, there is, over there on the right, near the fire-alarm box.

GÉRARD: Thank you.

LAMPLIGHTER: You know, I was just reading in the papers—Rockefeller is dead.

GÉRARD: Rockefeller?

LAMPLIGHTER: A relative?

GÉRARD: No. What makes you ask?

FIRST RAGPICKER: Even his millions couldn't keep him from dying.

SECOND RAGPICKER: How old was he?

LAMPLIGHTER: Eighty-seven.

GÉRARD: As old as that?

SECOND RAGPICKER: That old or not that old, when you're dead you're the same age as the next fellow.

FIRST RAGPICKER: Good evening, now. You're coming for a snort?

LAMPLIGHTER: Of course.

GÉRARD: What's that?

FIRST RAGPICKER: What?

GÉRARD: What's shining over there?

FIRST RAGPICKER: It's an old sardine can, my prince.

SECOND RAGPICKER: It's certainly no diamond.

GÉRARD: Look—it's funny the way it shines.

FIRST RAGPICKER: Going to have a drink?

LAMPLIGHTER: Of course.

GÉRARD: Well, then, let's go.

> *The door opens again, suddenly. Athenais appears. It is clear she has very little on now under her coat.*

ATHENAIS: Have you finished carrying on your discussions under my windows?

SECOND RAGPICKER: Did we disturb you, little lady?

GÉRARD: We weren't talking all that loud.

ATHENAIS: Tell me, what's that shining over there?

GÉRARD (*picking up the sardine can*): This?

ATHENAIS: What is it?

FIRST RAGPICKER: A sardine can, my little lady.

ATHENAIS: What a mess! Throw it away.

SECOND RAGPICKER: Lady, you don't usually find diamonds in trash cans.

ATHENAIS: Gérard, why haven't you gone home?

FIRST RAGPICKER (*to The Lamplighter and The Second Ragpicker*): Let's go have a drink.

LAMPLIGHTER: Let's go.

SECOND RAGPICKER: Good night, ladies and gentlemen.

   They go off.

GÉRARD: Good morning.

ATHENAIS: Why haven't you gone home?

GÉRARD: I'm going now.

ATHENAIS: To your house?

GÉRARD: Yes, to my house.

ATHENAIS: Seriously?

GÉRARD: Do you want it that way?

ATHENAIS: Certainly.

GÉRARD: Really? It's morning now. Let's take a walk.

ATHENAIS: It's cold out.

GÉRARD: We'll have a few drinks in the little bars that have just opened. You can see steam on the windows.

ATHENAIS: Steam?

GÉRARD: They're washing the floors. The coffee smells good. The gutters are limpid. The sky is streaming with light.

ATHENAIS: Gérard. They're washing the floors. And that smells like terrible coffee in those cafés. And the gutters. What an itinerary!

GÉRARD: Of course. Just what I was thinking.

ATHENAIS: What were you thinking?

GÉRARD: That you didn't love me.

ATHENAIS: Oh, no! Do change the subject.

GÉRARD: It's true—it's very cold out. Athenais, go to bed now.

ATHENAIS: And you?

GÉRARD: I'm going to bed too.

ATHENAIS: At your house?

GÉRARD: Do you want it that way?

ATHENAIS: It's as it should be. . . . Though . . . if you want . . . come and lie down on the living-room sofa.

GÉRARD: No.

ATHENAIS: What's wrong with that?

GÉRARD: That's just what I was thinking.

ATHENAIS: Yes, yes, I know, I know.

GÉRARD (*holding out his hand to her*): Therefore, good night.

ATHENAIS (*pulling him by the hand*): Come on, don't be so stubborn.

FIRST RAGPICKER: Have those two lovers gone in yet?

SECOND RAGPICKER: Don't worry about them; they're not likely to be bored.

LAMPLIGHTER: Bored? You never know what these little meetings will bring.

SECOND RAGPICKER: None of your fake disgust, you. You know you'd like to be in the place of our little friend.

LAMPLIGHTER: Me? No, no . . . Through with women. My bed is to sleep in, only. No sooner is my head on the pillow . . .

FIRST RAGPICKER: You wouldn't be trying to hand us a line, now, would you?

LAMPLIGHTER: I'm not trying to hand you a line.

FIRST RAGPICKER: You're just like everybody else.

SECOND RAGPICKER: Good night, friend.

CONCIERGE: Good night, gentlemen.

FIRST RAGPICKER: My lady, Countess, we have the honor to wish you a very good day.

CONCIERGE: Fine, fine. Look—when you pick up your rubbish, don't leave any lying around in front of the door.

SECOND RAGPICKER: Our rubbish. Our rubbish. It's just as much your rubbish.

LAMPLIGHTER: They're not the one who threw it there.

CONCIERGE: I suppose then it was the Pope, perhaps?

FIRST RAGPICKER: No, it was one of the tenants in Your Castle.

CONCIERGE: My tenants don't go around picking up rubbish, at least.

SECOND RAGPICKER: Oh, no—not even if one did pick up a little someone else, just now.

CONCIERGE: What my tenants do is none of my affair.

LAMPLIGHTER: Don't try and fool us. As if you didn't read all the incoming mail instead of passing it out.

CONCIERGE: Joke all you like. All that I want, and I'll continue to require, is that you don't dirty up my sidewalk with your filthy junk.

FIRST RAGPICKER: If that doesn't make you sick to your stomach —hearing nonsense like that . . . her sidewalk . . . our junk . . .

SECOND RAGPICKER: Come on, forget about it . . . let's go.

They go off. The Concierge goes back in.

ACT IX

Maxime's room. Empty. The window open. The quiet street. Very rarely, the sound of a passing car.

Silence, a very long silence. Then the clock strikes any hour whatsoever.

Suddenly, someone knocks at the door. First normally. Someone is waiting behind the door, then grows impatient and knocks again louder, then louder still, calls out.

VOICE OF FABRICE: Maxime! (*Knocks.*) Maxime! Maxime! (*Knocks.*) Open the door—it's me! (*Knocks. Silence.*) Maxime!

Continuing silence.

CURTAIN

one way for another

by JEAN TARDIEU

translated by George E. Wellwarth

Cast

ADMIRAL SEPULCHRE
MADAME DE SAINT-ICI-BAS
MONSIEUR GRABUGE
MADAME GRABUGE
BARONESS LAMPROIE
MLLE. CARGAISON
M. SUREAU
CÉSAR, valet de chambre.

The action takes place in the milieu of Jules Verne's novels. The admiral resembles Captain Grant: appearance of a naval officer of 1860, whiskers, tailcoat, tall naval cap, small telescope hanging round his neck, and so on. . . .

ADMIRAL SEPULCHRE (*steps bareheaded in front of the curtain*):
When we landed on the Nameless Archipelago—so named because no one had discovered it before—we found ourselves, to our great surprise, in the midst of a highly advanced civilization: newly built-up cities—which owed their creation to frequent bombardments; completely free citizens—thanks to an omnipresent and ever watchful police force; peaceful customs —defended by a militia armed to the teeth; and a government solidly based on the instability of opinions—in short, we discovered all the things ordinarily associated with the march of progress! Nevertheless, although we could see a certain resemblance between this society and our own, the customs of this country confused us completely. It was as if someone had taken a malicious pleasure in mixing up all our customs into an absurd hodge-podge so that the inhabitants understood something completely different by them. . . .

At first we were completely put out by these ways of doing things, but, with the help of our friendly hosts, we soon got used to them. I myself joined the navy of this country and remained in it for more than twenty years, attaining the rank of admiral. When I returned to my native country I could not understand why people shook each other's hands when they met or took off their hats when they came through a door or sat down with others at a table to eat or took pleasure in smoking or rubbed against each other to the sound of music. . . .

We have re-created for you a reception in one of the most distinguished salons of the Nameless Archipelago. Several days previously we had received a card inscribed as follows: "Mme. de Saint-Ici-Bas requests your presence at a reception which she will give on the 15th of May at 6:00 P.M. . . . Please come prepared to cough." (*Salutes and leaves.*)

The curtain rises on a luxuriously furnished salon. The furniture is in no way out of the ordinary, but there are a great many tables and no chairs. On the right, next to the door,

321

*a hatstand with a number of hats of all types. César, a butler
in livery and white gloves, stands in front of the hats.*

MME. DE SAINT-ICI-BAS (*enters left. She is barefooted*): César! Is
everything ready?

CÉSAR: Yes, Madame. . . . I think, Madame, that these are
Madame's guests now.

*Mme. de Saint-Ici-Bas sits down on a table. The door opens.
Enter Admiral Sepulchre, a distinguished-looking old man.
César takes an old-fashioned plumed naval hat from the hatstand and gives it to the admiral. The latter takes off his shoes
and gives them to César.*

(*Announcing.*) Admiral Sepulchre!

*The admiral, hat in hand, goes to Mme. de Saint-Ici-Bas and
respectfully kisses her right foot.*

THE ADMIRAL: Charmed, dear lady.

MME. DE SAINT-ICI-BAS: You're the first one, Admiral. Do put your
hat on.

THE ADMIRAL (*putting his hat on gravely*): Since I have the honor,
Madame, to be alone with you, allow me to take off my socks
and present them to you. (*He takes his socks off with some
difficulty and hands them to his hostess.*)

MME. DE SAINT-ICI-BAS (*taking the socks with a pleased smile and
putting them on the table*): Nothing could please me more,
Admiral! This precious souvenir will take a prominent place
in my collection.

*M. and Mme. Grabuge enter. They take their shoes off and
give them to César, who places them alongside the admiral's.
César then gives M. Grabuge a laurel wreath made of paper
and Mme. Grabuge a veil.*

CÉSAR (*announcing*): Monsieur and Madame Grabuge!

MME. DE SAINT-ICI-BAS (*jumps elegantly off the table and goes to
meet them*): How good of you to come! Do put something
on your heads!

*M. and Mme. Grabuge put their headpieces on. Mme. Gra-
buge sits on a table.*

(*Introducing.*) M. Grabuge, our national poet . . . Admiral
Sepulchre.

M. GRABUGE AND THE ADMIRAL (*rubbing their noses together*):
Charmed, my dear sir! . . . Honored, Admiral!

MME. DE SAINT-ICI-BAS (*taking the admiral to Mme. Grabuge*):
Admiral Sepulchre . . . Mme. Grabuge.

THE ADMIRAL (*in a gallant tone, after having respectfully kissed
Mme. Grabuge's right foot*): I had the pleasure of hearing
a great deal about you, Madame, during the course of my last
voyage. Everyone knows that your husband has no talent
whatsoever, and that such as he seems to have comes from you.
It is the privilege of beautiful women to domineer their hus-
bands to the point of robbing them of their own usefulness.

MME. GRABUGE (*artlessly, inclining her head to one side*): You
really are a most delightful admiral!

MME. DE SAINT-ICI-BAS: The admiral is just too modest! He pretends
that he has forgotten that it was thanks only to the incomparable charm of his own wife that he succeeded in losing the
Battle of the Gulf of San Pedro!

THE ADMIRAL (*burping*): How true! Ah, those were happy times!

*The door opens again. Enter Baroness Lamproie, Mlle. Car-
gaison, and young Sureau. Same business as before. The
guests take off their shoes, give them to César, and take the
hats and veils which he gives them in return.*

*While this is going on, M. Grabuge has taken a feather out
of his pocket. He gravely tickles the nostrils of his wife and
the admiral until they sneeze and say "Many thanks."*

CÉSAR (*announcing*): Baroness Lamproie . . . Mlle. Cargaison
. . . M. Sureau, Jr. . . .

MME. DE SAINT-ICI-BAS (*greets each one in a friendly manner and
at the same time "makes a nose" at them*): My good friend
. . . My dear neighbors . . . my dear child . . . Do cover
your heads!

*The ladies go and sit on the tables. The gentlemen kiss their
right feet and then rub each other's noses together. Then the
men gather in a group. César distributes canes on which the
men lean. Mme. de Saint-Ici-Bas sits on the center table.*

My dear friends, I have promised that you will be able to cough. For this reason I have asked M. Grabuge to read us one of his worst poems. Do your duty, my dear Grabuge, do your duty!

Everyone laughs knowingly.

M. GRABUGE (*advancing several paces and taking a paper out of his pocket*): This is an ode entitled "Ode to the Sea." This ode was inspired by the sea, as indicated by the title "Ode to the Sea." I wrote it on a day when I felt particularly bad. It is dedicated to my wife.

There is a murmur of approbation. Mme. Grabuge looks flattered. Mlle. Cargaison attempts a timid cough.

MME. DE SAINT-ICI-BAS: Our friend Mlle. Cargaison can't wait to begin coughing! Bravo, my dear! But have patience—in a few moments our national poet will give you real reason to cough!

M. GRABUGE (*reads with emphasis*): ODE TO THE SEA
All my ancestors went to sea
As far as I can make out from my family tree
I always find the sea to be the same old sea
That's why the sea is my mother
The sea is my grandmother
The sea is my grandaunt
The sea is the sister of my uncle
and the brother of my mother and the mother of my brother
and the grandaunt of my grandfather
All my ancestors went to sea.

MME. DE SAINT-ICI-BAS: My God, what a lousy poem! (*She coughs.*) That was absolutely the worst!! (*Coughs.*) And how badly planned and put together, don't you think so? (*Coughs louder.*)

THE GUESTS (*trying to outvie each other in coughing*): Absolutely frightful! It's stupid; there's no sense to it at all. I don't think I've ever heard a poem that was worse! Terrible! What a ghastly surprise!

Mlle. Cargaison goes into such a fit of coughing that everyone else stops and turns to stare at her in admiration. After a short pause, everyone starts coughing again. M. Sureau meanwhile shows signs of feeling unwell. When it seems as if he can't bear it any more, he goes to César and asks him something in a low voice, as if he were ashamed of being heard.

M. SUREAU: Tell me, my friend, where is the . . . the dining room?

CÉSAR (*pointing to the door left; in an equally low voice in which disdain and pity are mixed*): At the end of the corridor on the left, sir!

M. SUREAU (*anxiously*): Is everything necessary there?

CÉSAR (*almost reluctantly, but still in a low voice*): Yes, sir!

M. SUREAU: Thank you, my friend! (*He leaves quickly, trying to efface himself.*)

CÉSAR (*takes enameled spittoon and offers it to each guest, bowing ceremoniously*): Would you care to spit, sir? Be so good as to spit a little, Madame! Thank you! Spit here, please! Would you care to spit now?

The guests spit delicately into the spittoon.

MME. GRABUGE (*to the Baroness Lamproie*): This is one of the loveliest receptions I have ever been to. What style, what elegance in everything, don't you think?

THE BARONESS: How true! This is really one of the best places in the world for spitting and coughing. (*To Mme. de Saint-Ici-Bas.*) Did you go to the Harmonic Society's concert, my dear friend?

MME. DE SAINT-ICI-BAS: Of course! What an unforgettable evening that was! And what a success! The audience was so loud in its approval that it was absolutely impossible to hear anything!

THE ADMIRAL: I haven't seen anything like it since that evening the pianist couldn't go on playing. As that incomparable artist, overcome with gratitude and emotion, fled from the stage, the enthusiasm of the audience bordered on the delirious. They stormed on to the stage and literally pulverized the piano; everyone wanted some souvenir to take home—a key, a pedal, a string. A friend of mine made off with three white keys and two black ones!

MME. GRABUGE (*stupidly*): That is the proof of a really great love of music!

*M. Sureau comes back, wiping his mouth with his handker-
chief, and places himself unobtrusively next to Mlle. Cargaison.*

MLLE. CARGAISON *(in a low voice)*: Aren't you feeling well, young
man?

M. SUREAU *(low)*: Oh, just a little attack of hunger!

Mlle. Cargaison coughs indignantly.

MME. DE SAINT-ICI-BAS: César, pass the plate around!

César passes round a plate with balloon whistles.

CÉSAR *(in a low voice, bowing respectfully)*: A balloon whistle,
Baroness? A balloon whistle, Admiral? A balloon whistle,
sir?

*Each guest answers him, either with "Oh, yes, thank you very
much" or "No thanks, I don't whistle." Those who have
taken one begin to blow up the balloon and let the air whistle
out with the same natural movements with which we smoke
cigarettes.*

THE BARONESS: You spoil us, my dear friend!

THE ADMIRAL: I haven't whistled with such pleasure for a long,
long time!

MME. GRABUGE: These balloon whistles are really delicious! Where
did you get them?

MME. DE SAINT-ICI-BAS: I have them made up in the mountains—
there's a man up there who makes them specially for us.

M. GRABUGE *(whistling with a balloon that has a particularly good
tone)*: Listen to that! Marvelous! One would think this was
a whistle for a marriage or a baptism!

MME. GRABUGE *(always sounds equally naïve)*: There is no greater
proof of friendship than these balloon whistles.

MME. DE SAINT-ICI-BAS: You are too good, my dear friend! Alas,
since my husband died I have stopped whistling altogether!

THE BARONESS: My poor, dear friend! You must miss it terribly! I
really do pity you! I couldn't give it up at all—I even whistle
when I'm traveling!

M. GRABUGE (*to Mme. de Saint-Ici-Bas*): At least allow me to tickle you!

MME. DE SAINT-ICI-BAS: But of course, my dear poet!

M. GRABUGE (*takes his feather out of his pocket again, goes to Mme. de Saint-Ici-Bas and tickles her nostrils until she sneezes*): There you are! Of course, it's nothing like a good balloon whistle.

MME. DE SAINT-ICI-BAS: That is a really graceful feather! Is that the one you write with?

M. GRABUGE: No, this is my ceremonial feather!

MME. DE SAINT-ICI-BAS (*sneezes*): Thank you! . . . And now let's all do some gymnastics!

THE BARONESS (*stops whistling*): What an excellent idea! To tell the truth, I've been waiting impatiently for some time to do just that.

MME. GRABUGE: There is no greater proof of health than gymnastics!

MME. DE SAINT-ICI-BAS: My dear friends, please uncover your heads! We will start right away!

The men take off their hats and the ladies their veils.

I hope the dear admiral will be so good as to lead the maneuvers of our little squad!

THE ADMIRAL: With the greatest pleasure in the world, dear lady! César, hand me the gong!

César hands him a gong and stick.

Ladies and gentlemen, are you ready? Good! Then let's begin. One. Two. One. Two. One. Two. Bend the knees, and up again. Stretch the right arm, and the left, and the right arm, lower the head, good! Sit! Get up! Sit! Get up! Sit! Get up! (*He punctuates his commands by striking the gong. Music such as that sometimes heard when physical-culture lessons are being given on the radio emanates from the wings.*)

M. SUREAU (*while exercising*): What do you think . . . of the political situation?

The guests answer in jerky sentences while continuing to exercise.

THE BARONESS (*out of breath*): I think . . . that the government . . . will fall . . . this evening . . . and will be replaced by another one . . . tomorrow.

MME. GRABUGE: It's . . . a very great test for the government . . . even though it falls!

THE BARONESS: Have you read . . . the latest book . . . by Motus?

M. GRABUGE: I think it's a book that appeared . . . just at the right time.

MME. DE SAINT-ICI-BAS: What do you mean by that?

M. GRABUGE: It appeared just at the right time . . . to make us forget . . . its predecessors!

MME. GRABUGE: It is a great proof . . . of love of literature . . . to forget what one has read!

THE ADMIRAL (*very much out of breath himself*): I think the baroness is beginning to get out of breath. Allow me to end this marvelous performance, which, alas! is a little too strenuous for my age.

MME. GRABUGE: I could continue this for hours!

MME. DE SAINT-ICI-BAS: I am terribly sorry to have tired you, Admiral! But how could one have a party without gymnastics!

She signals César, who brings each guest his hat again.

THE GUESTS: It was wonderful! Very high class! One might think one was at Court! It's the most wonderful party game ever invented!

M. GRABUGE (*to his wife*): It's getting late, my dear! It's about time to put our friend outside the door.

THE GUESTS: Yes, yes, it's time! We don't want to make a nuisance of ourselves! It was such a wonderful evening! To the door! To the door! To the door!

MME. DE SAINT-ICI-BAS (*agreeing*): All right, all right, but before I go you'll give me a little present, won't you?

THE GUESTS: But of course, my dear friend! Why not? Naturally!

MME. DE SAINT-ICI-BAS: César, take the gifts, please.

CÉSAR (*carrying an empty tray to each guest*): For Madame's poor mother! For Madame's poor mother! For Madame's poor mother!

The guests put things on the tray: a gold watch, a ring, a necklace, a fountain pen, a lace handkerchief, a check, and so on.

THE BARONESS (*putting down her earrings*): We really can't thank you enough for everything, my dear friend.

THE ADMIRAL: I couldn't possibly leave you without first telling you how much pleasure your invitation gave me. I think I speak for all of us when I say that it would give us great pleasure to sleep here in your house tonight while you sleep outside the door. We all trust that a refreshing rainstorm will make your night a peaceful one on the steps of your own house!

MME. DE SAINT-ICI-BAS (*deeply touched*): You are too kind! Thank you so much, and au revoir! (*Exit.*)

CÉSAR (*hands out pillows and eiderdowns*): Pillows . . . eiderdowns! Pillows . . . eiderdowns! Pillows! Eiderdowns! . . .

The guests lie down on the floor and begin to yawn noisily.

CURTAIN

architruc

by ROBERT PINGET

translated by Michael Benedikt

Characters

THE KING
BAGA, the minister
THE COOK
DEATH, nonspeaking part

A shabby room, pretentiously furnished. To the right a canopied bed, an armchair, a table, a bearskin on the floor. At the center, rear, a door. To the left, rear, a screen arranged to hide a combination dressing room and toilet. At the far left a wall cabinet. In the middle of the stage a green plant in a flower-pot holder.

As the curtain rises The King is seated in his armchair. His crown is on his head. He is wearing a dressing gown. He inspects himself, adjusts his collar, scrapes a little spot off it, brushes off his sleeves, tugs at his pants. Then he takes a little mirror from the table, looks at himself in it, smooths down his hair, and sticks out his tongue at himself. Grimace. He puts the mirror back and picks up his nail scissors. He cuts his nails.

THE KING (*to Baga who is invisible behind the screen*): Ready yet?

BAGA'S VOICE. Not quite. In one minute.

THE KING: What are you doing? I asked only for simple things. What are you disguising as?

BAGA'S VOICE: An ambassador. I want it to be realistic.

THE KING: Realistic! You sadden me, Baga.

BAGA'S VOICE: A moment's peace.

> *Pause. The King continues to cut his nails. Baga hums something. The King makes as if to get up.*

THE KING: I'm going to peek.

BAGA'S VOICE: Peeking forbidden. I'm almost finished. (*Pause. Baga is heard flushing.*)

THE KING: Were you making?

BAGA'S VOICE: No, it was the cotton.

THE KING (*crying out*): For the thousandth time don't throw things into the john! The plumbing bills are awful.

BAGA'S VOICE: Pardon Y'r Majesty.

THE KING: Obviously you don't pay the bills around here.

BAGA'S VOICE: And now the finishing touch . . . There!

> *A long pause. The King arranges some objects on the table.*

333

THE KING: Ready yet?

BAGA'S VOICE: All ready.

> *Baga appears, wearing a ridiculous musketeer's costume. A cape, a sword, a plumed hat. False mustache. Heavily made up. He bows ceremoniously.*

BAGA: Sire, my respects.

THE KING (*bowing without rising*): That's me. What do you want?

BAGA: You don't say "What do you want?" you say "We're listening now."

THE KING: We're listening now.

BAGA: It's absolutely miserable that after all these years you haven't been capable of learning these few formulas. You don't even make an effort.

THE KING: Cut it out. We decided to have some fun. Now continue.

BAGA (*bowing again*): Sire. You are not without knowledge that my Master the King of Novocardia has rights to the succession. The law instituted by your great-grandmother

THE KING: You're not going to start that again, are you? Under the pretext of this disguise. I forbid you to speak about that.

BAGA: All right, all right. I'll begin again. (*He bows again.*) Sire, you are not without knowledge

THE KING: You may vary the formula.

BAGA: Vary it by finding something else yourself.

THE KING (*he stands up, bowing while lifting his crown*): Sire. Your Majesty loves tasty things. Permit us to propose a menu for this evening.

BAGA: An ambassador suggesting a menu to you!

THE KING: Why not? A menu always gives pleasure. It predisposes one to benevolence, to equity, to

BAGA: And then what does he ask for?

THE KING: The hand of my daughter for his king.

BAGA: Oh fine!

THE KING: What, that upsets you?

BAGA: No, but first we'd have to get us a daughter.

THE KING: Is the answer Yes or No?

BAGA: We must remain within the bounds of possibility.

THE KING: Possibility! You're making me feel sorry for you.

BAGA: And if all I did was sleep like you who is it would raise the taxes? You spend everything on stuffing yourself.

THE KING: Because I have nothing else to do. I can't exactly depend on your conversation. (*Pause.*) What are we eating today?

BAGA: We said we were going to have a moment of relaxation. What we said we said. I continue. (*He bows again.*) Sire. you are not without knowledge

THE KING: Still?

BAGA: that my Master wishes to marry. Various random rumors tell us that your daughter is the most beautiful of all the women in your kingdom.

THE KING: Wait one moment that reminds me that I haven't yet watered Fifille. (*He gets up, takes a little watering can from the corner and goes to fill it in the dressing room.*)

During this time Baga sits and meditates. He calculates, counting on his fingers.

(*The King comes out of the room with his watering can and waters the plant.*) Never forget to water Fifille. A rare plant

BAGA (*reciting*): which came to me from my Aunt Estelle which cost me a thousand rupees and which is female she has four hairy leaves a stem and a sex organ which is invisible she is

THE KING: Continue.

BAGA: she is very delicate you bring her indoors in the winter

THE KING: Not that. Back to the embassy.

BAGA (*he gets up, bowing once more*): Sire. You are not without knowledge that my

THE KING (*placing the watering can noisily on the table*): Cut it out! Find something else.

BAGA: I'm out of ideas. You discourage me. (*Pause.*) Deep down I liked your mother better.

THE KING: You slept with her, eh?

BAGA: A little bit. Not so hot. But at least in matters of government she let me take the initiative. If that crown still covers your skull don't forget you have me to thank for it.

THE KING (*calming down*): What don't we have to listen to.

BAGA (*stamping around the stage*): Yes, I've uncovered conspiracies. And I waged the Chanchèz war. And I signed a trade agreement.

THE KING: Your masterpiece! Let's talk about that! We don't even have a bite to eat.

BAGA: One must attempt restraint. A superior attitude. (*Pause.*) Besides you don't inspire pity.

THE KING: Continue.

BAGA: You are fat as an abbott, you take five

THE KING: Not that. The ambassador.

BAGA: I told you I was out of ideas.

THE KING: In that case discuss the menu.

BAGA: No I'm going to disguise myself as something else.

THE KING: If you change all the time the pleasure won't last for long.

BAGA: We're not concerned with pleasure here we're concerned with recreation. If now you want to effect pleasure . . .

THE KING: Oh the Gentleman is pulling a long face!

BAGA: You weary me, truly. Isn't it time that

THE KING: Don't tire yourself out.

BAGA: I'm going to disguise myself again.

THE KING: Go and disguise yourself again.

Baga returns to the dressing room. The King hardly knows what to do with himself. He takes a letter from the table, reads it in a low voice, shows signs of impatience, puts it down, picks up the mirror, puts it down. A long pause. Then he gets up and approaches the dressing room.

I'm peeking.

BAGA'S VOICE: No! It's a surprise.

THE KING: What's it like?

BAGA'S VOICE: You'll see. Read your love letter.

THE KING: It's too tedious. (*He walks toward the table again. He bends down and strokes the bearskin on the floor.*) My poor papa. My poor papa who hunted bears. He had domestic difficulties. Was he less bored than I am? (*Pause.*) Whatever can we invent next? (*To Baga.*) Shall we go look in on the kitchens . . . ? (*Pause.*) I can have a Pernod?

BAGA'S VOICE: Forbidden.

THE KING: Just this once you'd refuse me? Just this once.

BAGA'S VOICE: No and double no.

THE KING: Just this once while awaiting you!

BAGA'S VOICE: All right just for a moment of unanimity. But only to the bottom of the glass.

THE KING: Finally! (*He claps his hands. He goes to the cupboard, opens it, brings out a bottle and glass and serves himself, with water from the watering can.*) Would you like some?

BAGA'S VOICE: Later.

THE KING (*he sits down. He drinks*): Mmm it's good. (*He raises his glass.*) Do you remember when we were at Fantoine?

BAGA'S VOICE: What?

THE KING: When we were at Fantoine and our session with Pernod! Will we be going back again?

BAGA'S VOICE: It's not vacation time yet.

THE KING: You could at least consider it.

BAGA'S VOICE: Government before all. And leave me in peace, I can't do two things at once.

THE KING: You don't have to answer. (*He continues to drink. He rises a little tipsily, glass in hand, and mimics the ambassador.*)

Sire, please accept my deepest respects. (*Pause. To Baga.*) Is that correct? (*Pause.*) I'm speaking to you.

BAGA'S VOICE: Enough!

THE KING (*continuing his game*): My respects to mademoiselle your daughter. (*He laughs. Pause. To Baga.*) Isn't it the ambassador all over again? (*Pause.*) I'm speaking to you! (*Pause.*) What's it like? A king? A horse? (*Pause.*) Oh I know. A cook. (*While speaking he moves toward the dressing room.*)

BAGA'S VOICE: No peeking!

THE KING: If this is your performance, you're always in the wings. I'm coming in at three. One . . . two . . .

Baga comes out of the room. He is dressed as a woman, in the style of 1900. Dress with bustle, huge hat, veil, boa, parasol. He strolls along simperingly.

Not bad! One might almost say like my Aunt Estelle. (*Imitating Baga's walk, The King goes to sit down in his armchair.*)

BAGA (*in a woman's voice*): My dear nephew I love your room. It has such taste, such intimacy! And what comfort my dear! Dressing room and everything. You have inherited my taste for luxury, Architruc.

THE KING: No decidedly her belly stuck out less than yours.

BAGA (*woman's voice*): Oh I see that you still have my plant! That's very nice.

THE KING: Yes, Auntie. Her name is Fifille. I water her every day.

BAGA (*woman's voice*): You are right to, Nephew. It came to me from a Negro friend of mine who died recently poor thing. She left me this plant and her purse which I found five rupees in. But . . . didn't you once meet her?

THE KING: Yes. A little dumpy lady.

BAGA (*woman's voice*): No. A tall masculine type.

THE KING: That's right.

BAGA (*woman's voice*): Look here Nephew, talk to me about the government. Tell me about your minister, Baga.

THE KING: A real cunt, Auntie.

BAGA (*woman's voice*): Architruc that's unforgivable! Using that kind of language with me! Do you know that I could be your mother.

THE KING: How could that be, Auntie?

BAGA (*woman's voice*): Your father loved me first. We were in fact intimate. He had to give me up to marry my elder sister. That idiot

THE KING: I forbid you to insult the memory of my mother.

BAGA (*woman's voice*): All right, all right. (*Pause.*) But . . . I don't see Baga anywhere?

THE KING: He's in the toilet, Auntie.

BAGA (*woman's voice*): Really? How very amusing. I can see that you're making great progress in the art of conversation. (*Pause.*) In fact the King of Novocardia

THE KING: Did you understand what I told you? (*Pause.*) And how's my uncle, Auntie?

BAGA (*woman's voice*): The marquis is very, very weary. His lands are too heavy a load. I . . . But what's that I see? Some Pernod?

THE KING (*rising, eagerly*): Would you like some? I'll be glad to give you a glass. (*He goes to take a glass out of the cupboard, fills it, then reaches for another.*)

BAGA (*in his normal voice*): Watch out!

THE KING: Only one more! The last!

BAGA (*he pulls the bottle out of his hand. In his normal voice*): It's useless.

THE KING: Well then I'm not playing any more. (*He turns his back to Baga.*)

BAGA (*in his normal voice*): Excellent. I would like to speak to you of certain benefits realized as a result of the Chanchèz

THE KING (*turning around suddenly*): Really? Oh tell me!

BAGA (*in his normal voice*): If you continue.

THE KING: I'll continue.

BAGA (*in a woman's voice*): Tell me, Nephew, what do you think of your minister?

THE KING: He's an excellent minister, Auntie.

Baga nods approvingly.

I like him very much. We understand one another perfectly.

Baga nods.

But he keeps on forbidding me my Pernod. Is there any sense in that.

BAGA (*woman's voice*): Really? He probably has some reason. Your liver perhaps? No? Then your kidneys? Yes it's most likely your kidneys. What do you expect, Architruc? We're none of us getting any younger. (*Pause.*) You say he's an excellent minister?

THE KING: Excellent. Will you tell me something about the benefits?

BAGA (*normal voice*): Later. (*Pause. He postures restlessly. Normal voice.*) Now something dirty. We proceed. (*He approaches The King coquettishly. Woman's voice.*) Oh what a pretty little nose you have!

THE KING: Idiot!

BAGA (*woman's voice*): And what pretty little eyes! And what delicious little biceps! (*He tickles him. The King laughs.*)

THE KING: That will do.

BAGA (*woman's voice*): And what lovely little thighs! (*Pause. Normal voice.*) Well say something. Do something! (*He strokes his own breast and hips. Woman's voice.*) Come my love, I can resist no longer. (*He takes his arm and tries to lead him to the bed.*)

THE KING: Ai you make me sick. It's not funny.

BAGA (*normal voice*): All right, all right.

THE KING: Tell me about those benefits.

BAGA (*normal voice*): I'll tell you nothing.

THE KING: And if I continue to play you'll tell me? But not for love.

BAGA (*normal voice*): What a puritan you can be! (*He looks at his watch.*) Good we agree. There's a half-hour left yet. I'm going to disguise myself again.

THE KING: As what?

BAGA: As God.

THE KING: Good lord!

BAGA (*he goes to the dressing room*): Wait for me and don't peek. (*He goes into the dressing room.*)

THE KING: God the father or God the son?

BAGA: You'll see.

The King very mechanically picks up the letter on the table, rereads it, looks up, scratches his head, shrugs his shoulders. Pause.

THE KING: Government first! What government? Every man for himself. (*To Baga.*) Are you making fun of me?

BAGA'S VOICE: Me? Why?

THE KING: What government? What government?

BAGA'S VOICE: Your subjects for heaven's sake.

THE KING: My subjects! You've seen them then?

BAGA'S VOICE: I smell them. That will do.

THE KING: What do they smell like?

BAGA'S VOICE: Awful.

THE KING: It's true that they still pay? (*Pause.*) We must still look pretty good for our ages. (*Pause.*) Great benefits? (*To himself.*) And benefits in which respect? (*To Baga.*) That's it?

BAGA'S VOICE: That's it.

Baga comes out of the dressing room. He is dressed as a judge. Very dignified air. He creases his brow.

THE KING: What's that? You've changed?

BAGA: It's Judgment Day. I'm the supreme judge who will condemn you.

THE KING: For heaven's sake! And I thought it would be fun.

BAGA: One does not have fun with God. One listens to his sentence of death. On your knees.

THE KING: Why, since I am already condemned?

BAGA: In order to obey. On your knees.

THE KING: I'm tired. And then I've never been very fond of condemnations.

BAGA: You are deplorable.

THE KING: Possibly. I'm tired of having fun.

There is a knock on the door.

BAGA: Enter!

Enter The Cook, chef's hat in hand.

COOK: Your Majesty is served.

THE KING: What? And my beard?

COOK: Monsieur Baga said

THE KING: Who do you think is in command here?

BAGA: I had said to serve when ready.

THE KING: And do I seem to be ready?

BAGA: Just this once you can do without being shaved.

THE KING: And etiquette? And government? (*He makes a sign to The Cook to go.*) Go!

The Cook leaves.

Isn't that something! I can't do anything! I'm the slave of my servants! They order me around!

BAGA: Calm yourself. I'll go find the shaving dish.

THE KING: You'll go if I ask you to.

BAGA: All right, all right.

THE KING: Go find the shaving dish.

Baga goes into the dressing room. Still dressed as a judge he comes out again carrying a shaving dish which he places on the table. The King, waiting in his armchair, appears very bored.

BAGA: Not feeling well?

THE KING: I think not. I'd like to lie down.

BAGA: Do you want me to call the doctor?

THE KING: No. (*Pause.*) I think I've got my malady again.

BAGA: The last straw.

THE KING (*dreamily*): Baga, do you believe in government?

BAGA: Do I believe in it? What's got into you?

THE KING: My malady. (*Pause.*) Why not abdicate? We could live in the country, with nothing to do. Subjects complicate everything. Those walking odors, hiding in their holes. Have you ever seen them?

BAGA: I smell them I tell you, them and their smelly money.

THE KING (*indicating with a nod of his head the left-hand side of the stage*): Do you remember when the bed was over there? I think I liked it better that way.

BAGA (*making a gesture of resignation and sitting down on the bed*): Fine, pretend you have your malady.

THE KING: Yes I believe that I liked it better. It was much gayer.

BAGA: It's we who were much gayer.

THE KING: Do you think so?

BAGA: Since then we've done nothing. Not even a little war. We're getting rusty.

THE KING: We've changed so much? (*Pause.*) Baga, I want to speak to you of my childhood.

BAGA (*in consternation*): Oh no I beg you!

THE KING: Yes, I want to. (*Pause. Baga shrugs his shoulders.*) I don't know where to begin.

BAGA: At the beginning.

THE KING (*pause. He reflects a little*): It's funny the way they're all the same. (*Pause.*) I want to tell you mine but not the usual way. I want to change it a little. (*Pause.*) I want to . . . I want to speak to you of my soul.

BAGA: Jesus!

THE KING: To speak to you of my soul, yes indeed. . . And of life.

BAGA: What life?

THE KING: Life . . . life.

BAGA: You mean your life. What you do, what you've done, your government, your

THE KING: No more than that?

BAGA: How could there be more than that?

THE KING: It's not possible. And so I have no life.

BAGA: And do you think I have one! I have systems for getting you to sign things and I devise the menu.

THE KING: And you don't like that?

BAGA: I don't know any more.

THE KING: I don't either. (*Pause.*) At times I tell myself that we could change.

BAGA: Change what?

THE KING: I don't know. . . . Move the bed back, reupholster the chairs . . .

BAGA: Look here Archi that's not really changing things.

THE KING: And what is really changing things?

BAGA: I don't know myself. . . . Traveling?

THE KING (*getting excited suddenly*): Baga, it will be magnificent! We're going on a trip!

BAGA: Where?

THE KING: It doesn't matter. We'll pack our bags, polish up Papa's old runabout and be off!

BAGA: Where, I'm asking you.

THE KING: Well . . . to Chanchèz, for example.

BAGA: Chanchèz? A valley full of rats. What would you want to do there?

THE KING: Well then . . . to Dualie?

BAGA: So we can freeze? That's not for me.

THE KING: Well then . . . Oh I know. We'll go to Estellouse. Are the constructions there completed yet?

BAGA: I went there last week. The château will have to be rebuilt. The ceilings have fallen in and the cellars are full of water.

THE KING: Already? They must have worked like swine. When did they finish? And why didn't you tell me anything?

BAGA: My poor, dear old friend. It's been finished for a century. It's covered with moss already.

THE KING: A century! I forgot this château for a century!

BAGA: It's been there, forgotten. (*Pause. He gets up and helps The King to his feet.*) Listen, lie down a moment and things will be better.

The King stretches out on the bed. Baga pulls a cover up over him and then sits down in the armchair.

THE KING: Do you remember when I used to ask you my questions? (*Pause.*) I'm speaking to you.

BAGA: Eh?

THE KING: When I asked you my questions about nature.

BAGA: Oh listen now, why don't we go back to talking about your childhood.

THE KING: I don't remember it any more. (*Pause.*) Nature serves what end do you think?

BAGA: It governs us.

THE KING: You still think so? The sea, the trees, the mountains? (*Pause.*) I find the contrary true. Besides, what I was saying . . . No I remember I used to say that I would give them all up for a room overlooking a courtyard. (*Pause.*) Provided someone else were there.

BAGA (*he makes a circular gesture in the air with his finger, ending by pointing to himself*): And here we are.

THE KING: Not you Baga . . . I mean to say . . .

BAGA: Don't trouble yourself. I understand.

THE KING: No that's not what I mean. What I mean to say is that someone

BAGA: Someone you love?

THE KING: You know very well that I love you Baga.

BAGA: Then what?

THE KING: Then nothing.

BAGA: A good woman you make love with?

THE KING: I

BAGA: In a room overlooking a courtyard making love all day? And you don't think you'll have enough of it after three days?

THE KING: Well then let's say a room with a balcony overlooking the sea.

BAGA: That might take two days longer. And after that?

THE KING: Perhaps it will take the rest of my life. What do you think?

BAGA: What do I think? I think that together we've had enough of this for a century now.

THE KING: But since we haven't

BAGA: It comes to the same thing.

THE KING: You think so?

BAGA: Absolutely. (*Pause.*) We need to change

THE KING: Ah you see.

BAGA: to change before belief is lost. After that it's no use.

THE KING (*dreamily*): A room overlooking a courtyard . . .

BAGA: What if I were to say that I want to be a minister?

THE KING: A minister? You are.

BAGA: Well then you see.

THE KING: Oh you weary me. (*Pause.*) I'm tired. I'm not feeling too well.

BAGA: You want to sleep?

THE KING: No thank you.

BAGA: You want to stuff yourself?

THE KING: No thank you.

BAGA: Do you want me to tell you a story?

THE KING: Do you know one?

BAGA: I'll try. (*Pause.*) One day God said to himself . . . No. (*Pause.*) One day there was a king and his minister.

THE KING: I see it coming.

BAGA: Don't interrupt me. (*Pause.*) The king didn't know what to do and neither did the minister. They looked for something, and they didn't find anything. Then God said to himself I must do something for these people. He looks; and he finds nothing. He calls in his adviser, the serpent. He says to him you see that king and that minister? I want to give them some ideas. Find something. The serpent

THE KING: Why a serpent?

BAGA: Don't interrupt me. The serpent goes to find his bag and brings it to God. Take it he says. What should I do with it? says God. You take something out of it. No matter what? Yes the first thing you touch. God puts his hand in the bag and pulls out . . .

THE KING: Is that symbolic?

BAGA: and pulls out . . . Wait. Let me remember. (*Pause.*) Ah yes. A child. And God says to the serpent this king is upset because he is alone and concerned for the line of succession. This child is a good idea. I'll send it to him. It will keep him busy. And he throws the child onto the earth.

THE KING: Is that symbolic?

BAGA: The boy falls on the king's bed and the king wakes up and says what's this fat thing? His minister says to him Sire it's a gift from heaven, we have to adopt it.

THE KING: What are you leading up to?

BAGA: Don't interrupt me. The king says fine, what's his name? The minister reflects and says Junior, we'll give him a good, solid upbringing and he'll succeed you. The king is delighted, he forgets his cares, he devotes himself completely to his son. The son grows, becomes a distinguished individual, brings cheer into his father's old age, so his father can die in peace.

THE KING: Charming. (*Pause.*) And so you advise me to get married?

BAGA: No.

THE KING: Then to have a son?

BAGA: No: that's only for animals. But you could adopt one. I've been thinking about it for quite a while. Your succession

THE KING: And where could we get one?

BAGA: At the orphanage.

THE KING: And what guarantee do we have that he won't be a good-for-nothing?

BAGA: You have to choose between that and the succession of the King of Novocardia.

THE KING: Never! I prefer adoption. (*Pause.*) But what is this that's come over you all of a sudden. You're afraid that I'll kick the bucket?

BAGA: No I think only of your well-being, of your peace of mind.

THE KING: And that you're tired of me and that a son will keep you busy.

BAGA: Exactly.

THE KING: You're not very nice Baga.

BAGA: I'm a minister Sire.

THE KING (*pause*): A son that worries me a little. Bringing him up. (*Pause.*) Don't you want him to be yours too? Just a little?

BAGA: I'll be his godfather. We'll put a bed for him here and put his little things there in the closet. And I'll give him lessons in government.

THE KING: How old will he be?

BAGA: Seven. He won't piss in the bed and he'll understand you when you tell him something.

THE KING: I'll bet you've already taken steps without telling me.

BAGA: No but it's been on my mind. (*Pause.*) If you're better tomorrow we'll go buy one at the orphanage.

THE KING: How much?

BAGA: About a thousand rupees. It depends.

THE KING: Do you have the money?

BAGA: We'll borrow it from the chest of state.

THE KING: How much is there?

Baga pulls a chest out from beneath the bed. He rummages within and counts.

BAGA: One thousand . . . two thousand . . . three thousand . . . five thousand. Five thousand rupees.

THE KING: Extraordinary! They'll be able to rebuild Estellouse, and it'll be my summer home! (*Pause.*) Oh I'm feeling much better! Can I get up?

BAGA: No. Tomorrow.

THE KING: What will we do while waiting?

BAGA: What will we do? (*Pause.*) We can rehearse.

THE KING: Rehearse what?

BAGA: Your fatherly role. How will you go about it?

THE KING: That's a good idea.

BAGA: Yes we'll go over it all. I'll play Junior and you the father.

THE KING: By adoption.

BAGA: By adoption. (*He gets up.*) Here we are. Let's say that I've come back from the garden. On a scooter. I enter and I circle the room. (*He imitates a child on a scooter and circles the stage. In an idiotic child's voice.*) Good morning Papa! I love my new scooter!

THE KING: Oho! And who gave it to you?

BAGA (*child's voice*): You did. I'd much rather have had a motor scooter.

THE KING: A motor scooter at your age? Now look how silly you are.

BAGA (*child's voice*): I'm no longer a child, Papa. I'm seven years old.

THE KING: Do you think at the age of seven I had a motor scooter?

BAGA (*child's voice*): I'm sure you didn't! You were too dopey.

THE KING: And how are you speaking to your father?

BAGA (*child's voice*): Will you give me a motor scooter when I'm eight?

THE KING: Not until you're fifteen.

BAGA (*child's voice*): I'll ask my godfather for one.

THE KING: Who's your godfather?

BAGA (*child's voice*): You don't even remember! It's Baga.

THE KING: And what has your godfather taught you today?

BAGA (*child's voice. He continues to circle*): Division.

THE KING: Oho! (*Pause.*) How much is seven divided by three.

BAGA (*child's voice*): That makes . . . that makes . . . eight.

THE KING: No, no look here: that makes . . . that makes . . . two point three, three, three, three

BAGA (*child's voice*): How many times?

THE KING: Infinitely.

BAGA (*child's voice*): That's impossible.

THE KING: How is it impossible?

BAGA (*child's voice*): Only God Almighty is infinite.

THE KING: But

BAGA (*normal voice. Breathlessly. He continues to circle*): Don't you want to tell me to stop it? This doesn't bother you?

THE KING: Right. Junior stop when I'm speaking to you.

BAGA (*child's voice. Continuing to circle*): No I'm on a cross-country trip.

THE KING: Stop do you hear?

BAGA (*child's voice*): No it's a nonstop trip.

THE KING: Now what do I say to you?

BAGA (*normal voice*): You'll deprive me of dessert.

THE KING: Junior I'll deprive you of dessert.

BAGA (*child's voice*): What's for dessert?

THE KING: Euh . . . What's for dessert?

BAGA (*child's voice*): I don't know, I'm asking you.

THE KING: And I'm asking you!

BAGA (*child's voice*): But I don't know Papa!

THE KING: I'm talking to you Baga you jackass!

BAGA (*normal voice. Continuing to circle*): And suppose I'm not there.

THE KING: Why won't you be there?

BAGA (*normal voice*): Because I'm in the kitchen. What will you tell him then?

THE KING: Go and look in the kitchen.

BAGA (*normal voice*): O wonderful educational principles!

THE KING: Then what do I say?

BAGA (*normal voice*): Don't you say do you hear me there will be no dessert for you?

THE KING: Do you hear me there will be no dessert for you?

BAGA (*child's voice. Continuing to circle*): That's fine I never liked dessert anyway Papa.

THE KING: In that case . . . Oh shit.

BAGA (*child's voice*): O Papa said she-e-e-t Papa said she-e-e-et!

THE KING (*shouting*): Baga stop it!

BAGA (*he stops. Normal voice*): You are impossible. (*Worn out, he drops onto the bed.*)

THE KING: What should I have said? Are they all like that?

BAGA: All. You have to punish them.

THE KING: But after dessert what's left?

BAGA: Enough for today.

THE KING: It's not my fault. Couldn't we choose a more peaceful one?

BAGA: A sloth? Do you want him to be spineless?

THE KING: No but . . .

BAGA: He'll be either a real boy or else spineless.

THE KING: What I mean is why don't we get a little girl? They're calmer aren't they?

BAGA: And what about Salic Law?

THE KING: We've only to repeal it.

BAGA: Impossible.

THE KING: Baga you ought to be able to do that for me.

BAGA: I tell you it's impossible. We must have a boy.

THE KING: All right. (*A rather long pause.*) I'm sad, Baga. Everything we do is sad, this room is sad, life

BAGA: You're not going to start that again, are you?

THE KING: My soul is sad.

BAGA: Oh, cut it out.

THE KING: We're always forcing ourselves to do things. I told myself that that could be changed, I thought . . . (*Pause.*) If only we could retire. I don't even want . . . You see the main motive of life, want. One might call it a profound game of the connotations. (*Pause.*) Death's too. When you stop wanting, you die like a dog.

BAGA: Have you finished now? You're not supposed to think about that. After all I'm here aren't I?

THE KING: Yes, you're here. (*Pause.*) An enormous voyage! You don't want to go? Why don't you want to?

BAGA: I do want to. Where?

THE KING: No don't ask me. We'll pack our bags and leave to-morrow.

BAGA: Fine then we'll pack our bags.

THE KING (*brightening up*): Ah! (*Pause.*) Oh, I'm so much better!

Baga pulls the suitcase from under the bed. He opens it, then turns to the cabinet.

BAGA: How many pairs of socks? Three? Four?

THE KING: Five! We're going very far.

BAGA: Five pairs of drawers then?

THE KING: And five shirts and five handkerchiefs! And the tweed suit with the cap. It'll make me look like I'm on a trip. (*Pause.*) Don't forget the muffler and the dark glasses. We're traveling incognito.

BAGA: This passion for incognito! Anyway anybody can recognize us.

THE KING: Yes, but it simplifies etiquette.

BAGA (*he goes from cabinet to suitcase, packing things*): What do we do with Fifille?

THE KING: We'll leave her with the cooks. They'll water her.

BAGA: Aren't you afraid they'll flood her?

THE KING: Well then she'll be flooded.

BAGA: Decidedly, I'd hardly know you.

THE KING (*loftily*): One must know how to act when the time is ripe! (*Pause.*) Don't forget my slippers. (*Pause.*) Tomorrow! Tomorrow we go to sleep in a different room!

BAGA: Overlooking a courtyard perhaps.

THE KING: A different room, different walls, a different horizon. A huge, huge horizon, infinite!

BAGA (*continually busy with the suitcase*): And what will we say to the maids? Who'll keep an eye on them? They'll go absolutely mad.

THE KING: So much the better! Let them amuse themselves!

BAGA: And the chest?

THE KING: We'll bring it with us. (*Pause.*) Baga.

BAGA: What?

THE KING: The future is never as bad as it looks.

BAGA: Are we taking the camera?

THE KING: Twist the neck of the future. Consume it to the core!

BAGA: And show it who's the master!

THE KING: Baga, we're turning over a new leaf.

BAGA: It's about time.

THE KING: It's never too late. We're going to make up for lost time, we're going to live! We'll spend every cent in the chest! We'll free ourselves, no more ties, no more government, no more anything! We're off to adventure! Ah Baga, liberty!

BAGA: Don't excite yourself, old man. (*Pause.*) Where did you put the sunglasses?

THE KING: The sun! Stark naked in the sun! (*He picks up a hand mirror and looks at himself in it.*) Does my skin look old and wrinkled to you?

BAGA (*taking the mirror from his hands*): Put that down and lie down. You're upsetting yourself too much.

A knock at the door.

Come in!

Enter The Cook, his chef's hat in hand.

COOK: Sire it's not about lunch.

THE KING: Too bad. What then?

COOK: It's . . . I think it's . . . in short . . .

THE KING: Well what is it!

COOK: It's not exactly somebody who's there Sire. . . . I think it's somebody who's announcing himself. . . .

THE KING: How?

COOK: By a messenger boy.

THE KING: A messenger boy?

COOK: Yes on a bicycle.

THE KING: Is he still there?

COOK: No he went away again.

THE KING: What did he say?

COOK: He said this . . . He said . . .

THE KING: Well out with it!

COOK: I don't really know Sire, I couldn't quite follow him.

THE KING: But overall, Cook, he spoke about what?

COOK: I . . . I think it was about an extraordinary menu . . . Something like that.

THE KING: For who? For me?

COOK: I don't know Sire.

THE KING: But then you should have held him a little while, for amplification. (*To Baga.*) What does this mean?

BAGA: I don't follow. (*To The Cook.*) And that's all he said?

COOK: Yes I think . . . No he said all sorts of things but I didn't understand.

BAGA: He didn't say where he came from? Or for whom? Why do you think he was a messenger?

COOK: I don't know. . . . He said that . . . an extraordinary menu and he went off.

The King makes a sign to Baga indicating that The Cook is out of his mind.

THE KING: That's fine, Cook, that's fine. You may go.

The Cook goes out.

Poor fellow. Does he get enough to eat?

BAGA: It's obvious that he drinks sufficiently.

THE KING: At his age? He has love troubles?

BAGA (*he shrugs his shoulders. He goes back to the suitcase*): I was saying dark glasses . . . (*He takes a pocket notebook from the table and makes a notation.*) and some snacks.

THE KING: On a bicycle? An extraordinary menu? (*Pause.*) Do you know The Cook very well?

BAGA: Do I know him?

THE KING: Do you know his love troubles?

BAGA: Since when am I a doorman Sire?

THE KING: You don't mean to tell me that

BAGA: Don't bother going on. I don't know the troubles of The Cook.

THE KING: It's a fault.

BAGA: A fault? You're getting senile.

THE KING: I am the father of my subjects, I ought to know them.

BAGA: Well then recall him and ask him his secret.

THE KING: I have a minister, let him now officiate.

BAGA: Never. The secrets of others . . . I empty your chamber pot and that's enough for me.

THE KING: That's fine, that's fine. (*Pause.*) What are we taking for provisions?

BAGA: An extraordinary menu.

THE KING: What a bullshitter you are.

BAGA: I am a minister Sire.

The King stretches out. He turns his face to the wall. Baga snaps the clasps of the suitcase, takes the watering can from the table and goes into the dressing room. He comes out with the watering can and waters the plant.

THE KING (*without turning around*): What are you doing?

BAGA: I'm watering Fifille.

THE KING: That's very nice. (*He turns around and sits up. He smiles.*) Baga.

BAGA: Yes?

THE KING: We're going! Oh I'm feeling much better! (*Pause.*) Can we have another performance?

BAGA: Calm yourself.

THE KING: I'll calm myself but first disguise yourself, just once more.

BAGA (*he shrugs his shoulders*): If you want . . .

THE KING: As what?

BAGA: It's a surprise. Lie down and wait.

The King stretches out, face to the wall.

THE KING: You'll tell me when?

BAGA: Yes.

Baga goes into the dressing room. A very long pause. The King does not move. The door at the rear opens slightly. Death appears. He is taller than Baga. A skeleton wrapped in a shroud. He carries a scythe. He enters stealthily. The floor creaks. The King rolls over to look.

THE KING (*startled*): You frightened me! (*Pause.*) Not bad at all. One might almost say that you've gotten taller.

BAGA'S VOICE: What?

Death approaches the bed. The King is frightened again. He puts his hands over his eyes.

THE KING: Baga! You're frightening me!

BAGA'S VOICE: Just a minute! What's the matter with you?

Death lowers his scythe.

THE KING (*terrified*): Baga! Baga! No! No!

> *With a wide sweep Death mows the air above the reclining King. He drops his arms. He is dead. Mouth open. Death swiftly leaves by the door.*

BAGA'S VOICE: Now what's the matter with you? Did you see a spider? (*Pause.*) Eh? (*Pause.*) Answer me! (*Pause.*) It's all right. I'm here.

CURTAIN

La vie est un jeu, comme
on vieillit, on s'ennuie,
~~on~~ ce sont les repas,
                    la nourriture
les vacances et la postérité
à quoi on s'intéresse.

the painting

A GUIGNOLADE

by EUGÈNE IONESCO

translated by George E. Wellwarth

The Painting, as produced by Robert Postec—who had so admirably mounted *Jack, or The Submission*—was first performed in Paris, in October of 1955, at the Théâtre de la Huchette. It was not a success. In effect, the interpreters committed an important error: they adopted for the first part of the play a realistic, even naturalistic, manner, imagining that it was a question here of a critique of a capitalist exploiting the poor artist. The realistic style was evidently unable to "hang together" with the second part of the play, the theme of which is "metamorphosis"—with which I deal in a parody, in order, through indirection, to disguise its serious nature.

Actually, this guignol play ought to be performed by circus clowns, in the most ridiculous, exaggerated, thoroughly "idiotic" style possible. It is not necessary to give "psychological depth" to the characters; and as for the "social content" (!), it is incidental, secondary. The actors (The Stout Gentleman especially) should not fear to make horrible grimaces, to take tumbles, to pass without transition from one state to another. Reversals of the situations ought to be effected brusquely, violently, roughly, without preparation. In attempting to give a "social" bent to the characters, interpretation will only overload and, as a result, destroy the sense. What could the ending accomplish after a beginning played as it was?

It is only by an extreme, coarse, childish simplification that this farce's significance can be brought out: and become credible through incredibility and *idiocy*. Idiocy can constitute this type of revealing simplification.

EUGÈNE IONESCO

A large room furnished with a very large desk, a telephone, and an enormous leather armchair placed in front of the enormous desk. The Stout Gentleman is seated in the armchair. Doors right and left, and a window in the right-hand corner.

The Stout Gentleman, who has an air of being very much satisfied with himself, is in shirtsleeves, a rose pinned on his breast; loud-colored tie; cuffs rolled back, possibly; enormous gold wrist-watch on his wrist. As he speaks, he picks his teeth with a large gold toothpick and his ears with an ear-pick which he has on the desk. His jacket is slung over the armchair and has another rose in its lapel.

The Painter is very poorly dressed and ill-shaven. He looks almost like a bum. He is wearing a loose, flowing tie and is carrying a canvas rolled up under his arm.

Alice, a very old woman, is wearing a dirty apron and large, dirty shoes or sabots or slippers; white hair, hanging down in strands from her lace cap. She wears spectacles, has only one arm, and carries a white cane; she sniffs frequently and blows her nose either with or in her fingers.

The Painter is excessively timid and looks like a fool. Do not be afraid to progress from a style of apparent realism in the opening dialogue to a caricatural, outré, clownish one. Pass without transition from the "style" of Antoine to the "style" of the Marx Brothers.

As the curtain rises, The Stout Gentleman is seated at his desk. He keeps glancing at his wrist-watch and fiddles with his splashy-colored tie, picking his teeth, ears, and nose with the appropriate instruments. Opposite him, standing at a respectful distance, near the door on the right, is The Painter. He too would like to pick his teeth. He tries to do this, without success, whenever The Stout Gentleman happens to turn his head.

THE STOUT GENTLEMAN: Come closer, come closer. . . . (*The Painter does not budge.*) Listen here, it took me a long time to get started. Ah yes, it wasn't easy. I had to surmount unconquerable obstacles which I conquered! But I didn't reach the goal of my ambitions with one single leap; there wasn't anything miraculous about it, believe me, my dear fellow— you must understand me.

THE PAINTER: Oh yes, sir, I understand you.

THE STOUT GENTLEMAN: I'm a bulldog, relentless; I never let go. (*He shows his teeth, clears his throat; clenches his teeth, rolls back his lips, and growls like a dog.*) The main thing, let me tell you, my dear fellow, is to keep fighting.

THE PAINTER: To keep fighting, yes sir.

THE STOUT GENTLEMAN: Because nothing falls out of the sky for you ready-cooked, like the manna in the desert. (*He indicates the room, the desk, and himself with a sweep of his arm.*) But take a look at the result of my efforts—it's all mine. What do you say to that, my dear fellow? Eh? Tell me what you've got to say to that.

THE PAINTER: To be sure, yes indeed, to be sure . . .

THE STOUT GENTLEMAN (*dabbing at his forehead with a large handkerchief*): There you see the fruit of my labors—the sweat of my brow. I am proud of it.

THE PAINTER: You certainly have a right to be.

THE STOUT GENTLEMAN: Come closer. Come closer.

The Painter advances half a step.

Oh, yes indeed, my dear fellow, I certainly have the right. Without vanity I can hold myself up as an example. Let it be one for you and for others. Unlike most people who have become successful the way I have, through force of will-power, stubbornness, energy, and hard work, I, my dear fellow, am not an egotist. There aren't any miracles, my dear fellow, let me tell you. What there is, my dear fellow, is *the* miracle.

THE PAINTER: Oh, *the* miracle?

THE STOUT GENTLEMAN: Yes, make no mistake—one single miracle, the true miracle, the miracle of miracles: work!

THE PAINTER (*naïvely*): Ah yes, you're right; the miracle of work.

THE STOUT GENTLEMAN: There you are, you've said it yourself. I know I'm right. (*Again indicating the walls and the desk with a sweep of his arm.*) And here's the proof: the concretization of my efforts—this house.

THE PAINTER: There's no denying it. (*He puts the painting under his other arm.*)

THE STOUT GENTLEMAN: I am a self-made man. For me life has been one long struggle. That's what life is—a pitiless struggle. We trample onward over corpses! I don't know if you're of my opinion.

THE PAINTER: Oh yes, sir.

THE STOUT GENTLEMAN: A pitiless struggle, yes—but an honest one: free competition.

THE PAINTER: Free competition, yes sir.

THE STOUT GENTLEMAN: Finally one finds a sort of satisfaction, a deep and bitter pleasure, the joy of a job well done. . . . One can sleep well at night because one has a tranquil conscience. (*He closes his eyes for a moment, lays his head on his hand like a pillow, and pretends to snore.*)

THE PAINTER: Tranquil, yes indeed, sir. (*He tries to pick his teeth with a finger but does not succeed because . . .*)

THE STOUT GENTLEMAN (*reopening his eyes*): Yes, tranquil, but how? What tranquillity!! It's the tranquillity of the calm after the storm! Serenity beyond tranquillity!

THE PAINTER: Ah yes, after . . . after the storm.

THE STOUT GENTLEMAN: Come closer, come closer.

The Painter hardly moves; he is so sorry for himself that he is almost sniveling.

I've led a very hard life ever since the day I left my most tender years. My father . . . oh, well, let's not talk about him, perhaps it wasn't all his fault, and besides he's dead. Same thing with my grandparents. My mother—ah yes, my mother got remarried to a drunkard. My father drank a lot too, but after all he was my father; while the other one—how shall I put it?—was merely my adopted father—but still! In short, my mother died too. (*Growing sad.*) You can't imagine what it means for a young boy to be thrust out into life like that, out into the jungle. . . .

THE PAINTER (*also moved to tears*): Oh yes, sir, yes, I certainly can imagine.

THE STOUT GENTLEMAN (*hitting the desk with his fist*): No, my dear fellow, no, you cannot imagine it. But I triumphed over it all!! . . .

THE PAINTER (*timidly*): I've gone through all that too . . .
My mother . . .

THE STOUT GENTLEMAN: No, no, no, my dear fellow, absolutely not
—it's not the same thing at all. Everybody's completely
different!

THE PAINTER: Oh yes, certainly!

THE STOUT GENTLEMAN: Take a look at that window over there
looking out on the street. (*He signs to The Painter to go
over.*) Go on, go on.

THE PAINTER (*goes over, still carrying the rolled-up canvas*):
There?

THE STOUT GENTLEMAN: What do you see?

THE PAINTER: Passers-by.

THE STOUT GENTLEMAN: What are they doing?

THE PAINTER: Passing by.

THE STOUT GENTLEMAN: That's pretty vague. Take a closer look at
them: they're all different from each other.

THE PAINTER: That's true.

THE STOUT GENTLEMAN: I know that—I've looked at them before;
I'm always observing them when I don't see anybody, during
my hours of premeditation.

THE PAINTER (*going softly back to his original position, still carrying the canvas under his arm*): Yes, sir.

*The Stout Gentleman picks his ears; The Painter starts to
pick his teeth but is interrupted by . . .*

THE STOUT GENTLEMAN: I see right into them . . . Oh, do put your
picture down! . . . and they're all alike: there's the whole
mystery of life for you! . . .

*The Painter switches his canvas to the other arm again, not
knowing where to put it down.*

Don't keep changing your picture from one arm to the other
as if you were doing rifle drill.

THE PAINTER: Excuse me, sir, I . . .

THE STOUT GENTLEMAN: Change a picture from one arm to the other as if one were doing rifle drill!! That was a pretty good joke! Ha! Ha! Did you get it?

THE PAINTER: Oh yes! Ha! Ha!

THE STOUT GENTLEMAN: Have a seat, my dear fellow!

THE PAINTER (*again looking around vainly for a chair*): Yes, sir.

THE STOUT GENTLEMAN: You see, my dear friend, I've got twenty years on the Stock Exchange behind me. I've played and I've won. (*Pointing.*) I've got a telephone. You hear? It works.

The telephone rings.

I'm not sure if I've managed to convince you.

THE PAINTER: Oh yes, sir.

THE STOUT GENTLEMAN: Wait—once more! (*He points at the telephone again. It rings and then stops.*) But I'm not out to convince you absolutely. That has to come from within. What was I saying? Ah yes . . . The Stock Exchange, that stiffens a fellow's spine. The Stock Exchange—that's the life! . . . You have to make your choice.

THE PAINTER: Yes, sir.

THE STOUT GENTLEMAN (*sobbing*): I slept on straw, my friend, at the poorhouse—never mind where—I educated myself. I never had a real boyhood.

THE PAINTER (*also sobbing*): Don't cry, sir.

THE STOUT GENTLEMAN (*looking up after having buried his head in his hands*): I lived in this house—my house—with my sister . . . She's much older than I . . . I've always had— believe me, I'm not trying to puff myself up—you'll think I'm joking . . .

THE PAINTER: Oh no, sir! Oh no . . .

THE STOUT GENTLEMAN (*furiously signing to him to shut up*): I've always had a taste for the arts: good music, good literature, good painting, the cinema . . . Alas, I've never had much time to read or go to the museum or to concerts or to the theatre . . . one can never do everything one wants in life.

(*Strongly.*) Those people who pretend that they're doing what they want don't know what they're talking about, my poor friend.

THE PAINTER: Oh, no, sir! They don't know.

THE STOUT GENTLEMAN: I was always very tired in the evening after a hard day at the Stock Exchange; but I have an artistic soul. Let me tell you, my friend, that, far from despising creativeness, as perhaps you're inclined to think, because I know you people . . . (*He glares at The Painter, rises, and points his finger at him, practically sticking it into his eye.*)

THE PAINTER (*recoiling*): I don't . . . I don't think so at all. Not that! No! Oh, absolutely not!

THE STOUT GENTLEMAN (*going back and sitting down in the armchair again*): Lucky for you! (*Then in more honeyed tones.*) But do take a seat.

Same action by The Painter as before.

Far from despising creative people, I admire them—the "good!" the "true!" the "sincere" artists . . . because you see (*Big smile.*) in art . . . particularly in painting, since that's your field . . .

THE PAINTER (*embarrassed*): Oh, sir, I am unworthy . . .

THE STOUT GENTLEMAN: . . . And there, as in business, one needs professional integrity—that's the only way to get ahead! If you'll follow my advice, you'll make a sort of battle out of your art too. In its way art is a struggle for life just as much as war or business, the white slave traffic or the black market. The choice is merely a matter of temperament! In short, what we're all really searching for is happiness; we are companions of the same ideal; happiness—the satisfaction of one's instincts and one's needs! . . . of one's desires and one's self-respect! Is there a more noble ideal? No.

THE PAINTER (*approvingly*): Oh yes . . . that is to say, no!

THE STOUT GENTLEMAN: And that, finally, is why people can understand each other: a community can be founded only if there is agreement about its purpose. That's the principle of humanism.

THE PAINTER: What a wonderful thing humanism is!

THE STOUT GENTLEMAN: Yes, indeed, it's all part of being human
—and it's the human element which makes the human being!

Both men are lost in dreams for a moment.

But do sit down and put your picture down somewhere.

Same bewildered action by The Painter.

Since you have permitted me to confide in you, I want to tell
you everything. You have no objection, I trust? I like con-
fiding.

THE PAINTER: Oh, certainly, I am honored—I hardly expected . . .

THE STOUT GENTLEMAN: Many thanks for your attention; I like
to confide—but not to just anyone! I only confide in people
in whom I have confidence. You, my dear sir, are possibly the
first . . .

THE PAINTER: Oh, sir, I will try to deserve the confidence
which . . .

THE STOUT GENTLEMAN: Silence! Certainly you deserve it. I know,
I feel who I give it to. You've just come here to my house to
sell me your picture.

THE PAINTER (*timidly*): Yes . . . if possible . . . I would like to
. . . really . . .

THE STOUT GENTLEMAN: And you're not just anyone. You, my dear
fellow, are . . . I have a flair for telling these things—it's the
secret of my success . . . one of those noble spirits, so rare
in our days, sympathetic people who like to listen to others,
to share the next man's troubles. You are certainly, how shall
I put it? I don't think I'm making a mistake . . .

THE PAINTER: I hope not, sir.

THE STOUT GENTLEMAN: You are one of those for whom "the next
fellow," I should say: "THE *next* fellow" exists. You're not an
egotist—that's the word.

THE PAINTER: That's the word.

THE STOUT GENTLEMAN: Don't deny it . . . no false modesty . . .
I'm not saying this to flatter you—it's the truth . . . you
won't catch me lying, my friend!

THE PAINTER: I didn't say that . . .

THE STOUT GENTLEMAN: Well now, at the end of that battle I won and which made me what I am . . . which allowed me to realize . . . (*Large gesture.*) in short, I will not repeat it . . . what you see at the finish of that triumphant battle which gave me everything, my dear friend . . . is that there is something missing. Something which is perhaps essential. (*He gets up.*) I am not happy, my friend. (*He sits down again, looking very depressed, and sighs.*)

THE PAINTER (*sympathetically*): You are not happy? Oh dear!

THE STOUT GENTLEMAN: Alas! Oh yes, one would not suspect it; how complex the human heart is. I crave beauty. That's what I miss. (*He pounds his chest.*) My taste for the arts—I might even say my passion for them—has never really been satisfied. I who have succeeded in everything else—I have never, for example, found a woman who would have understood me, who might understand me, who would understand me: it's true that that isn't easy.

THE PAINTER: Oh no, it isn't easy! One can well say it isn't easy . . . since it isn't! . . .

THE STOUT GENTLEMAN: But is it perhaps impossible?

THE PAINTER: Perhaps it isn't really impossible.

THE STOUT GENTLEMAN: To tell the truth, it is impossible!

THE PAINTER: You're right—it is impossible.

THE STOUT GENTLEMAN: No. It isn't impossible.

THE PAINTER: To be sure, I quite agree with you—it isn't.

THE STOUT GENTLEMAN: No, no, I think all the same that it must really be impossible. In any case, it remains to be seen. A woman, my dear sir, who combines all the qualities of flesh and spirit psychosomatically . . . who is . . . intelligent, that's the word.

THE PAINTER: That's the word, yes.

THE STOUT GENTLEMAN: And who is also ravishing . . . ravishing!!! Beautiful and understanding! But beautiful, above all beautiful, my dear fellow . . . Alas, I have never found such a one on my way through life.

THE PAINTER (*dreamily*): On the way through life . . .

THE STOUT GENTLEMAN: Or at least if I could have the image, the photograph, the reflection of beauty in my house. (*Sweeping gesture.*) If you would believe me how these bare walls . . .

THE PAINTER: Oh, I believe you, sir.

THE STOUT GENTLEMAN: These bare walls weigh heavily on me because they are without weight! . . .

THE PAINTER (*showing the rolled-up canvas under his arm*): Perhaps . . . perhaps this picture would suit you . . . perhaps . . . to some extent . . . it could . . .

THE STOUT GENTLEMAN: I ask myself this: Can art replace the dreamed-of woman, beautiful and sweet, that I miss?

THE PAINTER: Try it—take a look. (*He shows the canvas.*)

THE STOUT GENTLEMAN: Of course, my sister, who is much older than I am, lives in this house, has not succeeded in life, and is not a bad woman. What would she do without me? I took her in, provide for her needs, give her a home, feed her— she's in the kitchen at this very moment; she looks after me as well as she can, she takes care of the housework—I wouldn't go so far as to say that she doesn't feel affection for me, but, after all . . . you can imagine a sister's affection is not what I need, it's not that . . .

THE PAINTER: No, it can't be that . . .

THE STOUT GENTLEMAN: I don't bear her a grudge, mind you; I don't bear her a grudge. Still, if she were good-looking I'd get some pleasure out of looking at her. (*Solemnly and lyrically.*) Coming home in the evening, tired with the ugliness of life, I'd like to be able to contemplate a beautiful face, a graceful figure . . . And she's all I have in life, my dear friend. She's ugly. (*Despairing gesture.*)

THE PAINTER: What a misfortune!

THE STOUT GENTLEMAN: Ah yes, alas, my dear fellow! Let's not close our eyes to the facts—there wouldn't be any point in that.

THE PAINTER: You're absolutely right, sir, there certainly wouldn't be any point in that.

THE STOUT GENTLEMAN: My sister, dear friend, has not managed to destroy that profound desire for beauty in me—no, indeed, she has made it even more alive, more pointed (*sigh*), more painful than before . . . You cannot imagine to what an extent.

THE PAINTER (*very sympathetic*): I understand you, sir.

THE STOUT GENTLEMAN (*in an outburst of gratitude*): Ah, my dear Maestro—let me call you my dear Maestro—I admire this generous understanding in you. From now on you will have a place in my house and in my spirit; we understand each other.

THE PAINTER: Oh, I am deeply honored, very happy to . . .

THE STOUT GENTLEMAN: You understand everything right away, despite the fact that so many others have understood nothing of my life and don't even suspect I exist! They have never seen me!!

THE PAINTER: They should have . . .

THE STOUT GENTLEMAN: My sister is far from being despicable. She's not a bad soul: the instinct for beauty is not entirely stifled in her. However, with her, beauty is as if buried deep down in shadowy chasms, swallowed up in the impenetrable darkness of oblivion. We'd have to uncover it in her subconscious. My sister lives only in the world of necessities, my dear friend; she forges her own chains; she has no liberty! For where would we be, my dear fellow, without beauty, music, painting, poetry, theatre, engraving, decorative art, movies, *haute couture*, design?

THE PAINTER: Eh, we'd be, eh . . .

THE STOUT GENTLEMAN: Yes, what would we be, I ask you?

THE PAINTER: Eh . . . I . . . I don't know, sir.

THE STOUT GENTLEMAN: I'll tell you (*Tremendous crash of fist on desk.*) —brutes, sir!!!

THE PAINTER (*slightly frightened*): Oh . . . perhaps not . . .

THE STOUT GENTLEMAN: Yes. Brutes!

THE PAINTER: However, however . . .

THE STOUT GENTLEMAN: What do you mean, however? There's no however about it, there's no contradicting it; didn't you just say that you understood me?

THE PAINTER: Yes, I understand you, sir.

THE STOUT GENTLEMAN: Well, then?

Pause. The Painter is somewhat embarrassed, and switches his canvas to his other arm again.

Sit down, my dear fellow, sit down.

Painter again searches elaborately for seat.

I have her in my care, I earn my living, I'm in a position to feed another mouth, of course.

THE PAINTER (*feebly*): Your sister's mouth, sir?

THE STOUT GENTLEMAN: We're talking about her, aren't we? Aren't you following me?

THE PAINTER: Oh yes, excuse me, I'm listening to you.

THE STOUT GENTLEMAN: Very well, then; in short, there's only one thing I can reproach her with; one thing, however—you see, I admit it because I'm just—for which she isn't responsible. I reproach her for not being an ornament, a jewel, something for the eye to repose on in this house, which is so drab, so austere, so severe . . . A work of art which would not force me, my dear sir, to buy paintings . . . It's all because my sister is plain that I have to buy paintings, and it's costing me a fortune!

THE PAINTER: Not all that much, sir—you know, for a man like you . . .

THE STOUT GENTLEMAN (*changing his tone abruptly to a hard, businesslike one*): Well then, let's put our cards on the table. How much do you want for your piece of canvas?

THE PAINTER (*taken off-guard and confused*): I . . . I . . . I don't know, sir.

THE STOUT GENTLEMAN (*same tone*): What's your price? Come on now! . . . Be specific and don't try to go any higher than the average for masterpieces in the field of painting.

THE PAINTER (*confused*): I simply came to ask you . . . to be so good as to glance at this work . . . and to be so good as to . . .

THE STOUT GENTLEMAN: Enough of this idle chatter. You've come to sell your merchandise. Let's not mince words. Now I, as I've just told you and for reasons which I've just permitted you to hear, I am or, to put it precisely, would be eventually —let me make myself clear—eventually, *e-ven-tually* a buyer, if your work satisfied my artistic as well as my financial requirements, requirements which are only the expression of a sincere and elevated artistic and economic ideal.

THE PAINTER (*more and more confused*): Yes, sir, to be sure . . . Naturally.

THE STOUT GENTLEMAN: As far as the economic requirements, which must be modest, are concerned, it's up to you to suggest a price; as far as the artistic quality is concerned, it must be of the first order and agreeable to my personal taste.

THE PAINTER: If you'll just take a glance at the picture first, you'll be able to tell me right away if you're interested in it. . . . The main thing is that it please you.

THE STOUT GENTLEMAN (*gets up, goes toward The Painter, sits down again*): It can only interest me within certain financial limits; that's a principle, my friend, believe me, it's nothing but a matter of principle.

THE PAINTER: Yes, sir, of course, I understand. . . .

THE STOUT GENTLEMAN: I'm very glad of that.

THE PAINTER: However . . .

THE STOUT GENTLEMAN (*offended by the "however"*): However what?

THE PAINTER (*stammering*): It's necessary, that is to say . . . It would be necessary, perhaps . . . that you'd see it first . . .

THE STOUT GENTLEMAN (*with a "coarsely cunning" smile*): The price first, my friend, the aesthetics afterward.

THE PAINTER: It's rather refined. Here, take a look at it.

THE STOUT GENTLEMAN: No, no, no! . . . As far as refinement is concerned, there's nothing you can teach me; and I don't

want to see anything before I know your price. I repeat—
that's a principle. You did say that you understood me?

THE PAINTER: Oh yes, oh yes!

THE STOUT GENTLEMAN: Well then. Your price?

THE PAINTER: Hum! Eh! you know . . .

THE STOUT GENTLEMAN (*very loftily*): What do you want me to
know? What do you suppose I don't know already?

THE PAINTER: You're certainly in the know . . . (*Making an
effort.*) A painter of my type, a contemporary painter, for
example, Rembrandt or Rubens . . .

THE STOUT GENTLEMAN: I don't know those gentlemen, even though
I'm not an ignoramus.

THE PAINTER: Oh, I know that, I know that very well . . . Rembrandt or Rubens . . .

THE STOUT GENTLEMAN: You're not talking about nonrepresentational painting, I hope?

THE PAINTER: Oh no, sir, I've done with that, I've been through
that stage—I've come back to reality now.

THE STOUT GENTLEMAN: Fortunately; you've corrected your mistake. My congratulations.

THE PAINTER: Well then, if you'll allow me, Rembrandt or Rubens
sell a painting like this one for . . . 500,000 francs. I'm
willing to let you have mine for 400,000.

THE STOUT GENTLEMAN (*stupefied*): 400,000 francs! You don't
know the value of money! That's a fortune, my poor friend,
absolutely a fortune. That would be like giving a high bonus
for *less* effort. I don't earn such a sum every day on the Stock
Exchange. And the Stock Exchange, as I trust I've been able
to make you understand, is a merciless struggle which wears
a man out; it's a racecourse, a foot-to-foot struggle—and it's
the most valiant who wins. . . . While as far as you're concerned, all you ever do is remain seated peacefully in front of
your easel. No, my friend, 400,000 times no!

THE PAINTER: My art isn't easy either; it's not within just anybody's
reach.

THE STOUT GENTLEMAN: Let's get back to the subject.

THE PAINTER: I can let you have it for 300,000 francs.

THE STOUT GENTLEMAN: 400,000 or 300,000—that's practically the same.

THE PAINTER: All right then, 250,000 . . . 200,000.

THE STOUT GENTLEMAN: 300,000 or 200,000—that's still practically the same thing.

THE PAINTER: 100,000.

THE STOUT GENTLEMAN (*lifting his arms above his head*): 100,000!!! 100,000 or 200,000—what *difference* do you see between the two?

THE PAINTER: 80,000.

The Stout Gentleman shakes his head.

70,000.

The Stout Gentleman shakes his head.

60,000.

THE STOUT GENTLEMAN: From 70 to 60, you know . . . (*He shakes his head.*)

THE PAINTER: 50,000.

THE STOUT GENTLEMAN: From 60,000 to 50,000 is no more than a step. Go on a little further, my poor fellow, go on a little further.

THE PAINTER: All the same, I've lowered my price pretty considerably, you must admit.

THE STOUT GENTLEMAN: What do you want me to admit?

THE PAINTER (*taking the bull by the horns*): In that case, sir, you must excuse me . . . I would be valuing my work at too low a rate. . . . (*With an effort, stammering.*) Because, you see, I too have principles . . .

THE STOUT GENTLEMAN: All the better. If you have principles, keep them, by all means. And your picture with them. (*Pause; he is standing with his hands behind his back.*) You'd be better off with a few good kicks in the ass than with principles! That would be much better for you!

THE PAINTER: In that case, I'm sorry. Good-bye, sir! (*He goes toward the door.*) I stand fast to my principles and I refuse— excuse me, but I absolutely must refuse—to be kicked in the ass!

THE STOUT GENTLEMAN (*suddenly becoming imploring and tearful*): One moment! You're not going to leave me, are you, my dear fellow, with these dirty, bare walls, these hideous walls, these walls whose absence of beauty horrifies me? Reflect, my dear fellow, think of others! Be charitable of your genius to me, denuded as I am . . . yes, from a certain point of view, denuded! . . .

THE PAINTER (*almost at the door, with a constrained smile*): Art, too, you know, has to be paid . . .

THE STOUT GENTLEMAN: Nonsense! An artist such as you, such as I hope you are, is not a bargainer; he must be a priest of beauty, like the vestal virgins!! (*Very much a mixture of Joseph Prudhomme* [1] *and Groucho Marx.*)

THE PAINTER: I have to live, my dear sir.

THE STOUT GENTLEMAN (*exaggeratedly humble*): And I, don't I have to support my sister? Try to be human, I beg you . . .

THE PAINTER (*coming back*): Perhaps you're right. We have to help each other!

THE STOUT GENTLEMAN (*exaggeratedly proud*): I'm not asking you for charity. You will offend me. I don't want to owe anything to anyone.

THE PAINTER: I'm willing to let you have it for 14,000 francs! . . .

THE STOUT GENTLEMAN (*picking his ear*): 4,000 francs? That's too much, my poor friend, you're not thinking clearly.

THE PAINTER: I said . . . I said . . . 14, not 4 . . . 14,000 francs.

THE STOUT GENTLEMAN: I'm not stupid and I'm not deaf either. You said 4,000 francs.

---

[1] A smug, self-satisfied, pompous bourgeois cartoon character, invented by the nineteenth century caricaturist Henri Monnier. [Translator's note.]

THE PAINTER: Oh no, sir, I assure you I said 14!

THE STOUT GENTLEMAN (*outraged*): So, you retract your word, which I don't agree to anyway. You are not a man of honor: a man of honor has one word only. One single word!!!

THE PAINTER: 14, sir.

THE STOUT GENTLEMAN: 4 . . .

THE PAINTER: Excuse me, I said 14. I really did say 14.

THE STOUT GENTLEMAN: 14 what?

THE PAINTER: 14 thousand.

THE STOUT GENTLEMAN (*stupefied*): 14,000. (*Sarcastically.*) And you think I'm going to believe that?! I'm not your dupe.

THE PAINTER: Nevertheless.

THE STOUT GENTLEMAN (*standing, arms folded, profile to the auditorium*): None of your neverthelesses. It would be better not to talk about it any more. Good-bye, my dear fellow . . .

THE PAINTER: Very well! Good-bye, sir! (*He goes toward the door again.*) Good-bye, my dear sir.

He leaves.

THE STOUT GENTLEMAN (*running after him*): One moment, my dear fellow, one moment . . .

He goes out and returns after a moment pulling The Painter in with him by the sleeve.

Wait a minute . . . I'd like to do something for you just the same. I'll offer you 400 . . .

THE PAINTER: 400,000 francs? Ooh . . . my dear, good sir!

THE STOUT GENTLEMAN: Ah! ah! (*Big laugh.*) You're joking. . . .

THE PAINTER: Hey . . . yes . . . no . . . yes . . . why not?

THE STOUT GENTLEMAN: I'm offering you 400 francs and not a penny more, 400 francs in all and for all.

THE PAINTER (*abruptly; after a moment's silent calculation*): Very well, sir, done!

THE STOUT GENTLEMAN (*giving The Painter a slap on the back which staggers him*): I felt that we'd understand each other! I understand artists, and artists should understand me too!

THE PAINTER (*with sincerity*): Oh yes!

THE STOUT GENTLEMAN (*condescendingly*): I esteem you, my friend.

THE PAINTER (*moved*): Thank you, sir. You know, I would have been desolate if we had not come to an understanding.

THE STOUT GENTLEMAN: Me too! Settlement out of court, even if it costs nothing, is better than lengthy proceedings, however costly.

THE PAINTER: I'm entirely of your opinion.

THE STOUT GENTLEMAN: That does me honor.

THE PAINTER: I'll unroll my canvas.

THE STOUT GENTLEMAN: Oh, I would have been able to do that by myself; it's not absolutely necessary anyway. A canvas, after all, is just a canvas. All I ask of it is that it be a work of art! It'll decorate the wall; it'll lighten this dim interior a bit; it'll make my life a little less painful to live. . . . (*Deep sighs and picking of ears or teeth.*)

THE PAINTER (*tries to pick his teeth but interrupts himself to say*): Certainly.

THE STOUT GENTLEMAN (*who has turned toward The Painter*): Certainly.

THE PAINTER: Certainly.

THE STOUT GENTLEMAN: Certainly. We keep using the same expression, which means that our agreement is perfect.

THE PAINTER: Yes, our agreement is perfect.

Stout laugh from The Stout Gentleman; thin laugh from The Thin Painter.

THE STOUT GENTLEMAN (*recovering himself*): All the same, we could look at the picture . . . just to do things right?

THE PAINTER: Ah!

THE STOUT GENTLEMAN: It won't embarrass you, I hope, my friend?

THE PAINTER: Oh. . . not at all . . . I may be in a bit of a hurry
. . . but, after all . . . for you . . .

THE STOUT GENTLEMAN: Ah, my dear fellow, I like to know what
I'm buying; that's my right! I don't buy anything with my eyes
closed! Not even paintings!

THE PAINTER: Quite right, indeed; it's your right.

THE STOUT GENTLEMAN: Well then, make it snappy, since you tell
me you're in a hurry.

THE PAINTER: Right away, sir. (*He unrolls his immense canvas.*)

THE STOUT GENTLEMAN (*as The Painter gradually unrolls the canvas
on the floor*): Well, now . . . well, now . . . well, now . . .

THE PAINTER (*timidly, not yet having unrolled the whole canvas*):
Well, what do you think of it?

THE STOUT GENTLEMAN: Nothing yet, my friend. I have to see it.
Unroll the whole thing. . . . Come on now, quicker . . .

THE PAINTER: Yes, sir, yes. (*He spreads the picture out on the floor
and gets tangled up in it.*)

THE STOUT GENTLEMAN (*looking at him without coming to his aid*):
How clumsy you are! Watch it! You'll spoil my picture.

THE PAINTER: Excuse me.

THE STOUT GENTLEMAN (*tapping his foot*): Dum de dum de
dum . . .

THE PAINTER: There, sir, there you are . . .

THE STOUT GENTLEMAN: Finished?

THE PAINTER: Well, what do you think of it?

THE STOUT GENTLEMAN (*playing the connoisseur*): Hmm! Well,
now, well, now . . .

THE PAINTER: That's it.

THE STOUT GENTLEMAN: It's a portrait. . . a portrait of a woman
. . . Yes, you're right, it's not nonrepresentational.

THE PAINTER: Yes, indeed.

THE STOUT GENTLEMAN: Don't step on it. You certainly are careless. I told you before to be careful with my picture.

THE PAINTER: Excuse me.

THE STOUT GENTLEMAN (*irritated*): It's no good! It's representational!

THE PAINTER: That's what you wanted; I told you that's the way
it was.

THE STOUT GENTLEMAN: We need to define our terms. I have taste,
you know. You can have confidence in my judgment. Obviously I would have preferred a nonrepresentational picture
or else a really representational one.

THE PAINTER: Aaah! You should have explained yourself.

THE STOUT GENTLEMAN: Anyway, it is what it is.

THE PAINTER: It is what it is, to be sure; but all the same, being
what it is, what is it really? You who have taste?

THE STOUT GENTLEMAN (*in a professional tone*): I don't want to
give you any definitive opinion yet, in view of the fact that
I've only seen your work under unfavorable circumstances—
spread out on the floor like that. . . . A play is written to be
performed; a picture is painted to be hung up. A canvas spread
out on the floor is no better than an ordnance map. You can
only see a few details on it here and a few there—a grouping,
an edge, some lines, a few colors—but the whole effect escapes you.

THE PAINTER: Yes, that does escape; it certainly does escape.

THE STOUT GENTLEMAN: You must also realize that there is an essential difference between a canvas and a carpet, even though
both words begin with the same letters.

THE PAINTER: Yes, they begin alike, but end differently.

THE STOUT GENTLEMAN (*without moving*): Since you're here, hang
it up for me; surely you can give me a hand.

THE PAINTER: It's a pleasure.

THE STOUT GENTLEMAN (*as The Painter begins to roll up the canvas
again*): You're not leaving with it, are you?

THE PAINTER: No, I'm re-rolling it in order to re-unroll it on the wall. (*He goes with the half-rolled-up painting to the wall at the rear.*)

THE STOUT GENTLEMAN: On the other hand, it's just as you wish—you're perfectly free to do as you please.

THE PAINTER: Oh! No, sir, I'm entirely at your disposal.

THE STOUT GENTLEMAN: Besides, you don't roll it up in order to hang it. . . . (*Profoundly.*) It would even be rather the opposite.

THE PAINTER (*near the wall*): We'll have to hang it pretty high up.

THE STOUT GENTLEMAN: Obviously, since we don't want it to trail on the ground. I have to tell you everything. (*He raises his arms.*) Tell you everything!

THE PAINTER: If we have to hang it high up on the wall, we'll need a ladder.

THE STOUT GENTLEMAN (*shouting in the direction of the kitchen*): Alice! Alice!

ALICE (*cracked voice*): Yes. (*She comes running in precipitately. She is, in fact, very old and stooped; strands of white hair hang down on her shawl; she wears large dark glasses, a mitten, and an apron; she has only one arm and carries a white stick.*) There, there! Oh, dear! My dear brother!

THE STOUT GENTLEMAN: Oh, go and get a ladder and hurry up about it . . . hop to it!

ALICE: What for, dear little brother?

THE STOUT GENTLEMAN (*thunderous voice*): That's none of your business! I told you to hop to it! Do I have to repeat my orders?

ALICE (*frightened*): Don't get angry, my little one, I'm going.
She leaves.

THE STOUT GENTLEMAN: That's my sister.

THE PAINTER: Oh, sir, alas, I see.

THE STOUT GENTLEMAN: Come on, come on, Alice, let's go . . . (*Tapping his foot.*) faster, hurry up, stop dawdling!

ALICE: I'm coming. (*She enters, the end of the ladder appearing first.*) It's heavy, little brother.

THE PAINTER: May I . . . give her a hand?

THE STOUT GENTLEMAN: She needs it; that'll give her two altogether. Go on.

ALICE (*to The Painter, who is helping her carry the ladder, while she uses her one good arm and her stump*): Oh, thank you, sir, it's heavy and I'm tired. I'm old, sir—just imagine.

THE STOUT GENTLEMAN: You're always complaining. That doesn't interest the gentleman.

Alice and The Painter carry the ladder and place it against the rear wall.

ALICE: There?

THE STOUT GENTLEMAN (*not moving*): No! There! Go on, go on, watch out that you don't damage anything—don't scrape my wall. Ah! . . . I don't like that. (*To Alice.*) Hand him the picture, hand him the picture. (*He taps his foot.*)

ALICE (*cracked voice; frightened*): Yes . . . yes, little brother!

The Painter gets up on the ladder and Alice hands him the rolled-up painting.

THE PAINTER (*trying to hang up the picture*): Here, sir?

THE STOUT GENTLEMAN: Wait a minute. (*He goes to the middle of the stage, reflects a moment, then:*) Higher.

The Painter moves the picture to various positions according to The Stout Gentleman's directions, while Alice wriggles around violently without speaking.

Too low! To the right! To the left! Farther left—no, no, no! Yes, that's it! No, no! To the right! Left! Right! Lower! Higher! Lower! No! [1] . . . To the right of the left, not to the left of the right. Just so it doesn't come out upside down. Mind the symmetry, I tell you: "the symmetry" is important. There, there, watch out there! To the left, to the right, vice-

---

[1] A comic routine can be played here: as a result of the automatism of The Painter's movements, The Stout Gentleman's orders, and Alice's shufflings, the ladder sways and is in danger of falling, but is held back by Alice.

versa, right, left, versa! . . . That's it! Don't move. Hang it there. Now leave it.

The hung picture unrolls; it is a large canvas, looking somewhat like a tapestry and representing a very beautiful, regal woman; the headboard of a throne can be seen; the woman has black eyes, is robed in purple, and holds a scepter.

(*Looking at the picture.*) Well, now, well now . . .

ALICE (*to The Painter*): Who is it? Who is that lady?

THE STOUT GENTLEMAN: Quiet!

THE PAINTER (*on the ladder, fearfully*): What do you think of it, sir?

THE STOUT GENTLEMAN: I certainly think something, but I can't tell you anything since you're blocking my view. Get down from that ladder—quickly, quickly.

THE PAINTER: Yes, sir. (*He scrambles down.*)

THE STOUT GENTLEMAN: Alice, get over to the side and don't block my view—and don't stick out your tongue.

ALICE (*who has been sticking her tongue out at the woman in the picture*): Yes, yes, right away, right away, little brother! I didn't stick out my tongue! (*She sticks it out again.*)

THE STOUT GENTLEMAN: Get that ladder out of the way, will you! You're not going to leave it there till Christmas, are you?

THE PAINTER: Right away, sir, right away.

THE STOUT GENTLEMAN: Get a move on, Alice; give the artist a hand with the ladder. Where's your common sense?

ALICE: Don't get mad, dear little brother! (*She sobs.*) He scolds me all the time, sir, if you only knew . . .

THE PAINTER: Oh, sir, don't scold her.

THE STOUT GENTLEMAN (*to The Painter*): That's none of your business. (*To Alice.*) I've told you before not to complain to everyone! Push that ladder out of the way, both of you!

THE PAINTER: Yes, sir.

Alice, in tears, and The Painter push the ladder out of the way.

THE STOUT GENTLEMAN: Enough! (*Trembling, the two others stop.*) Now let me take a look at it so I can judge it. (*He goes up to the painting and backs away again several times in the manner of an art connoisseur.*)

THE PAINTER: Tell me right out what . . .

THE STOUT GENTLEMAN (*to Alice*): Are you stuck to that picture, Alice? Ah! . . . shit . . . You're blocking my view. You don't look too good next to her anyway, you old hag! Turn around, hide yourself!

ALICE (*to The Painter*): You see, sir, you see—my mere presence irritates him. (*She turns her back to the stage and to the audience.*)

THE PAINTER (*to Alice*): I'm sorry for you. (*Timidly, to The Stout Gentleman.*) You're hurting her, sir . . .

Alice turns round again, showing a tear-stained face.

THE STOUT GENTLEMAN (*to Alice*): Idiot!

Alice redoubles her sobs.

THE PAINTER (*to Alice*): Calm yourself, Madam.

THE STOUT GENTLEMAN (*to The Painter*): Mind your own business.

THE PAINTER: Excuse me.

THE STOUT GENTLEMAN (*to The Painter*): She cries constantly, my dear sir, constantly—either for some idiotic reason of her own or just to annoy me. She's totally without a grain of artistic sensibility.

THE PAINTER: Not totally, perhaps . . . After all, she *is* a human being.

ALICE (*sobbing*): What's artistic sensibility?

THE STOUT GENTLEMAN: The sense of beauty.

ALICE (*crying*): The sense of what?

THE STOUT GENTLEMAN (*to The Painter*): You see—I told you so. . . .

THE PAINTER: Oh, sir! she is more to be pitied than to be blamed! It's just an infirmity like any other . . .

THE STOUT GENTLEMAN: Ah yes, infirmities . . . she certainly doesn't lack those! (*To Alice.*) Go back to your pots and pans.

ALICE (*drying her eyes with her apron*): Very well, very well, very well, very well . . .

She goes to the kitchen door, leaving it ajar; from time to time she will peep in and listen to what is going on in the room and then go back.

THE STOUT GENTLEMAN (*to The Painter*): Her brothers are all younger and don't resemble each other.

THE PAINTER (*timidly*): Do form your opinion, sir.

THE STOUT GENTLEMAN (*looking at the painting for a few moments in silence while The Painter waits nervously*): I'm forming it, my dear fellow, I'm forming it . . . hmm . . . it might be an unfavorable one, you know.

THE PAINTER (*with a constrained smile*): So much the worse, my dear sir, so much the worse—say what you like.

THE STOUT GENTLEMAN: Very well . . . look here, the more I think about your work, the less I know what to think about it: I'm trying to express myself precisely.

THE PAINTER: Yes, yes . . .

THE STOUT GENTLEMAN: Your work has its shortcomings; I can see very well what you tried to paint—a portrait . . . a woman's portrait, unless I'm very much mistaken . . .

THE PAINTER: No, no, sir, you're not mistaken.

THE STOUT GENTLEMAN: Yes indeed, well, this portrays a woman, a seated woman—I'm interpreting it, you understand—a woman seated in an armchair, holding a scepter in her hand. It's like a big photograph; a portrait. Right?

THE PAINTER: That's it, precisely.

THE STOUT GENTLEMAN: The armchair in which this woman is sitting bears a strong resemblance to a throne. It might indeed even be one. A throne with its lower part invisible; one can guess it's there, however. . . .

THE PAINTER: Yes, one can guess it's there—at least I hope so.

ALICE (*poking her head in*): If it can be guessed, that's the main thing.

THE STOUT GENTLEMAN (*to Alice*): Shut up! (*To The Painter.*) Since she has a scepter but no crown, she must be a queen. This lower part which can be guessed at consists of the feet of this armchair or throne. To the extent to which these can only be guessed at without being seen, your painting is a non-representational one.

THE PAINTER: Precisely to that extent, sir.

THE STOUT GENTLEMAN: This princess, this woman, is also treated in a half-representational, half-nonrepresentational style, since one does not see but can only guess at her feet, legs, thighs, and backside.

THE PAINTER: Oh, yes, sir, that's exactly true!

THE STOUT GENTLEMAN: How can one be sure that this woman is a woman? That's one of the mysteries of your art on which I congratulate you.

ALICE: It's all by suggestion.

THE PAINTER: Thank you, sir.

THE STOUT GENTLEMAN (*professionally*): Wait a minute! We must clear up this mystery. How can one be sure, since only the beginnings of the bosom can be seen, the nipples being carefully—I might almost say prudishly—hidden behind a lacy blouse. One doesn't see the woman's breasts, but still it can scarcely be doubted that they are there. . . . There's no disputing the value of suggestion—it's undeniable. As far as the woman's legs are concerned, one can only surmise that they are there by a process of pure logical deduction, since they are in no way suggested. (*Loud.*) That is a defect.

THE PAINTER: Excuse me, sir; I'm terribly sorry.

THE STOUT GENTLEMAN: Art and logic are, in fact, my dear fellow, two entirely different things, and if one has to appeal to logic in order to understand art, art goes out the window and only logic remains!

THE PAINTER: Yes, yes, I follow you, sir.

THE STOUT GENTLEMAN: Very good.

ALICE (*poking her head in*): I told him as much, oh dear, oh dear!

THE STOUT GENTLEMAN (*to Alice*): What are you mixing in for? Get out of here, get out!

Alice disappears and then reappears again a moment later.

By the same token, if you have to appeal to art in order to understand logic, logic goes out the window. That's just a way of speaking. Are you following me?

THE PAINTER: Oh yes, sir, I'm following you very well.

THE STOUT GENTLEMAN (*poking a finger up his nose*): Good. Here then we have the vulnerable point and at the same time the major criticism I have to make of your work: in your work— and then not always—we can guess at what we cannot see; but we do not see what we guess at. Thus there is a flagrant contradiction in your work and also, as a result, a confusion of styles, an impure mixture of the representational and the nonrepresentational.

THE PAINTER: Alas, yes, sir, I notice it myself. Your criticisms are just, but what can I do?

THE STOUT GENTLEMAN: It's too late to do anything now. . . . Perhaps you didn't sufficiently take into account the fundamental principle, according to which only logic demonstrates, while art suggests.

THE PAINTER: I never knew that principle.

THE STOUT GENTLEMAN: Well, think about it from now on. As to the rest, that's easy enough: this woman, real or imaginary, representational or nonrepresentational, whom you have painted, is neatly combed: she has brown hair, green eyes, a sallow complexion, lips, nose, chin, etc. . . . Moreover, to finish up, it's definitely a queen.

ALICE: A sidewalk queen . . . As soon as he sees a tit, he loses his head! (*She pulls her head back in again.*)

THE PAINTER: Yes, sir, it is a queen.

THE STOUT GENTLEMAN (*stamping his foot*): Quiet—don't tell me anything. Let me interpret it by myself. . . . I believe I've demonstrated my capabilities to you.

THE PAINTER: I won't say a word.

THE STOUT GENTLEMAN: Unfortunately, I observe that she doesn't have a crown. . . . Your portrait, whether real or imaginary, my friend, is incomplete . . .

THE PAINTER: How true. I'm in despair . . . absolutely in despair. What can I do? (*He wrings his hands.*)

THE STOUT GENTLEMAN: You should have been in despair earlier! Finally, there are also certain qualities in your work which I pass over in silence. For your sake.

THE PAINTER: Yes—absolutely.

THE STOUT GENTLEMAN: In short, your picture is distinctly in need of some essential patching up here and there. (*Brusquely decisive.*) I cannot take it off your hands in its present state.

THE PAINTER: Oh!

THE STOUT GENTLEMAN: You will bring it back to me later on. We'll talk about it again. For the present, the subject is closed. Take it away.

THE PAINTER: Oh, sir! . . . Sir! . . . It's heavy and a nuisance to carry. If you like, I'll let you keep it for 300 francs.

THE STOUT GENTLEMAN: Impossible.

ALICE (*speaking in a tearful voice from the angle of the door*): Come on, brother, come on . . . be understanding—it isn't nice to be that way. . . . (*To The Painter.*) He's not nice, sir, he's hard—he's always been that way! . . .

THE STOUT GENTLEMAN: Keep your nose out of this, Alice, d'you hear? Keep your nose out of it! Get back to your pots and pans!

ALICE: Yes, yes, yes, I'm going, don't get angry with me. (*She disappears for a moment, then pokes her head in again.*)

THE STOUT GENTLEMAN (*to The Painter*): As a personal favor to you, my friend, I'll keep it here . . . for a short while . . . on rental. I'll decide in a few months whether or not I'll keep it for good. Naturally, I can't pay you anything.

THE PAINTER (*practically tied into knots with gratitude*): Oh, thank you, sir, thank you from the bottom of my heart. Thank you for being so good as to keep it here.

THE STOUT GENTLEMAN: I'm just doing you a favor.

THE PAINTER: I know, I know, I appreciate it.

THE STOUT GENTLEMAN: This way you won't be bothered with it any more. I will, but, after all . . .

THE PAINTER: Alas!

THE STOUT GENTLEMAN: If I find time and if I think it's worth the trouble to improve your work, I'll take care of the necessary alterations myself.

THE PAINTER: I'd be very grateful if you would. How can I ever thank you?

THE STOUT GENTLEMAN: I'll ask you to pay me a small nominal fee for the rental—we'll arrange all that between ourselves, my friend—just understand that if I do it I do it solely for the love of art and because I'm interested in your future.

THE PAINTER: How generous you are, sir!

THE STOUT GENTLEMAN: Unless . . . well, anyway, we'll see . . . If I see that we can make a profit on it . . . I'll see that you get a good percentage. Do you have a telephone?

THE PAINTER: No, sir.

THE STOUT GENTLEMAN: Ah, these artists! They're all alike!

THE PAINTER: Um, well . . .

THE STOUT GENTLEMAN: Oh, well, it doesn't matter. . . . I have your address. I'll write to you or send you a telegram. Now then (*with a playful smile*), I'll show you to the door, and you'll see—leave it to me—you'll see. I have to work now. Business hours are over.

THE PAINTER: Thank you. Good-bye.

THE STOUT GENTLEMAN: Business hours are over.

While The Painter goes to exit, Alice comes into the room.

ALICE (*to The Painter*): Good-bye, sir, good-bye . . . take care of yourself! Good luck.

The Stout Gentleman contemplates the picture and becomes more and more humble in aspect; Alice, on the other hand, changes her personality too and becomes astonishingly aggressive. Since The Painter's departure, The Stout Gentleman has become stooped. This change of attitude in both characters is sudden, obvious, absurd, unexpected, and must be emphasized in a very marked manner.

THE STOUT GENTLEMAN (*pointing timidly at the picture*): It's nice, isn't it, it's nice enough. What do you say to it, my dear?

ALICE: What on earth put it into your head to buy that nasty picture? Stop picking your nose! What's come over you? Have you gone crazy? At your age! You're incorrigible!

THE STOUT GENTLEMAN (*already enfeebled, though still retaining a hint of his former authority*): That's my business; I've got a right to do it. Any way you look at it, we need something on the walls—you just don't understand me—so that things look nice.

ALICE: Snobbism! . . . Idiot! Who needs it? Just take a look at that! All this haggling and bargaining is just so much wasted time. We'll end up without a thing to eat or a stitch of clothes to put on our backs. You're ruining us with your imbecilic fantasies! You'd do better to think about contracts and papers —what's to become of all that? Eh? Time wasted means money wasted.

THE STOUT GENTLEMAN: Don't get upset, Alice; I'll earn some more.

ALICE: You'd do better to pay some attention to the certificate first.

THE STOUT GENTLEMAN (*looking furtively at the picture*): The certificate?

ALICE: Yes. And you needn't look as if you don't know what I'm talking about. I was called down to the Town Hall for the certificate.

THE STOUT GENTLEMAN: To the Town Hall?

ALICE (*walking round and round The Stout Gentleman, who twists his head to follow her movements*): To the Town Hall. But since I had already been called down to the Town Hall for the certificate, it can't have been on account of the certificate. . . . So it was clearly for some other reason. . . . (*As she walks, she taps her stick loudly on the floor.*) But it

can't have been for some other reason either, since I'd already
been called down for some other reason, so I wonder what it
can all be about. . . .

No reply from The Stout Gentleman.

Eh? (*She raises her stick.*) What could it have been for? You
don't bother to ask yourself that, eh? What do you do with
your time, anyway? Spend it all looking at her, eh, you lecher?
Dirty little snotnose! Get to work!

THE STOUT GENTLEMAN (*fearfully, as he goes to his desk, still furtively sneaking looks at the picture*): Yes, yes, I'm doing it,
I'm getting to work, Alice! . .

ALICE (*following The Stout Gentleman, who takes refuge behind
his desk*): Viper! Drunkard! You're spending your whole life
ogling at her. . . . Ah . . . I'm all out of breath, I can't get
any air. . . .

THE STOUT GENTLEMAN: Oh . . . my poor Alice, my dear, poor, little Alice!

ALICE: Hypocrite, liar, swine! Ah, if it hadn't been for me you'd
have been in jail long ago! That's all you think of. (*She points
at the picture and raises her stick as if to strike it.*)

THE STOUT GENTLEMAN: Now, now, Alice, my dear . . . Alice . . .
that cost a lot of money . . . but we'll make a profit on it.

ALICE (*hesitating*): Ah! I don't know what holds me back . . . I
don't know what holds me back. . . . Idiot! Just take a look
at that creature, that whore, filthy, ugly, rotten, disgusting . . .

THE STOUT GENTLEMAN: Don't hit me . . . don't hit me.

ALICE: Fine gentleman you are, can't get along without porno-
graphic pictures! . . . Showgirls . . . nude women. Just take
a look at that.

THE STOUT GENTLEMAN (*sheltering behind the desk*): She isn't
nude. On the contrary, I find her a little overdressed.

ALICE (*pursuing him with her stick raised*): Lecherous fool!

THE STOUT GENTLEMAN: It's a profitable acquisition—that's all I'm
thinking of. You just don't understand; I'm not thinking of
anything else at all—not at all.

ALICE: Just think: he hasn't even told you how much he'll pay you for keeping it for him.

THE STOUT GENTLEMAN: He'll pay plenty, don't worry; it'll work out. And meanwhile we'll both get a lot of pleasure out of it —out of this masterpiece; yes, you'll get pleasure out of it too.

ALICE: Me get pleasure out of it? Out of this filth? What do you take me for, anyway?

THE STOUT GENTLEMAN: I've done that painter a favor; I've taken this thing off his hands; he was very happy. I'll make money on this deal—you'll see—he's very grateful to me, and he'll pay plenty.

ALICE: He'll pay nothing, or almost nothing; I know that type. They never have a penny to their name, these poets . . . and their whores!

THE STOUT GENTLEMAN: You're unjust.

ALICE: He's glad enough to get rid of it—nobody wants it. You'll never see him again. He was shrewd enough—he certainly had you coming and going. You're the only one that wanted this thing, this obscenity. . . . I'm going to throw it in the garbage can—yes, the garbage can. (*She goes through the motions of taking the picture and throwing it out.*) I'm going to wring its neck. (*She makes the appropriate gesture.*)

THE STOUT GENTLEMAN: Don't go on like that. This is just a business matter. I've got great hopes for it—yes, indeed, great hopes . . .

ALICE (*hesitating*): We'll see about that! Meanwhile you'll spend days, weeks—whole weeks—months, your whole life looking at the thing, wasting time, making goo-goo eyes at her—toad's eyes! . . . (*Sniveling.*) Selfish! Instead of taking care of me, instead of thinking of me because I'm sick! I suppose I've got everything I need, eh?

THE STOUT GENTLEMAN: As far as possible.

ALICE: And my rheumatism!

THE STOUT GENTLEMAN: You've got that too.

ALICE: And my broken spectacles!

THE STOUT GENTLEMAN: I bought you another pair. You're wearing them.

ALICE: They're not the same ones.

THE STOUT GENTLEMAN: They're just as good.

ALICE (*shouting, stick raised*): That's not true—liar, liar, swine!

THE STOUT GENTLEMAN (*raising his eyes to heaven*): She'll never understand the nobility of my aspirations!

ALICE (*still menacing*): Don't you dare move from your desk! You'll stay there . . . there . . .

The Stout Gentleman sits down at his desk, precisely at the spot indicated by Alice with her stick.

Where are the contracts? Where are are they?

THE STOUT GENTLEMAN (*showing the drawer*): In there!

ALICE: You leave them lying around in your desk drawer? Are they ready?

THE STOUT GENTLEMAN: There isn't much left to do.

ALICE: Good-for-nothing! Get them out right away. What are your clients going to say? You'll lose them all—all.

The Stout Gentleman gets the papers out of the desk and spreads them out in front of him.

Get to work!

THE STOUT GENTLEMAN: Yes . . . one moment . . .

ALICE: You don't do a damn thing—all you ever do is chew the fat with anyone you can get to talk with you. . . .

THE STOUT GENTLEMAN: I didn't send for that painter. He came all by himself . . . because I'm a well-known man! . . .

ALICE: . . . braggart, bigmouth. That's all you're good for. That idiot of a painter, that talentless imbecile—anyone can do as well as that, a four-year-old child could paint better.

THE STOUT GENTLEMAN (*timidly*): That's not so.

ALICE (*menacing The Stout Gentleman, who disappears behind his desk to avoid blows from her stick*): Shut your mouth! Those painters just leave their pictures anywhere, with any old snob who's stupid enough to take them, with people who don't understand anything, who pretend . . .

THE STOUT GENTLEMAN (*hidden behind the desk*): I'm not pretending.

ALICE: Well, that makes it even worse!

THE STOUT GENTLEMAN (*timidly poking his head out*): . . . not true . . .

Alice strikes out with the stick, but The Stout Gentleman dodges back in time.

ALICE: Shut your mouth! Get busy with your contracts! If you haven't finished them by this evening, you'll get no soup, no dessert, no dinner at all. No work—no food . . .

THE STOUT GENTLEMAN (*appearing and disappearing timidly*): I'll be finished by this evening.

Alice strikes out but misses.

ALICE: Promises, promises! I have to keep an eye on you all the time, as if I didn't have anything else to do. . . .

THE STOUT GENTLEMAN (*again timidly poking his head out and back again*): If you don't leave me alone, I won't finish. . . .

ALICE (*again trying to hit him*): You just watch out if you're not finished. . . . A thrashing and no dinner, that's what you'll get! Understand?

THE STOUT GENTLEMAN (*same action as before*): Yes, Alice, I understand.

ALICE: I'm going now to wash your dirty dishes . . . but I'll leave the kitchen door open. . . . So mind what you're doing, I'm warning you. . . .

THE STOUT GENTLEMAN (*timidly poking his head out, then his entire body*): I'll be good.

ALICE: I'll be watching you. (*She points to the picture.*) Just mind I don't catch you eyeing that—just you mind I don't catch you at it. . . . Come here!

THE STOUT GENTLEMAN (*approaching her fearfully; Alice pulls his ears*): Ow! Ow! Ouch!

ALICE: Just you watch out I don't catch you leering at that picture! There! That'll teach you!

She looks at the picture and spits at it, while The Stout Gentleman, whom she has turned loose, cries like a little boy.

I'll get even with her. I know what I'll do to her! (*She exits stage left for the kitchen, hobbling and grumbling to herself; before leaving, she says again:*) I've got my eye on you! Get to your desk!!

She threatens him with her stick; The Stout Gentleman runs for the desk.

Alone, The Stout Gentleman looks at his papers, gives a sigh of relief after a moment and mops his forehead. Then he furtively turns his head for a moment toward the picture and once again concentrates on his papers.

ALICE'S VOICE: Don't play around! I'm here! I'm watching you!

THE STOUT GENTLEMAN (*startled*): No, no, Alice. No, no, my little Alice! . . .

He addresses himself to his work again. He throws an uneasy glance at the kitchen door, then another one, seemingly more assured this time. He gets up stealthily, a little more confidently; just at this moment he hears a crash of breaking crockery from the kitchen and Alice's voice saying, "Shit!" The Stout Gentleman sits down again precipitately, frightened, as if the pile of plates had been thrown at his head, and feverishly sets to work again.

Seven and eight, fifteen; fifteen times three, forty-five; forty-five divided by three, fifteen; fifteen less eight, seven; seven and one, eight . . . that makes eight million . . . eight million multiplied by ten makes eighty million, yes . . . eighty million, eighty million . . . eighty million . . . ten times eighty million makes eight hundred million . . . eight hundred million profit minus taxes . . . minus taxes . . . eight hundred million profit . . . not bad for two weeks . . . could be better, though . . . could be better! could be better! (*Alice is heard snoring.*) Is she asleep? Or is she just pretending? (*Very loud.*) Eight hundred million! Eight hundred! (*Alice continues to snore. He shouts at the top of his voice.*) Eight hundred million! Eight hundred million . . . million . . . million . . . million! (*He stops; the snores continue.*) She's asleep. I've earned eight hundred million so I deserve a little entertainment! (*He looks at the picture.*) A little entertainment that doesn't cost anything! (*He gets up, tiptoes to the picture, then changes his mind.*) I'd better make sure! (*He goes cautiously to the kitchen door and pokes his head through then brings it back. During all this, the snores continue. He closes the door softly, the snores becoming fainter and then fading away. Then he looks through the keyhole, puts his ear to the door panel, and finally rises reassured. He goes to the middle of the room, humming to himself but tiptoeing just the same and getting more cautious as he nears the picture, before which he stands with his back to the audience and his hands behind his back.*) A bargain! How beautiful she is! I didn't lose any money on that! I bet I've earned some. . . . Alice can say what she likes! (*He caresses the painted woman's arms.*) What a smooth skin she has! The painting even tastes good! (*He kisses the picture moistly.*) Darling! Oh, my lo-o-ove! (*He is enraptured, and sniffs.*) She smells good. . . . Ah, that lovely oil paint (*He is in ecstasies; he presses himself against the painting.*) . . . You're lovely. Ooh . . . darling . . . (*He backs off.*) Oh . . . woman! (*He holds on to the picture as if swooning; then he takes a step to the left and a step to the right.*) I take a step to the left, a step to the right, you shine from every angle. . . . The world is stiff and ugly only when one looks at it from the same angle all the time. . . . You have to keep moving. (*A step to the left and a step to the right. He declaims with ridiculous grandiloquence.*) The muddy marshes are turned to fragrant meadowland; the sky is an ocean of flowered islands . . . oases bubble through the deserts . . . rivers run through arid sands. . . . You are a stream of hawthorn blossoms. . . . You remind me of cities drowned beneath the waves . . . you remind me . . . you remind me . . . what was it you remind me of, what was it? I'm young, I'm budding, I'm flowering . . . tra-la-la-la-la-la-la . . . I'm even blossoming. . . . (*He goes to the picture and fondles the painted arms.*) I'm blossoming, I'm blossoming . . . Ah, I'm becoming a poet!

Alice sticks her head in; The Stout Gentleman does not notice her.

Oh, ooh, oooh, aaah . . . I love you! [1]

---

[1] The actor must play this as erotically as the censorship allows or as the audience will put up with; or he must be ridiculously lyrical and emphatic. But always clownishly.

ALICE: Swine! It's disgusting!

THE STOUT GENTLEMAN (*stuck right up against the picture*): I'm going to dissolve—that's it, I'm dissolving. . . . Ooh . . . (*He goes one or two steps up the ladder in order to embrace the portrait better.*)

ALICE (*coming into the room, unnoticed by The Stout Gentleman*): Lecherous camel!

THE STOUT GENTLEMAN (*same action*): Alas, art is long, life is short!

ALICE (*limping around the room*): Art is the opiate of the people. So is life.

THE STOUT GENTLEMAN (*coming down the ladder*): I'll go a little farther away so I can come up close to it again. . . .

ALICE (*same action; sobbing*): At his age! At his age! And she's so ugly, so ugly . . . if she were only beautiful at least!

The Stout Gentleman throws kisses to the picture; meanwhile Alice spits in his direction and menaces him with the stick.

What does he see in her that's so marvelous?

THE STOUT GENTLEMAN (*in ecstasies*): Darling . . . daaarling . . . da-a-a-arling! . . .

ALICE (*same action*): What's she got that I haven't got? To be sure, she's got two arms and I've got only one and a half, but I've got legs at least and she hasn't got any . . . And even if I have got only one arm, that's simply an accident of old age!

THE STOUT GENTLEMAN (*same action*): Beautiful young queen!

ALICE (*same action*): Queen of tricks! That picture dates from the last century, judging by its style!

THE STOUT GENTLEMAN (*same action*): Oh . . . how young you are . . . so young, so young . . .

ALICE (*same action*): That makes her eighty years old, no younger than me. . . . And if she were twenty years old, he could be her father . . . the lecher!

THE STOUT GENTLEMAN: Nevertheless . . . there's something missing.

ALICE: Oh, what's to become of us? He'll ruin himself for her, that's what will happen. . . .

THE STOUT GENTLEMAN (*to the picture*): I see what you need. . . .

ALICE (*tearfully*): He doesn't think of my rheumatism. . . .

THE STOUT GENTLEMAN (*satisfied with his discovery*): I see . . .

ALICE (*tearfully*): My nose hurts . . . my eyes hurt . . .

THE STOUT GENTLEMAN (*goes to the desk drawer, opens it, and takes out a crown; then he gets on the ladder again, trying unsuccessfully to put the crown on the painted woman's head*): I'm going to crown you . . .

ALICE (*same action*): Pointless expenses. (*To the picture.*) All because of you! because of you! (*To The Stout Gentleman.*) Dirty egoist! (*Alice sobs, hobbles around, spits, and threatens the portrait with her stick; the actions of the two players are separate; The Stout Gentleman does not see Alice.*)

THE STOUT GENTLEMAN (*climbing the ladder*): That's it, that's the way . . .

ALICE: What an idiot! . . . That lecher, all he thinks about is his own pleasure. . . . Never thinks of others. . . .

The Stout Gentleman is still trying vainly to fix the crown on the portrait's head.

THE STOUT GENTLEMAN (*exasperated*): Oh, it doesn't hold up there; I can't make it stay!

ALICE: I could have told him he wouldn't be able to do that—he's too old for that sort of thing. . . .

THE STOUT GENTLEMAN (*flying into a rage, stamping like a little child, hitting the canvas, and so on*): It won't stay . . . it won't stay up!

ALICE: Isn't that too bad!

THE STOUT GENTLEMAN (*despairing*): I didn't learn how to paint soon enough . . . it's too late now.

ALICE: Wasting his time on that! On that imbecilic bitch, on that monster!

THE STOUT GENTLEMAN (*on the ladder*): Let's try it another way. . . .

ALICE (*crying*): Oh, dear, oh, dear!

THE STOUT GENTLEMAN (*to the portrait*): Hold it, hold it, use your hands, help me! . . . (*He tries to put the crown into the painted woman's hands but is, necessarily, unsuccessful.*) I can't do it! She doesn't want to! (*He too cries.*)

ALICE (*same action*): Serves you right!

THE STOUT GENTLEMAN (*same action*): How sad it is!

ALICE (*same action*): That'll teach you.

THE STOUT GENTLEMAN (*same action, to the portrait*): I can't . . . I can't . . .

ALICE (*waving her stick*): You'll see! You'll be hearing from me!

> While The Stout Gentleman tries to put the crown on the portrait's head once again, and with equal lack of success, Alice, in tears, gets a bucket of water from a corner of the room or from the kitchen.

> (*Returning with the bucket and throwing its contents over The Stout Gentleman.*) There . . . that's for the lovers!

THE STOUT GENTLEMAN (*surprised, lets the crown drop; he shakes himself like a wet dog*): Ah! Ah! Ah! (*He comes down the ladder.*) I'll pay you back for this, Alice! (*He makes threatening gestures at her after having sneezed like a poodle; but "really" like a poodle.*) I'll pay you back for this! I'll pay you back for this! (*He tries to hit her.*)

ALICE: No . . . No . . . I don't feel well! Ah, I'm fainting! I feel dizzy, I want to throw up! I can't stand up any more. I'm going to fall . . . I'm going to fall! Get a chair—can't you even think of that? You'd do better to buy some chairs—that's a good deal more useful than pictures. (*She closes her eyes.*)

THE STOUT GENTLEMAN: I'm sorry . . . I'm sorry . . . oh . . . oh . . . my poor Alice! . . . I'm going . . . I'm going . . . I didn't kill you! They'll lock me up!

ALICE (*opening an eye*): Remove the bucket!

THE STOUT GENTLEMAN: Yes . . . yes . . . (*He takes the bucket.*)

ALICE (*sobbing*): I'm falling . . . hurry, hurry . . . I can't stand any more. . . . I'm i-i-ill!

THE STOUT GENTLEMAN: Ah . . . I'll never have any peace. . . . (*He goes reluctantly to the kitchen, carrying the bucket. After he exits his voice is heard saying:*) Never.

ALICE (*straightens up again during the few moments of The Stout Gentleman's absence and faces the portrait*): Disgusting bitch! (*She makes threatening gestures.*)

THE STOUT GENTLEMAN (*coming back with a rather high-backed chair with arms; Alice resumes her former attitude*): Here, sit down! (*He puts the chair down to the right of the picture.*)

ALICE: Not beside her! Not beside her! (*She sits down all the same.*)

THE STOUT GENTLEMAN: You just don't want to sit there because the comparison isn't to your advantage. (*It can now be seen that The Stout Gentleman is holding a large pistol in the hand he keeps behind his back.*)

ALICE: You don't see very well, you insolent fool; you haven't taken a good look at me! You don't know how to see! A rotten picture, ugly, ugly, ugly! (*She gets up and hobbles around, pounding on the floor with her stick.*)

THE STOUT GENTLEMAN (*sweetly*): You've got a blind man's cane and you use it as if you were deaf!

ALICE (*same action*): I hear you well enough, I hear you well enough, all right!

THE STOUT GENTLEMAN (*still more sweetly*): Do sit down . . . you're tired . . . rest yourself! Here's your chair!

ALICE (*same action*): What do you want with that chair? Leave things the way they are. You make a mess everywhere.

THE STOUT GENTLEMAN (*same tone*): You were going to faint . . . sit down, have a rest.

ALICE (*same action*): I don't have time. I've got work to do too. I'll die on my feet, like a horse. . . .

THE STOUT GENTLEMAN (*suddenly in a very hard tone of voice*): Don't move!

ALICE (*same action*): Don't think you're going to stop me!

The Stout Gentleman threatens her with the pistol.

(*She sits down, scared.*) Assas . . . sin!

THE STOUT GENTLEMAN: Didn't the doctor tell you you needed a rest?

ALICE (*trembling*): I'd rather you sent me to the mountains.

The Stout Gentleman aims the gun at her and laughs ferociously.

Your finger could slip on the trigger.

THE STOUT GENTLEMAN (*same action*): All the better . . . all the better . . .

ALICE: What do you want . . . tell me . . . speak . . . speak . . . brother . . . it's only words that count; the rest is just gossip.

THE STOUT GENTLEMAN: As far as I'm concerned, it's just the other way round! Quiet . . . don't move . . . I don't want to hear you any more, I don't want you to move any more, without my permission! (*He waves the gun.*) Pay attention!

ALICE (*crying*): Oh . . . brother . . . an accident could happen at any moment. . . .

THE STOUT GENTLEMAN: Precisely so. Stop crying! It's not allowed!

ALICE: Why are you frightening your sister? Why do you want to kill her?

THE STOUT GENTLEMAN: That's my business!

ALICE: Forgive me . . . forgive me. . . . (*She throws off her shawl with a movement of her head; her badly combed, dirty gray hair is seen.*) Now it's on the floor . . . You see what you've done! Let me pick it up!

THE STOUT GENTLEMAN: It's not my fault. Leave it there or watch out! This will go off. . . .

ALICE: It's my only one . . . I'm cold . . . It'll get dirty! (*She reaches out to pick it up.*)

THE STOUT GENTLEMAN: No! No tricks!

ALICE: Stop playing with your gun!

THE STOUT GENTLEMAN: No moving allowed, no crying allowed. And watch your step—this is loaded.

ALICE (*meekly*): I'm not moving, I won't talk any more—don't shoot, dear brother. . . . I'm not trying to trick you. . . .

THE STOUT GENTLEMAN: Sit up . . . lean on the back of the chair.

ALICE: That hurts me—it's impossible!

THE STOUT GENTLEMAN: Impossible is not a French word. . . . Kneel! . . . come on . . . come on . . .

ALICE (*scared, obeys painfully*): I've got the rheumatism. . . .

THE STOUT GENTLEMAN (*waving his gun dangerously*): I don't want to hear any more . . . hop to it, let's go!

ALICE: That might go off and kill the neighbor's birds . . . take care!

THE STOUT GENTLEMAN: I don't care! (*He sticks the gun under Alice's nose.*) Get a move on, faster than that! And don't move—don't talk either!

ALICE (*immobilized by fear; she cries*): You want to kill an old woman like me, your sister who always spoiled you. . . . If you don't feel pity for me, pity my age!

THE STOUT GENTLEMAN: Silence—once and for all! Talking's improper at your age! Look out! (*He waves the gun.*) One false move and it goes off!

She obeys, trembling.

You make an excellent target.

ALICE: Ooh!

THE STOUT GENTLEMAN: Remember, the gun is loaded! Head straight, head up . . .

Alice tries to speak.

Quiet! (*He stamps his foot.*) Don't fidget. . . . Smile! I told you to smile.

He puts the gun to her cheek. Alice smiles; she keeps a fixed smile to the end of the scene. He backs off a little, after having torn off Alice's second shawl, which he puts on her knees.

Watch out! I'm going to fire! (*He fires.*)

ALICE: Ah!

Her dress falls off, revealing a precise reproduction of the portrait's bust. In her startled movement her white wig and her spectacles have fallen off; her brown hair and eyes are revealed, exactly like those of the woman in the picture.

THE STOUT GENTLEMAN: Well, well, well!

At that instant, an arm grows out of Alice's stump.

And look at that—there's the arm too!

Depending upon which way is convenient in the staging, Alice can remove spectacles with her new-found hand at this point— spectacles, wig, and so on, lying on the ground like a sloughed- off skin.

Hurrah! Hurrah! (*He fires the gun in the air. Then he jumps with joy. Finally he calms down.*) And the scepter?

At this point Alice's white cane becomes luminous. If this is too difficult in the staging, The Stout Gentleman can throw Alice's cane away and hand her a scepter taken from the desk drawer; as for luminosity, it will suffice to have a small electric light bulb at the end of the stick. Alice is radiant.

There's the scepter! Bravo! Bravo! My congratulations, dear maestro! (*He shakes hands with himself.*) She needs the crown! (*He puts the crown, which is similarly illuminated, on Alice's head.*) A masterpiece! I've created a masterpiece! (*He sobs with joy as he looks at it.*) I've surpassed the model! I've done better than the painter. Who needs him? I don't want his pictures any more! I can make them myself . . . and better ones at that! I'll found an institute of beauty!

He makes grotesque reverences alternately in front of the picture and in front of Alice, who remains unmoving and radiant.

Your Majesty! Your Majesty! Your Majesty! Your Majesty! (*Then, to the audience.*) I'm perfect! I was right!

The door on the right opens, revealing The Neighbor, who looks exactly like Alice before her transformation.

NEIGHBOR (*coming in with a chair*): Oh, excuse me!

> *The Stout Gentleman stops, somewhat embarrassed.*

Am I disturbing you?

THE STOUT GENTLEMAN: Oh, no . . . to tell the truth, you're not . . . I was jumping around—like this—because I'm happy. . . .

NEIGHBOR: I came here to do some knitting and I brought my chair with me because I know you hardly have any. . . . It's cold at my place. . . . It's not much warmer here. . . .

THE STOUT GENTLEMAN: Come in, do come in!

> *This scene has taken place right in front of the door; The Neighbor now enters the room.*

NEIGHBOR (*noticing Alice*): Well, well, well, you're buying statues of queens! You're going in for interior decorating, are you?

THE STOUT GENTLEMAN (*proud, grotesque, solemn*): As you see!

NEIGHBOR: And a picture too? One would think that the picture was a copy of the statue . . . without the crown. . . .

THE STOUT GENTLEMAN (*lets out a laugh of satisfaction*): It's the other way round. . . . The statue is a copy, with the crown added. . . .

NEIGHBOR: Oh yes . . . it's better than the model . . . it's magnificent!

THE STOUT GENTLEMAN: I'm an artist!

NEIGHBOR: . . . this is heavier, fleshier . . . I didn't know you were such a genius! I congratulate you!

THE STOUT GENTLEMAN: Don't judge by outward appearances. . . .

NEIGHBOR: One would think she were alive. What a beauty!

THE STOUT GENTLEMAN: Ha, ha, ha! That's Alice!

NEIGHBOR: That's not possible. . . . Oh, sir, do the same for me. . . .

THE STOUT GENTLEMAN: It's a big job . . . doesn't come cheap.

NEIGHBOR: I'll give you the shirt off my back.

THE STOUT GENTLEMAN: Very well. Since you implore me, I'll give in. (*Aside.*) I'll sell her for billions. (*To The Neighbor.*) Put your chair there, sit down, do as I say, like this.

Alice and The Neighbor sit around the painting.

Ready! (*He draws his gun.*)

NEIGHBOR: Oh . . . painting by shooting, I adore that. . . .

THE STOUT GENTLEMAN: Don't move . . .

The Neighbor sits still in her chair.

Ready . . .

The door on the right opens, revealing The Painter.

THE PAINTER: Good morning, sir!

THE STOUT GENTLEMAN: What do you want?

THE PAINTER (*still timid*): Excuse me, sir. You told me to come back at the end of three weeks to find out if you'll take my picture . . . if you've decided . . .

THE STOUT GENTLEMAN: Better take a look at what I've done!

THE PAINTER: Oooh . . . that's wonderful. . . .

THE STOUT GENTLEMAN: My sister . . .

THE PAINTER: Oh, it isn't possible. . . . She is beautiful and pure, like a picture!

THE STOUT GENTLEMAN: I've re-educated her, using a little persuasion and a little terror. . . .

THE PAINTER: Terror!

THE STOUT GENTLEMAN (*showing the gun*): With this! (*He puts the gun to his temple.*)

THE PAINTER: Oh . . . look out . . . don't do that . . . you'll hurt yourself . . .

THE STOUT GENTLEMAN: Not at all, not at all . . . (*He fires.*)

THE PAINTER: Aah, sir!

THE STOUT GENTLEMAN (*laughing*): I told you it wasn't dangerous . . . that's for the terror part . . . you'll see, I've done better than you. . . .

THE PAINTER: Oh, by far, sir. . . . You told me that you had talent, but I must admit I didn't expect anything like this. . . . Such a successful masterstroke, you know, is better than a first attempt! . . . And what's left for me to do now?

THE STOUT GENTLEMAN: I've become an artist. You become a businessman now!

THE PAINTER (*desolate*): All I can do is take down my picture now!

THE STOUT GENTLEMAN: First you can pay me forty million for the rental!

THE PAINTER: I don't have that kind of money on me!

THE STOUT GENTLEMAN: You can pay it on the installment plan . . . a million a day for forty days . . . and ten million in interest!

THE PAINTER: Yes, sir, that's reasonable! Meanwhile I'll leave the picture with you. . . .

THE STOUT GENTLEMAN: That'll make it forty-five million! I accept. You can go.

THE PAINTER (*on the way out*): Good-bye, sir. I admire you. (*He stops on his way to the door; very naïvely:*) You had one twin sister, this gives you two twin sisters, and now with Madame (*He indicates The Neighbor.*) you will have three twin sisters.

Meanwhile The Stout Gentleman has taken two other crowns from his desk drawer.

THE STOUT GENTLEMAN (*putting a crown on The Neighbor's head*): And with her, that'll make three!

THE PAINTER: Wonderful! (*He goes out backward, but is stopped by the door.*)

THE STOUT GENTLEMAN (*shoots at The Neighbor, whose outer covering falls off so that she looks exactly like the portrait; then to The Painter*): And with you, that'll make four! (*He aims at The Painter.*)

THE PAINTER (*modestly*): Oh, not me, sir—I'm not worthy of it!

THE STOUT GENTLEMAN: Oh yes, you'll see!

He shoots at The Painter, whose old clothes suddenly fall off so that he appears as a Prince Charming.

THE PAINTER: Oh, thank you, thank you so much! (*He does not move.*)

THE STOUT GENTLEMAN (*putting a crown on The Painter's head*): As long as we're at it, let's make the best of it!

He gets up on a stool and shoots in the air; the lighting should be designed so that the whole scene is changed; flowers and paper streamers fall from the ceiling; firecrackers and fireworks go off. Do not be afraid to create a "fairground" atmosphere.

Oh! Oh! Oh! Bravo! . . . Aah, and me? And me? (*Despairingly.*) Oh . . . I'm still not beautiful! (*To the audience, offering the gun.*) Would you like to shoot me? Who wants to shoot me? Who wants to shoot at me!?

CURTAIN

1) Bill — Midwest
2) Muentscud,
3) D. O, (2)
4) Bank
5) Library (2) — Book (2)
   Xerox